Cause to Repine

E.M. STORM-SMITH

A PRIDE AND PREJUDICE VARIATION

Published by

Storm Haus Publishing, LLC
www.StormHausPublishing.com

Copyright © 2023
by E.M. Storm-Smith
ALL RIGHTS RESERVED

Cause to Repine / E.M. Storm-Smith – 2nd ed.
ISBN-13: 978-1-7374039-2-0 *electronic format*
ISBN-13: 978-1-7374039-3-7 *paperback format*

Original cover artwork by Louisa Cannell

For Charlie. Always and Forever.

Contents

Prologue

The crunching of the gravel along the drive was unusually loud in the early predawn morning calm as a single carriage ambled away from Pemberley Manor. George Darcy stood on the front steps and watched as his son's beautifully matched greys pulled him towards the road. Fitzwilliam Darcy, George's oldest child and only son, had come home after the end of the London season in July, then stayed for two months complete.

It was a gift to have his son home for such extended time. When George's great-aunt passed several years ago, leaving an independent estate in Wales for his son, the younger Darcy had started living most of the year at Cresselly Park. A naturally shy and unsociable young man, Fitzwilliam Darcy had been all too happy to bury himself into working on his new estate, learning all the tenants needs and taking his position as magistrate in the community seriously. It was extremely admirable. Everything that George had come to expect from his diligent, intelligent, and responsible son.

But it was also extremely lonely.

George was worried for his son. Approaching his twenty-seventh year, Fitzwilliam had few true friends and even fewer prospects for a bride. Though he professed a sincere desire for a wife and family, George had heard his son just the night before expressing lament over finding a woman with whom he wanted to spend his life. If the landscape of marriageable ladies and the London marriage mart did not change significantly in the next year, well, George did not want to think about alternatives. Fitzwilliam was tall, handsome, educated, and wealthy. Even without his eventual inheritance of Pemberley, Fitzwilliam Darcy was in the top one thousand landowners of the *ton* with just Cresselly Park.

Once the estates were combined, Fitzwilliam would be wealthier than most of the earls with permanent seats in parliament, and maybe even some of the nonroyal dukes. There was no shortage of titled women who would cut off their own heels to become the next Mrs. Darcy, which was essentially the problem. Fitzwilliam was not interested in any of the mercenary women who pursued only money and status.

He was too much like his late mother.

Several moments after the carriage was firmly beyond the bend in the road, George sighed, then he reached into his front breast pocket and pulled out a stack of letters addressed to his son.

The first two were from George's sisters-in-law, Lady Catherine de Bourgh and Lady Josephine Finch Fitzwilliam, Countess of Matlock. Having lost his Anne shortly after the birth of their daughter, Georgiana, Lady Catherine, as the elder sister of George's late wife, deemed it her duty to provide motherly guidance to George's children. Most of the time, her purposes were very well intended, even if her manner was always a bit intimidating. George had some disquiet about keeping her correspondence from his son and had even given Fitzwilliam one of the pages of the letter detailing Lady Catherine and her daughter's, Anne de Bourgh, summer entertainments, claiming that she had included the page with a letter to the whole family.

Lady Matlock, however, was much less interested in the Darcy siblings' general welfare and more interested in continuing to build her family's importance. George had not one ounce of guilt for holding back her letter, along with the third letter in the stack, which was from Lady Matlock's brother, the Earl of Nottingham.

George turned to go back through the large front manor doors and moved towards the master's study. Habitually an early riser, he was not surprised to see a fire already in the grate and a tea tray on the corner of his large mahogany desk. Mrs. Reynolds certainly ran a tip-top household establishment. The confiscated letters were laid on a larger stack of correspondence delivered to Pemberley in the past few weeks, and George picked up his perfectly prepared tea before starting on his ledgers for the morning.

Though, even midsummer rents and wool poundage reports could not keep George's attention for very long. Those dammed letters and his son's defeated demeanour kept creeping into George's mind. He glanced back at the stack of letters.

Am I doing the right thing, keeping the earl's request from William?

Suddenly, the sun burst over the tree line, through the high windows, and into the master's study, brilliantly illuminating two paintings hanging above the mantle. Many visitors to George's study over the years had commented on those two paintings, as they were quite unusual for a man of George's status and wealth.

The first was a small charcoal drawing of a modest tenant home. There were two stories, a thatched roof, only one window on the south-facing wall, and chickens roaming about the kitchen garden. Even without colour, George could easily make out the bright-vermilion front door and the dark-grey river-stone façade. Crushed, bright-white limestone circled the small drive, which led to a two-stall horse barn. One of the stalls always had at least three pigs living there, which the horses barely tolerated. The picture had originally been drawn on a piece of discarded butcher paper. But long ago, the drawing had been recreated using fine-point charcoal pencils from a very expensive art supplies dealer in London and preserved in gum wash. A beautiful cherry-wood frame and a fine piece of cut glass had been acquired when George's father desired to have it hung in the study.

The second piece was a slightly larger oil painting showing a lane in the centre of Derby. Modest homes lined both sides of the street, and several carriages ambled down the dirt road. In the middle of the painting was the main subject, a three-story home with a blue door and a sign declaring that the solicitor's office was open.

George stood from his chair and reclaimed the three letters. He strode confidently to the mantle with a merry fire fluttering in the grate. One long finger traced the bottom of the frame holding the charcoal drawing, and George smiled to himself.

He tossed the three letters into the fire and watched them turn to ash.

Dancing in the Country

"COME, SIR WILLIAM, YOU MUST HAVE SOMETHING more to say about our new neighbours than they are amiable and genteel! You find everyone amiable and genteel," Elizabeth Bennet laughed. "It rather more speaks to your character than theirs." She was having a marvellous evening. As a young woman with little in the world to cause her distress and a disposition not formed for melancholy, Elizabeth was a much sought-after companion at the Michaelmas public assembly in the town of Meryton, Hertfordshire, England.

"Now, Miss Elizabeth, that is nothing but the truth, as you can see yourself that our new neighbour is of a happy set." Sir William Lucas promoted his remarks with a pointed look in the direction of said new neighbour, Mr. Charles Bingley, a wealthy, young, and most importantly unmarried, man, who was at that moment dancing with Elizabeth's older sister, Jane.

"I will own to Mr. Bingley being happy and amiable, but what of the rest of his party? My father would say not one word about his call to them the other day, so I must beg your indulgence." Like many of the landed gentry throughout England, Elizabeth's father was a well-positioned estate owner with a moderate annual income that supported his family and kept his properties and tenants in good repair. Though certainly not of London Society, the Bennet family was among the wealthiest in the area. No one who lived in Meryton and the surrounding county could claim to be of high fashion or overly fine, but the country gentlemen of Hertfordshire were all well-educated, and their wives kept generous tables.

However, it was clear to the long-time residents that, though Bingley himself was outwardly enjoying his evening, the rest of the Netherfield party was feeling all the lack of high society.

Sir William shook his head and gave Elizabeth a slightly scolding look just as his daughter, Charlotte, joined their conversation. "Lizzy, are you attempting to goad Father into saying something ungenerous?"

Elizabeth bumped Charlotte's hip with her own and adopted an offended mien. "How you wound me, Charlotte. I am merely looking to gain a better understanding of our new friends."

"Of course, how could I ever believe such slander of my closest friend?" Charlotte took Elizabeth's arm and not so subtly steered her away from the circle of matrons and their husbands. "Come, dear, I am sure you are parched from dancing. Let us retrieve some lemonade and sit for a while, before my brother demands his turn around the room with you."

Elizabeth let out another full laugh at her friend's teasing. At one time, everyone in Meryton had thought that Elizabeth would make a match with the eldest Lucas boy, John, based mostly on their shared propensity to laugh and talk with animation during dances. As neither were inclined to marry the other, they had mutually decided, some years ago, to avoid each other during balls and assemblies to stop the gossip. Tonight was the first public dance since John married a kindly young lady from Weymouth, and he had been quite happy to be able to once again engage in diverting conversation with his childhood friend.

"We certainly cannot leave your brother dissatisfied, can we?" As Elizabeth promenaded around the room with Charlotte, she passed very close to the tall, dark haired gentleman introduced as Bingley's friend from Derbyshire. For a moment, while she was still chuckling about John's antics, their eyes met.

Fitzwilliam Darcy was miserable. He was only in Meryton to visit his friend, Bingley, who had taken a lease on an estate two days prior. The mayor of Meryton, a Sir William Lucas, had called on the new master of Netherfield estate the very morning before Darcy had arrived and provided tickets to the Michaelmas assembly for the entire Bingley party as a gesture of welcome. Darcy could not very well snub the local gentry by refusing to attend.

But he wished he had.

The Darcy family was squarely in *le bon ton* and had close connections to several peers of the realm. Even more importantly, the Darcys had money. While not holding a title himself, Darcy's father, the current Master of Pemberley, had an annual income which exceeded many of the lesser Earls and Barons with seats in the House of Lords.

Even for those who were not familiar with the name Darcy, it was apparent by the cut of his clothes that the newest addition to Meryton's society was a vastly wealthy man. Inside of five minutes after Darcy followed Bingley and his sisters into the hall, he had heard at least one of the local matrons whisper behind her fan that his inheritance was worth ten thousand pounds per year.

Add to the gossip a healthy dose of unceasing noise, and Darcy's misery was complete. Contrary to the easy manner of the country gentry, the highest ranks of society were conditioned to keep their emotions and their mouths under good regulation.

Women of the *ton* certainly never laughed in public.

As he was trying to avoid a massive headache, Darcy had taken up a place at the edge of the room where he could avoid much of the unfettered merriment.

"Come now Darcy, I must have you dance! It is too lovely an assembly with too many pretty faces for you to sulk in the shadows." Darcy jumped at the sudden declaration of his friend Bingley. His eyes had still been following the two young women headed towards the refreshments table and not noticed the other man walk up.

Coming back to himself, Darcy hung his head a little lower at Bingley's words. He was a tall man, over six foot, and had always towered over much of the other people in any room. If he ever hoped to be ignored in a crowd, Darcy learned he had to retreat to darkened segments of walls where the sconces did not quite reach. Bingley had found his friend standing in these shadows many nights in the five years of their friendship and was not fooled by the poor illumination.

"Charles, you know how I detest the activity unless I am particularly acquainted with my partner, and since both of your sisters are engaged for the next set, I believe I shall not. It would be insupportable to dance at an event such as this." Darcy sniffed as he finished his excuses and folded his arms protectively against his chest.

Bingley laughed at Darcy's attempt at intimidation. "I would not be as fastidious as you for all of the King's gold. Really, I am sure we can find someone appropriate for you to partner. My last dance partner has a sister who I believe is available. I can have her introduce you. I believe she is the one with that enchanting laugh."

This piqued Darcy's interest. He had indeed noticed the young woman who seemed to find humour in everything. She was fairly short, with a light and pleasing figure. Darcy also overheard one of her conversations with a young gentleman regarding the great threat that another war with the Americas posed to England's ability to defeat Napoleon in Spain. He had been very impressed with her analysis of the strength of the Royal Navy and its inability to sustain two shipping blockades. Darcy's eyes involuntarily swept the room looking for the lady in question and when he looked back, Bingley's expression told him his friend had already discerned Darcy was intrigued.

"Charles!" Darcy whispered harshly. "I cannot do such a thing. The local gossips are already loudly discussing my inheritance, as they are yours by the way, and I would not want to add any fuel to their fire. Dancing with a lady to whom I have only just been introduced will give rise to rumours. Those rumours will give rise to expectations, and then I shall be forced to hurt the lady when I quit the region for the season. You know my family's expectations of me!"

Bingley placed one hand on Darcy's shoulder. "William, calm down. No one is demanding you marry the lady. I know that the *London Times* gossip columnist has a special obsession with you, but we are not in London. One dance will not see you engaged. And I do believe you exaggerate your family's expectations. Surely, your father has made no demands on your marriage."

"No, he has not," Darcy sighed. "But the Earl and Countess have been exceedingly vocal in recent months about my marrying this year. I believe my aunt even has a particular lady specially selected. My cousin, Richard, wrote to me the last time he was in London saying the Countess was planning several early season dinner parties with limited guests in order to facilitate some level of discourse between myself and her chosen favourite."

After another heavy sigh and a moment to collect his thoughts, Darcy continued. "Perhaps it is for the best. I am so very awkward in social settings. I cannot catch the tone of conversation, or appear interested in the concerns of others, as I often see done. If I let the Countess choose me a wife, I shall at least be free to never spend another evening at Almack's. I have always hoped for at least some affection to be present in my marriage, but with my abominable temper for society, and general lack of ability to intelligently string two words together when in the presence of persons I do not know well, I am likely to leave Pemberley without an heir unless I allow the Countess to handle matters as she sees fit."

Bingley merely dropped his hands as Darcy walked away towards the refreshment table. He knew that the responsibility of living up to the Darcy name, with its noble connections and countless families looking to Pemberley for their prosperity, weighed heavily on his friend. In many ways, the trappings of wealth were indeed a trap.

"Well, girls, I do say that tonight was such a lovely success. So many gentlemen to dance with, and of course, our newest resident was obviously taken with my dear Jane!" Mrs. Bennet fanned herself and waved out of the window of their family carriage while pulling away from the Meryton assembly rooms. "Though, I cannot understand why you ever let John Lucas get away from you, Lizzy! He could have been married to you now instead of that plump, homely girl, if only you had done more to secure him."

Elizabeth and Jane shared a look. It was fruitless to argue with their mother about her favourite topic, the acquisition of husbands for her five daughters.

"La! Who cares if Lizzy dances with only the married men? Did you see how many of our *eligible* neighbours asked me for a dance,

Mamma? I will surely be married first out of all my sisters." Lydia, the youngest of the Bennet sisters at only fifteen years of age, though already the tallest with a well-developed figure, gave each of her older sisters a smug smile.

Elizabeth bit the inside of her cheek to keep from starting an argument in the cramped carriage. Jane patted Elizabeth's hand and redirected the conversation. "I also enjoyed the conversation of Mr. Bingley's sisters and friend during the breaks from dancing, Mother. Lydia, Kitty, what did you think of Miss Bingley's dress?"

Mrs. Bennet broke in before a discussion about dresses could start. "Oh, those sisters were finely dressed indeed, but their manners could not have been more formal. I thought the red-haired one had some foul smell under her nose all night. And don't even mention the friend. That Mr. Darcy may have some extensive inheritance and all the land of the Peaks, but he is so above his company that I will not be sorry to see him go back to London. Humph."

"I heard that he has his own estate in Wales somewhere, left to him by a distant relative, and that his father's estate in the north has more than one hundred tenant farms!" Kitty, the fourth Bennet sister leaned forward to produce her gossip before anyone else could speak.

"One hundred tenants! That cannot be true. How could one man manage one hundred tenants?" Lydia crossed her arms and challenged her closest sister in age and affection.

Kitty fiddled with her gloves and reticule. "Maria Lucas told me so. You know how Sir William likes to keep up with the holdings of the *ton*, and apparently, he wrote to his London solicitor for information on our new neighbours last week."

"Well, it was clear enough that he was uncomfortable with all the gossip this evening being so blatantly discussed, and with our neighbours' interest in his bank accounts. Who would not be uncomfortable?" Elizabeth pointed her finger at her youngest sisters. "I do not want to hear you two being so inconsiderate with your words and gossip. It is extremely impolite to discuss such things in a ballroom."

"Oh fie! Lizzy, let the girls alone." Mrs. Bennet waved off her least favourite daughter's scolding. "He was as unpleasant as any man I have ever seen, and what is impolite about the truth?"

"Mamma, please." Jane spoke softly in the voice which often placated their mother's nerves. "I am sure Mr. Darcy is a perfectly lovely person, though perhaps feeling out of place in this new society. He has been invited here as Mr. Bingley's particular friend and I am inclined to like him for no other reason than the connection to that amiable gentleman."

"Well," Mrs. Bennet squirmed in her seat. "As you say Jane, dear, he is a guest of Mr. Bingley, and I am sure when you are mistress of Netherfield Park you will be induced to invite him to stay for your husband's sake."

"Mamma!" Elizabeth warned. "One dance does not make them engaged, and we should not start spreading the expectation around our friends or else Jane might be harmed if he goes away."

Mrs. Bennet waved her fan around. "Nonsense! He was absolutely smitten with Jane. And it was two dances, not one. Mark my words, Miss Lizzy, Jane will not fail with Mr. Bingley as you did with John Lucas. I will have a daughter married before much longer, I am sure."

Elizabeth and Jane shared a look, then held their tongues. Fruitless indeed.

Just before taking to her bed that evening, Elizabeth heard a faint knock on the door that joined her room to Jane's.

"Come in dear, you know you need not knock."

Jane entered, went straight to the left side of Elizabeth's bed, climbed in, then covered her head with the blankets. Elizabeth laughed and proceeded under the covers herself.

"Janey, what has prompted this? You have not hidden in my bed for an age."

With downcast eyes, Jane spoke barely above a whisper. "I believe I liked him very much."

"Of course you liked him! Mr. Bingley was amicable and very attentive to you this evening. He was all that a young man should be. I am sure you can make up your own mind, but I certainly give you leave to like him as much as you will." Elizabeth booped Jane on the nose and smiled encouragingly.

"Do you really think he was especially attentive to me, or do you suppose it was just his kindly personality that made it seem so?"

Reaching for her sister, Elizabeth enveloped Jane in a tight hug. "I am certain that he was singularly attentive to you. Even Charlotte commented that he danced twice only with you and seemed to seek out your company between sets. Did he not introduce you to his sisters? That must also show his sincerity." Elizabeth could not fault Bingley for his preference shown to the eldest Bennet sister. Jane was by far the most beautiful of them all, and, in Elizabeth's biased opinion, the most beautiful gentlewoman in the whole county. Even Bingley's two sisters, who were dressed in fine silks of the very latest fashions, could not hold a candle to Jane's natural grace and beauty. Elizabeth was also aware that her older sister was quite shy and genuinely modest. She did not see herself as the most beautiful and was often unsure about the attentions bestowed on her, mostly by men. It was impossible to be jealous of Jane, for she was simply too good.

"I will bend to your opinion here Lizzy, though I will continue to guard my heart for a while longer."

Elizabeth squeezed Jane then released her. "That is entirely too sensible, but a good plan regardless. I was sincere with Mamma that one evening and only *two* dances does not see a couple engaged, but we shall give him time to enter our acquaintance. From what we have seen tonight, I believe you may get on exceedingly well."

"What about his friend, Mr. Darcy? I did have some conversation with him, though I must say it was but little. You seemed very much in his defence with Kitty's gossip and Mamma's dislike."

"Well, I was not actually introduced to him, but I did hear some of his conversation with Mr. Bingley." Elizabeth looked sheepish at Jane's scolding finger for her eavesdropping. "I did not mean to overhear, I promise. He was not aware how his voice carried around the room. I am surprised that more of our friends did not overhear."

Jane sighed. "Go on then, what do you want to tell me?"

"Some of it is that I am a bit ashamed of myself. You know that Father and I often take a sort of bizarre pleasure in reading the London gossip column and looking for the ever-changing reports of person A being in a torrid love affair with person B one day, then person C the very next, based on nothing more than a dinner invitation or passing conversation at the theatre?"

Jane nodded, knowing their father had passed on his enjoyment of laughing at their neighbours to her younger sister.

"Well, it seems that Mr. Darcy might be a person of particular interest for that column. Mr. Bingley said something about how the writer takes pleasure in following Mr. Darcy around in London. It seems that Mr. Darcy did not dance in part because he has been subjected to unfair expectations in the past based on a single dance." Elizabeth shook her head and sighed. "Also, he mentioned that he was uncomfortable hearing our neighbours, and probably Mamma, comment on his inheritance. The poor man probably felt very uncomfortable in a room full of people with whom he was not acquainted, but who were also speaking so impolitely of him."

"I am very sorry to hear that indeed." Jane's eyes had become very round with some small tears in the corners. "I am sure no one tonight was trying to make him uncomfortable. If only they could have known, I am sure they would have stopped speculating."

Elizabeth shook her head once more. "You are too kind to everyone. You know full well that our friends and family like to gossip." Tucking her hands under her head, Elizabeth turned on her back and staired at the underside of her bed's canopy. "Though I always suspected that no more than a quarter of what was printed in the gossip paper could be true, as an unconnected observer it has always amused me. I believe my feelings on the matter would be much different if I were personally acquainted with the unfortunate subjects or, heaven forbid, if I myself should be the object of such vicious lies and rumours. I feel very deeply for Mr. Darcy."

Jane smiled and closed her eyes. "It is good of you to think so well of our new neighbour."

"Yes, I am certainly very generous and all that is goodness!" Both sisters laughed, then yawned. It was nearly one in the morning already. "I believe that I shall make an effort to make the gentleman feel welcome here in Meryton. I am determined to do what I can to improve his comfort in our society. It is the Christian thing to do." *And has absolutely nothing to do with his clear blue eyes and strong shoulders*, Elizabeth added silently.

The only response was a small snore from her sister on the opposite pillow.

Blossoming Friendship

A S WAS HER FAVOURED ROUTINE, ELIZABETH BENNET rose early to go for a long walk on the cold morning following the Michaelmas assembly. She had slept fitfully the night before and risen well before the rest of her family, her thoughts consumed with the enigma of Mr. Fitzwilliam Darcy.

After sitting for a while in her favourite ash grove, watching the sun crest over the trees, Elizabeth began to ascend along the trail between Longbourn and Netherfield which led to the very top of Oakham Mount. Suddenly, a large black horse carrying a tall gentleman rider burst onto the wooded trail from a deer path. Elizabeth was so startled at their sudden appearance that she lost her balance and fell onto the ground.

Fitzwilliam Darcy had been equally engaged in the activity of re-living the Michaelmas assembly while riding his horse too fast down an unfamiliar path. He did not see Elizabeth until she fell hard on her backside.

Darcy immediately dismounted and reached out to aid Elizbeth. "I am exceedingly sorry for coming along the path at such speed. I did not think that anyone would be out at this hour."

"I dare say I also did not expect to see anyone this early after the assembly last night. It would be easy to imagine you and I are the only two persons of gentry awake in more than fifteen miles." Elizabeth laughed as she dusted off her skirts.

"Please let me help you back to your home." Darcy brought forward his large horse. "You can ride Knightly while I lead him."

Elizabeth looked at the horse, easily twenty hands tall, and shook her head. "No, thank you Mr. Darcy. I assure you, I am not made of porcelain. I shall be fine as soon as my pride heals itself."

Darcy was taken aback by being addressed by name. "I am sorry miss, but you seem to have me at a disadvantage. I was introduced to many new acquaintances last night and do not now recall your name. Though, it seems we were introduced, as you know mine."

"Everyone in Hertfordshire must know your name this morning after being introduced by Sir William to our society at yesterday's assembly." Elizabeth gave Darcy a small and kind smile, trying to convey that she understood some of how Darcy had felt the prior evening. "Though I am not surprised you do not recall all of us. My neighbours were in fine form and excess number last night. Miss Elizabeth Bennet, second daughter of Mr. Thomas Bennet of Longbourn." Elizabeth performed an exaggerated curtsy with a bright smile.

"A pleasure, Miss Elizabeth, truly." Darcy bowed low with his riding hat clutched tightly to his chest.

A moment passed after their ridiculous introductions before both let out a small chuckle at their situation. After another moment to regain their composure, Darcy drew together his brows. "I insist that you let me see you home safely, Miss Elizabeth. Please, will you not ride Knightly back home?" Darcy looked between Elizabeth and Knightly with anxiety clear on his expressive face.

Reaching out her hand, Elizabeth lightly patted the horse on his massive neck. "Mr. Darcy, I insist that I am perfectly uninjured. I have not yet been to the pinnacle of Oakham Mount this morning and I intend to make my personal pilgrimage before I must return for breakfast." Elizabeth gestured towards the path leading up to the highest point in the surrounding countryside.

"Well, would you do me the honour of allowing my company this morning? As a lifelong resident of the Peak District, I am well versed in the pleasures of a high vantage point." Darcy's shoulders relaxed seeing that Elizabeth was obviously not injured.

"Please. I would be glad for some company." Elizabeth turned back to the correct walking path and began leading gentleman and horse in the direction of the top of Oakham Mount.

A few quiet moments stretched out while both searched for some topic of conversation. Elizabeth spoke first. "I must say, even if I had been injured, I am not sure I would be able to ride your horse, sir. He is much larger than any animal we have certainly ever had at Longbourn. Where did you get him?"

Darcy turned to his black thoroughbred with obvious pride. "He was born at my father's estate of Pemberley in Derbyshire. His sire was my grandfather's favourite mount and his mare was a prized champion filly. Knightly was the second foal from our expanded breeding operation which my father started. I know he will have to be retired from being ridden in the next few years, but he is such a good horse, I cannot bear to be without him." Darcy's pride was evident in his whole demeanour. A wide, open smile lighting his whole face. "I was only sixteen years old when Knightly competed in the Flats at the Royal Ascot races. I was allowed to accompany my father to the races that year. He took home his Majesty's Plate that year, as well as three other championship titles at Jockey Club courses. We have had other horses win Royal Plates from the races at Winchester, but none are as impressive as Knightly."

"I cannot say I know much about horses, but even I am duly impressed with his accomplishments." Elizabeth's tone was jovial and her eyes sparkled. "Your horses are very important to you, I can see."

Darcy ducked his head. He was so engrossed in his favourite topic, furthered by Elizabeth's genuine interest in the discussion that he had simply forgotten to be his normal reserved self. Anyone who truly knew Darcy understood that his poor performance in public was mostly due to an extreme shyness and discomfort with the expectations placed on his station in life. Somehow, Elizabeth was able to relieve him of his timid mask as well as smooth out his social discomfort.

"Yes, Miss Elizabeth. My father's stables, and the ones I have built on my own estate in Wales, are extremely important to me. It is good to have something to do with my mind which is productive. The challenge of finding the best bloodlines, and breeding the best racehorses, has been a satisfying way to spend my time."

Shortly, Darcy and Elizabeth reached the top of Oakham Mount and enjoyed several quiet moments watching the countryside wake up with the sun. All too soon, it was time to turn back towards their respective residences.

That one stroll to the top of Oakham Mount quickly became a regular occurrence. Neither actively planned for those meetings, but neither could honestly say that they did not head out on most clear mornings with the express wish of finding the other along the path between the Longbourn and Netherfield estates. Elizabeth appreciated the way in which Darcy discussed intellectual topics with her. Darcy asked Elizabeth for her genuine opinion and was not offended when that opinion differed from his own. They debated literature, foreign policy, philosophy, and advancements in estate management during their early morning rambles, among a host of other topics. Darcy appreciated Elizabeth's easy manner and tendency to tease him into laughing at his own follies. Elizabeth was a welcome change from the ladies of the *ton* and their single-minded matrimonial efforts.

Unfortunately, there was one marriage-minded lady who Darcy could not escape in the Hertfordshire countryside, as she was currently residing under the same roof as himself. Miss Caroline Bingley, Bingley's younger sister, had set her sights on Darcy the second she laid eyes on his family's London townhouse. With eight bedrooms, two dining rooms, an indoor arboretum with a tropical flower conservatory, and a ballroom large enough to accommodate at least fifty dancing pairs, Darcy House in Grosvenor's Square was Caroline's ideal of high society and status. Caroline had yet to visit Pemberley, but if the Darcy London townhouse was any indication of the grandeur of the family's ancestral estate, she was certain the Darcys' ancestral home would be nothing short of magnificent.

A large part of Caroline's agreement to leave London for Hertfordshire had been the opportunity to show Darcy she was capable of running an estate household. She truly believed that the only thing holding Darcy back from making an offer to her was his reserve about her lack of experience with a country estate. This sojourn should have been the final piece to their courtship.

To her great chagrin, Caroline had not been able to spend any real time with Darcy during their stay. Even more worrisome to Caroline was her brother's continued infatuation with Jane Bennet. The Bennet and Bingley families had been socialising frequently at house parties of the local gentry, and each evening in their company had increased the fervency of Bingley's talk of Jane's beauty and serenity. If Bingley married that pretty, country no-body with no dowry and no connections of which to speak, Caroline believed she would become the laughing stock of London.

So, one morning a few weeks into their country stay, Caroline initiated her plan to both secure Darcy and remove her family party from Hertfordshire. Caroline awoke much earlier than was her wont, in order to accompany Darcy on his morning ride so they may have some much-needed conversation. Walking up to the stables just as the sun was cresting the house, Caroline beamed at finding her prey still attaching the bridle to his horse.

"Good morning, Mr. Darcy! It is a wonderful day for a ride, is it not?"

Darcy looked up sharply and did not quite keep the astonished look from his face at seeing Caroline out of her chambers before eleven in the morning. Knightly huffed loudly and nosed at his owner, clearly impatient for their race across the fields to begin.

"Yes, Miss Bingley. It is a lovely morning. Are you planning to walk the garden paths or ride out towards the folly by the small lake?" Darcy gestured in the opposite direction that he had been planning to ride. "I'm sure one of the grooms would be more than happy to accompany you."

"Oh, no, Mr. Darcy. I was hoping you might show me some of the more interesting paths around the estate. I know how you like to ramble in the mornings and thought it would be good to become familiar with the sights you particularly enjoy." Caroline glanced towards the stable hands and grooms with a slight sneer to her face. "I believe your *superior* company would be much better than that of a servant."

Barely managing to suppress a sigh, Darcy gestured for the stable manager to bring out Caroline's horse and the mounting block. Once both were seated on their mounts, Darcy and Caroline started on their sedate morning ride.

As expected, Caroline began complaining about the society in Hertfordshire and the lack of any quality entertainments before they made it out of the stable yard.

"I cannot understand Charles's insistence on staying in this backwater little town! There are no acquaintances of any fashion. Did you see that Miss Lucas wore the same gown at her mother's Guy Fawkes night dinner party as she wore to the Michaelmas assembly?" Caroline clutched the reins of her horses a bit tighter. "Why, I would certainly die if I had to re-wear a gown in company."

Darcy wrinkled his nose and sniffed. "I find the people and entertainment here to be superior to the hamlets near Pemberley and Cresselly Park. Being so near London on the great north road, Meryton is much more prosperous than near my family's estates."

"Surely, you don't mean that! How could any place be superior to your father's estate?"

This time, Darcy was not able to fully suppress his eye roll. "Really, Miss Bingley. Though I am very partial to Pemberley, I am not blind to the truth. Meryton is more than three times as large as Lambton village. Here, there are more than four and twenty landed families in the immediate society. One would have to travel more than fifty miles to find so many genteel persons in Derbyshire."

"I believe 'genteel' is not the world I would use to describe the society here," Caroline sneered. "Only Miss Jane Bennet might be considered truly genteel."

Darcy began to ride silently beside his best friend's sister while she continued to spew forth all of the reasons to return to London post haste, donning his London Society mask of feigned indifference, and applied himself to tuning out her ceaseless noise.

When the two riders finally neared the fork in the path that would take them to Oakham Mount and Elizabeth's typical morning ramble, Darcy was startled out of his internal musings by Caroline shrilly calling his name.

"Mr. Darcy! Are you quite alright? You just had the most curious look on your face and you have not answered my question regarding

Miss Jane Bennet. If I did not know you better, I would think you had not been attending to our conversation."

"Miss Bingley, I must apologise. I was distracted by considering the upcoming fork in the path. One direction shall take us back along the perimeter of Netherfield Park and return to the stables, and the other direction leads to the high point between the Netherfield and Longbourn estates." Darcy pointed towards the path which would take them to the top of Oakham Mount. "There is a lovely vista on the high point if you are inclined to see it."

Caroline smiled coquettishly and batted her eyelashes. "I would be happy to go wherever you are inclined to lead me, sir."

Darcy nodded and turned his horse toward Oakham Mount.

"Miss Bingley, I apologise again for not properly attending the conversation, but what was your question regarding Miss Jane Bennet?"

"Only what we should do about her and Charles. I have invited Miss Bennet to have dinner with myself and Louisa tomorrow evening while you, Mr. Hurst, and Charles are dining with the officers. We intend to learn more about her character and connections, but what else can be done?"

Darcy thought for a moment before answering. "I do not know if there is anything else to be done. She is certainly the most eligible young woman in the neighbourhood as the eldest daughter of the largest local landowner. Miss Bennet is certainly worthy of your notice for such a particular invitation. I am sure Charles will welcome your impressions on the lady as he becomes acquainted with her and her family. If they were to marry, she would be your sister after all, so your comfort and friendship with her would certainly be welcomed by Charles. I believe your invitation to dinner is a wonderful gesture of welcome."

Caroline's jaw opened in a silent scream and she sputtered for a moment before responding. "Mr. Darcy, I am shocked! Have we not been discussing at length how improper and vulgar the local population is, particularly including Mrs. Bennet and the youngest two Bennet sisters? You, not five minutes ago, agreed to help me convince Charles to take us all back to London for the holidays early. My purpose in having dinner with Miss Bennet is to *expose* her. The Bennets have one uncle who is a barrister and another in trade in London who resides in

Cheapside! We would be a laughing stock if Charles were to connect us to such a family."

"Miss Bingley, I fail to see the truth in your argument." Darcy wrinkled his nose and lifted his chin a bit in what most would see as an aristocratic posture. Though, truly, it was a gesture meant to focus his eyes on something other than his conversation partner's face, born out of Darcy's reserved nature and general discomfort discussing class and rank. "Your father is the current owner of a very large mill operation out of Yorkshire and has several warehouses in Cheapside. Your father has admirable ambitions for his son to become a member of the landed gentry, which is why he has sent you, Charles, and Mrs. Hurst out to lease a property and learn estate management, but as of today, the Bennet family decidedly outranks your family. Charles marrying Miss Bennet would make his sons the grandsons of a gentleman and able to hold the title themselves. Elsewise, Charles's purchasing of an estate would not produce true Bingley gentlemen until his great-grandchildren inherit the land."

Caroline's complexion was nearly sheet white. She knew that Darcy was correct in his assessment of her family's money being earned in trade, but they were part of the *ton*! Long before Caroline was able to form a response to Darcy's assessment of her family versus the Bennet family, one of the Bennet sisters appeared on the road as if summoned by evil spirits for Caroline's personal torture. Any further discussion would have to wait for another opportunity to be alone with Darcy.

Darcy was completely ignorant to Caroline's now sour mood. "Miss Elizabeth, what a pleasant coincidence to happen upon you this morning. As you can see, Miss Bingley and I are on a morning ride and were just about to point our mounts to the Mount." Darcy smiled and stepped out of his saddle. "Would you care to join us at the summit of your diminutive rolling hill, which is certainly not a mountain?"

Elizabeth chuckled at Darcy taking the first jab of the morning. "Tease all you wish Mr. Darcy, but I shall be content with my mountain. You proclaim the superiority of the Peaks near your home, yet still seem to enjoy the view from atop our humble hill well enough. I therefore must conclude that either the Peaks are much too high for you to reach the top, so you have never had the opportunity to observe the view such enormous height affords, or the vista atop Oakham Mount is substantially equal in splendour to the view from atop your beloved Peaks. Either way, my 'diminutive rolling hill' is at least as worthy of your notice as the Peak District. Finally, if these Peaks of yours are as high as you claim, I doubt that I would be able to make the journey to the summit twice in a single morning. But, as luck would have it, I still have enough stamina to join you at the top of Oakham Mount, even though I have just come down from that very spot."

Darcy let out a hearty laugh at Elizabeth's fresh arguments regarding the mountains. "Fair enough, Miss Elizabeth, you win today's battle of the wits. Shall we call a truce and make our way to the lookout point? Come, Miss Bingley, you shall enjoy the view, I am sure."

Caroline Bingley spent the rest of the morning paying close attention to the view around her but saw very little of nature. And she most surely did not enjoy any of what she saw.

A Better Understanding

"OH ELIZABETH, DO NOT BE SO DRAMATIC. NO one dies from a trifling cold. I am sure Jane will be well enough to take dinner with the family and then spend the evening with Mr. Bingley." Mrs. Bennet was sitting at the breakfast table and waved away her second daughter. Elizabeth had a death grip on a letter, just delivered from Netherfield in Jane's shaky hand saying she had taken ill the evening before, having gotten caught in a rainstorm after their mother insisted Jane go on horseback to the dinner invitation from Caroline Bingley instead of taking the carriage.

"Mamma, I would still feel much better if I was able to see Jane with my own eyes and ensure she is well." Elizabeth sat heavy on one of the dining room chairs. "Also, how rude would it be to inconvenience Mr. Bingley's sisters or servants in caring for Jane? No, I must go this morning and see to my sister."

"Fine, do what you will, child. Not like I have ever been able to stop you from your foolishness." Mrs. Bennet took another piece of toast and spread jam.

Elizabeth stared at her mother for a long moment, then folded the note in her hands and rose from the table. Not five minutes later, she was walking down the road towards Netherfield. The morning was clear and bright, but the walking path was muddy from the previous day's rain. By the time she completed the three-mile walk, her half boots and hems were covered in mud.

Even more embarrassing, Elizabeth had forgotten to grab a bonnet on her way out of the house after being so frustrated with her mother's cavalier attitude. So there she was, standing on the edge of the formal gardens on the deer path between Netherfield and Longbourn, muddy and bare-headed.

Around the back of the stables, a very distinctive black horse with a tall gentleman rider began to come in her direction. The moment Darcy recognised Elizabeth's presence, he steered Knightly to her and dismounted.

"Miss Elizabeth, are you well?" Worry lines formed between his blue eyes, taking in Elizabeth's mildly dishevelled appearance. "Do you need any assistance?"

Elizbeth looked down again to her muddy boots and tried to smooth the fly-away curls which never stayed in their pins. "No, sir. I am well enough. I have come to check on my sister. She sent a note this morning that she is ill. I believe, in my haste to get here, I have made a mess of myself."

"Not at all. Your constitution seems brightened by the exercise. Perhaps I can show you to Miss Bennet's rooms and let Bingley know you have come. I am sure he will be happy to know Miss Bennet is being well cared for." Looking back at Elizabeth's half boots and walking dress, Darcy continued. "I shall also send my carriage and valet to gather some additional items for you both. I am sure you would appreciate having a dinner dress as well as some more comfortable shoes."

"Oh! Mr. Darcy, that is not necessary, I am sure. I would not like to inconvenience your valet in such a way."

Darcy laughed. "When I left my dressing room, Connor was setting out several of my boots to be polished, a task I know he despises, which is why he does them all at once about every fortnight. You might find him grateful for the distraction."

"Are you sure you should be adding guests to Miss Bingley's table?" A teasing look in her eyes, Elizabeth chastised Darcy for overstepping his place. "I might imbalance her menu for the entire week."

"I am absolutely certain that the cook here can manage to feed one additional young woman without altering the menus. I have been impressed with the staff here, especially the kitchen staff." Darcy put his hands out to the side in a self-deprecating gesture. "I have often heard Miss Bingley bemoan the lack of a French cook in the country, but as a man of some height, I am not a light eater and I find the overuse of butter and heavy creams in French cooking much too rich for my gut. Simple, well-turned English roasts are much more to my taste."

"I appreciate the simpler food as well." Elizabeth took Darcy's out-stretched arm and they both moved towards the stables to lead Knightly into the side pasture. "Thank you for seeing me to Jane. I was beginning to dread having to face Miss Bingley with this mud on my shoes."

"Yes, I can see that would be a daunting possibility. Do not fret, she will be none the wiser and I shall discuss with Bingley the need to have you installed by Miss Bennet."

"Thank you very much, sir."

"Good morning, Miss Eliza. I trust you and your sister are well this morning. Has dear Jane been comfortable during her recuperation?"

Elizabeth tried to stifle a sigh. She was certain that Caroline Bingley was the most insincere person to ever come to Meryton and had no actual interest in Jane's health or comfort. It was a struggle to bring all her manners to bear to respond politely. "Good morning to you, Miss Bingley. Thank you, we are both quite comfortable here at Netherfield and Jane is much improved over two nights ago. I believe her fever broke during the night and she shall be feeling much better soon." Elizabeth resisted the urge to add *and then I can take her home and be rid of you.*

"Well, that is certainly a relief for all of us." Caroline bit her tongue and took a seat at the table opposite Elizabeth. "While we have a few minutes just to ourselves, I had a topic I wished to discuss which is of a bit of a delicate nature. Would it be alright if I dismissed the staff for a few minutes so we could be free to speak?"

For the first time ever, Elizabeth was exceedingly interested in hearing what Caroline had to say. "Of course, Miss Bingley, I am at your disposal to discuss any topic of import."

After the door to the kitchen closed, Caroline started in on her carefully prepared speech. "Miss Eliza, I could not help but notice that you have developed a *repartee* of sorts with Mr. Darcy over the few days you have been staying with us. I completely understand your interest in the gentleman, and it must be hard to separate out expectations for the future from harmless conversation in the present, but I wanted to caution you, as a *friend*, that Mr. Darcy would never make you, or any of the ladies in Hertfordshire, an offer."

Caroline poured herself a cup of tea from the large pot and added two sugar cubes. She lifted the cup to her lips then paused to look back at Elizabeth. "It is nothing against your character, but I know you are not of London Society and would not have the experience with high society to see the situation clearly. So, as someone who *is* part of the *ton*, I thought it would be kinder to let you know now, before a true tender could take root." She finally took a sip from her tea, then stirred in another sugar cube. "Mr. Darcy will surely marry someone in his own sphere, as is expected of such a wealthy gentleman." Caroline smiled into her tea.

Elizabeth was not fooled. She knew that Caroline wanted to marry Darcy, but she also was as certain as she could be without blatantly discussing the topic with him, that Darcy could not stand Caroline. While it was true Elizabeth was not familiar with London society or the habits of the *ton*, she knew it did not take a gentleman three years to make his proposal if one was to ever be forthcoming.

It was sad really. Caroline Bingley had all the material possessions that extreme wealth could procure. Unfortunately, bank notes could not purchase self-worth or a sense of security. Elizabeth decided to be kind to Caroline, at least mostly kind.

"Miss Bingley, I am grateful to know that my sisters and I have a true friend in you. Not many ladies would take the time to speak so plainly to spare the feelings of another." Elizabeth folded her serviette and placed it over her empty plate. "Now, let me speak plainly, so as to put you at ease. I am under no illusion that Mr. Darcy is at liberty to make me an offer. He is the nephew of an Earl for goodness sake!" Elizabeth laughed and sat back in her chair then gestured between herself and Caroline. "We Bennets and Bingleys are far too low to hope for any connection in the peerage. My father's sister is married to a Knight with a bestowed title for exemplary service to the Crown as a naval officer, but my other uncles are all either in trade or profession, like your father I believe." Caroline blanched at the last comment and set her cup down harshly on the table.

Elizabeth decided to finish this conversation, and drank the last dregs of her tea. "Certainly, we are not the calibre of lady who shall be the next Mrs. Darcy. While his inheritance is safely in the hands of his most excellent father, Mr. Darcy is free to indulge in friendships with lower society, but I expect even that is coming to an end." Elizabeth leaned in closer to the table to deliver her final nail. "It may seem indelicate, but Mr. Darcy has confessed that his family is anxious for him to marry this season and, to that end, his aunt, the Countess, has his future wife picked out. You certainly have the right of it when you say Mr. Darcy shall marry where he is expected."

Standing from the table, Elizabeth patted the back of Caroline's hand, which was limp on the table by her flatware. The look in her eyes was far away, focused on the windows out to the side garden, stricken and sallow. Elizabeth turned to make a hasty retreat from the breakfast room, however she looked back at Caroline just before crossing the threshold. In the few moments she had taken to cross the room, Caroline seemed to have bolstered. Where her posture had been small and unhappy, now Caroline was sitting straighter and more erect than proper posture would require. Her forlorn look was replaced with a determined mien.

Elizabeth shook her head and left the room.

After such a trying conversation with Caroline over breakfast, Elizabeth decided to make her way immediately back to Jane to assess her condition. However, no sooner had Elizabeth stepped onto the second stair leading to the guest wing than she heard her mother's loud proclamations in the foyer accompanied by her youngest sisters' giggling. Elizabeth sighed heavily, then turned towards the entrance hall.

"Ah, Miss Elizabeth," Mr. Bingley greeted when he noticed Elizabeth coming around the hall from the dining room. "Darcy and I happened to pass your mother and sisters in their carriage as we rode towards the turned fields and decided to see them to the house. They have come to see how Miss Jane Bennet does."

"I thank you for attending to my family, Mr. Bingley. Jane was asleep just an hour ago, but she is likely awake now. I was on my way to her room when I heard your entrance. Mamma, if you come with me, I will take you to Jane right away." It was too much for Elizabeth to hope that her mother and sisters would retire to Jane's sick room immediately.

"Now Lizzy, it would be very bad manners for us to abandon our hosts so soon, and certainly, Jane should sleep longer. You say she was still asleep merely an hour ago? Then, I'm sure we would be intruding on her much-needed repose. You would not mind our company for a few minutes more while we wait for the apothecary, would you, Mr. Bingley?" Elizabeth cringed a little at her mother's coquettish smile and attempted flirting with the young master of Netherfield.

"Of course not, Mrs. Bennet." Bingley was not the most observant, nor easily offended. "Shall we have some tea in the east drawing room?"

Mrs. Bennet and the three youngest Bennet sisters preceded Bingley into the drawing room while Elizabeth and Darcy hung back for a moment. Once Bingley had turned toward his newest guests, Darcy offered his arm to Elizabeth and they entered the drawing room together.

Upon steering Elizabeth to the overstuffed chair by the large window she seemed to prefer, Darcy noted the object she had been carrying. "I see you still have Bingley's copy of the *Odyssey* in your possession, Miss Elizabeth. Have you been able to make it past the sirens' call yet?"

Elizabeth smiled up at Darcy, glad for the distraction from her family imposing upon Netherfield at such an early hour. "I assure you I have not intentionally drowned myself in their song, and was just passing the whirlpool Charybdis this morning when breakfast was announced. I was hoping to find a sunny spot in the library today to complete the epic tale."

Before Darcy could respond, the other occupants of the room intruded on their discussion of classical literature in the form of excited squealing from Lydia Bennet, the youngest of the Bennet sisters. "Oh, Lizzy, you must convince Mr. Bingley to hold a ball!"

"Lydia, whatever do you mean?"

"Really Lizzy, have you not been paying attention to the conversation?! We have just been saying you must tell Mr. Bingley we have all been waiting for him to hold a ball for the neighbourhood, and we can help him with the names of the best families who should get invitations. It would be quite the event of the year."

Elizabeth could not quite find her tongue after such an extraordinary speech by her youngest sister, especially as they were all guests in Bingley's home. Thankfully, Darcy came to her aide before Elizabeth's dullness was exposed. "Miss Lydia, I do believe you are correct that it is the expected thing for the newest member of the neighbourhood to host some kind of festivity at the start of the Christmas holiday season. Your suggestion of a ball I believe is just the thing to celebrate new neighbours and such a wonderful time of the year." He turned back towards Elizabeth, sitting in the early morning sunshine. "Miss Elizabeth, might I entreat you to accept me for your first set, supposing, of course, that my friend does in fact host such an event and we are both free for the evening?"

"Mr. Darcy, you need not extend such an invitation in such haste. I know how you dislike the activity," Elizabeth said with a teasing smile.

"I assure you, I am happy to dance with my well-established acquaintances and neighbours."

Elizabeth looked down to the book resting in her lap and fought a blush taking over her face.

Mrs. Bennet was a loud, silly kind of woman, but she was not altogether stupid. A young Fanny Gardiner had used her beauty and lively personality to marry above her station twenty-three years ago at the tender age of sixteen. Even as a mother of five and nearing her fortieth birthday, Mrs. Bennet was a beautiful woman. Each of her five daughters had inherited something of her good looks and lively spirit. Jane was the most beautiful with golden hair and fair, almost delicate features. Kitty was still young, but another few years and her fine hair and fair features would rival those of dear Jane. Lydia had Mr. Bennet's darker colouring, but was still tall and slender with demure features and a wonderful lively personality. Mary was the least like Mrs. Bennet and took after her father almost completely in looks and personality. Thankfully, Mary was at least tall and slender.

Elizabeth was by far Mrs. Bennet's most troublesome child. She had always been particularly short, even as a child. Both Mary and Kitty had eclipsed Elizabeth's stature before they were all out of the nursery. Her dark colouring had also been obvious from the moment she was born sporting a full head of dark, curly locks. Only Jane was truly capable of taming Elizabeth's mass of hair, and even after more than half an hour putting in pins and clips, there were always tendrils of curls escaping her crown. Her eyes and mouth were over-large like her father's features, but her bosom left much to be desired with respect to size. The overall effect was pleasing in an unconventional sort of way, but no one would consider Elizabeth Bennet a classical beauty. Worst of all, in Mrs. Bennet's opinion, Elizabeth had inherited her father's bookishness and tendency to be impertinent in company to everyone. Mrs. Bennet had often worried that Elizabeth would never marry a man of any consequence.

Now, Mrs. Bennet had plans for her second oldest child that included considerably more wealth and prestige than had ever come into the Bennet family acquaintance before. Though she could not comprehend how it happened, Mrs. Bennet recognised the signs of infatuation on Darcy's face when he spoke to Elizabeth. Infatuation was the best inducement to marriage, according to Mrs. Bennet's personal experience. She reasoned that whatever Elizabeth had been doing on her own was good and clever enough that her interference was not needed.

"Oh, Mr. Darcy, I am sure that Lizzy is merely joking. She would never miss such a wonderful chance to dance with friends and neighbours either. Right Lizzy?" Mrs. Bennet gave Elizabeth a pointed look.

"Yes, you are correct Mamma, I do enjoy dancing very much. Especially with our close acquaintances."

"La! Lizzy, how droll. If you do not dance with Mr. Darcy after he asks, you will not be allowed to dance with all the soldiers, and I cannot imagine missing such dances." Lydia waved around her head and opened her fan in a mock flirting gesture.

In order to forward her new goal for Elizabeth's marriage, for once in her life Mrs. Bennet reined in her youngest daughter and spoke with a modicum of sense. "Lydia, do mind, if you cannot speak with more delicacy, you might not be allowed into the more superior society of the Bingleys' acquaintances. Take care child."

Mrs. Bennet stood suddenly and looked to Bingley. "I do believe we should see Jane now. I would not want her to be alone when the apothecary arrives. I believe we shall also stay for about an hour visiting in her rooms and give Lizzy a short break from her nursing duties. I know how she adores a lovely morning walk and a good book."

Elizabeth could only stay seated in her chair and look after her retreating mother and younger sisters with shock.

An Excellent Judge of Character

"MARY? MARY DEAR, MAMMA WISHES FOR YOUR presence. We are to walk out with our cousin to Meryton this morning and your company is much desired." Elizabeth called to the third Bennet sister as she ascended the stairs in search of the final member of the morning's walking party, which was the newest scheme to reduce the noise of the household and entertain the Bennets' newest guest.

Elizabeth and Jane had returned from Netherfield for only one night before another new person invaded their acquaintance and their home. Mr. William Collins was the Bennet sisters' second cousin through their father's aunt, and the only male heir to the Bennet family estate.

On the evening Elizabeth and Jane came home, Mr. Bennet had shared with Elizabeth a letter from Collins asking for permission to visit the Bennet family for an extended stay between Michaelmas and Christmas. One would expect that such a missive might have been filled with a discussion about why such a visit was requested, and as an introduction of the previously unknown relative. Instead, Collins's writing seemed filled with platitudes, sermon quotes, and descriptions of persons so wholly unconnected with the Bennets that it was inconceivable as to why such information was included in a letter to them. While he waited for his inheritance, Collins was the rector at a comfortable living in Hunsford, Kent. The living was bestowed by the owner of the Rosings Estate, which was currently Lady Catherine de Bourgh, of whom Collins had much to say to his cousin. There was also a good amount of toadying about the disagreement between Mr. Bennet and the former Mr. Collins which caused the current rift in the family such that the current Mr. Collins had never previously visited his 'fair' cousins or the 'place of his future felicity.'

By way of explaining his request to visit now, Collins only said he wished to offer an olive branch to his cousins as a means to heal such a rift, which of course was his great patroness's idea in the first instance, and such a fine idea was never had by anyone before. The letter went on again about Lady Catherine's unparalleled condescension in such a way that Collins never actually said what form such an olive branch should take.

So, it was with great surprise and no little humour that the young Bennet ladies found out at dinner the night of his arrival that Collins intended to take one of them as his bride, to merge the families and keep the estate of Longbourn as the Bennet family seat.

This news was received much more favourably by the Bennet matriarch. Mrs. Bennet was thrilled at the prospect of seeing another daughter married, and any suitor come to pay attention to her daughters was more than welcome. Within the space of moments, Collins had the full and unwavering support of the mistress of Longbourn for his plan.

As a man with functioning eyes and at least half a brain, Collins set his sights on Jane inside of five minutes after being shown into the parlour. Thankfully, Mrs. Bennet was convinced that Jane would be Mrs. Bingley before the Christmas cakes were cold, so she (not so tactfully) steered Collins away from Jane after dinner. The next morning, Collins turned his eye to Elizabeth, the next in age and beauty to Jane. But again Mrs. Bennet had plans for her second child that included ten thousand pounds per year and a house in Town, so she redirected Collins to the third Bennet sister.

Truthfully, Mary was the wisest choice for Collins. She was pious and thought she would enjoy life as a parson's wife until they came to claim the estate, hopefully many years in the future. She was also the only Bennet sister likely to entertain the idea of doing that which was necessary to provide Collins with children.

Elizabeth, being very grateful to her mother's scheming for once in her life, was quick to join in the effort to have Mary become the next mistress of Longbourn. Elizabeth shuffled through her own closet looking for any gown which might be offered as a sacrifice to Mary's cause. Three were chosen and trim added to the hem to make them long enough for Mary's taller stature. She was even successful in separating Kitty and Lydia from a few of their more attractive bonnets and ribbons by threatening them with Collins's attentions should he not find Mary to his liking. The once 'plain' Bennet sister was looking very well indeed. Thankfully, the efforts were not wasted.

Just over a sennight had passed since Collins's arrival, and he was a fair way to loving Mary. If only they could find the time together for a private assignation, Elizabeth was convinced her sister would be happily engaged.

"Mary? Is something the matter dear?" Elizabeth called into Mary's room when the woman of the hour failed to appear at the bottom of the stairs for their mid-morning excursion into town.

Mary was seated at her window, wearing the most attractive of Elizabeth's dresses which had been altered for her, hair arranged, gloves already donned, and beautiful bonnet from Lydia in hand. Unfortunately, tears streamed down her pretty face.

"My dear! Whatever is the matter!?"

"Tell me truthfully Lizzy, Mr. Collins would not have bestowed his attention on me if Mamma had not told him that you and Jane were already being courted, would he?"

Elizabeth took a sharp breath and grasped both of her sister's hands tightly. "I am sure that is not true Mary. It is clear to everyone that you and Mr. Collins match in personality and temperament. I believe you have always wished to marry a man of the cloth, no? And was our dear cousin not saying just last night how much he approves of your quiet steadiness and studious nature? While it is of course the expected thing for families to marry off elder daughters before younger ones, and Mr. Collins probably felt some pressure to consider Jane and myself before settling on you out of respect for our positions as the eldest sisters, I'm sure he would have always come to you as the natural choice for his bride. I will be happy to call him brother when the time comes."

"Then why have you painted me like a peacock in your dresses and Lydia's ribbons?"

"So that you may truly feel as beautiful as we all know you to be sweet sister." Elizabeth smiled and squeezed Mary's hands. "While I do not always agree with our mother about the best way to go about finding a husband, I believe she is correct in one respect. Men like to have something pretty to look at every now and again. You have always been pretty my dear. Clothes and ribbons cannot turn a sow into a silk purse, but they can help stupid men along the way to matrimony. Now. Let us to town! You look especially fine this morning and we should not waste such a beautiful day. What would God say if we squandered such a gift as sunshine in November?"

After a quick press of a cool wet washcloth to Mary's tear tracked eyes and cheeks, all the Bennet sisters and Collins set off for Meryton.

As soon as the Longbourn inhabitants crossed the high street into the town centre, Lydia and Kitty spotted a number of acquaintances from the ______shire militia being housed in Meryton for the winter. Lieutenant Denny was heading out of the tailor's shop with an unknown man in tow. Jane and Elizabeth followed the youngest Bennet sisters closely as they darted across the town centre to beg an introduction.

"Lieutenant Denny! Good morning, how are you? And who is the handsome new friend you have with you?" Lydia barely paused for a breath before dipping into a deep curtsey and fluttering her eyes at the stranger.

Denny and the stranger turned bright smiles towards the Bennet sisters and answered before either Jane or Elizabeth could scold Lydia for her flirting. "Miss Lydia, Miss Kitty, how fortunate that we have come across you this fine morning. Please let me have the great pleasure of introducing Mr. George Wickham to you. Wickham, these ladies are the Bennet sisters from Longbourn estate. Miss Jane Bennet, the eldest, Miss Elizabeth, Miss Kitty, Miss Lydia, and Miss Mary is there walking with the parson across the street. Ladies, Wickham has just today taken a position with the ______shire militia as a Lieutenant. I was taking him on a short tour of town before his meeting with Colonel Forster at luncheon."

Jane and Elizabeth corralled their youngest sisters and, after introducing Collins to the officers, managed to keep Lydia from more overt flirting as the group moved up the street towards the barracks and the milliners shop. After a few minutes of walking and talking, Jane and Elizabeth's attention was caught by two fine gentlemen coming down the road on horseback.

Bingley and Darcy rode up to the group a moment later and dismounted. "Miss Bennet! How fortunate we have come across you this morning. Darcy and I were just on our way to Longbourn to call upon you and your family, but here you are instead. Marvellous!" Bingley was all smiles and good cheer, while his friend was sporting a facial expression closer to having smelled something rotten. Elizabeth immediately went to Darcy's side without much thought to how her actions might signal her attachment to the rich man.

"Mr. Darcy, are you well? Your complexion has taken on an alarming red hue, and you look as if you have ingested something noxious. Can I fetch you water or perhaps a glass of wine to settle your stomach?" Elizabeth wrung her hands and looked around the square for a place to sit if Darcy required a rest.

Darcy looked at Elizabeth and willed himself to calm down. A feeling of extreme anger (and perhaps jealousy) had come over him when he saw Elizabeth talking with, and smiling at, George Wickham. Making a scene in the town square was the last thing Darcy wanted to do, so he schooled his features and responded calmly to Elizabeth.

"Miss Elizabeth, thank you for your concern. I was feeling flushed from the ride here, but I believe it has passed. Will you not introduce me to your friends?" Darcy attempted a smile of kinds, but only a grimace was achieved in his heightened state.

"Mr. Darcy, I would be happy to introduce you to the men in our party you are unfamiliar with, but we have just this morning been introduced to one of the group, a Mr. Wickham has apparently taken a commission with the ______shire militia as a Lieutenant and begins his duty today."

Darcy visibly relaxed at this news. "As it happens, Miss Elizabeth, I am already acquainted with Mr. Wickham and will only require an introduction to the other two men." Darcy turned to face the group.

"George, it is good to see you again. Miss Elizabeth tells me you are joining the militia quartering here this winter. Good man. I am sure my cousin, Colonel Fitzwilliam, will be glad to hear of your new post. We cannot have the homeland and our citizens unprotected with so many men away in the Peninsular War. Have you come from London or Derbyshire?"

George Wickham paled a bit at the easy manner in which Darcy spoke to him. "Darce, I am surprised to find you here and not enjoying London. I have just come from Town where I purchased a commission and came to meet with my friend Lieutenant Edward Denny." George gestured to the military man. "Denny, this is a long-time friend, Mr. Fitzwilliam Darcy of Pemberley in Derbyshire and Cresselly Park in Wales. My father was the steward of Pemberley and worked for Darcy's father until his death several years ago. We grew up together in Derbyshire and shared rooms at Cambridge."

Upon hearing the introduction of Darcy to the lieutenant, Collins became quite animated and inserted himself into the conversation. "Did I hear you correctly, that this is Mr. Darcy of Pemberley?!"

Mary tried to interject and perform the introduction. "Yes, Mr. Collins. Might I present to you our cousin, Mr. Darcy? This is Mr. William Collins, cousin to my father. He is staying with us for a few weeks. Mr. Collins, this is Mr. Darcy of Pemberley. He is a guest of Mr. Bingley at Netherfield."

"Well, such an honour, I'm sure!" Collins proceeded to bow incessantly and lowly to Darcy, Wickham, and Bingley. "I am so *very* honoured to be in the presence of the nephew of my noble patroness, Lady Catherine de Bourgh. I am the humble recipient of a living from her ladyship, the Hunsford parsonage near her estate, Rosings Park in Kent, and she has been most benevolent in her consideration to me. In fact, this journey to visit my fair cousins was her idea entirely, and I cannot be more grateful for the wisdom in her instruction to come to Hertfordshire and seek communion amongst my relations. Might I ease your mind sufficiently by saying that, when I was last in her presence not ten days prior, she and her lovely daughter Miss Anne de Bourgh, were both in very great health." Collins ended this extraordinary speech with more pronounced bowing. He bent over so low that Mary was required to catch his hat when it tumbled from his head and return the item to him after he regained an upright position.

Darcy looked at the toadying man with great amusement. He turned to Elizabeth to hide his smile, but one look at the twinkle in her fine eyes had him coughing into his elbow to regain some semblance of decorum. "Excuse me please. It must be the dust from the horses. Mr. Collins, thank you for that report on the state of my relations. I admit, I am a letter in her ladyship's debt and shall mention seeing you here, fulfilling her wishes by escorting the Bennet ladies around town on this fine morning, when next I write."

The look on Collins's face upon hearing that he would be mentioned in such a letter was nothing short of ecstatic. Before another coughing fit was required of both Darcy and Elizabeth, the gentleman offered his arm to the lady and steered her towards the book shop. "Miss Elizabeth, might I beg your indulgence in introducing me to the bookseller here in Meryton? I'm looking for a new item with which to entertain myself after having finished the book you recommended, *Sense and Sensibility*, by a lady. It was a fast read and did much to entertain in the evenings, but I believe I need something more masculine now. An introduction from one of the leading literary minds of the area will surely lend me credibility with the proprietor."

Elizabeth followed Darcy into the booksellers with an amused look on her face. "Mr. Darcy, please let me apologise for my cousin. We have only come to meet him recently and I had no idea of his connection to your family, or I would have warned you before subjecting you to such an introduction." Though her words were contrite, Elizabeth's face still shone with mirth and repressed laughter.

"Please do not trouble yourself, Miss Elizabeth. From what I know of my aunt, Mr. Collins perfectly fits with the type of person I would expect her to choose for her church. I would not be surprised to learn that she reviews his sermons ahead of their delivery to ensure the message conforms to her decided views on religion and morality. I cannot wait to hear what he might preach this coming Easter when my cousins and I make our annual visit to Rosins."

"So, your relationship with your aunt is a close one then?"

"I would not say we are particularly closely aligned in mind or share the same views on many subjects, but she is my mother's sister and has looked to my father and myself for support since her husband died many years ago. Regardless of her faults, I am close to her in familial affection. My cousin Anne, her daughter, is a close friend as well as a relation. We are of a similar age, and of similar temperament. That usually makes for quiet evenings when all in company." Darcy gave Elizabeth a pointed look and she laughed behind her free hand. "That is why we invite our other cousin, Colonel Richard Fitzwilliam. He treats life as a joke, even while facing Napoleon, and gives us all good entertainment."

Darcy suddenly remembered their actual errand for the day and reached inside his coat pocket to extract a large envelope addressed to Mr. and Mrs. Thomas Bennet. "Speaking of good entertainment, Bingley and I were on our way to pay a call to your mother this morning, with instructions to deliver this invitation to a ball being hosted at Netherfield by Miss Bingley on the twenty-sixth. I believe you already promised me the first set, did you not?" Darcy handed the envelope to Elizabeth just as several people came into the book shop.

"Of course, Mr. Darcy, you are correct as usual. I look forward to the event."

Tell Tale Letters

" **G**OOD MORNING, MA'AM."
The black-cherry, well sprung, two seat curricle was so often seen carrying Miss Anne de Bourgh and her companion, a Mrs. Jenkins, around the grounds of Rosings Park and the hamlet of Hunsford, that the local inhabitants barely paused anymore to bow or curtsey to the mistress of the estate. This morning was no exception as Anne commanded her mare around the perimeter road circling the two tenant farms on the south side of Rosings's land. Anne had fully inherited her father's estate when she turned twenty-five two years ago and spent much of her time keeping up with the concerns of the land and her tenants. Lady Catherine, Anne's mother, still managed the household and presented herself to society as the mistress of Rosings, but had long ago allowed her daughter to manage the economics of the estate. Lady Catherine had Anne educated in the economics of running an estate with help from her sister's husband and son. It would have been unthinkable to send Anne to university to learn the lessons taught to men expected to run an estate, but George Darcy was not opposed to giving his niece lessons in estate management.

"Mr. Smythe, good morning. How goes the repairs to the drainage pipe in the north field?" Anne spoke from the high seat of her curricle to her most competent, but also most troublesome, tenant.

"Yes, Miss de Bourgh, the work is all finished and well before the first of the cold rains. My boys got all the winter corn planted last week and spent the last days on that pesky pipe." Mr. Smythe stood his ground and matched Anne's stance, but twisted his hat a bit between his hands.

Anne nodded. "Very good. I am riding that way and will be well pleased to see the finished product. Make sure to put the cost of the materials on your next quarters' rent statement." She flicked the reins to her horse. "Good day Mr. Smythe."

Many ladies of society would consider Anne taking an active role in running her estate as extremely vulgar. The gently bred ladies in Anne's social class could not understand the independence of the Rosings women. But Sir Lewis de Bourgh, with the help of Lady Catherine's brother, Henri Fitzwilliam the Earl of Matlock, had ensured his daughter would be the rightful owner of his estate upon his death, even if she never married.

And Anne never intended to marry. She was mistress *and* master over Rosings. All the money, power, and privilege that came with owning her estate would be forfeit the moment she signed the church register. Instead of having nearly eight-thousand per year to spend as she saw fit, she would be relegated to a monthly allowance and pin money. Even if Lord Matlock could help her negotiate a hefty marriage settlement, the Rosings lands would be her husband's legal property to do with in life what he wished. No, Anne would never marry.

At one time, years ago, there had been talk of Anne marrying her cousin Fitzwilliam Darcy. He was kind, intelligent and not opposed to an educated woman, but Anne was not inclined to have him for her husband. Thankfully, her uncle Darcy made it clear there was absolutely no marriage contract between them, and if either she or he were not inclined to marry, they should not. Her mother had grumbled some, but not in many years now.

"We best be heading back now, Miss Anne." Mrs. Jenkins looked up at the sky with a wrinkled brow. "Your mother will have my head if you get caught in this coming rain."

Anne sighed. Lady Catherine would make a huge fuss about a little rain. "Of course, you are correct. I will just have to inspect the pipe tomorrow. It will be good to see the fields after a rain anyway." Anne turned the curricle around. "I have many letters to write this afternoon to my relations, so it is as good a time as any to turn home."

The young mistress's mind was occupied the whole drive back to the manor with thoughts of her family and the upcoming trip to London for the Christmas holiday. Anne started the list in her mind of all the letters that needed to be written to arrange their upcoming travel.

As if her internal musings had summoned them into being, Anne found a thick stack of letters from various family members and friends on her desk upon returning to her private study. No doubt each was filled with the individual travel plans and invitations to the various holiday parties which would start in early December. Flipping through the stack, Anne's interest was piqued by the unusually thick envelope with her cousin Darcy's unmistakable handwriting. Darcy was never overly verbose in his speech or his writing. He wrote uncommonly slowly and took several days to finish the front and back of even one sheet of paper, so his letters were hardly ever longer than that. Anne never quite could figure if he was slow because he wanted to make sure not to blot the ink, or if it actually took him such a long time to compose what he wanted to say internally. Whatever the reason for his usual slowness with a pen, this envelope seemed to hold at least three sheets of paper and Anne wanted to know what in the world could give Darcy so much to say.

October 11, 1811
Netherfield Park, Hertfordshire

My dear cousin,

I arrived safely on the 8th to the estate that Bingley has let. If you recall, it is named Netherfield Estate and the house is situated on a lovely park with a well-maintained road to the nearest town, Meryton, which lies on the Great North Road from London. It was an easy half day's carriage ride from Darcy House, London to Bingley's new residence. His sisters and Mr. Hurst are also in residence, though I am not sure why they came, as all they seem to discuss is how much better London is this time of year. I, for one, am much relieved to be out of the city for one cannot shoot game in London without causing trouble for himself. Miss Bingley and Mrs. Hurst also seem to find a great number of faults with the local society and keep a continuous stream of complaints rolling throughout the day. It has not helped matters that Bingley accepted an invitation for our party to the local public hall last night for a ball to celebrate the Michaelmas.

Now, you and I are much acquainted with the types of society one finds in a small country town. Landed gentry who are not of London society, gentlemen merchants, and the occasional second gentleman's son barrister or clergyman. It is not so very shocking to see unmarried ladies dance with married men not of their family, or hear genuine laughter fill the room at these country affairs, but you would think that Miss Bingley did not know that laughter could even exist while dancing. Whatever could there be to laugh at? Dancing is serious business and, per Miss Bingley, the only way to foster true inducement towards marriage. I tried to suggest this morning that if she was so very uncomfortable in the company of our new neighbours, perhaps they had better off to London and pass the autumn at Hurst's home. Miss Bingley somehow turned my words against me and began profusely thanking me for my generous offer to escort herself and her sister back to Hurst's London home. You will laugh at me dear Anne, as I am sure anyone less awkward than I would have seen her ploy coming from across the horizon, but I was genuinely confused. I believe I blurted out something resembling "Why in the world would I ever do that? You are the one who wants to go to London, not I."

Bingley nearly choked himself trying to stifle his laughter.

Unfortunately, my suggestion did not hasten their return to 'polite society' and I must endure Miss Bingley's fawning compliments to my person and grating complaints to everyone else for the time being.

October 18, 1811

I have been with Bingley just about 10 days now and he is making good progress at learning the estate. Netherfield is nothing to Pemberley or Rosings, but it is a good situation with profitable lands. You would love the country here. It is much like Kent, lush with mildly rolling hills. One of the highest points in the region, which the local citizens call Oakham 'Mount' – bless their hearts – is near the western edge of the Netherfield property, along the border with the second largest estate in the area, Longbourn. A Mr. Thomas Bennet, esq. owns Longbourn with his wife and five daughters. The second eldest, Miss Elizabeth Bennet, reminds me much of you, cousin. She is very intelligent and helps her father run the estate. She is also very kind and devoid of the artifice that is so pervasive amongst the upper set. Unlike you, or I for that matter, Miss Elizabeth is quite lively. She laughs at everything, but not in a vulgar way. Her laughter has a way of putting an entire room in a good mood. I believe you would enjoy her company very much. I know Richard and Georgie would adore her immediately.

Last evening, we were invited to a dinner party at the house of the Meryton mayor, Sir William Lucas. It was pleasant enough. I had been introduced to everyone present at the assembly hall last week, but you know how dreadful I am at remembering names. Thankfully, I have run into Miss Elizabeth on two occasions since the assembly and she designed to take pity on my poor memory. Miss Elizabeth and the eldest daughter of our hosts took me about the room. Having someone with me who is so effortless in conversation made it very easy to relax a bit and enjoy the society. Elizabeth introduced topics of conversation with each new introduction that seemed perfectly suited to the group as a whole. It was fascinating to watch. I must admit, I could not perform such a feat even in a room full of our closest relations. In fact, if Miss Elizabeth were to somehow join us at Rosings for Easter, I am sure she would still be the mastermind behind the dinner conversation.

October 25, 1811

Now in my third week with Bingley at Netherfield, I believe I have finally settled into the country. Three days ago, Mr. Bennet extended an invitation for Bingley, Hurst, and myself to the local gentlemen's club at the Fox and Lamb. There was not nearly the entertainments to be had at White's, but for a moderately sized hamlet, the gentlemen of Meryton have a well-organised outfit. There were three gaming rooms with billiards, darts, and card tables all set out. The smoking room had cigars from the Americas and the after-dinner port selection was top quality. Sir William signed a second endorsement, after Mr. Bennet, for Bingley's membership application and I believe a Mr. King was considering giving him the third he needs to be formally accepted. If Bingley could be accepted into the Fox and Lamb before Christmas, then his position in the local society would be set even if he removes to Town for the season. I do hope that Mr. King decides shortly.

After Mr. Bennet's introduction of Bingley into the gentle-men's club, it was only good manners to host a small dinner party at Netherfield for the families of the men whose company we enjoyed. The Bennet family, the Lucas family, the King family, a Mr. Long his wife and two nieces, Col. Forester, who is commander of the militia forces quartering in Meryton this winter and his new wife, plus several of the gentlemen officers serving under the Col. It was a relatively intimate affair, but well attended by all. Miss Elizabeth was sat too far from me during dinner to join in her conversation, but I was pleasantly engaged with her particular friend, Miss Lucas, and the eldest Bennet sister for much of the meal. Whatever conversation she had introduced to the young army Lt. sitting to her left must have been particularly interesting, though, as the man's eyes never left Miss Elizabeth's face through the whole of the meats course.

After the men re-joined the ladies, Miss Bingley invited anyone to exhibit on the pianoforte who had the inclination. Miss Elizabeth asked one of her younger sisters to play a specific song so that Elizabeth might sing. The playing of the younger Bennet sister was adequate, but Elizabeth covered any mishaps in the playing performance with her light and pleasing soprano. I believe that the younger Miss Bennet enjoys very much to play, but lacks the refinement that comes from in-struction with a master. It was kind of Miss Elizabeth to improve her sister's performance with her singing. At the end, the applause from the assembled group was genuine and both sisters looked very well pleased indeed. I thought that perhaps such encouragement would do wonders for Georgiana. While my sister is an extreme proficient on the instrument, she rarely performs for others due to her shy nature. If Miss Elizabeth sang to Georgie's playing, she might feel more confident in her ability and less on display during the performance.

Several of the other young women performed as well, then Miss Bingley performed last. She played a very complicated arrangement from La Clemenza di Tito and sang the high soprano part to the piece. I am well used to such a display, as many ladies of the ton *feel the need to showcase their skill by playing and singing the most difficult pieces they know, regardless of whether the music is actually pleasant for the audience. I can assure you, Miss Bingley showcased her superior skill at the pianoforte, but I do not believe she had the superior performance. Compared to the flawed playing of the young Miss Bennet accompanying the sweet singing of Miss Elizabeth, Miss Bingley fell far short of the mark that evening.*

Before I must start a fourth sheet of paper, I shall conclude this letter. Good luck for a bountiful harvest and safe travels this holiday season. I look forward to seeing you in London in December.

Yours, etc.
F. Darcy

Anne de Bourgh was stunned. She stared at her cousin's letter for some time trying to reconcile her twenty-seven years of experience knowing Darcy's quiet personality with the man who wrote such an account of people and places as those in the letter in her hand. What was most extraordinary, and perhaps a bit alarming, was his accounting of the young woman, Elizabeth Bennet. It did not escape Anne's notice, though she presumed it had completely passed over her cousin, that he had twice referred to her as simply 'Elizabeth' and not the more proper 'Miss Elizabeth.' He also twice referred to introducing Elizabeth to his younger sister, Georgiana Darcy, and once insinuated he would like to introduce this young woman to herself and their other cousin, Col. Richard Fitzwilliam.

"Anne! What has you looking so surprised?" Lady Catherine had entered the study several minutes prior and watched as her daughter opened and read what looked like a letter from their Darcy relation. "Is everything all right with my nephew and niece?"

"Yes, Mother." Anne looked up from the extraordinary letter in her hands and shuffled some other papers over the first few pages laying on the desk. "He is visiting friends and has much to say about the local gentry. It sounds as if he is having a very pleasant visit."

Lady Catherine hmphed and sat heavily in the wingback chair by the fireplace. "I hope this visit will not delay his arrival in London. You know he is expected at the Finch's annual ball. My sister Matlock has many plans for his dancing with her niece from the Nottingham branch of her family. He is much too old to be still unmarried."

Anne looked back to his letter, now hidden on the desk under the latest report from her solicitor. She worked on schooling her features so as not to give away her dismay at the scheming between her mother and aunt.

"I am sure that she has finally decided that Lady Fiona Finch is the right choice for Darcy," Lady Catherine continued without looking back to her daughter, nodding as if relaying the most important of information. "She is well bred, comes with fifty-thousand pounds, and a connection to the Nottingham earldom. Though I have not heard her play or seen her painted tables, Lady Nottingham would not have neglected her education, I am sure."

"Do you know if she reads many books or likes the out of doors?" Anne had very limited experience with the young debutantes of the *ton*, but she believed that Lady Fiona was more fond of town than the country. "Is she kind?"

Lady Catherine looked at her daughter sharply. "What does it matter if she likes books? And what about this nonsense of her being kind? Darcy needs a wife, not a governess."

Anne sighed. "I am sure that Darcy would much rather be at Pemberley in his library than anywhere else. I would think that his wife should have similar tastes."

"How extraordinary! Anne, marriage is about the preservation of rank and increasing one's coffers. After they produce the requisite heir, there is no need to further spend any time together if they do not wish." Lady Catherine stood and rang the bell on the wall near the door. "If you had needed a husband, I believe Darcy would have been good for you, but as my brothers ensured your father's legacy was secured in you, I believe my sister has the right idea to increase our family with new connections and an influx of dowry."

A servant appeared at the door to the study in very little time and waited for instructions from his mistresses. "Come Anne, I want tea and some cake before dinner. It will be brought to the east parlour." Without any additional acknowledgement of either her daughter or the servant, Lady Catherine swept out of the study.

Anne looked to the footman still standing to attention in the doorway. "James, please let Higgs know we are having tea in the east parlour and do warn cook that her ladyship is going to expect dinner to be very punctual today. Perhaps if there was an addition of a soup course to the menu, that would be very welcome."

James bowed and left to deliver his messages. Anne picked up Darcy's letter again. Without seeing Darcy in person and being able to discuss this development, she could not be sure if her cousin was on his way to developing a true tender for the lady, Elizabeth. Anne knew their aunt and uncle Matlock had long hopes for a noble connection with Darcy's marriage, but Anne was of the opinion that their plans would cause him nothing but misery. She would have to trust that her uncle George Darcy would intervene if Lady Matlock went too far pushing this match with Lady Fiona. For now, Anne hoped she could manage to meet this Elizabeth one day soon.

Dancing in Society

ELIZABETH SAT AT HER VANITY SEAT BRUSHING OUT her long, unruly curls and looking at her new evening gown. Well, mostly new. The base of the dress was a green satin gown her mother had worn more than twenty years ago at her coming out ball. She had kept the dress in a muslin bag hanging in her closet until, suddenly, five days ago, she had declared that Elizabeth was best suited to have the dress. A number of alterations were necessary so she could wear it to the Netherfield ball. Extra material from the original bustle was removed, the bodice was shortened by five inches, the lace overlay was updated with a lovely golden ribbon, the sleeves were shortened, and the neckline was altered for a more modern silhouette.

It had taken almost every second of the last several days and an emergency call to the local modiste, but the end result was truly stunning. Elizabeth could not remember ever wearing anything so lovely.

Now, it was time to make their final preparations, don their dresses, and drive the three miles to Netherfield.

Elizabeth kept telling herself this was just the same as every other ball she had ever attended before, and there was no reason for so many butterflies in her stomach. She also kept telling herself, nearly every time her thoughts drifted in the direction of a certain gentleman from Derbyshire, that her relationship with Darcy was strictly friendly. He was destined for a beautiful, accomplished, titled heiress who would dance this season at Almack's in a new white silk dress every week. A young woman whom his aunt, who was a Countess, had already specifically identified as his future bride. He could never be interested in a simple country miss wearing a twenty-year-old satin dress, no matter how well she looked in it.

A knock on her door brought Elizabeth out of her musings.

"Come."

Jane opened the door looking resplendent in her cream silk gown with a blue organza overlay. Their mother had ordered the dress for Jane at the start of the summer season that past year from one of the most exclusive dress makers in London, who also happened to be neighbour and business partner to their uncle Gardiner. As the oldest and most beautiful sister, it made sense to spend their limited clothing budget on silks for Jane.

Elizabeth had never before been jealous of Jane's looks or her finery, so why did she feel a pang of inadequacy today?

"Lizzy, why are you not dressed yet? Mamma has ordered the carriage be brought about in less than thirty minutes. Do you require help with your hair?"

Elizabeth sighed and dropped her brush. "No Jane, I am sorry, I was wool-gathering. I will finish straight away and be down. Sally has tied my stays so I only need to attach the ribbon and the buttons on the back of the dress. I am sure someone will be available to do me up. Go on downstairs for Mamma's inspection."

Jane tutted and stepped up behind Elizabeth. "There shall be time enough for Mamma after your hair is finished."

Only a few minutes later, Jane had worked Elizabeth's hair into a beautiful and modern style, leaving just a few curls across her cheeks. Sweet pearl hairpins capped off the look and stood out strikingly against the dark brown coiffure. "Lizzy, will you not tell me what has you at sixes and sevens today? Is it Mamma's dress? It is very fine and looks beautiful on you. I am sure no one shall know that it was originally our mother's coming out dress."

"Oh Jane, no! The dress has turned out quite well and I am very glad to be wearing it tonight. Even if there are those among us who will know, and I suspect our aunt Phillips will recognise the pattern on the lace as she has a nearly identical dress hanging in her own closet. I would not be ashamed to be wearing something so fine."

"Then what has you frowning so today?"

Elizabeth stood from her vanity and walked to the bed where her dress was laid out waiting to be donned. She fingered the fine lace and gently lifted one of the puffed sleeves. "I cannot say what has me melancholy. The most likely culprit is this dreadful rain. I have been quite confined to the house these past few days and I will be looking forward to a merry jaunt tomorrow morning if the clouds stay away."

"Perhaps Mr. Darcy will also be out in the morning looking to exercise his horse. You should find some way to mention your plans for the morrow while dancing this evening."

Elizabeth whipped around and stared at her sister with an open mouth. Jane calmly extracted Elizabeth's dress from her sister's tight grasp and helped place the fabric over Elizabeth's head. "Jane Francine Margaret Bennet! How could you imply such a thing! I most certainly shall not ask Mr. Darcy for any kind of assignation tomorrow or any day in the future. It is most improper and… and… and… obscene!"

Jane merely urged Elizbeth to turn so that she should fasten her buttons and ribbons. "Now, Lizzy, calm yourself. Of course I was not suggesting you ask Mr. Darcy directly for any assignation. But, it cannot hurt to let him know your decided preference for a morning walk. He is more than capable of deciding if he wants to have a private discussion with you away from the prying eyes and ears of our mother and sisters. There is always time to come home and make the proper call to our father afterwards. Many understandings come about in much the same way. Wholly proper and certainly nothing obscene."

For a brief moment, Elizabeth could see it. Darcy on his enormous black horse looking unbelievably handsome in his riding clothes and tall black hat. Or maybe he would be less formally dressed for a morning run like he had been that very first time they had come across each other on the trail to Oakham Mount. No hat, no waistcoat, no gloves and none of the trappings of a well-dressed gentleman. Contrary to what one might expect, Elizabeth found this relaxed Darcy more handsome than the formally dressed man who would make an appearance tonight. He would leap off his horse at the sight of her, come grab both of her ungloved hands in his and declare that he was bewitched and could no longer be parted from her. Then he would lean down and brush his lips to hers before grabbing her by the waist, placing her on his horse, and riding off straight to his estate in Wales.

It was a nice thought.

It was an impossible and foolish thought.

Elizabeth shook the images from her mind. "You and Mamma have this silly notion that Mr. Darcy is about to declare himself to me at any moment. Well, I am glad to be able to disabuse you of that notion. He has known about my habit of walking in the morning for many weeks now. We have even encountered each other on several occasions and walked to the top of Oakham Mount. Once, Miss Bingley even accompanied him on his morning ride. In all those mornings he had ample time to declare any intentions towards me and he has thus far resisted. I do not see why tomorrow morning should be any different."

"Lizzy, you astound me. Why have you never mentioned these meetings before? And of course tomorrow will be different. He will be struck dumb by your radiance tonight and unable to resist the call of the morning. I anticipate that you shall come to an understanding quite soon."

"Please, Jane. I know Mamma has grand plans for myself and Mr. Darcy, but do not tell me that you too have fallen victim to this folly?" If her sweet, even-tempered sister started speaking of such things, it would be difficult to keep a tight rein on her own daydreams.

"I do not see why you say it is such folly. Even Charlotte has spoken on his decided preference for your society."

"Yes, our friend has said on several occasions that she believes he is partial to me, but I assure you, it is only a friendship. He and I are nothing more than like-minded persons with a similar taste in books. We are nothing more to each other and I do not have any expectations of him."

Jane appeared wholly unconvinced. After a moment of silence, Jane looked Elizabeth directly in the eyes and asked, "Do you love him?"

The look in Elizabeth's eyes was all Jane needed for an answer.

Elizabeth turned away and walked to the mirror to fiddle with her neckline and hairpins before becoming master of her voice once again.

"Jane, I am not so foolhardy as to lose my heart to a man of Mr. Darcy's standing. Whether Mamma wishes it or not, he will never be free to make an offer to someone of our standing in society. I have always known this, from the first day of our acquaintance."

"A true gentleman would not have shown such preference if he did not intend to pay his addresses!" Jane clasped Elizabeth by the shoulders.

"He has never deceived me." Elizabeth turned away from her sister towards her vanity and pretended to check her hair in the glass. "From the first day of our acquaintances, I have known he is all but promised to some favourite of his aunt. I will admit to enjoying his company very much and I will be sad to lose his society when he leaves for London, but I have kept my heart safe from him and will not be overly dismayed at his departure. Now, enough with this foolishness. You must submit yourself to Mamma for inspection. Mr. Bingley is more than able to make his match from our sisters and you, dear one, are likely to meet with more success on this front than I am tonight."

As Elizabeth breezed past her sister and headed for the stairs, she felt a lone tear slide down her cheek. She chastised herself for such a silly display. There would be no more tears over Mr. Darcy.

All the torches lining the drive of Netherfield Hall had been lit and the effect was so striking that Elizabeth could barely catch her breath. Every family of any distinction for thirty miles had been given an invitation tonight as well as several guests from the Bingleys' acquaintances in Town. From the length of the carriage line, it seemed that few had declined the invitation. Now Elizabeth was worried they may miss the first set if the line did not start to move faster.

When their carriage finally pulled up to the front door, Elizabeth had to resist the urge to fidget or push her sisters out of the door. It was equally difficult to stand in the receiving line instead of running up the stairs to the ballroom to find Mr. Darcy for their set. At last, her mother and father had greeted their hosts and Elizabeth was free to enjoy her evening.

As soon as she straightened from her curtsey to Miss Bingley and Mrs. Hurst, a gloved hand was held out into her field of vision. "Miss Elizabeth, I believe you are promised to me for the first set. May I escort you into the ballroom? The musicians are nearly ready to start."

"Mr. Darcy, you are certainly prompt!" Elizabeth took the offered hand and laughed with some relief. "I would be glad to accompany you and you well know you reserved my first set weeks ago. I promise I have not given it away to anyone during the long ride between Longbourn and Netherfield."

Mr. Darcy's eyes sparkled with mirth. "I am glad to know that you have not accepted any offers to dance from travellers on horseback, though I would not be surprised if some of the guests had gone carriage to carriage in the line asking for your dance card. You look exceptionally well this evening and I am sure I will have to fight our neighbours for your company after this first set."

Elizabeth's laughter rang above the crowd just as the first strings of the musicians began to play. "Do not worry, Mr. Darcy. After this set is concluded, we shall find a corner of the ballroom in which to start a discussion of the book you purchased from Mr. Brathorn on the fall of the Roman Senate. I am most interested in your thoughts regarding the horse that Caligula planned to make a consul. My friends and neighbours know better than to try and interrupt me while discussing ancient history, even to dance. You shall be able to command my company for as long as you can stomach the topic."

"While I would no doubt enjoy such a discussion with you for many hours, I cannot speak of books in a ballroom filled with such lovely sights. My mind would be much too distracted with the present company to do the subject justice. We shall just have to leave Caligula and his horse for one of our morning walks up your little Mountain."

"Mr. Darcy, are you trying to start another fight which you are doomed to lose?" Elizabeth adopted a false scolding visage. "I believe we have exhausted the topic of my mountain and its superiority to any of the heights of the Peak District."

It was now Darcy's turn to laugh loudly. "Miss Elizabeth, I would never act in so ungentlemanly a fashion as to start an argument with a lady while dancing. I do not believe I have conceded any comparison between Oakham Mount and the Peaks, but I will just have to let you make the final judgement yourself sometime when you visit Pemberley. For now, we shall speak of more mundane topics that will not disrupt our dance. Shall I comment on the size of the room or the number of couples on the floor?"

"If you were to make such a comment, I would most likely follow it with how private balls are much pleasanter than public ones." Elizabeth's voice sounded slightly reedy to her own ears as she had lost all her breath at his mention of her visiting his estate near the Peaks.

"Well, we must have some conversation arranged, for it would be odd to spend an entire half an hour in silence, especially with one as given to entertaining conversation as yourself."

"Is that a nice way to say that I am long-tongued? I am shocked! I have always thought we were of a great similarity in the turn of our minds being that we are each of an unsocial, taciturn disposition, unwilling to speak unless we expect to say something that will amaze the whole room and be handed down to posterity with all the éclat of a proverb." Though her words were biting, Elizabeth's eyes sparkled, and her mouth was not cooperating with her attempt to maintain a stern set to her lips.

"Now, Miss Elizabeth, while you are more gifted with words than many people I have ever known, I know for a fact that you are not a gossip and would never betray a confidence. As to your description of our characters, there is no striking resemblance of your own, I am sure, though it is quite true that when you speak at least a portion of the room is surely amazed. I, however, am guilty as charged with your faithful portrayal of a taciturn young man afraid to say something unless it is of great value to the conversation."

"Please, do not make yourself uneasy. I understand your shy and reserved nature. Playing to strangers will never be your strong suit, but you are not required to play to placate people who know nothing of your character. It is nothing to let your manners and reputation speak for you instead of trying to force conversation with strangers." As neither had a ready comment to follow such a turn in the conversation, they were silent for a few moments until they had gone down the dance again.

"Miss Elizabeth, do you and your sisters often walk to Meryton?"

Elizabeth startled slightly at the tone of his question, but could not merit where it had come from. "Yes, Mr. Darcy. We often walk to Meryton whenever the weather is fine. There is much to be seen in our fine town and many friends to meet along the way. We had just made a new acquaintance when you met us there the other day."

"Yes, I remember you saying that George Wickham had just been introduced to you as a new lieutenant in the ______shire militia. I must apologise to you for my behaviour when we first dismounted. I believe you observed my ire and were kind to offer relief. I should have been more circumspect in my reaction to meeting with Wickham again."

Elizabeth was truly astounded and more than a little intrigued with this revelation. "I do remember you looked peculiar when you first arrived, but you spoke so civilly to Mr. Wickham that I would not have known there was any difficulty between you had you not said anything just now."

"Perhaps I should not say any more, but I would not want to leave you without a caution. It does seem that Wickham is starting a new life as a gentleman officer, but he has not always conducted himself as a gentleman." A darkness took over Darcy's expression that Elizabeth had never seen before. "He is blessed with such happy manners as may ensure his making friends wherever he goes, but whether he may be equally capable of retaining such friends is less certain." Shaking his head as if to clear his thoughts, Darcy continued after a moment. "He has caused a great deal of heartache for my father over the years. I have taken the liberty of writing to my cousin, Colonel Richard Fitzwilliam of the Household Calvary. Richard is familiar with Wickham and would have the ability to order him into behaving as an officer should. Hopefully, such measures are not required, but I feel better knowing my cousin plans a visit to the ______shire militia for shortly after I depart."

"I can hardly account for such a description of someone who seems very convivial, but from what I know of your character, I must credit it. It seems interesting to me that you are cautious in your hope for Mr. Wickham's reversal in character. Did you not once say that you hardly every forgave and that your resentment once created was unappeasable? I must assume that Mr. Wickham has not gone so far as to engage your resentment."

Darcy was quiet for a moment as he considered his history with Wickham. "I recall that conversation one evening here during your sister's convalescence. It is true that my good opinion once lost is lost forever, however, I hope I am very cautious in creating such resentment as to lose all good opinion of a person. Also, I hope I never become blinded by prejudice to such a degree as to cast off a friend."

"It speaks highly of your character."

Darcy looked down towards his feet as they waited for their turn in the line. "I hope that you are not attempting to sketch my character at the present moment, as there is reason to fear that the performance would reflect no credit on myself."

"Why ever would you think that, sir?"

"Well, for starters, I have made a lovely lady uneasy during the first set of the night at a society ball." He cleared his throat and seemed to observe his surroundings for the first time since beginning their conversation. "And moreover, I have spoken of indelicate matters relating to persons who are not even present. I am certain you must find me very dull."

Before Elizabeth could respond to Mr. Darcy's misgivings, Sir William Lucas appeared very close to them, meaning to pass through the set to the other side of the room, but on perceiving Mr. Darcy, he stopped with a bow of superior courtesy to compliment him on his dancing and his partner. "I have been most highly gratified indeed, my dear sir. Such very superior dancing is not often seen. It is evident that you belong to the first circles. Allow me to say, however, that your fair partner does not disgrace you, and that I must hope to have this pleasure often repeated, especially when certain desirable events shall take place. What congratulations will then flow into our society!"

The look of confusion on Darcy's face at Sir William Lucas's last statement was enough to make Elizabeth wish for a hole to open directly below her feet. She averted her eyes to the floor and tried to will away the crimson blush spreading across her cheeks.

"Sir, I am certain that any superior dancing on my part is all due to my fine partner this evening, and if there are any future events which present an opportunity to escort the lovely ladies of Hertfordshire, I will be happy to once again add to your pleasure in the dance." Satisfied, Sir William Lucas moved out of the way of the dancing and left Elizabeth and Darcy to move down the line.

After a moment, Elizabeth attempted to bring their conversation back to the topic of character. "Mr. Darcy, I believe we were discussing the sketch of your character which can be made tonight."

"Are you having any success?" Darcy asked with a small smile. "I would still rather you wait until another time."

"But if I do not take your likeness now, I may never have another opportunity."

He bowed his head. "I would by no means suspend any pleasure of yours."

"I thank you sir, and to your earlier question, I do not find you dull in the slightest. I also do not find you indelicate. You have given me something serious to think on, but I cannot help but be thankful for your confidence in me."

"There is no better lady of my acquaintance in whom to confide such matters, I am sure." Darcy nodded with assured confidence. "Your intelligence and education make you a uniquely suited young woman to hear such things and act accordingly."

Though it was a great pleasure to hear Darcy praise her intellect, Elizabeth could not help but make a remark about his subtle commentary on the fairer sex. "'My own sex, I hope, will excuse me, if I treat them like rational creatures, instead of flattering their fascinating graces, and viewing them as if they were in a state of perpetual childhood, unable to stand alone.'"

Darcy's eyes became round and wide. "Wollstonecraft, Miss Elizabeth! Where did you ever come to have that book?"

"My father's library is very complete sir, and he does not restrict my access to anything within."

"Then, I believe I have underestimated your father."

"Quite, sir." Elizabeth smirked.

Shortly after, the first set was finally at an end. Darcy escorted Elizabeth back to her mother just as Bingley returned Jane in the same manner. A quick nod between the gentlemen and each found themselves with another Bennet sister on their arm for the second set. After a pleasant half an hour partnering with Jane Bennet, Darcy found himself being able to converse with Elizabeth, Jane, and Bingley for a few minutes until several of the officers in attendance braved the finely dressed gentlemen to ask for the hand of the most beautiful ladies in the room. After Elizabeth and Jane departed with their partners, Darcy invited Bingley into the men's card room for a drink and a cigar.

While her brother and his friends were hiding in the card room, Caroline was becoming more and more put out with the evening. Though she considered it beneath her skills as a hostess to invite the rabble from Hertfordshire to her ball, it was the expected thing. Even Darcy had said it would be rude not to host some entertainment for the neighbourhood. So, she had planned the event with her usual grandeur and elegance. Not that the people of Meryton would know any different from the public assembly ball they had all attended at the beginning of their stay in this backwater town. As luck would have it, her sister's great-aunt-in-law, Lady Sefton, had expressed a desire to visit Hurst and escape the London air for a few days before Christmastide. Lady Sefton was one of the patronesses of Almack's and a great paragon of the *ton* and Caroline let the fact of the great lady's attendance slip to a few choice individuals. When news of the Bingleys' ball had sufficiently made the rounds of the ladies' tea parlours, Caroline had taken the liberty of inviting a select few society acquaintances, including Darcy's titled relations, all of whom accepted immediately. The unfortunately timed rain had delayed their guests' arrival until that very afternoon, but at least she had been able to enjoy the distinction of setting out a luncheon for no fewer than five titled ladies and their companions and chaperones.

With Lady Sefton presiding over the dancing in an ornate chair placed on the side of the room specifically for her enjoyment, along with the London guests, this ball should have been Caroline's triumph. It was with no little dismay she learned that both her brother and Mr. Darcy would be opening the ball with Bennet ladies. Caroline had to dance with her brother Hurst for the first set. Then, she was disappointed when Hurst delivered her to her sister instead of her brother following the set, since Louisa was nowhere near Darcy in between the first and second set. Thankfully, the brother of one of her society friends partnered her for the second set so she was not required to dance with any of the local gentlemen, if they could even claim the title.

But that was the end of her good fortune.

The third set had been a disaster. The toadying little man who was expected to inherit the Bennet's estate had boldly asked to pay his respects to his future neighbour and hostess with a dance, and Caroline could not refuse and expect to be available to dance with Darcy later in the evening. Thankfully, the third was a short set and Caroline made her escape as quickly as possible.

"Miss Bingley, I require an introduction." Being addressed so unexpectedly from behind, Caroline startled before turning to find Lady Sefton with Darcy's aunt, the Countess of Matlock, and a beautiful young woman. Though Caroline had personally written the invitations, she was actually but little acquainted with Darcy's relations. Based solely on the accepted invitations, she assumed that the young heiress was Lady Fiona Finch, the daughter of the Earl of Nottingham, and Lady Matlock's favourite niece.

Reflexively, Caroline curtseyed to her titled guests and let out a long settling breath. "Of course, Lady Sefton. I would be more than happy to provide introductions to anyone with which you wish to acquaint yourself. Shall we take a lap about the room or is there someone in particular you desire to know?"

Lady Sefton nodded in the direction of Elizabeth Bennet at the exact moment she let out a loud laugh at something her dance partner said. Caroline pinched her lips, but nodded, and led the three ladies over to where Jane and Elizabeth were being returned to their family party in between dances.

Loudly enough that the small grouping of young officers who were perpetually loitering around the Bennet sisters could hear her, Caroline performed the introductions.

"Mrs. Bennet, Miss Jane Bennet, and Miss Elizabeth, may I introduce you to my brother Hurst's great aunt, the honourable Countess of Sefton. Lady Sefton, these are our neighbours, Mrs. Bennet, Miss Bennet and Miss Elizabeth of Longbourn Estate." All the women curtsied, and Caroline looked to Lady Matlock and Lady Fiona. Technically, neither had asked for an introduction and Caroline was not sure whether one was expected.

Thankfully, Lady Sefton took over the conversation quickly. "Mrs. Bennet, you have such beautiful daughters who dance with more grace than some of the young women who come to Almack's in London."

Mrs. Bennet tittered behind her fan. "Oh my, Lady Sefton, thank you. They are quite the most graceful and beautiful ladies from Hertfordshire, as you can see. I have three other daughters also. My youngest, Miss Lydia, is also very beautiful and quite lively. A favourite amongst the officers, for certain."

Elizabeth's cheeks flamed under her mother's boastful demeanour, but saintly Jane was as even and polite as ever. "You are much too kind Lady Sefton. Elizabeth, myself and our sisters are merely honoured to be included in the invitations this evening. The Bingley family have certainly provided our community with the most elegant entertainment of the entire year. Have you come from London lately?"

"I have, Miss Bennet. I spend most of my time in London these days, unless I am visiting my favourite nephews, Reginald Hurst and his brother at their family estate. It might not be very *fashionable* to live in London all year, but as an old lady with high standing and my own portion at my disposal, I believe I have earned the right to do as I like." Lady Sefton winked at Elizabeth at an angle that neither Lady Matlock nor Caroline could see.

A lively smile formed across Elizabeth's face. She was very pleased with this new acquaintance. Unfortunately, a moment later, her happy bubble was squeezed tightly and popped.

Lady Sefton motioned to her companions. "Mrs. Bennet, may I introduce you to my good friend, Josephine Fitzwilliam, the Countess of Matlock, and her niece Lady Fiona Finch, the eldest daughter of the Earl of Nottingham."

Another round of curtsies found Ladies Sefton and Matlock conversing with Mrs. Bennet about the local families in Hertfordshire while Lady Fiona turned towards Elizabeth and Jane.

"Miss Bennet, your dress is very beautiful. Where did you get such beautiful silks?" Lady Fiona seemed genuine and open in her affect, not the snide highly placed lady Elizabeth had feared she might be.

"Oh, thank you, Lady Fiona. My mother's brother owns the largest imports business in London, Gardiner Imports. His wife, my aunt Gardiner, selected this blue silk specifically for me, and their business partner, Madame Devy, sewed the gown. It was a gift for my birthday and this is only the second time I have had occasion to wear it." Jane, always full of humility and grace motioned to Lady Fiona's own gown. "Though I am sure your gown is of the very latest designs. It is the perfect shade of pink to match your cheeks."

Lady Fiona blushed prettily, highlighting Jane's observation, and ducked her head. "Yes, my mother chose the colour for exactly that purpose. I am given to a flushed complexion."

Elizabeth reached out with the tip of her fan and lightly tapped Lady Fiona on the arm in an affectionate and comforting touch. "It was an inspired choice. And, as Miss Bingley shall be the only lady here tonight with even the slightest possibility of joining the balls of the little season, you shall have no worries wearing it again in London this winter." Elizabeth gave Caroline, who was still hovering near their group, a side glance. "You will not tell anyone, will you Miss Bingley?"

Caroline's pinched expression came back for being addressed directly by Elizabeth, but she schooled her face quickly under Lady Fiona's scrutiny. "Of course, you must not fear wearing such a lovely gown again in London, though you may want to change the ribbons or trim, as of course you shall see Mr. Darcy and my brother again shortly."

Lady Fiona fiddled with the golden ribbon around her waist with a worried expression, but Elizabeth just laughed. "Miss Bingley, men do not remember the gowns we wear from one day to the next. I am certain that I could wear this exact gown to breakfast in the morning and my father would look at it as if it was the first time he'd ever seen it." Jane playfully smacked Elizabeth on the arm, the sisters laughing at the private joke knowing their father certainly would not recognise Elizabeth's gown, even though it was the gown their mother wore when he fell in love with her.

"That is a very beautiful shade of green, Miss Elizabeth." Lady Fiona commented. "And the lace is quite intricate. I do not believe I have seen that pattern before. Quite unique."

"Yes, unique," Caroline sniffed. "Though you might not have seen it before as the most fashionable shoppes in London do not often stock *satin*, as silk is the most preferable. Tell me, Miss Eliza, who made your gown?"

Elizabeth raised her eyebrow and answered truthfully, "Madame Devy." She purposefully left off the fact that this was the *very first* ball gown Madame Devy had ever made when she was still a young woman working out of her father's tailor shoppe.

In a fit of pique, Caroline removed herself to some excuse about checking on supper. Lady Fiona sighed a heavy breath and visibly relaxed at her departure. Both Bennet sisters noticed the reaction, but had too good of manners to comment on their hostess. Their conversation shifted to more congenial topics until the end of the fourth dance set.

As the fifth supper set was lining up, Darcy and Bingley reappeared near the Bennet family with the intent of asking the two eldest sisters to dance the supper set then accompany them into the dining room. They were surprised to find Darcy's aunt and her party conversing with the Bennet women.

"Aunt Matlock, Lady Sefton, I was not aware you were in company tonight. I would have come to greet you earlier." Darcy bowed to the ladies and looked to Bingley, who was just as ignorant of their attendance as his friend.

"Yes, I expected you had not asked Miss Bingley for the guest list for the evening and as you spent the afternoon in your rooms you were not here when we arrived." Lady Matlock had a sharp quality to her speech then she turned towards Lady Fiona, stepping fully in front of Elizabeth in an obvious attempt to create space between the Bennets and Darcy. "You remember my niece, Lady Fiona, Lord Nottingham's daughter, yes Fitzwilliam? You danced last year at my cousin's anniversary ball, then again at Almack's the single week you attended during the season."

Darcy looked back and forth between Lady Fiona and Elizabeth with some distress. Lady Matlock's manoeuvring was obvious but also skilful. He had already opened the ball with Elizabeth and the first notes of the supper set were starting as Lady Matlock basically placed Lady Fiona's hand into Darcy's. It was impossible to not take Lady Fiona to the dance floor for the supper set without being very rude.

Elizabeth caught his eye, smiled kindly and nodded her head as if to say, 'go on.'

"Oh, of course. Lady Fiona, how lovely to see you again." With one last, longing look at Elizabeth, Darcy held out his arm to Lady Fiona. "Would you care to dance with me for the supper set, Lady Fiona?"

The young heiress ducked her head shyly and spoke so softly that Darcy nearly missed her words. "Yes, thank you Mr. Darcy. I would be honoured."

As soon as the dancing couples took their places in line, Elizabeth excused herself to the ladies retiring room. Only one of the matrons near her caught sight of the single tear which escaped down her cheek.

One Proposal and Two Broken Hearts

ELIZABETH WAS ABED MUCH LATER THAN HER USUAL want, but she still managed to rise before the majority of the family. Only her father was dressed and downstairs when she made her way to the breakfast room. He was taking a full cup of tea and a scone into his book room as Elizabeth perused the sideboard. Feeling unequal to the quiet of the house, Elizabeth took her own scone with a smear of clotted cream and stepped out of the back door into the full sun of the late morning.

Choosing the path to her favourite pond just below the main trail to Oakham Mount, Elizabeth headed out into nature. The late night combined with her unsettling dreams, that progressed from dancing with Darcy to playing with children who shared his striking blue eyes and wry smile, had made Elizabeth rather melancholy. It seemed that no matter how many times her head had firmly stated that Darcy would never be at liberty to form a connection to her beyond friendship, her traitorous heart had formed a tender for the distinguished gentleman from Derbyshire.

Dancing in his arms had been a pleasure beyond reason. His bright smile and gentle embrace, which was both very proper and sensuously intimate, had made her feel safe and special. She was the only lady he singled out for a second dance. After spending the supper set with Lady Fiona, he had secured Elizabeth's hand during the mid-ball meal for the first set post-supper. They danced a Quadrille with Mary and Collins as their partners, then spent much of the next set regulating their laughter from the atrocious dancing skills of the portly clergyman. At least Collins had been paying affectionate attention to Mary and seemed to genuinely enjoy dancing with the woman he was courting.

In fact, Darcy had asked Elizabeth for three dances last night, which was not very proper, but she had been enjoying the evening too much to really think about the consequences of a third dance. No doubt the neighbourhood would be forming expectations of their engagement after such forward behaviour. After he departed for the holidays, if the rumours and her mother's laments become too difficult, she decided she would have to beg her aunt Gardiner to spend some time in London over the winter. With any luck, she would be spared her mother's wrath while planning Jane's and Mary's weddings. With the estate secured by Mary's marriage to Collins, and Jane's fortune gained through Bingley, Elizabeth entertained a sliver of hope that the expectations on her own marriage would be relieved.

The sun had crested its zenith and was on its way back to the horizon by the time Elizabeth started towards home. Upon entering the house, Elizabeth was immediately confronted with multiple members of her family in various states of agitation.

"Where have you been, you ungrateful child? You were much needed here at home and instead spent the morning out doing goodness knows." Mrs. Bennet cried from her position, laying on the chaise with smelling salts in one hand.

Before even being able to answer her mother, Kitty and Lydia flounced into the parlour in a fit of giggles. "Oh la! Lizzy, what a good joke! You shall soon be Mrs. Collins and will have to spend your mornings tending Mr. Collins's chickens instead of getting lost in the woods."

This was wholly unexpected and Elizabeth was unable to come up with any kind of response. Looking around the parlour, Elizabeth could see Jane looking uneasy and Mary had tear tracks visible down her cheeks.

Finally deciding it was time to get some answers, Elizabeth walked over to Jane and took the open seat near her. "Jane, you must tell me, what in the world is happening?"

Jane merely shook her head and bit back tears of her own. Beginning to become really alarmed, Elizabeth stood without another word then went in search of her father with the determination to demand an explanation to the bizarre state of the parlour.

Mr. Bennet was where he could usually be found, in his book room, and he was not alone. In her distress, Elizabeth failed to notice the absence of Collins from the parlour, but he was clearly sitting with her father drinking what appeared to be brandy, which was unusual for the man who often complained of indigestion and warned against the habit of over-imbibing.

"Papa, I came to see what has so upset my mother and sisters, but I will come later if you are having a private discussion with our cousin."

Collins stood up so quickly that he sloshed some of his brandy onto his sleeve. "No, Miss Elizabeth! Please, we have been waiting for you to come back to the house! I have a conundrum most difficult, you see. My most gracious patroness, the grand Lady Catherine de Bourgh, whom you know is aunt to the distinguished Mr. Darcy of your esteemed acquaintance, had given me very direct instructions to come to my cousins and heal the breach in our families by taking one of my lovely cousins as a wife. Fully anticipating that my future happiness dwelt within these walls, I hastened to this house of felicity and was not disappointed by the reported loveliness of my cousins and my future home. It was such a grand gesture and condescension from her ladyship and I have been extremely satisfied with her advice."

"Yes, Mr. Collins, we have heard much about your patroness and your purpose here." Elizabeth looked to her father for some explanation of why Collins's widely known purpose was being restated at length. "I will be glad to call you brother someday, but I do not understand what about this situation has caused a conundrum. Furthermore, I am confused about the melancholy of my sister Mary which I just observed in the parlour."

"Therein lies the true problem, Miss Elizabeth, I knew you would see directly! You see, my great patroness bid me come and make all haste to marry the eldest unattached daughter of my cousin. When I came, Miss Bennet and yourself were assumed to be attached to the gentlemen from Netherfield, and two finer men I have never met and could not imagine ever calling brother myself. It seemed that all was in order and I would make Miss Mary the object of my future happiness. But now, well with the gentlemen from Netherfield departed without any understandings solidified, I cannot but follow my patroness's advice and ask for Miss Jane Bennet to be my wife. Though my cousin's wife does say that she shall not allow the match but instead I must marry you my dear cousin. So, it is with all of the anticipation of felicity that comes with the decision to marry that I apply for your hand."

Elizabeth could barely breathe. "But you cannot be serious Mr. Collins! You cannot have a strong attachment to me, no not even the slightest!"

"Believe me, my dear, your modesty, so far from doing you a disservice, rather adds to your perfection. You would have been less amiable in my eyes had there not been this little unwillingness; but allow me to assure you that I have respect for your mother's advice in this choice. You can hardly doubt the purport of my discourse, however your natural delicacy may lead you to dissemble; my attentions to you have been subdued in deference to Mr. Darcy's superior company, but they should not be mistaken for indifference. Almost as soon as I entered the house, I singled you out as the companion of my future life. But, before I run away with my feelings on the subject, perhaps I should ease your mind in saying how much I admire you sister Miss Mary and her fortitude in accepting the natural order of the world and her stepping aside to see her sister advantageously matched with the man she had hoped to partner. I am sure that this is the way it has been ordained by the almighty. My patroness has said the very same. And nothing remains for me but to assure you, in the most animated language, of the violence of my affection and I shall be quite content with our situation once we are married."

Mr. Bennet was white knuckled and looking quite red in the face at the entire speech but looked to Elizabeth to answer Collins's speech.

"You are too hasty, sir." Elizabeth replied with caution. "You forget that I have made no answer. Let me do it without further loss of time.

Do you believe that I could countenance myself to such a situation which brings my beloved sister so much grief? An alliance between us shall always wear a shadow and you and I shall always know that our union was tainted with unkindness towards dear Mary. I am very sensible to the honour of your proposals, but it is impossible for me to do otherwise than decline them."

"I do not understand. Our families need to be united and Lady Catherine has declared that I must marry the eldest unattached sister. We must marry."

If she had not been so very angry, Elizabeth would have laughed at the expression of extreme perplexity on the foolish man's face.

"Mr. Collins, just because Lady Catherine told you to marry the eldest unattached of my sisters does not make that match a prudent one. She cannot know our characters, or our minds, and she cannot impress upon me her will from afar." Elizabeth began to be really angry and took a moment to gather herself before she raised her voice any further. "Nay, were your friend Lady Catherine to know me, I am persuaded she would find me in every respect ill qualified for the situation of your wife. I will not have you, under these circumstances or any other in the future. I am, however, willing to overlook this entire episode and put it from my mind forever if you go directly to my sister Mary and make your declarations to her instead of me. Though I must warn you, a delay of even a moment will likely stroke my ire and you may find me ill inclined to forgive such an infraction of publicly jilting my sister. What say you sir, shall you keep your word to my family and do your duty to my sister? The whole neighbourhood expects your engagement after your attentions to her these past weeks. You have engaged not only her feelings, but your own honour with the community and a change now will reflect badly on you and the Bennet family. Think carefully and do that which is expected of your honour." Elizbeth hoped that her bluster about honour would pay off and make the man see some kind of reason.

"Mr. Bennet, is this true? Does the neighbourhood expect me to make my addresses to Miss Mary?"

Mr. Bennet took a deep breath and a deeper pull from his glass before finding his voice. "Mr. Collins, I believe the rumours and gossip from our neighbours does tend in the direction of your attachment to

Mary. However, my position on this has not changed from when you came to me less than an hour ago. I will not give my permission for you to marry any of my daughters, regardless of the talk about town, unless the lady is inclined to accept you. Lizzy has stated her disinclination to your proposal. I will not beg her to change her mind. I am also in agreement with my Lizzy. I would be willing to forget your ill-guided attempt to persuade her to marry you, *only* if you make amends to Mary. If she is inclined to accept your addresses and you never again make *any* of my daughters shed a tear, I shall forget this has ever happened. You now only have to decide your course."

After a moment of hand wringing and unintelligible muttering, Collins stood from his chair, threw back the last of his brandy and looked to the door of the book room with a mixture of fear and fortitude.

"Faint heart never won fair lady, sir," Elizabeth urged. "Go now or forever be estranged from us."

Collins nodded once, then strode to the door with purpose.

Neither Elizabeth nor Mr. Bennet followed, but after a few moments, Mrs. Bennet's wails of joy could be heard coming from the parlour. Mr. Bennet audibly blew out the enormous breath he had been holding inside, stood from his desk, poured Elizabeth a small glass of sherry, and sat beside her on the couch.

"Now child, you have shown fortitude in the face of the events of this day, but tell me truthfully, how are you feeling? And what has kept you from the house for so long? Did Mr. Darcy impose upon you in any way that I should know about?"

Elizabeth nearly choked on her drink. "What has brought this on, Papa? Of course Mr. Darcy has not imposed upon me in any way. He is a gentleman of the utmost character and reputation. I have always been safe in his company. I was out of doors this morning for no reason other than I have been confined to the house for three days with the recent rains and I required some rambling in the woods to right my disposition. It can hardly be a surprise to my family that this is my first response to a sunny day."

"You are correct, but I had to ask given the news we received this morning." Mr. Bennet fiddled with the pocket of his morning coat and pulled out a single sheet of paper.

"What news, Papa? Mr. Collins referred to something about the Netherfield party departing without any understandings being solidified, but I cannot understand of what he was speaking."

"Your sister, Jane, received this missive from Miss Bingley this morning." He started to hand over the letter, then seemed to think better of it and placed it back into his pocket. "I will not bore you with the entire contents, but I will say that she wrote, in some part, to apologise for not taking proper leave of us. Mr. Darcy and Mr. Bingley rode for London sometime this morning and the ladies were left to pack the house and follow on the morrow. Miss Bingley does not anticipate being back to Hertfordshire before the end of the full London season." Mr. Bennet raised his eyebrows in a pointed look. "She also made some specific claims in regard to Mr. Bingley's marriage to Mr. Darcy's sister. Now, with your sister's dashed hopes, I find I congratulate her. Next to being married, a girl likes to be crossed in love a little now and then. It is something to think of, and gives her a sort of distinction among her companions. I was also inclined to think this of you and Mr. Darcy until Lydia began saying some very disheartening things about your young man."

"Papa, I find I am not equal to this discussion at the present, there is too much in what you have just said, but I must ask you to elaborate upon the last point you have made about Lydia and accusations against Mr. Darcy." Elizabeth pinched the bridge of her nose in fear of a large headache coming quickly to the front of her mind.

Mr. Bennet paused for a moment then spoke in a direct and fatherly tone. "Upon hearing that Mr. Darcy quit the region this morning, Lydia began to loudly say that she was glad of such news and would rather not set eyes upon such a man again as the Darcys of Pemberley. She claims that Mr. Darcy's father has disregarded a contract made for one of the curate livings under Pemberley's direction. According to a Lieutenant Wickham, Mr. Darcy Senior made a promise that upon some living becoming vacant, the young man was to be given the living. Lieutenant Wickham confided in Lydia that the living became vacant this past year and when he presented himself to Mr. Darcy Senior to take the position, the elder gentleman denied such a contract existed and refused to bestow the living, which is why the man now finds himself as a lieutenant in the militia instead of a curate. Lydia also had some other things with which to charge our young Mr. Darcy. That he is prideful and above his company is evident to the entire neighbourhood, but if this Lieutenant Wickham is to be believed, he is also none too careful with the affections of young ladies. Now, I will repeat my question. Has Mr. Darcy imposed himself upon you?"

"I believe I understand Mamma's need for smelling salts all of a sudden," Elizabeth muttered. Then, in a stronger voice, she replied, "Papa, I cannot relate in strong enough language how untrue all of this slander is against Mr. Darcy and his esteemed father. I know nothing of any living or contract, but I know enough of Mr. Darcy to be sure in my position. If such a living is under the direction of Pemberley, then the current master of that estate must have the right to dispose of it as he chooses. If Lieutenant Wickham has not made any recourse in the crown courts, then he cannot have a legitimate claim to the living. Secondly, I cannot believe any word against Mr. Darcy in regard to the affections of young ladies. He has been nothing but proper to me."

Elizabeth stood abruptly and walked to the window overlooking the back garden. She wrapped her own arms tightly around her body. "I have always known he will seek a wife from the titled heiresses of the *ton* in the coming season and that he was not inclined towards me. I have no expectations of the gentlemen and he has done nothing to excite any such expectations. In fact, the things of which Lieutenant Wickham accuses Mr. Darcy are the exact things which Mr. Darcy accused Lieutenant Wickham on our very first day of acquaintance. I was witness to their meeting that day and both men's reactions to each other. Mr. Darcy looked almost angry to be in the same company with Lieutenant Wickham, and Lieutenant Wickham looked frightened at facing Mr. Darcy." She turned back to her father and narrowed her eyes. "In light of these accusations, I would now say Lieutenant Wickham looked *guilty* of something. However, Mr. Darcy showed his good manners and decided to give Lieutenant Wickham the benefit of doubt, hoping that the man had turned over a new leaf and was finally taking responsibility for his own life."

"How can you know all of Mr. Darcy's inner thoughts?"

"Simple. He has spoken them aloud to me last night at the ball. While we danced, he warned me against Lieutenant Wickham as a man who is not to be trusted, but also hedged his comments with hope that this new post with the militia showed that he was seriously pursuing his career. I would also dispute the claim that Mr. Darcy is proud or above his company. He is perhaps shy with strangers and does not perform well in a crowded room, but he is perfectly amiable when engaged to speak with sensible individuals in a calm setting." Elizabeth motioned between herself and her father while taking a seat again on the sofa. "You, yourself, have engaged him in pleasant conversation."

Mr. Bennet shook his head. "He also danced with you three times last night and has not once given a thought to how his desertion would affect your reputation. If you say you never had any expectations of the gentleman, how could you allow him to present the vision of such an attachment to you to all our neighbours?"

Elizabeth looked down to her hands folded in her lap. "I am sorry that I allowed the third dance last evening, especially if it causes harm to our family. I only have the defence that it was quite late by the last dance and I did not think of it being our third until we were already standing in the line. Also, I doubt our neighbours will remember any such infraction in the face of Jane and Mary's double wedding this Christmastide."

"There will be no double wedding. Did you not listen earlier? Jane is abandoned by Mr. Bingley who is, according to the sister, set to marry Miss Darcy."

Elizabeth waved her hand. "Miss Bingley says many things which are not so. I am sure she may wish for him to marry a girl who has all the importance of money, great connections, and pride, but I do not believe him to be inclined towards a child of only fifteen years. Miss Bingley's bluster shall come to nothing, I am sure."

Mr. Bennet hummed and smirked, his general good humour in the face of female intrigue restored for now. "We shall have to see, child. Now, run off to your sister, Jane. I am sure she is in need of an escape from your mother."

Departures

AFTER LEAVING MR. BENNET'S STUDY, MR. COLLINS went straight to Mary and dropped to one knee. In a very long-winded and meandering speech about duty, honour, position, and the wishes of his patroness, Mr. Collins finally got to the point of his ramblings.

"My dear Mary, all impediments to our match have been cleared between myself, your father and your older sisters. I am now free to make my addresses to you as the object of my future happiness and ask for you to become my wife. I am sure you will be quite content living so close to such a grand and condescending lady, and Lady Catherine de Bourgh and I shall be quite content knowing I have been given the power to heal the breach between our families."

Later that evening, Mary knocked softly on the door to Elizabeth's room. "Lizzy, may I come in?"

Elizabeth smiled warmly. "Of course, you are always welcome here. How are you feeling? It has been an exciting day, has it not?"

"Yes, very much has happened today." Mary sat softly on the bed next to her sister. "I feel as though I have no more emotions left inside my body, as first I was as downtrodden as I have ever been, then I was brought back to life and lifted to the height of happiness. It has left me quite numb, actually."

"That is very understandable. I am sorry you were so low waiting for our cousin to make his proper proposals." Elizabeth reached out to hold Mary's hand and put some escaped curls behind her ear.

"I was convinced that you would agree to marry William to protect our family." Mary hastened to add, "Which I would have absolutely understood and supported. I do not blame you for what happened. It is the normal course for older sisters to marry first, and of course you would have had to take him with such prospects of inheriting Longbourn."

Though Elizabeth thought to herself that neither herself nor Jane were in any danger of accepting Collins, even to protect the family from losing their home at her father's passing, she kept those thoughts to herself. "It may be the normal course when younger sisters do not come out until the elders are married, but I was not inclined to accept him knowing it would bring you such pain, dear one."

"I am glad that it has been worked out between William and Papa." Mary ducked her head into the pillow. "While you were in Papa's book room, I was considering plans to leave Longbourn after your wedding."

"Where would you have gone?" Elizabeth exclaimed.

"I thought of joining the Clapham Saints in their mission to abolish slavery and serve the poor, or even going to Ireland to find sanctuary in a catholic nunnery." She smiled, wryly. "I was certain that I would not be able to endure the times when you and William would visit our family or come to claim the estate after Papa's passing. If that had come to pass, I would have to be away."

"Well, while you were planning to cross the sea in search of Irish nuns, I was telling your intended that I would never accept a man who had harmed my beloved sister." Elizabeth lifted Mary's face so their eyes could meet. "I made it very clear that he was to go directly to your side and profess his intentions or forever be estranged to us all."

Mary giggled, then settled back into Elizabeth's side. "It has worked out as it should."

"I could not agree more."

Exactly three weeks later, time enough to call the banns and arrange for Mary's personal items to be sent to Kent, Mrs. Bennet had the satisfaction of seeing a daughter married and the estate secured for herself and her remaining daughters.

The wedding of Mr. William Collins and Miss Mary Bennet was a simple but elegant affair with Christmas flowers decorating the church of Longbourn. The bride wore a pale green muslin dress with satin lavender ribbon trim. Mrs. Bennet wanted to go to London for a trousseau, but Mary was firm that her station in life as a parson's wife would be ill served by silk dresses or lace. Sturdy muslin dresses of a fashionable cut were ordered from the Meryton dressmaker and each of the five sisters took to their needles and embroidery to give Mary a well-trimmed start to her life as Mrs. Collins. Lydia, especially, had some fun with the task of making Mary's wedding dress the shining star of the event. She worked a beautiful lavender brocade rope around the bust and patterned the sleeves in such a way as to mirror one of her favourite styles in a recent addition of *La Belle Assemblée*. Many of their neighbours, who had known the Bennet sisters since they were in their cradles, could not remember any other day in which Mary outshone her elder sisters. But walking down the aisle, everyone thought Collins a supremely lucky man.

Elizabeth and Jane each served as Mary's attendants while one of Collins's friends from theology school attended the groom. The wedding breakfast was hosted at Longbourn and everyone had their fill of food and wine before sending the couple off on their trip back to Collins's home in Kent.

"Well, Jane, it is done and done for the better. I am persuaded that Mary has a true regard for him and that they shall be well matched in their future lives." Elizabeth turned closer to her elder sister and spoke softly. "I am heartily glad that it is not me married to such a pompous, narrow-minded and silly man, but Mary shall manage him well and perhaps make him more sensible as the years progress."

"Now Lizzy, be kind." Jane admonished. "He is today our brother and he will be caring for us in our spinsterhood. We should learn to respect him, and trust him as we trust our father to provide."

"Jane! How uncharitable of you. I am certain that Mr. Bingley will return in all due haste once the little season is ended."

"But, how can you doubt his sister's assertion of his attachment to Miss Darcy?" Jane shook her head and looked stoic. "No, I am convinced that he shall return no more, or if he does, it shall be of no consequence to me."

To Caroline's assertion of her brother being partial to Miss Darcy, Elizabeth paid no credit. That he was really fond of Jane, she doubted no more than she had ever done, but she allowed some resentment that he should allow his sisters to treat him so ill as to make Jane doubt his affections.

Not moments after the newly married couple had driven away in their hired carriage, Mrs. Bennet had returned to her favourite subject, which was her general irritation about Netherfield, its master and his friend. Jane continued in an uncharacteristic outburst, though it was a long time coming. "Oh, that my dear mother had more command over herself; she can have no idea of the pain she gives me by her continual reflections on him. But, I will not repine. It cannot last long. He will be forgot, and we shall all be as we were before."

Elizabeth looked at her sister with incredulous solicitude, but said nothing.

"You doubt me, but you have no reason." Jane directed a very pointed look at her sister. "As I have taken your word that Mr. Darcy is nothing more than a friendly acquaintance, please give me the same courtesy. Mr. Bingley may live in my memory as the most amiable man of my acquaintance, but that is all. I have nothing either to hope for or fear and nothing to reproach him with. It may have been merely an error of fancy on my side and has done no harm to anyone but myself."

"My dear Jane, you are too good. I shall still carry hope that the man shall be unable to stay away from your beauty and goodness. You wish to think the whole world respectable, and are hurt if I speak ill of anybody, but I only want to think you perfect. There are few people who I really love, and still fewer of whom I think really well. The more I see of the world, the more I am dissatisfied with it." Elizabeth sighed and frowned. "The false words of Miss Bingley and Lieutenant Wickham have confirmed my belief of the inconsistency of human character, and shows that little dependence can be placed on appearance of either merit or sense."

Elizabeth had heard enough of Lt. Wickham's complaints in the weeks since the Netherfield party had departed, and was growing tired of his smiles and flirtations spoken in the same breath as his sufferings. While the gentlemen of the neighbourhood and some of the more discerning ladies were not moved by his slander against the Darcys of Pemberley, many of the young ladies, taken with his society, and the gossiping mothers won over by his platitudes, had taken up his cause. Elizabeth's own mother was overly distressed with the story about the living which was supposed to have been granted by Darcy's father and used this as both a complaint against the younger Darcy who had deserted her second eldest daughter but also as a blessing that such a man was not now among their family party.

Elizabeth and Jane tried to put around that there must be extenuating circumstances unknown to the whole of society, which would materially alter the extent of any such grievance, but Darcy and his father were soon condemned by most of their friends as the worst of men.

After listening to the complaints of their mother for nearly four weeks, Jane and Elizabeth were both feeling unequal to the usual cheer of the Christmastide season. Even the arrival of their London family, with Elizabeth's favourite aunt and uncle Gardiner and their four lively, cheerful children, did nothing to raise Elizabeth's spirits.

Elizabeth's melancholy mood was especially worrisome for her father, elder sister, and aunt Gardiner, each of whom expressed some anxiety over how many days had passed since Elizabeth had enjoyed a morning stroll in the woods or played the pianoforte after supper. Mr. Bennet conspired with his brother-in-law to take his two oldest children back to London for the new year and away from the gossip flowing around Meryton and inside their own home. His chief goal was the gift of a sensible household in which to bury their personal disappointments with time and entertainments.

"My dear brother and sister, pray, take Lizzy and Jane to at least one play, a funny one preferably. And if you can manage it, bring them to a ball or two of the little season. I do not expect you to find them replacement suitors, but a bit of distraction is most seriously in order."

"Yes, Thomas, we shall take them to entertainments." Madeline Gardiner began to run through the list of all their acquaintances who generally entertained during the winter little season, mentally noting events which would be appropriate for two young unmarried women. "I feel very poorly for Jane, because with her disposition she may not get over such disappointment immediately, but I am most distressed over

Lizzy's reaction to this abandonment. Before this moment, I would have guessed Lizzy to have laughed herself out of any such situation in all due haste, but now. Well, I see she is most affected and must have had a violent attachment to Mr. Darcy. But she is still denying it all and refuses to even hear a word about how they were much of a mind with each other."

Mr. Bennet sighed. "Yes, she has been most vehement that she never had any expectations of Mr. Darcy, and while I believe that to be true, she is determined that it also means she never had any true feelings for him. I am most profoundly glad she is intelligent and has attempted to protect herself from the disappointment of his unavailability, but deceiving herself will do her no good. A change of scene might be of service, and any relief from home will be as useful as anything."

Both Jane and Elizabeth accepted their aunt and uncle's invitation with pleasure, and looked forward to removing to London at the conclusion of the Christmas celebrations. The last week of the Gardiners' visit was filled with so many engagements that the family hardly ever took a meal at home without some invited guests. Twice the officers came to Longbourn to dine, which Lieutenant Wickham was always a party to, and Madeline narrowly observed the officer with her nieces. The widely varying accounts of the young man, and Lydia's plain preference for his society, made her uneasy, and she was resolved to speak to her sister, Mrs. Bennet on the subject before quitting the area.

"Now sister, you know that before my marriage to your brother, I came from Lambton, a small village in the north of Derbyshire. But, you may not know that the village Lambton is the closest town to Pemberley and the Darcy family lands. I have known Mr. Darcy Senior all my life, and many of my friends and relations work for his household or serve the needs of his family. My own father was the town's attorney and served as under-magistrate for Mr. Darcy when the family was away. I also know something of young Mr. Wickham."

Mrs. Bennet waved her handkerchief in the air and cried, "Oh sister, really! I had quite forgotten the name of the estate which your town served. How extraordinary! Tell me, what think you of Mr. Wickham? I believe he is very handsome and will do nicely for Lydia. And I'm sure that once that nasty Mr. Darcy sees he is married to a gentleman's daughter with uncles in the law, he will finally give Mr. Wickham the living he was promised. Then Lydia will have a very nice life indeed. And then, Lydia will be able to throw Lizzy back into young Mr. Darcy's path and she can finally catch him. Then, I am sure that Lizzy would invite her unmarried sisters to live with her and throw them in the way of other rich men."

Madeline managed to take a steadying breath without rolling her eyes. "Now, sister, let us leave the discussions of any of your unattached daughters marrying for another day. I was speaking specifically of Mr. Darcy the elder, and Mr. Wickham. Mr. Darcy is kind to his servants, generous with the poor, and often frequents the shops in Lambton instead of saving all of his money to purchase necessities in London. On the contrary, I have not heard such general good of Mr. Wickham. I believe that the young man left behind many unpaid debts with the merchants in Lambton. My good friend, whose family owns the inn on the town square, has spoken of how he is not welcome to stay in their rooms even were he to have the money to pay upfront as he has been much too free with the maids in the past."

Mrs. Bennet looked aghast and shrieked for her smelling salts, but it was Lydia who spoke against her aunt. "I am certain that such slander against my poor Wickham has been circulated by that nasty Mr. Darcy and I shall hear not one more word of it. I shall be glad once you are away this year and take my eldest sisters with you, for they are most ungracious in their words and have refused to hear any of the proof against Darcys. It is such hypocrisy! Just because the Darcys are rich, they have the power to make people believe whatever they say and my dear Wickham pays the price. Well, when I become Mrs. Wickham, I shall encourage my dear husband to seek out that living by starting proceedings in the law, and I shall certainly not use such a connection to throw Lizzy into the way of Mr. Darcy again. I do not wish for such a relation!"

Seeing that the endeavour was lost, Madeline withdrew from the fray. She hoped that her young niece's general immaturity and lack of fortune would be enough to save her from such an imprudent match, but only time would tell.

The very next morning, the Gardiners left Hertfordshire with Jane and Elizabeth in tow and left the remaining Bennet family to their own devices.

Grey January Days

"I TELL YOU TRUTHFULLY, CHARLES, I COULD DIScern in her no symptom of particular regard. Her look and manners were open, cheerful and engaging as ever, but I remain convinced that while she received your attentions with some pleasure, she did not invite them by any participation of sentiment." Darcy handed Bingley a tumbler of his best aged scotch. "I cannot claim a particular insight into the minds or hearts of young ladies, but after a most acute observation on my part, I am of the belief that her temper is amiable but her heart is not easily touched. I fear if you return to her now, you risk a marriage of unequal affection which would bring you pain through your life together, for surely she would accept you based on her prospects and age and her mother's none-too-subtle exclamations of joy at such a match."

Darcy sat in his chair behind the massive oak desk in his father's study for several minutes in silence while Bingley stared out of the window into the London fog from his seat. He had been anticipating an argument over the nature of Jane Bennet's affections, but Bingley merely stood, set down his full glass, thanked Darcy for the call, and walked out of the front door. Darcy took his friend's actions as confirmation that Bingley knew the truth of Jane's heart and was only waiting on confirmation from those who knew them both. It was unfortunate, but at least no lasting harm had been done and no declarations made.

"What has that happy young man looking so downtrodden?" George Darcy asked from the doorway to his study.

"Father! Please excuse me. I was answering some correspondence." Darcy stood and stepped from behind the desk and gestured for his father to take back his own chair. "Do you require the room for yourself this morning?"

George waved off his son and sat himself in one of the plush, low chairs in front of the desk. "No William, I just came to let you know that I will be on my way north shortly. Please do not disturb your work, this room is as much yours as it is mine."

Darcy crossed back to the spirits cart and poured his father a small glass of his favourite brandy. "I wish you would reconsider staying for the little season, Father. Georgie will miss you and Richard has particularly enjoyed your company this past month."

"And I am sure your aunt Matlock has been putting it in your ear that I must stay if either of you is to make fine matches." George huffed affectionately and sipped his drink. "Your sister is still just fifteen and Lady Matlock would have her betrothed already with a contract even though her own daughter is still unattached at nearly twenty. No my boy, another year in the nursery and with her masters would be just fine for Georgiana."

"I am glad you are giving my sister the time to focus on her studies without coming out this year. She is more shy than even I was at her age."

George chuckled. "It is hard to imagine any person more uncomfortable in company than you, William. However, Georgie does come close. At least she is not so tall as you are. Even as you tried to hide in the shadows of ballrooms all across town, it was a bad job. Every matrimony minded lady could easily find your handsome face floating well above the heads of the crowd."

"Father! I hardly would consider myself uncomfortable in society and it is not polite to refer to oneself as handsome." Darcy looked down at the stack of papers on the desk, reaching for several unopened on the side.

"I was not referring to myself, I was referring to you." George smiled and winked at his son, enjoying the rare moment when he could fluster his stoic son.

Darcy shot back a mock serious look. "Well, I have heard it said enough that we are so alike in the face that you may as well be referring to yourself."

At this, George laughed heartily. "Oh my boy, your wit, as dry and seldom seen as it may be, never fails to cheer me. While I am more outgoing and jovial, it was your mother who always managed to bring laughter into our lives."

"Yes, I remember." Darcy smiled and looked to the portrait of his mother, Lady Anne, hanging above the mantle. "She was always teasing me, up until the very last."

"We should speak about Georgiana's entertainment during the little season before I leave." George said after a moment of reflection. "I am very much of a mind with Lady Matlock in one item. Georgie should have a family season this year and attend balls given by family until after supper, dancing only with her close relations of course, and attend the theatre with you or the Matlocks, as long as the performance is not an opening night and you do not stay for the after entertainment. Also, I have agreed that she may spend at least one day a week taking calls with her aunt at Matlock House, but she should not attend Lady Matlock's visiting days. Georgiana may also be allowed to attend dinners given at Matlock House and if you both wish, she may act as hostess for dinners here at Darcy House with select guests such as family and very close friends."

"Yes, Father, I will make sure she only attends appropriate events." Darcy could not resist one last plea for his father to stay in town. "However poor a substitute I shall be for your presence and guidance to us both."

George pointed his finger at his son. "That was low." The elder Darcy sighed and set down his glass. "I hope you will not take your duties to Georgie so seriously that you will neglect your own introductions and entertainments."

Darcy shifted in his seat. A fleeting thought of Bingley and his extreme disappointment passed through his mind. If Bingley never returned to Netherfield, Darcy might never see Elizabeth again. She was unlikely to show up at one of the events he was invited to this season. They were not of the same class or social circle and he could not write to her to inquire of any plans she may have to be in London with her aunt and uncle. He knew he wanted to return to see the superior lady, but he did not know how to accomplish such a feat or what his relations would say to the match. He *was* getting on the high side of the age that most of his acquaintances had married. And if he was honest, he wanted to find a wife with which to share his life. He wanted children of his own and someone to share his most intimate moments. And, if his sister were to marry in the next year or two, he would like to have his own house established instead of finding himself all alone in the evenings. In order to find his match, Darcy needed to be in London for the season, no matter how much he disliked society's expectations or the marriage mart.

As his son remained quiet and lost in his own thoughts, George waited. Darcy was never best at spontaneous speech, and his father had learned to let the silence stretch for a long moment before interrupting Darcy's internal monologue.

"Father, I know that everyone has expectations of my marriage. Even myself, I want a wife and family." He paused again. "I just do not know if she is waiting for me in the ballrooms around London."

George's eyebrows rose into his hairline at this admission. If Darcy was mentioning looking for a wife in any place other than the London Marriage Mart, it sounded suspiciously like he might have somewhere *specific* in mind. "And where do you believe she might be waiting for you?"

Darcy blushed deeply but was mercifully interrupted from having to formulate a reply by his sister entering the room.

"Father, there you are! I was worried you had left without saying goodbye to me." Georgiana came and placed a kiss on her father's face, then sat on the second seat in front of the study desk.

"Never, my darling. I was just speaking to your brother about your family season this winter." George booped his daughter on her nose. "I expect you to be on your best behaviour for William and not complain when you must retire after supper at the ball next week."

"I promise, Father, I shall not complain." Georgiana looked over at Darcy with a mischievous smile on her face. "Though it is perhaps not me you should be worried about in regard to complaints about leaving balls early."

Darcy narrowed his eyes at his sister. "What do you mean, you little troublemaker?"

"Oh nothing, just that I have had it from *several* sources that you danced the first set, the supper set, and the last set at the Bingley's ball before Christmas." She clapped her hands and bounced a bit in her seat. "Aunt Matlock was very animated to report that you danced the supper set with her Nottingham niece, the Lady Fiona Finch."

"Did you really, William?" George looked back at his son with a small smile. "She is a lovely lady and comes from a very well established family."

Darcy cleared his throat. His mind wandered to how disappointed he was to have to dance the supper set with Lady Fiona instead of Elizabeth. In his annoyance with his aunt's meddling, he'd forgotten himself and danced with Elizabeth for two dances after dinner. Three dances in total that evening. It seemed like Lady Matlock was not speaking about that bit of gossip as it would certainly not help her scheme to marry him off to her niece, but he was worried that it might get back to his father through some other acquaintance.

"Lady Fiona is perfectly tolerable company, but perhaps not really handsome enough to tempt me. And we hardly know each other after one dance at a country ball." Darcy's rigid mask of social anxiety was firmly in place.

"Fitzwilliam!" Georgiana admonished. "What a terrible thing to say about a young lady. Really now, '*not handsome enough.*' Who could ever be good enough for you if Lady Fiona is not handsome enough?"

Elizabeth, William's heart whispered. Elizabeth was lovely, accomplished, kind, and generous. Everything he wanted in a wife. Darcy hoped his father would support such a match, but he worried about what the Matlocks would say. He did not need his uncle's blessing, but he did have familial affection for them, and he respected his uncle's opinions very much. If he chose to make Elizabeth an offer, he needed to be sure his family would welcome her with the openness and love she deserved. The indignation of the world which might be excited by his marrying a young gentlewoman of little fortune would matter little to Darcy or his immediate family, but he would be grieved if his family treated his wife poorly. Though he hoped that society in general would have too much sense to scorn his choice.

"I am sorry, poppet. You are correct that I should not have said such a thing about Lady Fiona. I only meant that I am not thinking of her seriously for courtship." No matter the reactions of his relatives, Darcy would likely not hear of Elizabeth for more than three months, when Bingley would return to Netherfield to inspect the planning, and he had his sister to attend in the meantime. Checking the mantel clock, Darcy knew his father wanted to be on his way to make it to his first stop before nightfall. "Come, now, let us put aside talk of young ladies and balls. Father, your carriage is likely ready to depart and I would like to step out for a shopping trip to Hatchards before our dinner engagement this evening."

Elizabeth was truly enjoying her visit with her aunt and uncle Gardiner very much. She could not be more pleased with the absence of her mother's complaints regarding Darcy and her youngest sister's constant praise of Lt. Wickham. However, she had not yet regained her typical happy demeanour. She kept telling herself, and her aunt and sister, that it was the cold of the season, the grey clouds, and the lack of rambling nature-filled walks in London, and most definitely not at all the absence of a tall handsome gentleman from Derbyshire.

If she was being honest with herself, it was a combination of all the above which had her spirits still feeling down. Elizabeth was also more than a tad bit angry with Bingley's duplicitous sisters. Not two days ago, Jane and Elizabeth had presented themselves to the Bingley townhome, which Caroline herself had given them the direction of in her farewell note to Jane. Her sister was eager to renew the acquaintance, which had been quit barely a month before, and despite the manner in which they had been cast off by Miss Bingley, Jane was still hopeful for a welcoming return from her friends.

All such hopes were destroyed within moments of presenting themselves at the door to the house. Jane applied to see Caroline, but the butler turned up his nose and asked them how they came to have this address. In her innocence, Jane pulled out Caroline's letter and checked the address to the numbers on the house and showed it to the butler asking if they were mistaken with the direction. Seeing his mistress's handwriting, he was obliged to bring the sisters into the foyer, but he did not ask to take their outer things. Instead, they were instructed to wait in the entry hall while he went up the stairs to the parlour to ask whether the ladies were welcome to call. Caroline's distinct voice could be heard all the way down the stairs. Though the exact words were difficult to make out, the tone was clear. And it was anything but friendly.

A short fifteen-minute call was conducted with all the patience on Caroline's part of a hungry bear eying its dinner. She barely asked after their family, did not have any interest at all in the Christmastide celebrations of their Hertfordshire neighbours and kept making vague references to planned guests coming to tea. Elizabeth understood that Caroline wanted the Bennet sisters gone before their tea guests arrived, but Jane was unaccustomed to thinking so meanly of anyone, and instead continued to make polite conversation asking after their entertainments during the past month. Finally, when a coach could be heard passing in front of the house, Caroline stood abruptly and thanked them loudly for their visit. Elizabeth and Jane had nothing to do except stand, thank their hostess, and collect their coats and gloves.

Before leaving, Jane remembered that one purpose in their calling had been to leave the direction to their uncle's house and pulled out one of her aunt's cards. Instead of taking it directly, she paused for too long a moment and Jane's brows knit together in confusion before Caroline finally snatched the card from her hand and bid them good day.

All that evening, Jane had commented about the oddness of the visit, but she concluded that Caroline must have been under some distress that she could not speak of directly and wished for solitude. Elizabeth concurred with the wish for solitude, but she was sure that the odd behaviour was more due to lack of enjoyment at the company, and at least for Elizabeth herself, the feeling was mutual.

Yesterday, Jane had insisted on waiting in the parlour all day as it was her aunt's stated day at home printed on the calling card which had been left. She was sure that Caroline, and probably Mrs. Hurst (and she hoped silently, Bingley,) would come to return the call as was the custom for friends newly arrived in Town. But the fashionable calling time came and went without so much as a by-your-leave note from either of Bingley's sisters.

Today, Elizabeth had asked their aunt if they might have a fun adventure with the children in Hyde Park. Jane loved feeding the ducks at the Serpentine and some fresh air would do Elizabeth a world of good. So, just before teatime, they packed a picnic basket, bundled the Gardiners' four young children into their coats and headed off in the landau with two of the warehouse men from Gardiner Imports attending.

Elizabeth was determined to put any Darcys and Bingleys out of her mind and instead enjoy some childish fun with her young cousins.

Chance Meetings

AFTER BIDDING THEIR FATHER GOODBYE, DARCY and Georgiana opted to stroll along the Rotten Way towards the bookshop instead of driving the curricle. The sun had finally decided to make a glorious return from its prison behind the clouds. As they approached the south end of the park, Georgiana noticed a group of ladies with some children feeding the ducks. "Look, brother! How happy those children appear. Do you remember when Father used to bring us to do that? Maybe for the sake of nostalgia we could bring some old bread one day and join the children."

Smiling indulgently at the memories of his sister splashing around in the water at the park, Darcy looked towards the shore of the Serpentine.

"Elizabeth!"

The three ladies near the water and Georgiana all stopped what they were doing to look towards Darcy, startled by his sudden outburst.

"Brother?"

"Come, dearest. I want to introduce you to some friends of mine." Darcy changed direction swiftly, nearly dragging Georgiana towards the lake, and did not stop to acknowledge his sister's surprise.

By the time Darcy and Georgiana reached the group at the shore of the lake, Elizabeth still had not recovered from the shock of Darcy calling her name, then coming towards their party with determined strides. Her emotions in the last thirty seconds had gone through such a whirlwind. Alarm at hearing someone shout her name. Elation at seeing Darcy waving at her with a bright smile on his face. Then utter dejection at seeing a young, beautiful, fashionably dressed blond woman on his arm. She had already suffered an introduction to Lady Fiona at the Bingley's ball, whom she knew to be a contender for Darcy's hand. Was she now going to have to suffer another introduction and be pleasant to the most elegant and lovely woman she had ever seen? How was she ever to compete for his affections in the company of such ladies?

Jane was the first to find her voice. "Mr. Darcy, how lovely to see you sir. Might we have an introduction to your companion?"

"Yes! It gives me great pleasure to introduce my sister, Miss Georgiana Darcy. Dear, this is Miss Jane Bennet and Miss Elizabeth Bennet." Darcy beamed back at the Bennet sisters. "Their father owns the estate which borders that which Mr. Bingley and his sisters let this past autumn, and I had the great pleasure of spending many pleasant evenings with the Miss Bennets, their three younger sisters and parents. Would you do us the honour of introducing your friends?"

Elizabeth had once again been rendered mute at the relief she felt learning that the young woman was his sister and not his potential future wife, so Jane was again required to perform the pleasantries of introducing their aunt Gardiner and the four children. Darcy bowed in genuine pleasure at meeting Madeline Gardiner. She was very fashionable in her look and manners. If he did not know from Elizabeth that her husband owned an imports business, he would have taken her for a lady of fashion. If Gardiner was as gentlemanly as Madeline was lady like, Darcy could have them to dine with his relatives without any reason to worry over Matlock's objections to Elizabeth's connections.

"What a wonderful surprise to find you in London, Miss Elizabeth! I had not heard of your removing from the country. We must have you and your aunt and uncle for dinner some time. What do you say Georgiana? Would you like to have a little dinner party for friends?" Darcy was smiling much brighter than he normally would in company, but he was too excited over seeing Elizabeth. It was almost as if his musings of that morning had conjured her from the ether.

"Mr. Darcy, my sister and I have been here barely a sennight and plan to stay though until Easter." Elizabeth finally found her voice. "Our third sister, Mary, has lately been married to our cousin Mr. Collins, and they removed to Hunsford in Kent just before Christmas. Jane and

I plan to visit our sister and new brother for the Easter celebrations and will stay about six weeks before travelling home to Longbourn."

"As you know, our aunt, Lady Catherine de Bourgh, and her daughter, Miss Anne de Bourgh, hold the estate that Mr. Collins's living serves, and we make a yearly visit to her ladyship at Easter. Now, I must insist that you come to dinner some evening to meet our relations. Perhaps Georgiana can host afternoon tea some day for Anne and our other female cousin, Lady Marianne Fitzwilliam. Then we will all be a merry party in Kent at Easter indeed." Darcy and Elizabeth merely looked at each other with matching smiles. Jane, having seen the pair together before, was less dumbfounded than their other companions at the turn in the day's events, but only mildly.

Madeline finally inserted herself into the conversation. "Mr. Darcy, my husband and I would be happy to consider any invitation you or Miss Darcy would like to extend to our nieces. Perhaps it would be prudent, before we send Jane and Lizzy off to so many engagements, to have you to our home for dinner so you may be introduced to my husband. Would you and your sister be free in two days' time for dinner?"

Darcy looked radiantly at Madeline and bowed deeply. "Madam, we would be more than honoured to dine with your family in two days' time."

A sudden splash and cry broke the spell of the most enthusiastic introductions to which Darcy had ever been party.

"Mamma! Henry fell in the water!"

All five adults had forgotten for a moment that they were escorting four young children at the edge of a large lake. "Oh! My! Henry, are you all right?"

"I'm a duck, Mamma! Quack Quack!"

"You are all wet is what you are, young man! Mr. Darcy, Miss Darcy, I am so sorry but we will need to leave immediately."

Darcy was not at all keen to have Elizabeth away from him now that he was being given exactly the chance he had wanted to introduce her to his sister. "Madam, if I may. Our townhome is less than a five-minute carriage ride from here and as the weather is quite chilly. I must insist that you bring young master Henry to our home to get dry and warm before making your way home. This time of day the traffic might delay your arrival by more than three quarters of an hour which is much too long to be wet and cold."

"Mr. Darcy you are much too kind, but I am afraid that we could not fit you and your sister in our landeau." Madeline fretted and looked around their fairly large party.

"That is no matter. Georgiana shall escort you and the children in the landeau and I am sure that Miss Elizabeth can make the short walk escorted by myself," responded Darcy, then he hastily added, "and Miss Bennet as well, of course. We will be only a few minutes behind you."

Madeline was stunned at the invitation to come to the Darcy townhome, but she admitted that he was right about the chill and the time to get back to Cheapside. "Girls, will you be alright walking back to Mr. Darcy and Miss Darcy's townhome?"

"Aunt, of course we will be more than fine and perfectly safe with Mr. Darcy. Go and take care of Henry. We will see you very shortly." Elizabeth shooed her aunt and the children towards the horses and footmen.

The Gardiners' men had brought the landeau around in all due haste, and Madeline, the four children and Georgiana, who had yet to say more than a polite hello, piled into the equipage and trotted off towards Darcy House. After finally looking at his sister's pained face, Darcy had a moment of regret at throwing his sister into such an unfamiliar situation, but he was sure that she would be fine for the ten or so minutes it would take him to return with Jane and Elizabeth on foot.

"Mr. Darcy, thank you for your hospitality. Little Henry is forever finding something in which to get wet or dirty." Elizabeth said while following the landeau with her eyes. "I am certain that it is the purview of little boys to always be trying the patience of their mother's saintly hearts. Perhaps we should have anticipated this eventuality and we certainly should not have taken our eyes off of him for more than a second."

"Miss Elizabeth, it is nothing, and I would certainly not leave the young man to catch his death of a cold. Also, I am sure it is not just little boys who try their mother's patience." Darcy caught Elizabeth's eye and smirked. "Did you not once tell me that you also fell into the Serpentine at the age of about seven chasing after a line of baby ducks?"

"Sir! I would certainly not admit to such an unladylike thing in such a fashionable place as Hyde Park! Just think who might hear such a tale and then spread it all over London by tomorrow at tea. Your reputation would be quite destroyed."

Darcy laughed heartily. "My reputation? How do you figure such a thing?"

"Simple, no one knows me here, but you are instantly recognizable with your stature and posture." Elizabeth gestured widely with her hand which was not resting on Darcy's arm. "They shall all say 'Mr. Darcy was seen with some ladies of disreputable character who admitted in public hearing to be less than perfect paragons of fashion and society. How tragic!'"

"Let them talk, Miss Elizabeth. I believe I can withstand some tongue wagging from the *ton*." He leaned in closer and lowered his voice. "In fact, my father would say that until I have caused a minor scandal, I cannot truly inherit the title of Master of Pemberley."

"Really? How intriguing. I did not know I was keeping such un-fashionable company. Tell me, what scandals have the men of Pemberley caused that give them such a reputation for misbehaving?" Elizabeth smiled widely.

"Now, now, Miss Elizabeth. You cannot expect me to tell you such tales here. We shall have to save the airing of my family's dirty laundry for another day."

Darcy and Elizabeth made pleasant small talk for a few minutes while they headed towards the Darcy family townhome on Grosvenor Square. Jane followed a pace behind, forgotten but not unhappy. Finally, they all arrived in front of a magnificent five storey Georgian house with red brick and white limestone columns. Elizabeth could not remember ever being in any home so large and stately. In a fit of self-consciousness, Elizabeth ran her hands over her pelisse and bonnet as the Darcy's butler opened the front door.

"Thank you, Smith. Has my sister returned with the Gardiners?" Darcy helped Elizabeth remove her pelisse before removing his own outer coat.

The butler bowed as he directed two waiting maids to take the Bennet sisters' outer things. "Yes sir. Mrs. Gardiner and the young master who fell into the lake have been shown to a room in which to dry off and rest. The other children were taken to the music room by Miss Darcy. I believe that Mrs. Annesley was going to find some games to entertain the youngsters."

"Excellent, Smith. This is Miss Bennet and Miss Elizabeth Bennet, Mrs. Gardiner's nieces and friends of mine from Hertfordshire. I shall escort them to the music room. Please have some tea, chocolate and sweets brought to us, enough for all our guests. Also, send a tray to Mrs. Gardiner and Master Henry with a full pot of chocolate for the young man."

"Right away, sir."

Darcy conducted a short tour of his home for the two eldest Bennet sisters while escorting them to the parlour floor music room. "My great-great-grandfather purchased this home in his dot-age during the original plotting. He was friends with Sir Richard Grosvenor and was able to obtain the land licence at a very good price. My father has spoken of adding another storey, as has been the fashion recently with many of the original homes being redone in a more modern gothic style as of late, but we like the look of the original blue Georgian roof."

"The elegance of such a design quite adds to the ease and grace of your home, sir. It seems a place that is comfortable and well situated to please." Elizabeth was quite overwhelmed at the grand home. She had always known Darcy was wealthy, well beyond her own family, but it was quite another thing to walk through his home and see the grandeur around every corner. Even among such finery, the home looked easy and comforting, like a place people enjoyed living. It was not garish in the slightest.

"Thank you, Miss Elizabeth." Darcy said, very pleased that Elizabeth liked his home. "My mother was frugal by nature and desired comfort over frippery or keeping up with ever-changing fashions. Unfortunately, my town home which is on Hans Place Garden in Knightsbridge was completely redone in the more fashionable form about eight years ago. I hope to rectify the problem of the servants' living space being in the hot attics one day, but as it is currently let out, I do not have the ability to disrupt the family living there to make modifications."

"Mr. Darcy, did I hear you correctly? You own a *second* town home?" Elizabeth was dumbfounded at hearing that Darcy had two homes in Town. Even one townhome was extravagant! How much wealth did the Darcy men command? Elizabeth did not think that even ten thousand per year would support *two* London residences.

Darcy looked a bit sheepish at the flippant way he had referred to the extent of his family's holdings. "Yes. Though, it has only been in the last few years that we came into the second townhome. My father's great-aunt, Helen Darcy, married Benjamin Mildmay, the nineteenth Baron FitzWalter, later the Earl FitzWalter. They were never blessed with children. The lands of the Crown Estate in Kent reverted into trust for future heirs, but the non-Crown lands in Wales were titled to the Lady FitzWalter in her widow's estate. She lived until a very old age and having been closest in age and affection to my great-grandfather, decided to name his line as heir to her estate, Cresselly, which came to me after her death.

"Lady FitzWalter was also quite eccentric in her beliefs and managed her lands independently of any of her brothers, nephews, or great-nephews. She has also placed a requirement in her will that, should I have a daughter who reaches her majority of twenty-five years without a husband, I should leave Cresselly Park to that daughter for her independent use. The women of my family have done well with property management when they desired and I am sure that were I to have a daughter in need of an estate, she would be perfectly capable. Time will tell how my family will evolve and we shall not, as they say, cross that bridge until we come to it."

"How extraordinary!" Elizabeth could not readily come to a response for such a speech and was relieved that the need for a reply was negated by their arrival at the music room. Georgiana was quite happily playing draughts with little Madeline, the eldest of the Gardiner children who was nine years of age, while Georgiana's companion, Mrs. Annesley, had James, seven, and Sarah, five, engaged with a book of fairy tales. A tea tray followed Darcy, Elizabeth and Jane into the room and the entire group was corralled into taking some refreshment.

Jane quickly settled herself into helping Mrs. Annesley with the two younger children and left Elizabeth to continue her conversation with Darcy. Though she had been nearly forgotten by her sister and the gentleman during their trip back to Grosvenor Square, Jane was in no way offended. She was delighted at the opportunity to meet with the Darcys and observed her sister's manner with a keen eye. Elizabeth had been startled to meet with Darcy and his sister, but it was obvious that she was very much pleased to see him again.

Georgiana and young Madeline took seats near Darcy and Elizabeth and the women engaged in a polite conversation about music. Darcy reverted to his more reserved self during tea but listened with much enjoyment as his sister and Elizabeth engaged in a lovely and friendly discourse. He started daydreaming about pleasant afternoons spent visiting the entertainments of London and even more pleasant evenings dining with friends.

Just over thirty minutes later, Madeline appeared in the doorway of the music room with a dry Henry and announced that they should be going home. "Mr. Darcy, I cannot thank you enough for your kind hospitality to my children and nieces. As you can see, Henry is back to rights and we should head home before we infringe on your kindness any longer. I fear we also cut short your walk and whatever afternoon plans you had, so please accept my apologies for disrupting your schedule."

Darcy waved his hand dismissively at her regrets. "Georgiana and I were merely on our way to the book shoppe and I am certain that there was no great loss from this diversion. We have spent a much more pleasant afternoon in the company of friends. The books will still be there tomorrow. I wish you a pleasant journey home and we shall see you two days hence for dinner at your home."

With the efficiency of a well-run home, the Gardiners and Bennets were presented with their outerwear and bundled into their landeau with hot bricks at their feet expeditiously. Maybe even too expeditiously for Darcy's liking.

As they walked back to the music room together, Darcy turned to his sister. "Tell me dear, what do you think of Miss Elizabeth and her sister? Would you like them as friends?"

Georgiana failed to hide a smile. "I believe that both Miss Bennet and Miss Elizabeth would be wonderful friends, brother. They are obviously of the highest manners, and very intelligent ladies. Miss Elizabeth also enjoys to play and sing. I believe I have finally found someone who will indulge me in a duet or two."

That was a nice thought. His sister and Elizabeth sitting together on the pianoforte bench playing something lovely. Maybe Elizabeth would even sing. Darcy sighed in contentment as he took a seat again in the music room. A nice thought indeed.

Grand Introductions

"**P**OPPET, WHY IN THE WORLD WOULD WE TAKE ourselves to the art museum today for an art exhibit that shall last through until the end of the full season? I do not understand why you insist on dragging me on this adventure. It is not even a nice day! The rain outside shall make it impossible to traverse the steps up to Montagu House without making us wet. Let us stay home and enjoy some quiet entertainment and forget this nonsense of going out today."

Georgiana Darcy was not insensitive to her cousin, Colonel Richard Fitzwilliam's complaints. Her favourite cousin was not a great art lover and, as a military man, he much preferred the spectacle of the Changing of the Guard or the delights of Drury Lane to the British Museum. But Georgiana was on a mission.

The last week had been an unparalleled joy for the shy young woman. Since meeting with the Miss Bennets and Madeline Gardiner in Hyde Park, Georgiana had enjoyed seeing her new friend at a lovely spontaneous tea at Gunter's, two dinners, one each at the Gardiners' home and Darcy House, a planned afternoon tea at Darcy House, and a morning visit to the Gardiner's home two mornings ago. The two families had finally exhausted all the expected polite invitations and return invitations and now propriety would dictate that they should wait at least a few days or a sennight before issuing another formal invitation.

But Georgiana did not want to wait a whole week before seeing the Bennet sisters, or more specifically, Elizabeth, again. What she wanted was for there to be a closer friendship between the ladies that would justify as many invitations as Elizabeth could entertain.

So, regardless of the weather or her companion's dislike for stuffy museums, Georgiana was determined to go to the new art installation that morning. Elizabeth had specifically mentioned they had advance tickets for the eleven a.m. tour of the sculptures. Without a shred of guilty feelings, Georgiana employed her most put-upon pout. "But Richard, I have been cooped up in this house for three days straight and the museum is perfectly dry inside. Did William not ask you to come and see to my enjoyment today? And now you would deny me this very small thing?"

Richard eyed his baby cousin with suspicion. "Now I know there is something afoot. For you have ever been a most agreeable companion and I have sat in this very room hearing you argue that all you truly wish for in life is to play your pianoforte. What can make one so wholly devoted to her instrument as you wish to go out in a rainstorm and stare at dusty old canvases with coloured mud smeared about?"

Georgiana harrumphed and turned her head. "I am sure I do not know what you mean."

"Out with it poppet. Give me one reason, that *I* will like, to put on my boots and take you to an exhibit."

Eyeing her cousin, Georgiana debated what reason Richard would like best. "I will tell you there is someone I hope to meet at the exhibit today. Someone you would probably find very interesting."

"Oooohhhh, no! I shall not have you doing my mother's bidding and introducing me to some dull lady with a great dowry. I will stay right here, thank you very much." Richard emphasised his point by raising his feet to the opposite side of the couch and laying back with his hands behind his head.

"What nonsense is this? A young woman not yet out has better connections than one of His Majesty's most decorated soldiers?" Anne de Bourgh stepped into the room without being formally announced and swatted Richard's feet down from the furniture. "Who are we meeting, Georgie?"

"Do not be silly. I am not in a position to play matchmaker and I would not want to anyway." The young woman crossed her arms across her stomach and leaned back in her chair. "The person of whom I speak is a new friend of mine, but she is a better and older friend of William's. You might even say she holds some specific interest for him and I am trying to be an accommodating younger sister by becoming the closest of friends."

That revelation got Richard to sit up and pay very close attention. "What do you mean '*she*' and how could this mystery woman be an old friend of William's? I know all of William's friends."

"Apparently not." Georgiana attempted to play a little coy and looked away, fiddling with a book on the side table and picking up her tea cup.

"Poppet…" Richard warned in a bit of a growl.

"Would this young woman be a Miss Elizabeth Bennet, by any chance?" Anne asked.

"Yes!" Georgiana exclaimed and leaned forward. "Do you know her too?"

Anne shook her head. "No, I have not yet had that pleasure. However, Darcy mentioned her in several letters this past autumn and winter."

Georgiana nodded her head. "William met her and her family, including an older sister Miss Jane Bennet who is also in London, while visiting Mr. Bingley in Hertfordshire. Miss Elizabeth's father owns the estate which borders the estate that Mr. Bingley has let, and they apparently were very good friends over autumn. Now, the two Miss Bennets are staying with their relations here in London for the little season before travelling to Hunsford in Kent for Easter. I very much enjoy the company of Miss Elizabeth and simply wish to see the art installation with her this morning."

Richard did not know whether to be amused or alarmed, but he settled on suspicious. "And why would Miss Elizabeth, who happens to have such interesting timing for extensive travel, be staying in Kent, so near our dear aunt at Easter, the exact time our family usually visits the region?"

"Oh! That is easy." Georgiana said. "Her next oldest sister, the former Miss Mary Bennet, has married their cousin, Mr. William Collins.

He is the rector at Hunsford. Evidently, he is the heir apparent to Mr. Bennet's entailed estate and was also in Hertfordshire this past autumn looking to take his bride from among Miss Elizabeth's five sisters to keep the estate in the family, as it were. I understand from William that it was originally Aunt Catherine's idea. It seems very practical as well as kind of him to care for his cousins after their father passes."

"It certainly seems sensible, especially coming from our wholly insensible aunt, but is leg-shackling some young woman to Mr. Collins really kind?"

Anne swatted his arm. "Do not be crass, Richard. I know Mr. Collins seems a bit over-eager to please Mother and myself, but my friends in Kent say that the new Mrs. Collins is very kind and seems happy with her new situation. Also, the last letter I had from our neighbours said that Mr. Collins does improve under his wife's sensibility and affection. I am most eager to meet with the new couple next month as they returned to Hunsford after we had travelled to London for Christmas."

"I am convinced, *for now*, that these Bennets seem to have a surprisingly high number of connections which are genuinely parallel to our own, and are not somehow manufacturing introductions into your circle of acquaintances." Richard looked between Georgiana and Anne. "But, dearest cousins, you must admit it seems uncanny that your brother is introduced to a family with *five sisters* of marriageable age from an estate of no consequence, then it just happens that he not only sees the eldest two again in town, but that he shall be in close proximity with them again during the Easter break. Especially in a place where the lack of genteel society will ensure we shall meet with them often and in a relatively intimate gathering."

Georgiana was seething. "Richard, I am going to tolerate this attitude in the spirit that it was meant, as an expression of your love for my brother and myself which leads you to being overly protective of us without just cause. However, I will say this exactly once, I will not tolerate such slander against the Miss Bennets or their family again. I know that I also speak for William as he is very fond of the Bennets generally and Miss Elizabeth specifically. Do not let your pride blind you to the worth of good people born without titles. There are more of us than you."

Richard smiled indulgently at his young cousin. She had lived a sheltered life in Pemberley and, while he was grateful that she had not yet been exposed to the evils of society and the grasping manner of many of the people who call themselves genteel, she would soon learn. Her dowry of thirty-thousand pounds was large, even amongst the nobility, and there were plenty of men who would wish to use his cousin ill to gain such a sum. And the ladies of society were often much worse. "I shall keep my tongue for now, poppet. You have convinced me. Let us hurry to the museum so we do not miss your friends. You were correct that I am most intrigued to meet with the Miss Bennets and their family. Come Anne, join us."

It took only ten minutes before Richard, Anne, and Georgiana were riding comfortably in the Darcy carriage towards the British Museum.

Once relieved of their outerwear, Georgiana drifted towards the crowd gathering for the eleven a.m. tour. She heard soft tinkling laughter coming from the right side of the gathering and knew instinctively that it must be Elizabeth. "Miss Elizabeth, Miss Bennet, how lovely to see you!"

"Why, Miss Darcy, I am glad to see you as well and to know that this dreadful rain has not hindered your entertainments." Elizabeth curtsied and gave her friend a quick peck to her cheek before looking about for her tall brother. With a quick look of concern, Elizabeth did not see Darcy anywhere in the vicinity but instead she noticed a man in regimentals looking between them with an open smile but assessing eyes. Elizabeth did not like his look and instinctively tried to move the younger woman out of the man's field of view. She was thwarted in her attempt by the man unexpectedly addressing Georgiana.

"Poppet, come now and introduce us to your friends."

"Yes, of course! Miss Elizabeth, Miss Bennet, might I introduce my cousin, Colonel Richard Fitzwilliam. Richard, this is Miss Bennet and Miss Elizabeth Bennet of Longbourn Estate in Hertfordshire." She turned slightly and also addressed a slight but tall woman standing behind Richard. "And this is Miss Anne de Bourgh, daughter of my mother's sister, Lady Catherine de Bourgh. Cousins, these are the young ladies I told you about who met Mr. Bingley and William over autumn and whose younger sister is now married to Aunt Catherine's rector."

Richard made a bit of a show of clicking his heels, crossing his chest and bowing formally to the ladies. "Miss Bennet, Miss Elizabeth, it seems that we have very many connections in common and I have heard much good about you both and your family. It is my pleasure to make your acquaintances."

Jane blushed at such a gallant display, but Elizabeth resisted the urge to roll her eyes. The Colonel's showboating seemed a tad over the top for her taste. "Charmed Colonel Fitzwilliam. We have much enjoyed your cousins' company. I am all that is hopeful that you will prove to be as good a companion as the rest of you family."

With a winning smile and a tilt of his head, Richard replied, "I aim to please, Miss Elizabeth."

Anne perked up at Elizabeth's unimpressed manner with Richard. She had not yet had an opportunity to interrogate her fastidious cousin regarding his letter detailing the Bennet family and Elizabeth, but this was her chance to get to know the lady without worrying about Darcy's interference. Her first impression was not a disappointment. "Miss Bennet, Miss Elizabeth, I am glad to make your acquaintance. I have heard of your family through correspondence from William, and while I have yet to meet your sister, as I have been in London since her marriage to Mr. Collins, I believe I shall become acquainted with her quite soon. We are to travel back to Rosings for the Easter celebrations. I believe my mother has some level of entertainment planned when we arrive, to formally welcome the new Mrs. Collins to Kent."

"Miss de Bourgh, you and your family are exceedingly kind to recognise our Mary upon her marriage into your parish." Jane spoke softly.

From behind the crowd, Madeline appeared, calling for her nieces. "Lizzy! Jane! We are all set and ready to join the tour. Oh! Hello Miss Darcy. It is a pleasure to see you again. Are you here to see the art installation?"

"Yes, Mrs. Gardiner. May I introduce my cousins, Colonel Richard Fitzwilliam and Miss Anne de Bourgh, to you. This is the Miss Bennets' aunt, Mrs. Gardiner." Both bowed and curtsied in response. "Might we join your group on the tour? I do so dearly want to see the exhibit."

"We would be delighted to have you. We are ready to go in if you would come with me?"

Richard hastily extended his arm to Elizabeth and motioned for Georgiana to walk ahead with Jane and Anne. "Go on, we shall follow."

Elizabeth was forced out of politeness to take the Colonel's arm when she would have much rather walked with her good friend. She took a moment to assess her new companion. Richard seemed to be slightly older than his cousin Darcy and not nearly so handsome. However, he held himself with good posture and had a friendly smile about his face. Except for the unnerving look he had worn when first approaching their party, he seemed quite the gentleman in person and address. Once they started their tour, Richard was polite and stood with his face towards the pieces, however it was not hard to tell that he was not at all interested in the exhibit.

"Tell me Colonel, how did you come to escort Miss Darcy and Miss de Bourgh to the museum today? It seems you take little enjoyment in the art offered." Elizabeth looked up at Richard with an arch look and a quirk to her left eyebrow.

At first, startled by such an observation, Richard quickly chuckled and took his opportunity to have the more open discussion with Elizabeth. "I believe you have caught me, Miss Elizabeth. I do not often enjoy art exhibits over other entertainments, but alas I have been conscripted into escorting my young cousins today while William does all kinds of boring things with his solicitor and business partners. As I have no head for business and am very much used to going where I am bid, it was no hardship to walk sedately around this art exhibit at the pleading of my fair cousins. The inclusion of such lovely new acquaintances has merely added to the ease of the afternoon."

Elizabeth was not very convinced that the good Colonel was truly enjoying the inclusion of her party, but could not find a polite way to say so. "I must agree with you that new friends almost always make an afternoon very easy. We have been so fortunate as to see Miss Darcy several times since our arrival in Town."

"So I have been hearing. It seems I have missed quite the entertainments while I was out whipping young boys into men for His Majesty's army."

"But I am sure that your relations are pleased to have you with them now, ahead of the season. I understand that Georgiana is to have a practice season this spring and summer. I imagine that your entire family shall play their parts to ensure she has the freedom to enjoy the amusements without having to entertain suitors." Elizabeth gave Richard a very deep look and practically begged him with her stare to disagree with her statements.

Richard saw something unusual in Elizabeth's look, but could not quite figure out what she was trying to say with her arched eyebrow. "Yes, I believe you have the right of it, Miss Elizabeth. Our family is somewhat known for keeping young ladies out of the marriage mart until they are slightly older. My sister is nearly twenty years old and has only this year seriously considered her prospects. Anne is twenty-seven and still not married. Though she is of a different bent and has an estate of her own and no need for a husband. Georgiana will surely enjoy this season and several more before having to consider her prospects. So, instead of worrying over the married state of my relations, it is my lot in life to play at the disposal of my rich cousins who like to arrange their business just as they please."

"I can well believe that, and even when Mr. Darcy or Miss de Bourgh cannot please themselves in the arrangement of their schedules, they have at least great pleasure in the power of choice." Elizabeth chuckled softly.

"It is true that they like to have their own way very well," replied Richard, "but so do we all. It is only that William and Anne have better means than most due to their fortunes. I might also add that neither William nor Anne are much given to worrying what society shall say of them. As long as they have friends enough to enjoy their days, and money enough to pay their own way, what need does either have for society? As a younger son, you know, I must be inured to self-denial and dependence."

"And it seems a fair amount of showboating." Elizabeth gave a bit more of a genuine smile to the Colonel. "In my opinion, the younger son of an Earl can know very little of either self-denial or dependence. Now seriously, when have you been prevented by want of money from going wherever you choose or procuring anything that you had a fancy for?"

Richard looked down at the slight woman on his arm who spoke with such wit and fire and began to fully understand how the immovable

Fitzwilliam Darcy might have come to admire this country nobody so far as to introduce her into his sister's society.

Anne chose that moment to take over Elizabeth's conversation and attention. "Well said, Miss Elizabeth. Richard likes to play the poor relation, but he is well enough in the pocket. Come now, tell me about your estate in Hertfordshire. I know it is considered vulgar by the debutantes of the *ton*, but I like nothing more than to discuss crop yields and how good the sheeping fields do."

Elizabeth laughed loudly and easily fell into a conversation with Anne about her father's estate as well as the neighbouring lands. Anne was impressed. Elizabeth seemed genuine and engaging. Most remarkably, she had not spent their entire conversation attempting to extract information about Darcy. In truth, Elizabeth had spoken more of Georgiana than William in their brief conversation. While it would take more than one turn through an art gallery to ensure that Miss Elizabeth Bennet was exactly what she seemed, Anne and Richard were both inclined to put aside any lingering concerns about her intentions with Darcy.

Revelations

AFTER THEIR ART GALLERY ADVENTURE, ELIZABETH and Georgiana finally gave up the formality of address as well as the formality of timing their engagements. Elizabeth and Jane became frequent visitors to Darcy House and even spent one very lovely afternoon at the Matlock townhome with Richard, Anne, Georgiana, William, Richard's sister Lady Marianne, and the eldest of the Fitzwilliam siblings, Henri Fitzwilliam, the Viscount Huntley. In addition to all the calling between their respective London homes, there had been numerous trips to the theatre, a lovely outing to the Vauxhall Gardens and one exhilarating trip to Astley's Royal Grove for the circus acts. Elizabeth and Jane were so overwhelmed with entertainments and excitement that they hardly could catch enough sleep each night to be refreshed for the next day's adventures.

Tonight was Jane and Elizabeth's first London Society Ball. Their host for the evening were Sir James and Lady Miranda Finch. Before being knighted for his service to the crown, Sir James had served in his Majesty's Navy and rose to the rank of Captain. He was the grandson of the 4th Earl of Nottingham and first cousin to the current 6th Earl of Nottingham. Sir James and Edward Gardiner had become very good friends while studying at Cambridge, and maintained their correspondence during their adult lives. When Sir James came home to retire his commission and take a wife, Edward had taken his good friend to several events and introduced him to the former Miss Miranda Craven, a cousin of Edward's new bride, Madeline Gardiner, who spent the summer with her cousins in London.

Now connected by both affection and marriage, the Gardiners were frequent guests at the parties hosted by Sir James and Lady Finch in their lavish Mayfair townhome.

Elizabeth was planning on wearing her new ball gown, which had been patiently waiting in her closet for this evening since it was delivered two days prior. The original three gowns made for their excursion in town had not gone far. Inside of a sennight, both Elizabeth and Jane had worn all their new clothes and spent several mornings in dedicated work to finish over-making several older gowns. After one particularly stress-filled day, Edward Gardiner had practically demanded they each order two more full dress evening gowns, an opera gown, and a day walking dress.

If Elizabeth had been intimidated by wearing her mother's twenty-year-old satin gown to the Netherfield ball, it was nothing to how she felt now. Her aunt had insisted that both Elizabeth and Jane get a true silk masterpiece for the Finch's Ball. Elizabeth's gown consisted of a light green silk underdress with a low-cut square neckline, capped puff sleeves, and an A-line gathered bust. The under dress was long and slim, showing off Elizabeth's slight figure. The over dress was sheer organza with a rich pattern sewn into the fabric using a gold thread and draped around the bodice in a diagonal wrap with a scalloped edge. It was the most extravagant costume Elizabeth had ever seen, let alone worn. She mused that if Caroline Bingley could but see her in this gown, the snobbish lady would have an apoplexy.

Bingley. There was a troublesome thought.

Their frequent socialising with the Darcys and their cousins had been all that was wonderful, except for one small item. There had not been even the smallest mention of Bingley. Elizabeth and Jane had expected that at least one of the dinners or evenings out would have produced a sighting of him, but it had not come to pass. Elizabeth had asked Georgiana about Caroline and Bingley the other day, and the answer she received was most puzzling.

> *"I had not given it much thought before now, but you are right that we have seen much less of the Bingleys than we usually would this time of year. I am not overly friendly*

*with Miss Bingley being that I am so much younger and not
yet out, but William does usually include Mr. Bingley in
invitations to dinner. Perhaps he is back at the estate near
your family which he let?"*

Elizabeth had hardly known how to respond except to say that she
had not heard that he was back at Netherfield. No, apparently, Bingley
and his sisters were missing in action, completely out of the norm. Also,
Caroline had not yet returned their call and it was now more than
three weeks since the initial visit. Her behaviour was decidedly rude.
It also did not seem that Darcy had any positive role in keeping his
friend away, except that, perhaps, invitations had not been as frequent
as in the past.

Jane had decided that the only explanation was that Bingley was,
in truth, not interested in Jane's society. She came to believe that,
with the Bingleys now back in London where the entertainments and
acquaintances were much more varied, a young country miss held no
attraction for either the brother or the sister. Jane went on, in true Jane
fashion, to absolve both from any kind of malice, saying that it was not
so unexpected. Of course, they had so many friends that it was surely
difficult to keep up with their social requirements.

Elizabeth was much less convinced of the attitudes of both Bingleys
and reasons behind the sudden cutting of the acquaintance, but she
could not help but admit that Jane had been abandoned.

However, Elizabeth also mused, there was nothing she could do
about the situation. Elizabeth and Jane were stuck waiting for one or
the other of the Bingleys showing themselves to the Gardiner's home
for a call, and the chances of that seemed less and less likely with each
passing day.

A soft knock on the door to Elizabeth's room startled her out of
her daydreaming. She bid the person enter and was quickly swept up
into preparations for the evening by her aunt's maid. Contemplations of
Bingley's abandonment would have to wait for another time.

Fitzwilliam Darcy escorted Georgiana into Sir James and Lady Finch's beautiful ballroom with a calculating eye, looking to scare any young rakes away from even daring to think about asking his baby sister for a dance. This evening's invitation for the Darcy siblings had been arranged by their Aunt Matlock. Sir James was her cousin and quite a favourite of his Matlock relations. The Earl of Nottingham, Lady Matlock's brother, was also in attendance with his three grown sons and daughter, Lady Fiona. While Darcy didn't think that the event really counted as a 'ball given by family,' which was one of the limited categories of events that his sister was allowed to attend, Lady Matlock had insisted it was exactly that, and there would be plenty of family members to dance with Georgiana. This particular ball was an annual tradition for the wedding anniversary of Sir James and Lady Finch, and the extended Finch family, as well as much of Lady Finch's family, always attended. With such an attenuated connection to Sir James and Lady Finch, Darcy had never before attended, but he had to admit, looking around the room, he did know many of the guests very well.

Lost in his own thoughts of pleasant dancing partners, Darcy almost missed when his sister removed herself from his side and called out "Lizzy!"

A moment later, Elizabeth, Jane, Madeline and Edward Gardiner, and Lady Finch were standing in front of Georgiana and Darcy.

Elizabeth smiled widely and brought Georgiana in for a warm hug. "Good evening, Georgie. I did not know we would have the pleasure of seeing you this evening. How delightful!"

Darcy was stuck, his mouth agape, and his head spinning. Elizabeth was a vision in soft green and gold with silver and pearl tipped hair pins dotting her dark curls. He had never, in all his days of dancing with the wealthiest debutantes in the whole of England, seen any lady shine so brightly.

"Oh! Maddie, I did not know you were already acquainted with Mr. and Miss Darcy! You know how I dearly love to make introductions." Lady Finch tapped Madeline on the arm with her closed fan. "I was specifically guiding you this way in order to introduce Jane to Mr. Darcy. Do you not think our dear Jane looks a vision in blue,

Mr. Darcy?" Lady Finch was a sweet-tempered woman but lacked something of wit. She was also known to enjoy matchmaking for all her friends and relations. As soon as Lady Matlock mentioned that she had convinced the younger Mr. Darcy to attend their ball, Lady Finch started combing through her relations for a suitable match for the rich, but untitled, gentleman. She knew that her husband's cousin wanted Darcy for her own niece, Lady Fiona. But Lady Finch also knew that Lady Fiona was not nearly as handsome as her own cousins and nieces.

Darcy shook himself from his stupor and attended to the conversation. "Why yes, Lady Finch, my sister and I are very much acquainted with the Miss Bennets and Mr. and Mrs. Gardiner." He finally tore his eyes away from Elizabeth and was startled to see Jane looking very well indeed in a blue silk gown. Bowing slightly in Jane's direction, Darcy replied, "I dare say you are correct that Miss Bennet looks as lovely as always."

He then turned fully back to Elizabeth and continued "Miss Elizabeth, please let me say that you are also looking exceedingly fine this evening. I believe that shade of green does match your eyes perfectly." Darcy reached for Elizabeth's hand and bowed low over it with a brushing kiss to her knuckles. "Might I ask for the honour of your first set if you are not engaged?"

Elizabeth blushed a deep shade of rose all the way to the décolletage of her gown. "I am not yet engaged, Mr. Darcy and I would be very pleased to dance the first with you." She handed him her dance card so that he might officially claim her dance.

Glancing down at the card, Darcy impulsively put himself down for her first and her supper dance. "I hope you do not mind, but Georgiana and I shall be leaving after supper, so I must claim what time I can now as I am sure your entire night will be full the moment the musicians begin playing."

In a small voice that she hardly recognised as her own, Elizabeth replied, "I do not mind at all, sir. I shall look forward to our dances."

Darcy and Elizabeth continued to stand close to each other and next to Jane and Georgiana who chatted amiably, neither saying much but enjoying the company immensely.

After a few minutes, Col. Richard Fitzwilliam came to claim Georgiana for the first dance, dragging his brother Henri with him so that the Viscount could escort Jane for the first set, and all three couples moved into the line.

During the respite between the fourth set and the supper set, Darcy stood by his sister simply observing her conversation with Elizabeth and Jane. The evening had been a wonderful success. His sister had danced each set so far, one each with their cousins Richard and Henri, one with Darcy himself, and one with Darcy's very good friend and their Aunt Matlock's nephew, the youngest son of the Earl of Nottingham, Bernard Finch. Her final dance was going to be with the Earl of Nottingham's eldest son, and then they would all sit together for supper. After the supper, Darcy had consented to allow Georgie to stay for the musical entertainments and Elizabeth suggested they play the duet they had been working on for the past week. Then he really was determined to take Georgiana home, much as he would rather stay and enjoy Elizabeth's company.

Not long before the supper set was to begin, his Aunt Matlock came up to him with his cousin Lady Marianne and her niece, Lady Fiona, in tow. Darcy had only danced the first set with Elizabeth and the second with his sister thus far, and Lady Matlock was determined to see her recalcitrant nephew dance the last set before he left for the evening, preferably with Lady Fiona.

"Fitzwilliam! There you are dear boy. I feel we have not had a second to greet each other all evening. Do tell me, have you enjoyed the entertainments thus far?"

Darcy sighed, knowing that his Aunt Matlock was coming to start something he would find at least a mild annoyance. She had been trying for several days to have him stay for the entire evening and forget his father's strictures regarding Georgiana's scheduled entertainments. "Aunt, it is good to see you. I agree that the ball has been quite full this evening. I apologise if I have not done my share of socialising as I have been sticking close to Georgie in order to ensure her enjoyment and appropriate dance partners."

"Oh, of course! She has been doing so well tonight and hardly seems tired at all. Perhaps you might consider letting her stay for the after-supper dancing. I am sure that one little ball will not test her too greatly." Lady Matlock looked to Georgie, who was still deep in conversation with Elizabeth and had not yet been drawn into their discussion. She sniffed slightly with a subtle shift in her posture, minutely raising her eyebrow. "Besides, with such *quaint* friends to entertain her, I daresay Georgiana is not in dire need of your devoted attention. Come, you must dance more, for the ladies outnumber the gentlemen tonight, and we would be at a loss if you were to leave after supper."

Suspecting something was not quite right with his aunt's inspection of Georgiana, but being unable to determine exactly what she found objectionable to his sister's conversation with Elizabeth, Darcy decided to leave his aunt's rather snide comments without a retort. "She has been doing quite well, and I must say I am glad to have found the Miss Bennets are relations to Lady Finch so that Georgie had some female companionship between sets. We will, however, not be altering our plans. We shall both dance the next set, enjoy supper, then leave after Georgiana has exhibited on the pianoforte. I am sure that our departure will be no true loss since we shall take one gentleman and one lady out of the partnering and leave the ball in no worse shape than it is currently."

Hearing her own name, Elizabeth finally spared some attention for their new conversation partners. "Lady Fiona, Lady Matlock, how lovely you both look this evening." Elizabeth gave both ladies a very correct curtsy. Jane and Georgiana followed the example and made their own polite greetings.

Lady Matlock took control of the conversation again. "Charmed to see you here Miss Bennet, Miss Elizabeth. Did I hear correctly that you are connected to my cousin's wife, Lady Finch?"

Elizabeth quirked her eyebrow. Though Lady Fiona was a bit shy in company during the Bingley's ball, she had been kind to Elizabeth and Jane. On the three occasions that Elizabeth had been in the company of Lady Matlock since coming to London, the countess had been polite, if distant. Elizabeth surmised that Lady Matlock was not so snobbish as to refuse an acquaintance with the gently born Bennet sisters. Now, it seemed that the superior lady was less than eager to be in their company.

"Yes, my lady," Jane answered before Elizabeth could say something overly witty. "Sir James and my uncle Gardiner have been the closest of friends since their university days and Lady Finch is my Aunt Gardiner's cousin. Though this is the first evening my sister and I have had the pleasure of their hospitality, I understand that my aunt and uncle Gardiner are frequently in company with our hosts and have been coming to this particular ball for many years."

Georgiana began to pick up on some discord between her favourite aunt and her very good friend, so she tried to interject and steer the conversation towards something more neutral. "Cousin Marianne, I believe that colour is very flattering with your complexion. I know I would not be able to wear such a bold shade of yellow given how it would contrast with my hair."

"Thank you, Georgie. I loved this silk as soon as I saw it in the window of Madame Devy's shoppe. I dare say she had only the one bolt used on my dress and no one else shall have such a fine dress in the same fabric." Lady Marianne preened a bit at the praise for her new favourite gown. It was one of her greatest finds for the season and she was exceedingly proud of how well the dress had turned out, even if there had not been enough fabric left for matching gloves or a shawl.

Jane interjected herself next. "Lizzy, did you not get one of your new opera dresses in that same yellow silk with the bolt we found at Uncle's warehouse? I believe Madame Devy mentioned she had run out of the same in her store but was glad to find another in the warehouse. It is very much a shade for ladies with dark hair. As you say Georgie, those of us with golden hair would only achieve looking sick in such a colour."

Lady Fiona, who had been anxiously watching her aunt's discussion with the Bennet sisters, decided to finally interject. "Oh, Miss Elizabeth, did you really go to the fabric warehouse? My abigail once worked for a drapers shoppe and she told me the warehouses have crates and crates and crates-worth of the most beautiful fabrics."

Elizabeth turned to the quiet young heiress with a genuine smile. "Why yes, Lady Fiona. My uncle's imports warehouse is so very large that Jane and I spent nearly four hours digging through the hundreds of bolts of silks and only managed to make it down two aisles of crates stacked from floor to ceiling. I'm not sure that Uncle even knows the extent of what he has in that warehouse!"

"That is a sight I would very much like to see for myself." Lady Fiona spoke softly but with warmth.

"Oh! You should join us sometime." Jane said. "I am sure my uncle could find a time to accommodate us."

Finally, the musician's soft playing took up again, and before any of his relations could continue their hostility towards Elizabeth and Jane, Darcy suggested they dispose of their punch glasses before the supper set was to start.

"Of course, you are correct, Fitzwilliam. It would be a shame to not be asked for a dance and have to sit out the entire set just because one was holding onto refreshments for too long." Lady Matlock finally was given the opening she had hoped for. "I believe the next set is a cotillion. Did you not dance the cotillion on the last night of Almack's last season with my niece? I believe that a more handsome couple was not seen that night. What say you Fitzwilliam, will you do your duty to the ladies present and dance the supper set?"

Lady Fiona took a small step forward in anticipation of the gentleman's address after such a directive from his aunt.

Darcy was finally sure of his aunt's motive and stiffened significantly at her meddling. Thankfully, he had the perfect excuse to avoid a repeat of the supper set at Bingley's ball. "As you say, Aunt, I must do my duty to the guests as a gentleman. I have actually signed a dance card for this set as much as it is not my normal habit." Darcy turned fully toward Elizabeth and held out his hand for his lady of choice. "Miss Elizabeth, are you ready for our set? The line looks to be starting."

Smiling, with an impertinent twinkle in her eye, Elizabeth took Darcy's outstretched hand and curtsied to the other ladies present. "I am most certainly happy to follow you to the dance floor, sir. Ladies, it has been a pleasure."

Darcy left his aunt standing in a disdainful silence while he escorted Elizabeth to the dance floor. Thankfully, Richard had been nearby and stepped up to take Lady Fiona onto the dance floor before anyone could comment on Lady Matlock's obvious scheming.

Supper was highly enjoyable for the Darcy and Bennet siblings, then the musical exhibitions took nearly a full hour with so many ladies interested in performing. Darcy was extremely proud of Georgiana for getting up to the pianoforte, though he knew she was extremely nervous. It was truly Elizabeth's influence and presence that gave Georgiana the courage to perform in front of so many guests. Hopefully, with a few more duets and other practice exhibitions, she would be ready to take her full place next year and perform the expected three pieces during her own debut ball.

Once Darcy and Georgiana were finally ready to depart, it was nearly two in the morning, though there were another four sets to the dancing before the rest of the guests would depart. With a fond goodbye to their friends and a short leave taking from their relatives, Georgiana and Darcy left before the dancing recommenced.

Elizabeth did not have long to mourn the loss of the Darcy siblings. Nearly as soon as she had straightened from her parting curtsey, Col. Richard Fitzwilliam came to claim her for their dance.

"Miss Elizabeth! Finally, I get my turn to escort the loveliest lady in the room around the dance floor." Stopping abruptly in front of the lady, Richard clicked his heels loudly, clasped his sabre to his chest, and bowed dramatically. He had noticed upon their first meeting that his flair for the dramatic never failed to get a reaction from Elizabeth, and this time was no disappointment.

Elizabeth rolled her eyes in exaggerated fashion and curtsied very deeply to perform an equally ridiculous greeting. "My, my Colonel, you are in fine form this evening, are you not? I know for a fact that you have already danced with my sister and your fair cousin, so please do not attempt to flatter me with such empty words. I have always been second fiddle to Jane's brightness, and I am not so vain as to be upset by forever being beset by other beauties."

Richard was genuinely taken aback by Elizabeth's admission. "Miss Elizabeth, I cannot disagree more. Though your lovely sister is indeed a beautiful lady, I do not offer empty words. You are indeed a vision this evening and I am sure you cannot have missed my cousin's attention to you or his inability to see any other lady."

"Please, let us not speculate on your cousin's attentions. Mr. Darcy is an agreeable dance partner and I am glad that I can offer him pleasant conversation between sets. He is uncommonly devoted to his friends, which speaks well of him." Elizabeth looked over to Lady Fiona, who was being partnered by the younger son of some Baron she was not acquainted with. "I am convinced that any attention to myself this evening was to keep close to Georgiana so that she was properly chaperoned at her first ever ball."

"You are correct that to speculate on any persons attentions in a crowded ballroom would be unwise. I hope you do not misinterpret my cousin's attentions to you?" Richard frowned.

Elizabeth misinterpreted Richard's words as a warning instead of the inquiry he had meant. "I assure you Colonel, Mr. Darcy and I understand each other very well. I am clear on his attentions and intentions."

Both parties satisfied for the moment, Richard moved their conversation on to other shared connections. "Speaking of Darcy's friends, Miss Elizabeth, have you been much in company with the Bingleys since coming to town? I have missed Bingley's company these past weeks. He usually comes to our club for the regular Thursday lunch and cards, and we run in such the same circles that we often see each other at least once a week while in town, but I have not seen him anywhere since returning to London. I understand from Georgiana that you and Miss Bennet have an acquaintance with Miss Bingley?"

Elizabeth was not quite prepared for this turn in the conversation, but managed to hide her surprise and regulate her features before turning back to Richard. "You have actually hit on a point of mystery for Jane and myself. We have, in fact, not seen Mr. Bingley at all since coming to town and we have only managed one visit with Miss Bingley nearly three weeks ago when we called at her home. She has not returned our call and we have had no communication from any of the Bingleys or Hursts. I must say, I am most perplexed at their disappearance."

"Well, that is very strange. I asked William the other day about Bingley and he seemed upset but would not give a reasonable excuse for their continued absence."

"Did he give any excuse?"

"Oh," Richard looked suddenly uncomfortable. "You must know that Bingley is forever falling in love with some lovely creature or another. Well, William would only say that he was upset over a recent heart break. But I did not think that made much sense as he has been nowhere other than Netherfield and London since I was in his company last, and I cannot imagine he has come into lady problems in such a short time."

Elizabeth was now nearly desperate to hear anything else the good Colonel might say, and she was not disappointed, as Richard continued in a distracted manner as if he was really speaking to himself instead of to her.

"But, though William was extremely tight-lipped about the whole affair, he did say that it was better this way and Bingley would hopefully come out of his depression with a better understanding. He seemed relieved that Bingley was separated from the lady."

From where Elizabeth found the ability to speak calmly, she did not know, but she was able to address the conversation. "Did Mr. Darcy give you his reason for this interference?"

"I do not know if he interfered directly, but he did say there were some strong objections to the lady from Miss Bingley and Mrs. Hurst. I understand it would have been imprudent at the least and potentially embarrassing." Richard frowned. "However, I am not sure I would take Miss Bingley's assessment of what is embarrassing."

Hearing all that she had always suspected of Darcy's views on marriage from one of his noble relations sent Elizabeth into a bit of a head spin. How could she have been so silly as to believe that their socialising could ever mean anything beyond that the Bennets were mannered enough for genteel entertainments, but not highly born enough for marriage into *le bon ton*. Mercifully, the first dance of the set came to a close and Elizabeth chose to ask Richard to take her to get a glass of refreshments.

When the music began again, Elizabeth cried off, saying she was fatigued and required a rest. Without waiting for Richard to answer her, Elizabeth took off in the direction of the Ladies retiring room and prayed it would be sparsely used at that time in the evening.

It was a small miracle that Elizabeth found the Ladies retiring room devoid of anyone. Fighting back tears, she took up a seat near the fire and stared into the flames. It was time to finally deal with her own heartache. Pretending she was not in love with Darcy was no longer working. He had been the most interesting, attentive and engaging companion for their entire acquaintance.

It also did not hurt that he was the most handsome man she had ever seen.

And finally, everyone in her life had been telling her since the beginning that he was showing her a particular interest. Beyond his estate or his connections, Elizabeth admired his quiet sturdy nature. He was judicious in his words and generous in his actions. She knew instinctively that he was a man upon which she could always depend. Most important to Elizabeth, he treated her thoughts and opinions with interest. She believed that Darcy respected her intelligence and admired her mind. How could she not fall desperately in love with this intelligent, kind, and respectable man?

Tears streaming down her cheeks, Elizabeth missed when the door to the room opened quietly. "Excuse me Miss Elizabeth, I could not help but see that you left the dance floor in some distress. Might I be of assistance?"

Elizabeth jumped at the newcomer and looked to the door to see a kind-faced older lady dressed in a beautiful evening gown fit for a princess. "Oh my, please excuse me. Lady Sefton, correct?" Elizabeth searched through her reticule for a handkerchief. "I was overcome for a moment and came in search of some quiet to right myself."

A fine silk handkerchief came into view, and Elizabeth looked up once again to her new companion with a small smile of thanks.

"Please dear, do not make yourself uneasy. I have seen many young women in various states of upset at a ball. I am a mother and grandmother, so your tears shall not offend me. I would say that I am more than willing to thrash that Colonel Fitzwilliam for you if he has importuned upon you in any way."

Elizabeth's eyes grew large with alarm. "No! My lady, no, he has not importuned upon me. He did relay information that I found distressing, but I do not believe he was aware of the true extent of how his intelligence would affect me."

"Well, that is a relief. I have to say, it would not be the first time I have delivered a tongue lashing to a young man for his behaviour on a dance floor, but it would be the first time that one of the sons of

Matlock exhibited such bad behaviour." The elder lady paused for a moment. "Please do forgive me if I seem forward, but did he say something to you about his tall, dark haired cousin from the north?"

"How could you know that?" Elizabeth blurted without thought, then retracted. "Please forgive me, I was not expecting your inquiry."

"Dear, it was obvious all during the first half of the night that Fitzwilliam Darcy has an interest in your society, and knowing that Mr. Darcy and Colonel Fitzwilliam are thick as thieves, and also knowing that Colonel Fitzwilliam likes to tease, I thought that perhaps he took a joke too far."

Elizabeth hung her head and fiddled with the handkerchief in her hands. "You certainly have the right of Mr. Darcy and Colonel Fitzwilliam, but no, it was not a joke. He merely relayed some information about Mr. Darcy that I found distressing and now I realise that I do not know how to proceed. I thought that Mr. Darcy had always been a good friend to my family, but perhaps I was mistaken."

"Hmmm." Lady Sefton considered the young woman. "Perhaps, you might take a moment and remember why you have always thought of Mr. Darcy as a good friend and, if there is something with which you would charge him, you should perhaps discuss the matter directly."

"Oh, I am sure I could not do that. Why would he tolerate someone so wholly beneath him in consequence questioning his decisions?"

"Well, I am not a mind reader, but I do know the Darcy family relatively well, in this generation and the previous. I would say that they do not hold with those in society who look at class and birth as the preeminent classification of worth. You are obviously a gently bred young woman. I would suggest talking to Mr. Darcy before you give him up or think ill of him."

Elizabeth looked into the elderly woman's eyes and saw a profound kindness that not many people possessed.

"Now, we should go back to the ballroom before we are missed, but perhaps you will let this old lady give you one more piece of advice. Do not be too hasty in your judgements. Whatever you might choose in a hurry is sure to be regretted at length."

Confrontation

THOUGH SHE HAD BEEN IN ATTENDANCE AT SIR James and Lady Finch's ball until nearly four in the morning, Elizabeth was out of her bed again just after eight. She could not close her eyes without seeing Darcy. At first, he was smiling and asking her to dance, then his face would transform into a sneer while he sidestepped her and clasped the hand of some beautiful rich debutante wearing jewels, furs and a superior smug smile. Both the mystery lady and Darcy would laugh at Elizabeth and walk away arm-in-arm.

Elizabeth's rational mind was screaming that the Darcy siblings and most of their cousins were not snobs, but it was clear from her reception by Lady Matlock that Darcy's aunts and uncles had expectations for his marriage. She had never met Mr. Darcy Sr., but it was hard to imagine he would be much different from his siblings-in-law.

Then there was the disturbing information that Richard had relayed about Bingley's abandonment of Jane, and Darcy's comments on the situation. Richard had not known, and Elizabeth did not have positive confirmation, that the lady from whom Bingley was separated was Jane. But by Richard's own admission, the only place Bingley had recently been besides London was Netherfield.

Most disturbing to Elizabeth personally, was Richard's belief that Darcy considered the separation for the best. If the Bennet sisters were objectionable and imprudent in Darcy's mind for marriage to Bingley, he would be categorically opposed to a connection for himself. Lady Sefton had urged her to discuss the matter with Darcy before making any decisions or taking any actions that might not do credit to either party. But as Elizabeth thought about confronting Darcy, she was completely lost. How to start such a conversation?

Have you seen Mr. Bingley, or given him any advice recently?

Do you believe Mr. Bingley will be returning to Netherfield anytime soon? No? What makes you say that?

I wonder if I might ask you about how you betrayed my sister. Perhaps over tea?

Deciding to try and quiet her mind with a walk, but not wanting to worry anyone over her toilette or breakfast, Elizabeth dug out from the back of her closet one of her older day dresses with a front closure, her warmest apron, and her brown overcoat. The Gardiner house was less than one mile from the great St. Paul's Cathedral. It was a poor substitute for the hundreds of acres of woods surrounding her father's estate, but the trees and quiet of the churchyard were beckoning Elizabeth.

Fitzwilliam Darcy was up early the day after the Finch's ball. He and Georgiana had returned late, but not nearly as late as usual after a society ball. Darcy would have much rather stayed and danced with Elizabeth again, but it would have likely caused a minor scandal. His aunt's not so subtle prodding to dance with some of the titled ladies present was also sure to have become unbearable if he had stayed. Darcy detested the expectation that he should partner his aunt's niece, Lady Fiona, and the other unmarried eligible society ladies in attendance held no special interest for him.

Having always been an early riser, Darcy was awake only an hour later than his normal schedule, which was still a full two hours before the normal breakfast hour of the *ton*. Darcy decided to exercise his horse and try to keep his thoughts under control.

Seeing Elizabeth at the Finch's ball last night had been a revelation! She may not have a significant fortune and some relations in trade, but her connections were obviously top notch. If she was a welcomed guest at Sir James and Lady Finch's home, their relations and connections were not all that disparate. It would be hard to argue that a gently bred lady from a respectable estate with relations in the first circles was an inappropriate choice for Darcy.

He did have to admit that his Aunt Matlock's reception of the Bennet sisters was not as warm as he would have hoped, which was somewhat concerning. However, his family surely wished to see him happy in his choice of wife over making a selection which merely increased the amount of money in his bank account.

The morning bells of the many London churches began to ring all around Darcy, announcing the new day and the top of the hour. The noise startled Darcy out of his musings only to find that he had given his horse its own head for so long that they were somehow now walking past St. Paul's Cathedral. He should really let Knightly rest for a bit before making his way home.

Upon walking into the garden of St. Paul's Cathedral, Darcy was surprised to see another person sitting on one of the old stone benches near the north entrance to the chapel. Then, upon a second look, he was stunned to realise he recognised the posture of the young woman, as well as the bonnet and overcoat, as belonging to Elizabeth. Leading his horse around the path to a hitching post, Darcy tried to brush his riding breeches free of horsehair and straighten his hastily tied cravat. It was too much a gift to find Elizabeth on her own to worry about his attire.

"Miss Elizabeth, what an extraordinary coincidence! I would not have imagined that you would be up so early this morning given the late night of the Finch's ball last night, but I am certainly not disappointed to find you here."

Elizabeth startled at the unmistakable sound of Darcy's voice. The morning's thoughts had weighed overly heavy on the young lady and she was finding it hard to keep the hurt and anguish from her eyes.

Darcy's smile slowly faded as he registered Elizabeth's facial expression. "Miss Elizabeth, are you in some distress? Can I be of any assistance?" Darcy sat next to Elizabeth on the stone bench and out of true concern for her wellbeing, took one of her hands in his own.

Elizabeth stared at his hands surrounding her much smaller one and rubbing soothing circles with his thumb. Tears started to form in her eyes, and she looked into his face, so precious and thoughtful. The alarmed look in his own eyes gave Elizabeth the strength to finally speak.

"Mr. Darcy, I am not in any physical distress. Please do not be alarmed at my attitude. I find I awoke this morning with heavy thoughts and came here looking for some clarity or, if clarity is beyond my reach, peace."

This was not the interview Darcy had hoped to have with Elizabeth this morning, however, she was in need of support and he would give her anything. Everything. "My father has often said that 'a burden shared is a burden halved'. Perhaps I might take half of your burdens." *Or all of them if you will allow me.*

Elizabeth managed a small smile. He was such a dear hearted and kind man. Truly, the best of men. And this would be the moment that her fears regarding his intentions would be revealed.

"In fact, sir, there is something in particular which I wanted to discuss with you. Will you speak to me of Mr. Bingley?" As the words came from her mouth, a fresh wave of tears flooded Elizabeth's eyes.

Darcy was taken aback sharply. Without much thought, Darcy answered defensively. "I cannot say that I have seen him in many weeks. What interest does he hold for you?"

Elizabeth looked down at their still entwined hands. "He holds very little interest for me personally, but certain members of my family have been aggrieved by his sudden and continued absence."

"Your mother, no doubt, chief among them."

The sharpness in his voice brough Elizabeth up short and she looked up abruptly. "Whatever does that mean? Why would my mother have an interest in the gentleman?"

"Well, she has made her hopes for a match between Bingley and your eldest sister very clear to the whole neighbourhood surrounding Meryton."

Elizabeth withdrew her hand from Darcy's. "My mother may be a bit freer with her words than is strictly polite, but she loves her children very much and only wishes that they should be happy in life. Her hopes for Jane are no more than Jane's hopes for herself."

Darcy snorted a laugh at Elizabeth's description of her mother. "That is putting your mother's attitudes and actions mildly. I know you are not insensitive to Mrs. Bennet's total want of propriety as displayed regularly in company, an attitude that she has passed on to your two youngest sisters. I have seen your embarrassment at their public displays of poor comportment."

At this recitation of the defects in her family, Elizabeth withdrew completely and stood, taking a few steps away from Darcy.

Darcy's brain finally decided to take over the discussion from his mouth. "Forgive me, Miss Elizabeth. That was poorly done. I should not have spoken of your family in such a way. We were speaking of Bingley. What do you wish to know of him?"

Elizabeth did not return to the bench, and spoke with her back to Darcy, trying to control her temper. Unleashing the full weight of her imprudent tongue in this moment would only lead to more hurt feelings. "Please, I beg the truth from you. Has Mr. Bingley been discouraged from calling on my sister?"

Darcy gasped and stood, extending a hand out towards Elizabeth. "Where did you hear this?"

Elizabeth turned to Darcy in a flash of anger. "It matters not where I heard such things, I only care if they are true!"

Taking a large breath that turned into a sob, Elizabeth continued in a much weaker voice. "Please, sir. I must know the truth and I know you too well to believe that you will lie to me. I thought we were too good of friends for such deception and prevacation."

Darcy stared at her for a long moment, then sighed and answered. "Yes. From both myself and his sisters, Bingley has been discouraged from pursuing Miss Bennet."

"Why?"

"Does the reason truly matter?"

"It matters a great deal to me."

Darcy sat back on the stone bench with a heavy sigh then ran his hands through his hair and across his face. Elizabeth longed to go to him, to draw comfort from him and provide comfort in return. She resisted this urge and stood waiting for his excuses.

"I believe that Miss Bingley and Mrs. Hurst have some objections to the financial standing of your family. I cannot repeat most of their objections since I normally tune them out when they begin to complain and gossip about people they believe below their station. Miss Bingley has a uniquely skewed view of the world and clings to some unwarranted belief that money is the most important quality one can possess. She refuses to understand that genteel behaviour and a long connection to duty and responsibilities to one's community bound by land are the more important qualities of superior society."

Elizabeth closed her eyes. Miss Bingley's objections were well understood and easily dismissed as ridiculous. But there was one more set of objections she needed to hear directly from the source. "And you sir, what are your objections?"

"Only that I believed Miss Bennet indifferent."

That was not what Elizabeth was expecting to hear. "What can you mean, Jane indifferent? How can you know a young woman's heart, a heart which is now nearly destroyed from disappointed hopes? Are you certain there was no other objection? Perhaps an objection to my mother who displays a 'total want of propriety' in company or my lowly placed relations in trade here in London and in Meryton?"

"Miss Elizabeth, you must allow me to tell you how ardently sorry I am for saying such a thing about your mother. I cannot pretend that her behaviour is all that is respectable, but she is your mother and deserves my respect for no other reason than you love her." Darcy sighed. "As to your relations here in London, they are lovely people and fashionable. Bingley could not have any objection to your relations in trade since his father is currently the owner and operator of a set of large factories in Scarborough. In fact, your father would be the one with reason to object to Mr. Bingley as a man without an estate into which to install your sister. Truly, the only objection I ever had to your sister's match with Bingley was the possibility of a marriage of unequal affection. Her look and manners were open, cheerful, and engaging as ever, but without any symptom of particular regard that I could decipher; and I remained convinced that, though she received his attentions with pleasure, she did not invite them by any participation of sentiment. If you have not been mistaken here, I must have been in error. Your superior knowledge of your sister must make the latter the most probable. If it be so, if I have been misled by such error to inflict pain on her, your tears and anger are warranted."

Darcy looked up from his hands towards Elizabeth, who stood silently crying in the sunlight cresting over the trees of the churchyard. The sun created a radiant halo around her head and Darcy was struck by how beautiful and fragile she looked in this quiet moment. He slowly stood and took a faltering step in Elizabeth's direction, giving her time to step back from him if she did not desire his approach.

When she stayed still, Darcy closed the distance between them and handed her his handkerchief. Georgiana had embroidered it for him recently with Sweet William flowers surrounding a delicate *D* on one corner of the silk cloth. As Elizabeth dabbed at her eyes, Darcy laid his hands on her shoulders. For a long moment they stayed in that silent moment. Elizabeth ran her fingers across the stitches of the flowers and traced them reverently.

"Bingley came to my townhome shortly after the Christmas season was ended and asked me if I would return to Hertfordshire with him." Darcy spoke softly. "In fact, if memory serves me, he came to see me on the same morning that Georgiana and I later met you and your family in the park."

"You mean the day little Henry fell into the Serpentine?" Elizabeth said with a small laugh and smile.

Darcy was cheered considerably by her smile. "Yes, exactly that day. So, you see, he had not given up on Miss Bennet as late as the end of January. I have not seen him at all since that day, but I promise you now, I will do what I can to correct my error and withdraw my objections to his pursuit of your sister."

"It is not your doing alone which has taken Mr. Bingley from my sister. You cannot promise to fix it all with your superior persuasion. And I would not have you feeling so guilty over the abandonment." Elizabeth shook her head and dabbed her eyes with Darcy's handkerchief. "No, Mr. Bingley must answer for his own part in this whole affair."

"Thank you for that defence of my character. I know that I cannot make a man who knows his own mind bend to mine, however Bingley is often swayed more than he ought to be by the opinions of his friends. I will remove any part that my opinion played in his abandonment of Miss Bennet and provide him the direction to your uncle's house. He may do with the information what he will."

Elizabeth looked up into Darcy's smiling eyes and nodded. The moment was perfect, but the emotion of the heavy discussion left both feeling a bit hollow.

"Come now Miss Elizabeth, let me escort you back to your uncle's house, then I have some calls to make."

"Lead the way Mr. Darcy."

Atonement

IMMEDIATELY UPON SEEING ELIZABETH BACK TO HER uncle's house, Darcy ran his horse back to Darcy House to ready himself for making calls. Little more than one hour later, Darcy was out the door and on his way to Bingley's townhouse. However, instead of finding his friend, Hastings, the butler at Bingley's house, informed Darcy that Bingley had left not two hours ago on his way to Netherfield in Hertfordshire.

"He left this morning?" Hastings nodded. "And you say he is on his way to Netherfield." Hastings nodded again. "Well, good on you, Bingley."

"Yes, Mr. Darcy. He left in some haste. He even went on horseback and ordered his valet to come with the carriage and his trunks at a later hour. Grayson is just about ready to depart. The horses have been hitched; he is just waiting on some bread from Cook before making his way north."

Darcy thought quickly. Bingley was not aware that Jane was here in London. Bingley would be better served to come back to town and call upon her here, but Darcy would have to make significant haste to catch him up and bring him back to town before the Bennet sisters left for Kent in two days.

"Mr. Hastings, I know that I am not master here, but I would beg you to delay Grayson's departure. I intend to go after Bingley and bring him back here to London. I happen to know why his is going back to Netherfield and he will not find what he is looking for in

Hertfordshire. If I am swift, I shall catch Bingley at the coaching inn between here and Hertfordshire and bring him home before evening sets in." Darcy glanced at the mantle clock. "If I am not lucky, I shall go on towards Netherfield and bring him back in the morning. If we do not return tonight, the coach and Grayson can leave at first light tomorrow and we shall meet him at the coaching inn by nine a.m. to bring everyone back to London. If Bingley is not with me at the coaching inn by nine a.m., then Grayson can go on to Netherfield. I shall inform Bingley of my atrocious manners ordering about his servants."

The aged butler was not overly comfortable with following orders which directly contradicted his master's, however, Darcy was Bingley's oldest friend and commanded such a presence that very few would deny him anything for which he designed to ask. So, arrangements were made to delay the servants and the carriage until the next day. Grayson was dispatched to Darcy House with a note for Georgiana letting her know that her brother had left on a very urgent matter which he hoped would be resolved within the day, but he might be gone at least one night. Then Darcy rode off towards the great north road on his fastest horse.

Darcy hit his first bout of bad luck when the coaching inn reported that a man matching Darcy's description of Bingley had been there for a meal and to rest his horse, but had left about forty-five minutes prior. Darcy quickly had a bite to eat and exchanged his grey horse for one of the coaching inn horses, with the promise to be back the next day to reclaim his horse, then made his way towards Netherfield. The horses available at the inn were not of the highest quality and showing obvious signs of age and continued use, so the second half of the journey did not proceed as quickly as Darcy would have liked.

Finally, Darcy rode up to the Netherfield manor house with his tired horse and handed the animal off to a groom waiting by the front drive. A familiar carriage was in the drive as well, and Darcy inquired after the butler if Bingley had guests.

"Aye sir. Mrs. Bennet and her two youngest daughters came calling not ten minutes past. They are all in the blue parlour. Shall I show you to a room to change or announce you?"

Looking down at his dust covered boots, Darcy considered taking a few minutes to clean himself, but since Bingley was not expecting his arrival, Darcy decided to be announced to the master.

As soon as they approached the east parlour, Darcy could hear Mrs. Bennet's voice cutting through the halls.

"Oh no! Jane is not presently at home. You see, both of my eldest daughters are visiting my brother Gardiner and his wife and children in London. Jane and Lizzy have been in town for more than six weeks now. I am surprised that you have not known this. They called upon your sister during their first week in town and have been much in the company of Mr. Darcy and his sister these past weeks. I was sure that you would have seen Jane many times since their leaving us in January."

Darcy heard a bit of a pause in the conversation and imagined Bingley was trying very hard to come up with an appropriate response to Mrs. Bennet's revelation. He decided that now was the right time to intercede and nodded to the butler to announce him.

As soon as the door was opened, four sets of surprised eyes moved to him.

Darcy made a polite bow to Bingley but addressed Mrs. Bennet first. "Mrs. Bennet, it is a pleasure to see you. I am sorry for the dust about my person, but I have lately come from London and without a proper invitation. So, here I am, throwing myself on Bingley's mercy for one nights' lodging."

Bingley did not display his normal good cheer at the arrival of his best friend. His look was, in fact, quite hard. Darcy considered the tongue lashing which was his due.

Mrs. Bennet, however, was ecstatic at the arrival of both Bingley and Darcy. Her sister Phillips had been out shopping when Bingley had ridden past the centre of Meryton more than an hour ago. She had run nearly the entire way to Longbourn to tell her sister of the unexpected arrival of the young master of Netherfield. Not wanting to miss even one day's opportunity, Mrs. Bennet had hastily set out to invite the young man to dinner that very evening, reasoning that the Netherfield cook could not have known he was arriving and had no time to prepare a fitting dinner. Now, with Darcy unexpectedly arriving after his friend, Mrs. Bennet was sure her wildest dreams were about to come true and both Jane and Elizabeth would be matched with the wealthiest men who had ever stepped foot into their acquaintance.

"Mr. Darcy!" Mrs. Bennet exclaimed. "What an unparalleled pleasure to see you again. Have you come to Netherfield for any specific purpose?"

Darcy bowed again to the Bennet family matron. "Madam, I had some urgent business to discuss with my friend, and when I called at his house in town, I found that he was not at home. His butler directed me here and I followed post-haste."

"Well, all this urgent business shall have to wait until tomorrow. I insist that you both come to dinner this very evening at Longbourn. I know for a fact that Netherfield has not a pound of good meat in its stores and such young and strong men as yourselves cannot have a dinner so wanting."

"I am afraid that we shall, neither of us, have appropriate dinner attire this evening. I left without even packing a valise with a change of clothes, and I delayed Bingley's servants hoping to catch him at the coaching inn to bring him back to London with me tonight."

"Really Darcy, why would you do that? And why would Hastings and Grayson agree to such a thing?" Bingley exclaimed in an uncharacteristic angry outburst.

Mrs. Bennet was now beginning to suspect something was not right between the two men. Darcy had been unfailingly polite and soft voiced, while Bingley was now nearly shouting. It seemed that there was some dispute between them that needed righting. It was clear that the best thing would be to depart from Netherfield now, but still insist that they come to dinner at Longbourn. "Oh Mr. Darcy, never mind your clothes. I am sure whatever you do have will be fine after a good brushing. We are such good friends, we shall not stand on such formalities as proper dinner attire for just a small party. I must insist that you both come. In fact, with you two, we shall be even in ladies and gentlemen. My husband has not had that pleasure at his dinner table in almost twenty years. Now, girls, say your goodbyes. We must be off home to ready cook for our guests tonight."

The gentlemen bowed and the ladies curtsied while the Bennets outer things were handed over. Darcy handed Mrs. Bennet and her daughters back into their carriage, then took a steadying breath before going back into the parlour to face Bingley.

He did not have to wait long.

"What is this about Jane Bennet being in London since *January?* And apparently '*much in company with*' you and your sister? Tell me truthfully, are you trying to steal her from me? I shall call you out. I do not care how long we have been friends."

"Charles, please calm down." Darcy held up his hands in a placating gesture. "I promise I am not in any way interested in your Miss Bennet. But I have been much in company with her and her sister, Miss Elizabeth, and their aunt and uncle Gardiner."

"Then why would you not tell me this?" Bingley was nearly shouting with six weeks of heartache and anger bursting forth. "I have been nearly dead with heartache since last we talked, believing she was indifferent to me. I have secluded myself inside my house in London, even driving Caroline to seek refuge in Hurst's house to escape my black moods. And now I hear that my supposed best friend has been seen all over town with my angel! What am I supposed to think?"

"Charles, I was not in company with Miss Bennet for her sake. I have been enjoying much time with Miss Elizabeth Bennet."

"Miss Elizabeth?"

"Yes, Miss Elizabeth. Miss Bennet just happened to be everywhere Elizabeth could be found due to their being sisters. Not that I dislike Miss Bennet, she is a lovely young lady. I just prefer the company of her sister." Darcy fiddled with his signet ring and shifted between his feet.

Charles sat heavily on the sofa and covered his eyes with his hands. "But still, why would you not tell me that they were in town?"

Darcy sat down opposite his oldest friend. "I have two excuses for why I never told you, well three, though they are not very good. Firstly, after our last talk, I thought that seeing Miss Bennet again would be damaging to your resolve to give her up. Second, most days I was much too busy enjoying Elizabeth's company to even spare you a thought. Finally, and this is the only excuse I shall defend, I honestly thought you knew she was in London, as Miss Bennet and Miss Elizabeth called upon your sister, at your house, in January."

"Answer me one question truthfully. If you had known I was ignorant of her presence in town, would you have actually told me?"

Darcy signed and looked at his hands clasped in his lap. "I do not think I would have before today."

"And what, pray tell, is so special about today?"

"This morning, I spoke to Elizabeth." Darcy took a great breath. "She was very upset and revealed that Miss Bennet is suffering from your abandonment. I spoke of my prior belief that her sister was indifferent to you and Elizabeth insists that she is not. In fact, according to Elizabeth, Miss Bennet is very much missing you and would welcome your call, if you should choose to call upon her."

Bingley stood up and paced a bit in front of the sofa. "Truly?"

"I promise you, I have never lied to you about this. I was mistaken before about Miss Bennet's regard, but when I was given reliable intelligence that my thinking was incorrect, I set out without delay to inform you of my error." *And to ease Elizabeth's distress. Mostly for Elizabeth, but some for Bingley and Jane too.*

Bingley stopped pacing and looked at his friend with hard eyes. After a moment, he seemed to see in Darcy what he was searching for and broke into a bright smile. "Well, what are we waiting for? Let us back to London poste-haste!"

Darcy looked to the mantle clock. It was nearly five p.m. "Bingley, it is very late indeed. We would not make it to London before nightfall and the horses are overworked. It would be foolhardy to try and leave now. We shall take dinner with the Bennets in just over two hours and then return here to sleep. I intend to return to London at first light. We shall meet your man at the coaching inn north of Hampstead Heath and let him know we shall all return to town together."

Bingley agreed to the plan and both gentlemen decided to retire and have what clothes were available to them cleaned before leaving for Longbourn.

As soon as Mrs. Bennet returned home, she ordered her cook and Mrs. Hill to start on a fantastic dinner plan. The silver was polished, and the best China laid out on the table. An additional soup course was added to the menu along with some lemon tarts for after dinner. Finally, Mrs. Bennet rushed into her husband's library with all due haste.

"Oh Mr. Bennet! Such wonderful happenings, yes, wonderful indeed! You must make yourself ready for our dinner guests tonight."

Mr. Bennet looked up from his book with one eyebrow elevated above the other. "Now, who in the world could be coming to dinner that requires my attention more than one hour prior to the proper hour? You know I am not much in the habit of changing for dinner and I do not see why any of our neighbours should expect it of me now."

"Oh, you have no compassion for my nerves! Tonight, Mr. Bingley and Mr. Darcy are both coming to dinner. I insist that you at least change into a more formal waistcoat and put on a new set of evening breeches and hose. I tell you they are coming to speak for Jane and Lizzy!"

"How can you know that for certain? Did they declare themselves to our daughters in London? Neither Jane nor Lizzy have written me of such expectation?" Mr. Bennet did not like the thought of losing both of his sensible daughters in one night. Even more troublesome, he had heard nothing of the feelings of his daughters on the matter. He was determined to reserve his full blessing and consent for any understanding until hearing on the subject from his children directly.

"Well, I cannot know the mind of a man on my own of course. And there did seem to be something of a dispute between them when I left Netherfield just a while ago. Mr. Darcy was trying to get Mr. Bingley to come back to London and delay his speaking to you. I cannot understand why that would be the case, but who knows what goes on in men's heads?"

"Quite." Now, Mr. Bennet was a bit more interested in what would happen over dinner. He dutifully went to his rooms and had his valet dig out some formal dinner breeches and hose. He even changed into a new cravat which had recently been starched. Mr. Bennet might have been a lethargic type of man, preferring his books to most other things, but he was not insensitive to his children's future happiness and the prosect of some entertainment from his neighbours.

Darcy and Bingley presented themselves at Longbourn at the exact hour and sat down to a very small dinner with just Mr. Bennet, Mrs.

Bennet, Miss Kitty and Miss Lydia Bennet. It was both the most comfortable Darcy had ever felt in the Bennet home and the most anxious. He did not know if he should ask for permission to call upon Elizabeth or leave it be for now. She would be under the care of her uncle for a few days more then moving into her brother's home, but neither of those gentlemen could object if he carried Mr. Bennet's approval for a call. There was also the issue that he had not been able to discuss his intentions with Elizabeth. He would like to speak to the young lady directly before engaging her father.

Bingley was considering similar thoughts as his friend and remained uncharacteristically quiet. Mrs. Bennet asked general questions of the gentlemen, and Lydia and Kitty giggled together but kept their voices low between themselves. Their mother had threatened them within an inch of their lives if they behaved loudly at this dinner and ruined their elder sisters' chances at marrying so well. Lydia had wanted to protest based on what she considered the infamous treatment of Mr. Wickham by Darcy's father. But Mrs. Bennet had required that she stay singularly quiet on that topic. It did not matter what was in the past between the Darcys and Mr. Wickham. The young Darcy would be welcomed as a suitor for any of her daughters, especially her most troublesome and headstrong daughter.

Mr. Bennet spent the entirety of the meal watching, with significant amusement, the unease of his guests.

After dinner, the gentlemen retired to Mr. Bennet's study for cigars and brandy. Here, it was Mr. Bennet's turn to make sport of the young gentlemen.

"So, Mr. Darcy, my daughters tell me that you and your sister have become something of a constant in their London entertainments. I've been hearing all about teas, shopping excursions, the opera, balls, art exhibitions and everything in between."

Darcy nodded. "Yes sir, my sister and I have had the pleasure of Miss Bennet and Miss Elizabeth's company for a number of engagements since they came to town. I must say, I have never seen my sister so taken with social engagements. Your daughters, and Miss Elizabeth in particular, seem to bring out the best in my sister. Just last night, Georgiana took a very big step and exhibited on the piano for the first time in full company at a ball thrown by some mutual connections of ours, Sir James and Lady Finch. I believe she was only able to overcome her shy nature because Miss Elizabeth played with her in a lovely duet."

Mr. Bennet chuckled a bit. Of course his Elizabeth would be making a splash and exhibiting at a London society ball without any fear, and indeed helping another young woman overcome her own fears. "That certainly sounds like my Lizzy. She is small in stature but makes up for every lost inch in fearlessness. I trust you did not repeat your bad behaviour from the Netherfield ball and kept your number of dances to the appropriate two?"

Darcy looked chagrined. "Yes, sir. I danced with Miss Elizabeth only twice, then departed with my sister after the supper entertainments as she is not fully out yet." He cleared his throat and left out that, given his druthers, he would have stayed and danced every dance with Elizabeth, hang the consequences. Well, not hang the consequences, since he was more than prepared to protect her from any negative consequences.

Mr. Bennet nodded and turned fully to Bingley. "Now, in contrast, I have heard nothing at all of you, Mr. Bingley. Not one word in any of my daughter's letters, and none of the missives I get from my brother Gardiner have been devoted to any account of seeing you. My wife insists that you must be coming to ask for Jane's hand in marriage, but I am at a loss as to how you could have come to any understanding without seeing her since November twenty-sixth of last year."

Bingley blanched and choked on the sip of brandy he had just taken. But Mr. Bennet was not done.

"And add to my confusion the report that Mr. Darcy here tried to stop you from returning to Netherfield at all today. Now, that is peculiar. I believe I would like to hear from you both what was the purpose of this hasty visit to Hertfordshire." Mr. Bennet sat back in his chair and waited for the young gentlemen to start coming up with some excuse that made any sense at all.

Darcy started to speak on both of their behalf. "Mr. Bennet, sir, it was not my purpose to stop Mr. Bingley from seeking any audience with you, but to give him information he lacked. I assumed he came here to call on Miss Bennet and knowing she is currently in London with your brother and sister, I wanted to catch Bingley up to redirect his adventure."

"So, you wanted to bring him to call on *my* daughter without my permission?" Mr. Bennet's eyes were positively sparkling with joy and mirth.

"NO!" Darcy was panicked. "Of course, I would never disrespect you in that way. I believe I did not consider the matter of your consent to a call at your brother's house."

"I can well see you did not consider the matter since you have been calling on my family without my consent for quite some time now. Is that not right?"

"No sir, I mean … I have been … that is we, my sister and I, have been in company with Elizabeth many times, but always with Mr. Gardiner's permission and Mrs. Gardiner acting as chaperone." Darcy took a large gulp of his brandy. "I assumed that you had been informed and provided consent to such entertainments or Mr. Gardiner would have objected. He seems a very upstanding man and protective of his nieces. I certainly would not have done anything I thought would be objectionable to you as Elizabeth's father." Darcy was very flustered at the turn in this conversation. His leg was shaking with the repressed need to pace and his hands were wringing together while his eyes looked around fitfully for something upon which to land. He also completely missed his slip into using less formal language for Elizabeth's name, something that, had it registered with him, would have been mortifying in the extreme.

Bingley, for once in his life, kept his mouth shut. He had never seen his friend so discomforted. It was highly unexpected to see Darcy struggle for words. Bingley spared a look towards Mr. Bennet and was further shocked to see something akin to joy in the elder man's features. Bingley leaned back in his chair and tried to make himself look smaller.

Mr. Bennet was not a cruel man. "Mr. Darcy, do not become sick over this. You are correct that I was informed of your socialising with my family, and I am not truly worried over your association with my daughter, *Miss* Elizabeth. I do want to warn you that while your behaviour here in Meryton has not caused any serious harm to Lizzy's reputation, if I hear that you have caused expectations to rise in London, and her or my family's reputation is harmed, I will not hesitate to insist you do what is required to correct the situation."

Darcy finally calmed and looked Mr. Bennet straight in the eye. "I promise you sir, I have nothing but the purest intentions when it comes to Miss Elizabeth. You would not have to press the issue at all as I would have rectified any negative gossip before it could reach your door."

Mr. Bennet nodded and turned once again to Mr. Bingley. "Well, young man, what have you to say to all of this?"

Bingley looked at the father of the woman he hoped to pursue, then finished his glass of brandy in one drink. "Mr. Bennet, I would like your permission to call on Miss Jane Bennet while she is in London and ask her for a formal courtship."

"Here, here! That was very well done, my boy." Mr. Bennet raised his glass towards Bingley. "I will give you my answer, then we should join my wife and youngest daughters for some sweets in the parlour. I give you my permission to call on Jane while she is with my brother Gardiner in London, and her sister Mary and brother Collins, for she and Lizzy leave in two days to go to Kent. However, I shall reserve any permission for a formal courtship or anything more," Mr. Bennet turned quite pointedly to give Darcy a significant look, "until you have secured the consent of my daughter. I expect to have news from Jane and my brother Gardiner soon."

All three men then nodded, stood, and went to face Mrs. Bennet in the parlour.

Caught in the Rain

A S SOON AS THE SUN PROVIDED ENOUGH LIGHT FOR Darcy and Bingley to safely ride out in the morning, both gentlemen were mounted on their horses and headed for the coaching inn between London and Hertfordshire. After about one hour of riding, it became apparent that the weather for the day was going to turn stormy. Rain came from the south and began heavily falling when Bingley and Darcy were only thirty minutes from their destination.

Thoroughly soaked, both gentlemen were shown to rooms to attempt to dry themselves and clean the mud from their clothes and boots. When the hour arrived that Bingley's valet was supposed to arrive at the inn, there was nothing but an increase in the amount of rain falling. After a full three hours past the appointed nine a.m. hour that they were supposed to meet Grayson and Bingley's carriage, Darcy spoke to the inn proprietor about reserving two guest rooms and two servants' quarters for their party overnight. Finally, at two p.m., Grayson, Bingley's coachman, and his coach, with four very dirty, tired horses arrived at the coaching inn.

"Mr. Bingley, sir. I am sorry to say that the road 'tween 'er and London is too much washed ou'to be able to travel 'gain today. Maybe 'morrow. We only made it through some o'the muck while Johns and I walked by the horses to lighten the load for a long way."

"You did not need to go through all that trouble, though I am exceedingly glad to see you and a change of clothes after the wet ride from

Netherfield. I will arrange for the men here to take my trunk upstairs and once the horses are safe in the stables, you and Johns should retire for the rest of the day. I will have some hearty dinner sent to you in the rooms we arranged for you both."

"Thank you, sir. I won' be saying no to a rest after walkin' so many miles. Mr. Darcy, sir. Connor sent me with a change o'clothes, your shave kit, and some paper in case you have directions to send back o'your house. He just about came with me, but decided you would rather he stay to add an additional man in the house with the young miss there. He also says to tell you that your cousin, Colonel Fitzwilliam did come at your sister's biddin' to stay while you was away. I saw Conner this morning early with getting your things, and the storm had already started to threaten the skies in London, so Johns and I thought we would be stuck here for the day. Connor will tell your house o'the likely delay in our return." Connor Grayson, Darcy's valet, was younger brother to Bingley's valet, John Grayson. Darcy had suggested Grayson to Bingley in his first semester at Cambridge when the social expectations and dress code for gentlemen of means had become more than Bingley could manage on his own. The Darcy family preferred to hire staff from their most trusted families to build loyalty with those persons who care for the family's most intimate requirements.

"Thank you, Grayson. That is very kind of you and exactly the sort of excellent service I have always known from your family. I agree that a change of clothes is exactly what is in order after the stress of the day."

Grayson and Johns set off to see to the horses and then enjoy their afternoon of rest.

After changing clothes, Bingley and Darcy retired to a private sitting room on the second floor near their rooms, with a roaring fire and some scotch. "Well, this is a debacle. The Miss Bennets will be leaving for the Collins' home tomorrow at dawn and I shall miss the chance to call on Miss Jane Bennet until May!"

Darcy considered the problem for a moment. They had both been hoping that if Bingley called upon Jane or her uncle Gardiner that afternoon that she would delay the trip to Kent, or not go at all, to give their relationship a chance to advance. Now that Jane and Elizabeth would most likely depart early in the morning before Darcy and Bingley could reach London, another plan would need to be discovered to bring the two back into each other's acquaintance.

"What do you say to a trip to Kent?" Darcy asked.

"What are you talking about?"

"Well, you know that Georgiana and I spend nearly every Easter with my aunt, Lady Catherine de Bourgh and her daughter Anne. You may also know that the Hunsford parsonage, where Mr. Collins and his new wife live, is within walking distance of the main house at Rosings. Mr. Bennet specifically mentioned his approval for you to call on Miss Bennet at her brother's house and I can ask my cousin if you would be welcome to our party for at least some of the visit. Anne will likely perceive the reason without even being told, but I suggest full disclosure on your purpose, especially if you plan to become engaged during the next six weeks. Anne can be a forceful ally in all things, but would be especially useful in creating appropriate entertainment for our party, which will include the Collinses and Bennet sisters, so we might be in company with them often."

"That is a capital idea," Bingley exclaimed, his good mood restored. "I could call on Miss Bennet and her sisters at the parsonage and have our courtship away from the prying eyes of *my* sisters. I do not know how I shall face Caroline right now. I am very angry at her deception and keeping Miss Bennet's visit to our London home from me. If she were to come to me now, I might regret what I would say."

Darcy coughed uncomfortably. "Yes, Miss Bingley has always been vocal of her dislike for Miss Bennet. I am surprised that she kept the visit a secret from you, however, I do not know why it comes as such a revelation. After leaving Netherfield in such a rush after the ball in November, I should no longer be shocked at your sister's rude behaviour."

"I have not even really dealt with that episode." Bingley looked pensively into his cup. "It was abominably unmannerly of Caroline and Louisa to quit for the little season without taking proper leave of the neighbourhood. How is one to make amends to their neighbours after so long a time?"

Darcy chuckled under his breath, "I imagine, if you come back engaged to one of the 'jewels of the county' all will soon be forgiven."

Bingley blushed slightly. "You are correct. I shall just have to make sure to treat them all with respect, and host some entertainments in anticipation of our wedding."

"Do not get ahead of yourself. As Mr. Bennet so pointedly said, you still must win the fair maiden's heart."

"Correct again old chap. And what better way than an exciting cross-country pursuit against the flourishing spring backdrop of southern England. It nearly sounds like one of those romance novels written '*by a Lady*' that are all the rage now." Both men laughed. "Miss Bennet loves the country better than town anyway, so we could both discover the sights in Kent together! With a proper chaperone of course."

Darcy smiled at Bingley's enthusiasm. "I shall call on Anne as soon as we make it back to town and seek an invitation for you. It may take a few days for me to be ready to depart, I had not planned on removing to Kent for another week. But, I am sure that Connor can put together one week's worth of clothing for an early departure, then send the rest of my requirements with my sister and cousin when they leave at the originally appointed time. You and I can ride ahead in a few days and meet with the Miss Bennets before the full party arrives. Does that sound like a viable plan?"

"It sounds capital, just capital!"

Though the rain stopped near dawn the morning after Darcy and Bingley left Netherfield, it took a full day of sunshine for the spring roads to be in good enough condition for the carriage and four men to travel back to London. Darcy and Bingley would have taken their horses, however Bingley's coachman, Johns, advised that they had found heavily washed out roads, and with the thick mud there was too high a risk of harming one of the horses. So, instead, Darcy and Bingley spent the day at the coaching inn devising their plan for Kent.

Darcy started by composing a letter to his cousin, Anne. As the official mistress of Rosings, she was the correct person from whom to beg an invitation. Additionally, he was not sure that his aunt, Lady Catherine, would be overly warm to the idea. She had many nonsensical ideas about status and strict separation of the social classes. In Lady Catherine's opinion, having money, though a requirement for a truly highly placed family, was not enough. Men deserving of the title of 'Gentlemen' and therefore deserving of respect and attention, according to Lady Catherine, must have a long-standing and respectable connection to *land*. Bingley was educated as a gentleman, had never worked in trade himself, was a welcomed member of the social activities of the *ton*, and was looking to purchase an estate. But he was not *technically* a gentleman. It would take three generations of owing an estate to be considered a true gentleman. If he did not marry into the gentry, the Bingley men could not call themselves gentlemen until Bingley's great-grandson was born on the estate he purchased.

Anne, in contrast, was not a follower of such strict social guidelines. If Bingley was going to have a chance at making amends to Jane before she returned to her father in May, they would need Anne's help. Darcy wrote a very complete letter to his cousin. He detailed all his bad behaviour regarding Bingley and Jane's relationship. He also described how Elizabeth believed that Jane suffered from Bingley's abandonment. It was a risk to be so open in a written communication, but he planned on having his trusted valet deliver it to Anne's maid by hand. The letter also included an invitation to dinner for three nights hence to plan some appropriate entertainments for the whole Kent Easter party.

Not a whole hour after returning home to London and sending Connor to deliver his letter, Anne barged into Darcy's parlour with a sour look on her face. It was times like these that he saw the most striking resemblance between Anne and her mother.

"Fitzwilliam George James Darcy! Tell me you did not do this?" Anne scolded while waiving around his letter.

Darcy sighed. "Unfortunately, yes. I did do all the things in that letter or else I would not have written them down for you to read. Please come in and sit here by the fire with me. I have finally warmed after two days of being in a draughty coaching inn and riding on horseback through a rainstorm. I shall call for some tea."

"Well, I shall not berate you anymore after this, but you must know how much pain Jane has been suffering." Anne huffed her dissatisfaction. "She would never speak of her abandonment in company, but I extracted some information from her one evening after hearing Lizzy ask Georgiana about the Bingleys. The night we were at the theatre, I do not believe she saw any of the entertainment, as her eyes constantly swept the audience for any view of Mr. Bingley or his sisters. You must tell me how you came to get Lizzy to confirm Jane's feelings."

Though it was not in his nature to admit to such impropriety, Anne was a trusted confidante. "The day after Sir James and Lady Finch's ball I, completely by coincidence during a morning ride, came across Miss Elizabeth in the churchyard at St. Paul's and she seemed in distress. She revealed that her sister was suffering from Bingley's abandonment then insisted on knowing my part in his disappearance." Darcy laughed without mirth. "I was not at all proud of that admission, and she was very angry with me. I set out immediately that morning to meet with Bingley, but he had already, of his own volition, set off for Hertfordshire. We are now a full day too late to catch the Miss Bennets before they left for Hunsford. Do you think you can help reunite them?"

Anne stirred honey and lemon into her cup from the tea service which had been delivered. "I have always liked Mr. Bingley, and I adore Jane and Lizzy, so I would love to help reunite them. However, the invitation will *not* include those horrid grasping sisters of his. Miss Bingley is the worst kind of harpy and I do not wish to play hostess to her during what should otherwise be a very pleasant holiday."

"No, I agree wholeheartedly. Though I would never be so rude as to gossip about my best friend's sister," Darcy gave Anne a stern look, which she simply shrugged off and continued to drink her tea, "our group would be, um, crowded with the addition of Miss Bingley and the Hursts."

"Wonderful! Now, call for Georgie and she and I shall work on some entertainments designed for the Bennet sisters to be in company with the party at Rosings. Only my mother shall also be in company as your father and our uncle Matlock have both declined to visit this year. We shall be a merry band of young people." Anne shooed Darcy out of his own parlour, to fetch Georgiana.

As he went in search of his sister, Darcy frowned. He had suspected his father would bow out of the trip to Kent this year since Darcy and Georgiana would be returning directly to London for the season, but he had not yet read his father's letter confirming the elder man's long confinement at Pemberley. Nearly five years ago now, George Darcy had suffered an apoplexy of the heart. It had taken more than six months for his father to regain his strength. Now, though the doctors insisted that his health was very good, it seemed like Darcy's father was afraid of his own shadow. The trip between Pemberley and London was certainly not the most exciting trip, and a plush wingback chair was decidedly more comfortable than the swaying carriage, but there was no strain on his father's health to make the journey. However, to hear his father's excuses, anyone would think he was on death's door after fewer than ten miles of well-kept roads.

There was the added strain of the attention his father attracted in London, with which Darcy was very familiar and could commiserate. His father had aged well, as they say, and was still a very attractive man in his early fifties. A widower of some significant time, as Lady Anne Darcy had passed away less than one year after Georgiana was born, it was the general opinion of the marriage mart that he was fair game. Almost universally, the ladies, and some of the fathers, of the *ton* adhered to the belief that a single man in possession of a good fortune, must be in want of a wife. No matter his age.

Whatever his reasons, George Darcy was now absent from their lives for a majority of the year. It often felt to Darcy that he had guardianship over Georgiana. He found her masters and interviewed her servants. Last year, it was Darcy who had hired Georgiana's new companion after she outgrew the need for a governess. There had been several candidates who had applied to his father, but it was left to Darcy to make the final selection. One woman, a Mrs. Younge, had been his father's favourite, but Darcy did not like something about her manner. It also happened that he asked Richard to check up on her references and they discovered that one was completely forged. Thankfully, a very kind, gently bred widow, Mrs. Annesley, had been recommended by his Aunt Matlock. Mrs. Annesley was much more appropriate and familiar with the social requirements of the London season.

After Georgiana had joined Anne for a social entertainment planning session, Darcy excused himself from their company to search his neglected correspondence waiting on the master's study desk for a letter from their father. Sure enough, a letter with the Pemberley wax seal was set on the silver tray on the desk reserved for the most important letters. Cracking the seal, Darcy read his father's apologies for missing Easter at Rosings and instructions for the coming season and Georgiana's care. It was a blessing to still have his father's guidance in his life, even if it was from afar.

One passage in the letter caught Darcy's full attention.

Now, my boy, it is time that you take your responsibility to find a wife seriously. I know you are healthy and young and feel that there is plenty of time in the future for wives and babies, but I do not want you to miss out on years of happiness for the sake of what you now believe to be freedom. A wife, well chosen, will not inhibit your freedom. She will enhance your spirit. I implore you not to be hasty in your decision, but also do not let someone pass you by who makes your heart sing. Also, do not blindly follow the dictates of your Aunt Matlock. She means well, and will always have, what she believes to be, your best interests first in her heart as she has served as a loving substitute for your lost mother all these years. However, I am not convinced that her methods for making matches always bring happiness. We have all suffered from the loss of your mother, but perhaps none more than your sister. Georgiana has grown into a beautiful and accomplished woman, but her shy nature handicaps her in many ways. You also share this Darcy trait, however, you have always had such lively companions in Richard and young Bingley to keep you from hiding yourself away too much. For Georgiana's sake, chose someone kind, lively, and witty. For my sake, choose someone who makes you happy. And for your own sake, choose someone without whom your soul cannot live.

Reunited
At Last

ELIZABETH BENNET WAS SITTING IN THE MOST LAVISH parlour she had ever seen. Many times more ostentatious than the Darcy family London townhome, stuffed to the girders with furniture, paintings in gilded frames, wall coverings from a much older era, and endless bric-a-brac. William Collins, her sister Mary's husband, had spent the entire twenty minute walk between the Hunsford parsonage and the manor house of Rosings Park discussing the cost of the glazing to the windows, the finery of the home, and the *extraordinary condescension* of his patroness to invite their little family party to dinner so soon after his sisters had arrived.

"I confess" he had said, "that I should not have been at all surprised by her Ladyship's asking us yesterday after services to drink tea and spend the evening at Rosings this week. I rather expected, from my knowledge of her affability, that it would happen. But who could have imagined that we should receive an invitation to dine there for our whole party so immediately after your arrival!"

Elizabeth admitted to being impressed with such an invitation and Jane was very pleased to be able to meet with such elevated company. Scarcely anything was talked of the whole day or the next morning but their visit to Rosings. Collins had carefully instructed them in all the particulars of what they were to expect, the sight of such rooms, so many servants, and so splendid a dinner, so that the experience might not wholly overpower them.

The dinner was exceedingly handsome, and there were all the servants, and all of the articles of place which Colins had promised. And, as he had foretold, he took his seat at the bottom of the table, by her Ladyship's desire and from being the only male in attendance at the dinner, and looked as if he felt that life could furnish nothing greater. He carved, and ate, and praised with delighted alacrity, and every dish was commended first by him before being served around the table.

Collins was also overwhelmed at the gowns that Elizabeth and Jane had to present themselves to Lady Catherine. The wardrobe they had acquired in London would do them well at Lady Catherine's table over their time in Kent. Especially considering the expected socialising with the Darcy siblings, Anne de Bourgh, and Col. Richard Fitzwilliam. Elizabeth had insisted to their aunt and uncle Gardiner that at least two new fashionable dresses be acquired for Mary, along with several measures of cloth for overmaking some of her wedding clothes. Gardiner even included, as a gift to his niece and her husband, several lengths of cloth in black for a high-quality reverend's coat and trousers. Collins was suitably impressed at his new family's generosity.

Lady Catherine also did not disappoint Elizabeth's expectations for the evening. So much had been said on the topic of Collins's patroness, and much of it sounded very foolish to Elizabeth. However, Anne was such an intelligent and delightful companion that Elizabeth did not know exactly what to expect.

What they found in the parlour of Rosings was more marvellous than Elizabeth could have imagined.

Lady Catherine was dressed in a gown of the most expensive looking silk imaginable with a much longer sleeve than was strictly fashionable, but so adorned with gold thread embroidery that the effect was unmistakably fine. Her overdress had the shape and fullness of a court gown usually worn for presentation to the Queen and certain other court affairs. Definitely not a gown for a country dinner party. And her hair! Elizabeth was not sure how it was possible for her hair to be so highly styled. Both curled and braided, with large ostrich feathers sticking straight up from an elaborate turban style headdress. The entire ensemble, most strikingly, was in a shade of chartreuse that was excessively fashionable right now in the Parisian fashion magazines, but which made the elderly lady look slightly sick. Elizabeth thought this was a vision of what Caroline Bingley would look like in twenty-five years or so, except Caroline would be wearing a shade of orange which very clearly clashed with her hair colour.

Oh my! To see the two of them standing side by side. It would be so much a collision of particular tastes but still somehow natural that the two women would be drawn together by those personality traits which must bind them together. The image was too much for Elizabeth and she had to pull out her handkerchief to disguise a laugh as a cough.

"Here now, Miss Elizabeth, you are not sick, are you? I cannot abide by sick people who come to other people's homes and expose them to sickness." Lady Catherine's shrill voice raised above the assembled company. "I expect my Anne and some other guests this evening and you know my Anne is of a fragile constitution. I will not abide by someone endangering her health."

Elizabeth looked down to her hand and handkerchief, gently stroking the Sweet Williams daintily embroidered around a scrolling *D* in the corner. It was Darcy's handkerchief which had been hidden in her reticule since he had handed it to her nearly a week ago in the St. Paul's churchyard. She smiled again at the memory before answering. "Forgive me my lady, I do not believe I am afflicted with any specific ailment. I just believe that some of the dust from the road must have tickled the back of my throat. I am well now. Thank you. I would certainly not wish to harm Miss de Bourgh in any way, however it is hard to see her as having a fragile constitution. She always seemed so strong and lively when we met in London. I very much appreciated her companionship and intellect."

Lady Catherine harrumphed and fiddled with her teacup. Ordinarily, she would not abide by such insubordination as to have someone of such low rank disagree with her, but since Elizabeth's comments were so complimentary of Anne, Lady Catherine did not answer right away. "Well, of course you are right that my Anne is the most intelligent of ladies and extremely strong in spirit. *However*, she does have a delicate physical constitution and I take no risks with her health. You shall all remember this while you are visiting my estate and be mindful of not exposing her to anything. Even a trifling cold could be too much for her constitution."

Collins was ever at Lady Catherine's right hand ready to make his devotions. "Of course, Lady Catherine. I shall personally ensure that my family is well enough to be in Miss de Bourgh's company and if any of us are exhibiting even a headache, we shall not risk a visit to you."

"See that you do not." Lady Catherine sniffed, took a sip of tea, and moved on to other topics of conversation. "Now, Miss Bennet and Miss Elizabeth, I have been very impressed with your sister, Mrs. Collins, but I am interested in how the younger sister came to be married before the elders. Especially two such pretty and gentile ladies. How can your mother expect to marry you at such an age with younger daughters already married? I have never heard of such a thing as younger daughters being allowed out before marrying off the eldest sister."

Elizabeth felt very much for her two sisters, one with a broken heart and the other in such an awkward position of being compared to her elder sisters. "My lady, we were very much happy to have our cousin, now our brother, stay in our home for some time, as you know since I believe you were the originator of such a scheme. So, our brother Collins was part of our family party and able to meet all my sisters at the same time. It was apparent from nearly the first moment of his arrival that my sister Mary was the most suited in character and temperament to be a parson's wife. I also believe that Mary and my brother are of a like mind, more so than that the rest of my sisters share with our brother. Not that we do not get along as a family, however, I believe there is something more that must be shared between a man and his wife."

"I suppose you are correct. And Mrs. Collins has been a very great boon to our community since she arrived. She is appropriately demure and dresses to her station within the community." Lady Catherine looked at the gowns being presented by Elizabeth and Jane, which were of much higher quality than those Mary often wore. "I am very glad that Mr. Collins took my advice to go to your father and marry one of his cousins. I understand that your father's estate is entailed upon Mr. Collins, and though it has all worked out as it should, I see no occasion for entailing estates away from the female line. It was not necessary in Sir Lewis de Bourgh's family. Do you not agree Miss Elizabeth?"

"You are very much correct that Miss de Bourgh has been successful with the Rosings estate. Though I am delighted for my sister's marriage and happiness, I do wish we could have grown up knowing that my mother and family would be cared for after my father's passing. Perhaps my mother would have been less nervous these past years with a more solid plan for her dotage." Elizabeth reached over and patted Mary's folded hands. "My sister and brother Collins provide us with significant peace of mind in the future."

Collins fairly beamed at Elizabeth's praise and turned his smile back to Lady Catherine. He could not believe how wonderfully this first visit of his new family to his patroness was progressing. Jane had been serene and silent in her beauty, which greatly suited her ladyship. And Elizabeth had directed her impertinence into compliments to Lady Catherine and her daughter, which was as good a use of her lively disposition as any he had ever seen before. Yes, indeed, his wife's elder sisters were making quite a fine impression upon his patroness. He was most pleased with himself and his dear Mary. Collins even spared a kind and loving smile for his dear sweet wife and congratulated himself on having seen her worth from the moment he walked into his future home (at least that was how the event went in his memory).

Before her ladyship could introduce any more mildly inappropriate and somewhat uncomfortable topics, the butler entered with a most pleasant distraction.

"My lady, Miss de Bourgh has arrived with her cousin Mr. Fitzwilliam Darcy and their party."

"Thank you Higgs. Has my daughter retired to rest from her travels?"

"Yes, ma'am. All the travellers have been shown to their rooms to change from their travelling clothes and shall join yourself and the guest in a few moments."

"Very well. Please leave the door open and show my family in once they are refreshed. Another tea service with fresh water as well as some cold meats and cheese for the travellers please."

"Yes, ma'am."

"Well, it looks like you shall not have to wait very long to meet with my family. I understand that Miss Bennet and Miss Elizabeth have been in company with my daughter, but Mrs. Collins has not yet been in company with my Anne, as she has been in London since

Christmas. I never stay for the little season, but of course Anne is much in demand at the events given by the *ton* and this year expressed an interest in staying through until our family retired here for Easter. I believe that my nephew Darcy is also in the party, and perhaps my niece Miss Darcy."

At that moment, Darcy walked into the room and went to his aunt to bestow a bow and a kiss to her cheek. "Forgive me Aunt, but Georgiana and Richard will be coming in another few days on our original arrival date. I came to escort Anne early and brought our friend, Mr. Charles Bingley with me as Anne indicated in her last letter." Darcy then turned to the Bennet sisters and Mr. Collins to greet his friends.

"Mrs. Collins, it is lovely to see you again. I have not yet had the pleasure to provide my facilitations for your marriage. I wish you much joy." Darcy bowed respectfully to Mary and extended his hand to an rapturous Collins. "Mr. Collins, congratulations on your lovely wife."

Mary curtsied very prettily and thanked Darcy for his kind words while Collins genuflected repeatedly and was unable to speak for the surprise at being directly addressed with so much familiarity by one such as the great Fitzwilliam Darcy.

Darcy next turned to Elizabeth and Jane who had been sitting together on a settee and gave a very friendly bow then took a seat on the chair nearest Elizabeth, leaving the chair by Jane open. "Miss Bennet, Miss Elizabeth, how nice to see you again. It has barely been a week since the Finch's ball, but it seems like much more time has passed with all that has happened recently."

"You are right Mr. Darcy, we have had such excitement in the past week." Elizabeth spoke softly and continued to give Jane side glances. Her older sister had gone stiff at the mention of Bingley being part of the arriving party and not yet regained her voice. "Meeting with new and old friends, and such a long journey here to my sister and her husband's home. We have had many adventures since last we all danced with Sir James and Lady Finch."

Darcy laughed. "Truly, Miss Elizabeth? A long journey? I know you must jest, for I would say it must be very agreeable for Mrs. Collins to be settled within so easy a distance of her own family and friends."

"An easy distance, do you call it? It is nearly fifty miles."

"And what is fifty miles of good road?" Darcy teased. "Little more than half a day's journey. Yes, I call it a very easy distance."

"I should never have considered the distance as one of the *advantages* of the match," cried Elizabeth. "I should never have said Mary was settled *near* our family."

"It is a proof of your own attachment to Hertfordshire. Anything beyond the very neighbourhood of Longbourn, I suppose, would appear far."

As he spoke, there was a sort of smile which Elizabeth did not fully understand. "I do not mean to say that a woman may not be settled *too* near her family, but I am persuaded my sister would not call herself near our family under less than half the present distance." Seeing a small frown forming on Darcy's face, Elizabeth went on. "However, it is the way of the world that women should leave their family and take their place with their husband. Though Mary is resigned to missing our family much of the year, I believe she is very happy here with my new brother."

Darcy drew his chair a little towards her, and said in a soft, somewhat intimate voice, "You cannot have a right to such very strong local attachment. You cannot have been always at Longbourn."

Elizabeth laughed and backed away from the intensity in Darcy's eyes. "Of course, I have not *always* been at home. My aunt and uncle Gardiner have often had us in London. However, I must admit that the travels of this year are not typical. I have never been further north than one trip with my father to Cambridge to purchase a special book he had arranged for with the head librarian of King's College. And except for one trip to Brighton when I was only three years of age, and do not particularly remember, this is the furthest I have ever been from my home. My uncle Gardiner has invited Jane and myself on a trip to the Peak and Lake Districts this summer, and I am most excited for the excursion."

Darcy was very interested in hearing more about this trip so close to his home, however a small gasp from Jane drew both Elizabeth and Darcy's attention away from their conversation. One look in her direction and it was apparent what had occupied Jane's attention. Charles Bingley and Anne de Bourgh walked into the parlour together. After bowing to his hostess, Bingley let his eyes roam over the room's occupants, and then they stopped on Jane.

The colour, which had been driven from Jane's face, returned for a half a minute with an additional glow, and a small smile of delight added lustre to her eyes as she thought for that span of time that his affection had not weaned. However, she could not be secure. Bingley was likewise looking pleased, embarrassed, and nervous. The persons who were privy to the significant feeling going between Jane and Bingley were all suspended in significant misery, which seemed to stretch into years in only a few moments. Yet, the misery, for which years of happiness might not have offered enough compensation, soon received material relief from observing how much Jane's beauty, serenity, and forgiveness did rekindle the admiration and devotion of her former lover.

Unfortunately, Lady Catherine intruded on the happy mood of the four good friends. "Anne, introduce me again to your friend here. Mr. Bingley, is that your name? I have not heard of your family. Pray tell, who is your mother's family?"

Anne interceded. "Mother, this is Mr. Charles Bingley. He and Darcy were at Cambridge together. His elder sister is married to Mr. Reginald Hurst. He and his sisters are much the favourite of Lady Sefton who often takes her summers at Mr. Hurst's country estate."

Lady Catherine's eyes bulged, and she pulled herself up to her tallest height in the wingback chair she was inhabiting. "Do you mean to tell me that you have brought the son of a *tradesman* to stay in *my* home?"

"No Mother," Anne replied calmly. "I have brought a good friend of myself and Darcy who has been educated as a gentleman and has nearly completed the acquisition of his own estate to be a guest in *my* home."

At Anne's reminder that she was the legal owner of the whole of the Rosings estate, Lady Catherine puckered her lips in such an exaggerated way that Elizabeth had to hide another smile behind her (Darcy's) handkerchief.

Lady Catherine turned to Bingley. "Is this right? Are you purchasing an estate for yourself?"

"Yes, it is." Bingley nodded. "I currently have a two-year lease on the estate nearest to the Bennets' family home called Netherfield. I have not made a final decision on whether to purchase the property, as the owner and I have not come to agreeable terms, however it is the wish of my father that I purchase an estate within the next few years."

"So, you are acquainted with the Miss Bennets' family, and Mr. Collins?" Lady Catherine asked.

"Yes! We have all known each other since Michaelmas when I came to the neighbourhood." Here, Bingley directed another bright and adoring look towards Jane.

"Well, then you shall stay with Mr. Collins and his family at the parsonage." Lady Catherine stated firmly. "It is a much more appropriate arrangement than having the halls of Rosings polluted with such *tradesmen.*"

Everyone in the room looked aghast at Lady Catherine. Collins, who would normally not dream of going against his patroness, was very uncomfortable with this plan. For one, he did not have the appropriate room for an unmarried male guest plus Bingley's personal servant without having his sisters share a very small room with only a single person bed. Additionally, and more concerning, he knew that Jane and Bingley were courting. He did not want to host the man in his home with the possibility that he and Jane could have inappropriate contact under his roof. It was unsupportable.

Thankfully, Anne spoke up before Collins had to oppose his patroness. "Mother! I am appalled at you. Mr. Bingley is a particular friend of myself, Darcy, and Richard. He is a well-respected member of the *ton* and is regularly invited to the best homes of the highest persons in town. He is educated, mannerly, and *my invited* guest. Besides, it would be inappropriate for Mr. Bingley to stay in a house with so many unmarried ladies present without their father in residence. I shall hear no more of this. Not one word. He is already installed in the guest wing and shall share the room attached to Richard's. Now, I must beg my share of conversation with the new Mrs. Collins. If we are to be neighbours, we must also be friends. Come and join me here on the settee by the fireplace as I am still a bit chilled from the trip."

The Collins party stayed another thirty minutes, but none of the people present regained their easy demeanour. Collins spent the time trying to placate Lady Catherine. Anne and Mary had a pleasant conversation as they began their acquaintance, however it was not very deep on the topics covered. Darcy, Elizabeth, Bingley and Jane sat together drinking tea and not saying much beyond general inquiries after each other's family and shared acquaintances. There was too much hanging in the air after Lady Catherine's officiousness for any of them to regain their ease. The only joy in the remainder of the evening was Elizabeth's observation of Bingley, for while he spoke but little, every five minutes he seemed to give Jane his full attention with an adoring look. Jane was anxious that no difference in her demeanour should be perceived and tried to come up with topics for conversation, but her mind was so busily engaged that she did not always know when she was silent.

In both too short a time and an eternity later, Lady Catherine's butler came into the parlour to announce that the carriage was ready to take the Collinses and the Miss Bennets back to the parsonage. A few stilted farewells later and the party was broken up for the evening.

Pleasing Company

ON THE CARRIAGE RIDE BACK TO THE PARSONAGE, everyone was uniquely quiet. Elizabeth was overwhelmed with the treatment of Bingley by Lady Catherine. It seemed to confirm all her worst fears about Darcy's family. And Jane was desperately trying to control her blush over the heightened emotions of seeing Bingley again after so long a time.

As soon as they all alighted from the carriage, Elizabeth announced that she had had quite enough excitement for the day and was ready to retire. Once in her bed shift, Elizabeth went to Jane's room to see how her sister was faring. Jane was sitting at the mirror, fully dressed and holding her brush, but not taking down her hair. Elizabeth took the brush from Jane and started to take down her hair pins then brushed out her long blond locks. Not much was said for several minutes.

"Now," Jane finally said, "that this first meeting is over, I feel perfectly easy. I know my own strength and I shall never be embarrassed again by his company. I am glad that he will be in the neighbourhood. It will then be publicly seen, that on both sides, we met only as common and indifferent acquaintances."

Elizabeth laughed. "Oh yes, very indifferent indeed."

"Lizzy, please! You cannot think me so weak as to be in danger now."

"I think you are in very great danger of making him as much in love with you as he ever was." Elizabeth spoke plainly but kindly.

Jane finally stood to disrobe and hang her dress in the closet. "I cannot understand why he has come to Kent. His arrival was certainly not met with pleasure from Lady Catherine, though Miss de Bourgh had some stern words on the subject."

Elizabeth sat upon the bed and hugged her knees to her chest. "Yes, her ladyship was very firm in her opinion about Mr. Bingley's welcome in her home. How much more should she be disinclined to have any of us under her roof? It was very uncomfortable to be so strongly faced with the feelings of superiority displayed by Lady Catherine."

Jane eyed Elizabeth suspiciously. It had been many weeks since they had argued over Darcy's interest in Elizabeth. All their time in London showed that the gentleman definitively had some feelings for her. However, there had been nothing at all close to an understanding. He did not even come to call on Elizabeth on the day after the Finch's ball, which Jane thought he should have given that he danced with Elizabeth twice at that event. Jane was beginning to worry that Elizabeth's initial impression of Darcy was accurate and the gentleman did not have serious intentions for her sister.

For many reasons, sparing Jane's feelings chief among them, Elizabeth had kept her discussion with Darcy in St. Paul's churchyard to herself. The tender moments were much too dear to her to be able to share with her sister and she did not wish to have any expectations or demands from their private encounter raised by her aunt and uncle. Darcy had ridden directly home after seeing Elizabeth to her uncle's door, so none of her family had seen him in the street and they were not aware that the two had met the morning after the ball.

"Lizzy, what do you think of Mr. Darcy's relations?" Jane asked, pulling Elizabeth out of her pensive thoughts.

"Well, Georgiana is delightful, but you know that. Anne and Colonel Fitzwilliam are lovely companions and I am glad they shall be with us for much of our visit here. It shall be a pleasure to see them often in a more relaxed setting than London. Maybe we can ask Mary to organise a picnic or other outdoor entertainments as the weather promises to be quite fine."

"And what of the Matlocks and Lady Catherine?"

Elizabeth sighed. "What of them, Jane?"

"Well, what do you think of them?"

Elizabeth rested her head on her knees and looked at Jane from the side. "They are what I would expect from such highly placed persons. I did not much speak to Lord Matlock in London, but Lady Matlock seemed to be slightly disdainful of our company. Lady Catherine sees us as entertaining company with manners enough to invite to a small country dinner party, but her opinion of where the Bennets and Bingleys place in the social hierarchy was made quite clear this evening. She would not welcome a close connection to us, I am sure." Elizabeth sighed and tried to lighten the mood. "And why should either welcome our connection? What good is a title if not to inflate the ego? It is silly to be offended at their attitude. It is the way of the nobility, is it not?"

Jane felt badly for her sister but could not dispute what she had said after witnessing Lady Catherine's attitude that evening.

After a moment, Elizabeth rose from Jane's bed and kissed her sister goodnight. Both young unmarried ladies slept with considerable unease all night.

The next morning, promptly, at eleven a.m., Anne, Darcy and Bingley knocked on the door to the Hunsford parsonage to ask after the inhabitants of the house. Anne took Mary by the arm and declared that they should enjoy a stroll around the grounds of Rosings as the sun was shining and it was such a lovely day.

Collins declined and instead made mention of attending to his routine and working in his garden, which was large and well laid out. Mary had been encouraging him in his endeavour due to the healthfulness of the exercise as well as the practicality of growing such a fine kitchen garden. The surplus of which was shared with the needy members of their congregation.

As soon as the whole party was beyond the Collins's garden fence, Bingley quickly claimed Jane's companionship, leaving Elizabeth and Darcy to stroll around the path arm-in-arm. Bingley had spent the entire night coming up with topics of conversation which might lead to a more direct line of communication between himself and Jane. He had mostly decided on starting with the information that he had recently taken dinner with her family when Jane surprised him and herself by asking directly of his purpose in Kent.

"Mr. Bingley, I was astonished to find you travelled here with Mr. Darcy and Miss de Bourgh. We have been planning this excursion to my sister and her husband for many weeks and Mr. Darcy, with his sister, has been very involved in those plans. Miss Darcy and Lizzy have planned many outdoor games once she arrives later in the week. But we have seen and heard nothing of your involvement in the party. What has made you now come to Kent when you have been so absent in London?"

Bingley stopped on the path and allowed some distance to separate themselves from the rest of the walking party. "Miss Bennet, I fully intend to answer your question, but I would like to ask you something first. Has my absence caused you pain?"

"That is unacceptably forward, sir! What is your purpose for asking such a question?"

Bingley took both of Jane's hands between his own. "My purpose in asking is to determine how much grovelling I must engage in before you will forgive my foolishness."

Jane looked up sharply into Bingley's eyes and gasped at the depth of feeling in them. "I fear that your absence has been extremely trying for me. Some days I despaired of ever knowing happiness again. I was certain I would never trust a man again with my heart. Why were you so absent? We called upon your sister and spent *weeks* with Mr. Darcy and Miss Darcy. Did you even care that I was in town and missing you?"

"I swear to you that I did not know you were in town. My sister did not tell me of your visit for her own purposes, and she will not escape my displeasure at such deception. Also, Darcy and I had not seen each other nor spoken since before he was aware of your presence in town. I only learned all of this about a week ago, when I went to visit Netherfield and had dinner with your mother, father, and youngest sisters."

"What do you mean you took dinner with my mother? You truly did not know I was in town?" Jane ended in a whisper.

Bingley sighed and turned them both back to the path to continue walking. Elizabeth and Darcy were still in sight but would shortly be too far ahead to maintain strict propriety. Bingley did not want Jane to think he was taking advantage of her emotional state. "We should continue on the path. I shall relate the story as we walk, though I beg you to let me finish before judging me too harshly."

Jane nodded and took Bingley's arm as they continued to walk. He took care to relate all of his time in London and his black moods since January.

"Eventually, I decided that I had to find out for myself if you and I could match in affection. I called for my horse to be saddled and rode straight to Netherfield, being unaware that you were at your uncle Gardiner's home in London. I am sorry that my foolish behaviour kept me from seeking you out sooner. We might have been reunited weeks ago had I not sequestered myself in my house. That brings me to now, here in Kent. I came here to Rosings for the express purpose of calling on you and asking for your forgiveness. I intend to stay here and prove my faithfulness to you, then when you are ready, if you ever wish it, I shall ask you to be my wife. Until then, I will do your bidding. I shall be here as much as you desire and if you wish it, I shall leave you be."

It was too much to be endured! Jane walked arm-in-arm with the man whom she had hoped and wished would make exactly this declaration for many months, and now she was seized with fear. What was the right course of action?

She decided to be honest. "Mr. Bingley, that is an extraordinary story. It seems there has been much between us that has never been said. As much as I have hoped for your declarations, I find that I am in this moment not prepared to hear them. I have been very hurt by your abandonment these past months. And though you have not intentionally inflicted such pain on me, I do not know how to begin to trust that you will not cause me similar pain in the future. I believe I need some time before I will agree to a more formal understanding between us."

Bingley stopped them again and turned Jane towards himself. "You shall have all the time you require. I promise you, from this moment on, I shall be constant. You shall never have one moment to doubt me, and I shall never doubt you. I will never marry another and shall wait for you all my days. If you choose to put your trust in me, I will never give you one moment to repine."

After the Rosings party said their goodbyes and plans for a picnic the next day were made, Mary, Elizabeth and Jane retired to the sunny south-facing parlour in the parsonage.

"So," Mary began, "what happy news might we be able to share, hmm? Jane, anything to discuss about your walk with Mr. Bingley? You did seem to lag behind the group at such a distance to make private conversation quite easy. Pray tell, how is his family?"

Elizabeth jumped in with sisterly teasing. "Yes, do tell us all about Mr. Bingley's family. How is Miss Bingley enjoying the little season? Has Mrs. Hurst had her fill of dancing while in town? When are they all to visit the seaside?"

Jane blushed under the attention of her two sisters. "You are both completely incorrigible. I am sure we only had a very sensible conversation which did not discuss anything of his sisters except their general health." She picked up her sewing basket and started to concentrate on the shawl she had begun to embroider as a gift to Kitty.

Neither of her sisters were inclined to let the moment pass. "Oh no! That is not at all true, and I am sorry to say sister, but your fair colouring gives you away in how brightly you blush. Now, tell us all about it." Elizabeth snatched the sewing basket and put it out of Jane's reach.

"I am not sure what you want to hear."

Mary had found, in her few months of marriage, that forthright communication and kindness were the best tools for forcing a confidence where one was not inclined to provide disclosures. Her husband, used to being on his own, had been unexpectedly tight-lipped early on in their relationship about his likes and dislikes. He was quite verbose on everything else in his life, but what dinner dishes he preferred, how much starch he liked in his clothing, and how often he wished to enjoy the marriage bed had been difficult to get him to opine upon. Mary had learned quite quickly how to broach sensitive topics and decided to exercise her right as the only married lady present to force the issue with her older sister.

"Now, Jane, I know that it might be embarrassing to speak of confidences from Mr. Bingley, but as your hostess, and your chaperone and protector along with my husband, I must hear how today's interview progressed. What are his intentions and what are your feelings regarding those intentions?"

"Oh Mary, forgive me, sister, for not giving you your due as our hostess." Jane began to fidget with her dress and the edge of her wrap. "Well, if you must know, we spoke of why he has been absent these past months. It was a combination of not knowing I was in London and being unsure of my affection. He claims he had determined to know the truth and went to my father to seek permission to call upon me last week."

This was new information to Elizabeth and Mary. Neither Anne nor Darcy had discussed the gentlemen's harrowing trip to Hertfordshire and back to London in a rainstorm. "He spoke to Papa? How did he come to be here in Kent?" Mary asked.

"Yes, he says he went to Netherfield to see if he might call on me. Apparently Mr. Darcy followed him, and they both took dinner with our father, mother, Kitty and Lydia."

"So, he comes for you." Mary stated firmly.

Jane could only nod in response.

"Well, this is marvellous!" Mary clapped her hands. "I cannot think of a better time for a courtship than springtime and Easter, which is the promise of rebirth and new beginnings. I shall see you as happily married as I am before many more months. How splendid!"

"I have not agreed to a courtship yet."

Mary considered her sister for a moment. "I shall not press you to make any understanding with Mr. Bingley, but I would like to know what has you upset, dear. Was Mr. Bingley's reappearance not everything you wanted when you left for London in January?"

"Well, yes. I am sure it was. However, it has been so many weeks, months even, since we last saw each other! And I have been so miserable since. If he was so easily swayed by others' opinions, what assurance do I have that he will not be swayed again and set me aside?" Tears began to prick at the corner of Jane's eyes.

Elizabeth was alarmed at Jane's reaction. "Janey, my sweet sister. I have never heard you in such a state. You are always so assured of the goodness of others."

"And *you* have always teased me for that trait!" Jane cried in earnest. "Is it not you who once told me that my goodness, and my belief in the goodness of all around me, was illogical? That literature and history are overflowing with examples of men of ill repute? And even in our real lives there are men and women who are not to be trusted! What of the stories that Mr. Wickham has been telling of Mr. Darcy's father? One of the two of them must be at fault there. Either Mr. Darcy's father is unkind and has abandoned his orphaned God son, or Mr. Wickham is lying. And there are the stories of that man who used to work for the butcher. Laudie Kellogg says he promised to marry her, and that her baby was his natural child. How is one to ever trust a man if they can just disappear for months and it is women who always bear the consequences?" Jane was now worked up to a point of nearly gasping for air.

"Dearest, do calm down." Elizabeth brought out her handkerchief from Darcy and gently wiped away Jane's tears. "Yes, of course some men are scoundrels and liars and rakes. But certainly not all men. Even Laudie Kellogg did not suffer for long. Mr. Wainwright married her even before little Jeremiah was weaned. It was unfortunate for a time, but Laudie now has two beautiful boys and another child on the way. We cannot fear living, or distrust everyone around us. Now, I do not want to tell you that this new attitude is wholly bad. You are right that Mr. Wickham is a liar and we should take care with our hearts and our reputations. However, some men may be trusted. Papa for one is a man who loves us and would not let us suffer a scoundrel." Elizabeth was rubbing soothing circles on Jane's back trying to stem the tide of tears streaming down her face.

Mary spoke up next. "Lizzy is correct. Papa was kind to me in my choice of husband and we had known Mr. Collins much less time when I was married than we have now known Mr. Bingley. All we know for sure is that Mr. Bingley takes matters of the heart very seriously. I believe that we may take him at his word and in the future, you shall be the chief influence on your husband. Good men are made better with steady and faithful wives. This is one of the reasons God gave us matrimony. You shall not suffer if you put your faith in a man who can come to make amends and freely admit he was wrong. If you are very much worried over the choice, I shall ask my husband to write to Papa and we shall hear what he thinks of Mr. Bingley."

Collins, who had come in from the garden when he saw the ladies return to the house, was approaching the door to the parlour when he heard Jane's distress. With a wife such as Mary, he was not well accustomed to female hysterics. However, he listened at the door to ensure that all was well with his sister for which he was now responsible. He decided that, at the mention of writing to their father, it was a good time to come and deliver some news which had been brought in the mail.

"Sister Jane, I am sorry for listening to your distress, but I have some correspondence from your wise father which might be of use in this moment. You see, I wrote to your esteemed father before your arrival to ask him for any specific instructions he might have in the time that you shall be under my care, and his reply has come this very morning while you were all walking with the party from Rosings. It appears that Mr. Bingley asked permission to call upon you and Mr. Bennet has given his permission. He says specifically that I should, and I quote, 'Give the young man a stern look and be sure to guarantee that he treats my Janey with all the respect that is her due, but do not be too hard on him as he has already dared to face my frightening presence.' I shall not fail you sister. He shall be all that is respectable while in your presence or I shall send him away."

Jane smiled at Collins and her sisters. "Well, if my family finds that he is not too bad, and my brother and father approve of his suit, then I could do much worse than consider his courtship. I shall watch, and if I find that he is all that a young man ought to be, sensible, good-humoured, lively, with happy manners, and *constant*, I shall give myself leave to like him once again."

Happy News

"NO! I GIVE UP. THIS GAME MUST BE RIGGED. I SHALL go back to drinking lemonade under the shade with Miss Lizzy and leave this ridiculous hoop tossing to my equally ridiculous cousins." Richard tossed his dowel rods towards Georgiana and waved off the laughter of Darcy, Bingley, Jane and Anne.

Elizabeth was even less inclined to leave Richard alone. She greeted him laughingly. "Poor Colonel! *Le jeu des graces* is certainly not your best game."

Richard harrumphed. "I have never had much time for games designed for young girls. I cannot think why Anne pulled it out from the attic."

"She asked Mary which games we Bennet sisters loved from home and this was one of my mother's absolute favourite games. It was supposed to teach young ladies to be more graceful. She read about it in *Le Belle Assemblée* and determined to have us each play. We used old embroidery hoops and sticks that my father whittled for us. I was always the best, though I do not believe I was ever very graceful playing." Elizabeth laughed heartily. "I was known to, on more than one occasion, dive to the ground to make a catch. I had more grass stains from playing that silly game than all the times I would wander off into the woods or climb trees."

Richard huffed a laugh and poured another glass of cool lemonade for both himself and Elizabeth. "I must say, I saw something of that urge when you soundly defeated Darcy. There was one moment when he dropped his rods thinking you were going to fall and heroically sacrificed the point to be ready to catch you."

Elizabeth blushed deeply. It had been a close call and quite embarrassing. As Richard said, her childhood instinct had taken over for a moment and she leapt forward to make a difficult catch. She had managed to maintain her footing, but barely. When she righted herself, Darcy had been inches away with his arms outstretched waiting to catch her. Thankfully, it was the tenth point of the game and she was able to pass her rods on to Jane then go take a rest on the lawn chairs set up under a tree. It was not that Elizabeth felt winded from the game, but her heart was beating quite fast, and her face was very flushed.

Clearing her throat again, she turned back to Richard from watching Darcy play opposite his sister while Jane was patiently teaching Bingley how to correctly launch the hoop into the air. "Yes, of course Mr. Darcy would never let a lady fall. He is all that is chivalrous."

"I do not know, Miss Lizzy. I do believe he might have competition for which of our companions is the most chivalrous. Bingley is acting very much the knight in shining armour these days. Why, yesterday he used his own hat to shield Miss Bennet's bonnet from the start of the rain while escorting her to the carriage after dinner. It was barely sprinkling! In fact, I am sure I felt fewer than five drops the entire five minutes I was outside handing Mrs. Collins into the carriage. I have never seen the man so in love as he is with your sister. It is a good thing that he left behind that supposed heartache from the winter and came with Darcy to Kent. I believe I have rarely ever seen a couple more well matched than Bingley and Miss Bennet. In fact, I can think of only one such couple."

Richard gave Elizabeth a significant look, but she missed it as she was wringing her handkerchief in her hands. The same handkerchief that Darcy had given her in the churchyard of St. Paul's.

She had not spoken of what Richard revealed at the Finch's ball to anyone since talking to Darcy the morning afterwards. Not even to Jane. At first, Elizabeth did not want to further upset Jane with the added knowledge that persons whom they all counted as friends had actively tried to separate her from the man she hoped to marry, even if some of those people had good intentions. Then, it was a moot point after Bingley came riding into Kent with Darcy and Anne. After Jane's revelation that Bingley came to Kent for the express purpose of courting her sister, Elizabeth decided to let all the past rest and see what the future would bring.

The last week of entertainments had been a joy. Mary and Anne were becoming quite good friends and all the young people at Rosings and Hunsford were spending each afternoon together. Picnics, open carriage rides around the countryside, or lawn games had been arranged each day. On the one afternoon of rain three days ago, Anne had sent the carriage to Hunsford parish house and invited them all to a game of charades at Rosings. Even last Sunday there had been some light entertainment after church to accompany the cold meats. Elizabeth and Mary had performed several musical numbers and duets during the evenings at Rosings. Anne, who loved music but never learned to play due to the lingering pain in her hands from her childhood illness, invited Mary to come whenever she wanted to play on the fine pianoforte in the Rosings music room. She might as well have given Mary her own pianoforte, it was such a kind gesture.

It was lovely to see her sisters enjoying the company so much.

Richard and Georgiana had arrived two days ago and jumped right into the fray.

Elizabeth knew that Richard was not aware of who had been at the centre of Bingley's 'winter heartache' or how that had been resolved, but it was outside of Elizabeth's acting skills to not react to his words.

"Miss Lizzy? Are you alright? I did not mean to bring up indelicate topics."

"Richard! Might I speak to you for a moment" Before Elizabeth could reply to Richard's inquiry, Darcy had come over and in a rather demanding attitude commanded his cousin's attention.

"A moment Darce. Miss Liz."

"No, I believe you have importuned on Miss *Elizabeth* quite enough. Come, I must have your attention."

Darcy nearly pulled Richard from his chair and dragged him across the lawn to another large shade tree. "What in the world were you saying to Elizabeth? She looked positively stricken!"

"Nothing! I merely commented on how much Bingley looked smitten with her sister and that I was glad he accompanied you here to recover from his winter depression."

"What? Why would you say something like that to her?"

"It is not like Miss Lizzy and I have not discussed Bingley's mood over the winter before now. We spoke of him at the Finch's ball during our dance."

Darcy took in a sharp breath. "It was you!"

"What was me? I have done nothing untoward, I promise!"

Darcy shook his head and laughed a bit humourlessly. "You are the person who told Elizabeth that Bingley had been discouraged from pursuing Miss Bennet."

"What? Why in the world would I have said that? And when could I have said such? He has just come to Kent and they are clearly enjoying each other's company now! I just said to Miss Lizzy that it was a good thing he left his heartache behind as he was most perfectly matched with her sister."

"This is not the first time that Bingley and Miss Bennet have been in close company. In fact, Miss Bennet is the young woman over whom Bingley despaired all winter."

Richard stared dumbfounded at Darcy. "I… what… It was Miss Jane Bennet from whom you separated Bingley?"

Darcy nodded. "Yes. Though I did not overtly do anything to separate them, I certainly did not encourage he return to her side. I told him that I believed she was indifferent."

Richard scoffed. "How can you know what a woman thinks? They are unknowable creatures at the best of times, and Miss Bennet seems a rather shy young lady. I imagine she is not overt with her heart. However, having known her in London and now in Kent, the difference is too pronounced for even this perpetual bachelor to notice. She is fully smitten with Bingley and he with her. I think you should turn your powers of persuasion on Bingley again and get that man to propose and put the rest of us out of misery."

"I agree with you. However, I interfered once. I will allow their relationship to grow at the pace they choose from now on. I will, though, give hearty congratulations once he secures her hand, and stand up with him at the wedding if he wishes."

"Darce, I must ask, this *unpleasantness* with her sister and Bingley, it is not the reason *you* have been dithering over a particular question for Miss Lizzy, is it?"

Darcy coughed and ran his hands through his hair. "I have not… that is to say, I have been waiting for a moment of relative privacy to… to… speak with Elizabeth."

"'*Faint heart never won fair lady.*'"

"I do believe I have heard that one before, however I would like to strangle the sage for it." Darcy grumbled. "I just want the moment to be special and outside the hearing of our respective families. If a moment comes, I promise I shall not waste it."

"I shall leave you for now, but be sure that you do not waste one moment. I do not believe *Miss* Lizzy is a lady well suited to waiting."

"Noted. Shall we rejoin the party?"

Richard gave Darcy a bolstering clap on the shoulder. "Lead the way, old chap."

As soon as Darcy and Richard walked away to have a private chat, Jane came over to beg her sister to come for a short walk. "Please, there is a pretty sort of grove just on the other side of the line of pine trees that I wish to see, and I am sure you would like to stretch your legs for a bit after sitting in one attitude for so long. Take a turn about the lawn with me."

"Very well, Jane. I shall come. Let me grab one of the parasols that Lady Catherine sent out to us. If she sees us escaping through the yard without one we shall be subjected to a very stern discussion at dinner, then again from our brother in the carriage ride home."

Jane plucked a sweet pink parasol from the basket sent out with the refreshments from their hostess. "Now, be kind Lizzy. Her ladyship has been very solicitous of our entire party and the entertainments have been beyond gracious. I have not had such fun in many years!"

Elizabeth smiled at her sweet sister and took her arm as they walked away from the ears of their companions. "You are correct, I shall be civil, nay even kind, to her Ladyship. It is no hardship to endure her *solicitations* when the company is so fine. Now we have separated our-selves from the group, what is it you wish to speak of?"

Jane blushed. "Why do you think I have something I want to talk about? This was just a nice little walk in the sunshine."

"Out with it Jane. I know you well enough to know that this is not a simple walkabout. I promise I shall listen and hang on your every word."

Jane fiddled with the handle of the parasol. "Charles has been rather attentive this past week, has he not?"

Elizabeth raised her eyebrows at the use of Bingley's Christian name, but let it go. "Yes, I would say that he has been wonderfully attentive and most *solicitous* of you."

"Yes, he has been wonderful. And I find myself wishing for him to move along and maybe bring up talk of a formal courtship or more, but he has not said anything at all." Jane spoke so softly that Elizabeth had to strain to hear her words.

"Does this concern you? Without any joking, he has been excessively attentive to you. I am sure he acts much a man in love."

"That is just it, he acts it, but he does not speak of it." Jane looked very frustrated. "I was thinking last night of what he said to me on our first full day in company here. I told him I was not prepared to hear his declarations at that time and then he said, '*You shall have all the time you require.*' Do you think he is waiting on *me* to say something?"

Elizabeth thought for a moment. It was not entirely proper for a lady to initiate conversations of such a forward nature, but Bingley *did* start this dialogue, even if it was nearly a week ago. It would also be good for her shy sister to have practice in leading her husband a little and expressing her wants to him. Elizabeth was also sure that Bingley would not be offended if Jane took the next step for them.

"Dear Jane. I believe that you are the best person to know how your relationship with Mr. Bingley should unfold. If you believe he is waiting on some sign from you that you are ready to proceed with a courtship or something more, then I shall not dissuade you from that action. He is a man uniquely given to good moods, and he loves you dearly. I do not believe that he would ever be offended at your hinting of your feelings or desires."

"How does one even go about such a conversation?"

Elizabeth laughed at the distress in Jane's voice. "Sweet Jane! It is not something of which to be afraid. All you need say is that you have been enjoying his company and that you are exceedingly glad he came to Kent. It has already been said, by him, that he came here for the sole purpose of courting you. So, any acknowledgement of your happiness at his presence will rather be a confirmation of your receptiveness of his suite."

"You make it sound so easy."

"Dearest, not all things must be hard."

After completing their circuit of the yard and bypassing the path to the grove behind the pine trees completely, Elizabeth steered Jane back to the group. Bingley greeted the sisters with his usual unbridled enthusiasm.

"There you both are, come and play lawn tennis with us. The footmen have just finished putting up the net and Miss de Bourgh has procured four rackets. It looks to be good fun."

Before Jane could respond, Elizbeth took the racket from Bingley and stepped away from Jane. "I have been looking forward to lawn tennis, but Jane was just expressing a desire to make another circuit about the garden. She has never been much of an enthusiast for games with a racket."

Bingley looked back and forth between Jane and Elizabeth, then seemed to realise what Elizabeth was suggesting.

"Well, I would be honoured to escort Miss Bennet around the garden while the others play tennis. Shall we?" Bingley held out his arm to Jane with a look of contentment and joy at his chance for a relatively private interlude.

Jane took Bingley's arm and gave Elizabeth a nervous look. Elizabeth simply smiled and waved a small goodbye before flouncing off towards the tennis net.

"It certainly has been a wonderful afternoon. The sun has provided just enough warmth, but not so much that it is too hot. I thoroughly enjoyed the hoop and sticks game, even if Richard declared it was a game for little girls. And now a stroll through the garden with the most beautiful of ladies on my arm. What could be a better afternoon? Nothing,

I do say." Bingley was babbling a bit, wondering how much he should say, or if he should take advantage of their privacy to advance his cause.

"Mr. Bingley, might I say, that… well, I have very much enjoyed your company here in Kent," Jane stammered. Immediately after speaking, she flushed bright red and ducked her face under the brim of her bonnet.

Bingley was stunned and elated! Did Jane just admit to enjoying his company? Was she perhaps receptive to his declarations now? Bingley had only a few moments to contemplate this turn in the conversation when Jane interjected again.

"I might even say that your purpose in coming has been successful."

Bingley stopped them on the path and turned directly to Jane. "My purpose was to please you and win your heart before asking for your hand. Is this the purpose of which you speak?"

Jane was too embarrassed to look at Bingley, but she found her courage in her voice. "Yes. I have not been under false pretence about your purpose and I believe if you were to speak now, you would find positive answers to any questions you wished to ask."

"You mean that you would agree to a courtship with me?"

"I daresay, I would be amenable to a courtship… or… something more." Jane flushed an even deeper red all the way to the tips of her ears.

Bingley breathed heavily for a moment, then dropped to one knee.

"Jane Bennet, I promise to love you for as long as I live. I shall always put your happiness and the happiness of any children with which we are blessed before all else. Please, relieve my suffering and make me the happiest of men. Please be my wife?"

Jane looked into Bingley's sincere eyes and found her voice once again. "Yes."

Bingley whooped and stood in a rush, catching Jane in his arms, and twirling her around twice before setting her down again on the ground. Cheers and clapping could be heard from their friends and family across the lawn who had watched in rapt attention when Bingley fell to his knee, assuming correctly what was taking place. Richard whistled loudly while Elizabeth and Mary rushed over to their sister to provide hugs and kisses. As the acting head of Jane's family as well as her guardian, Collins went directly to Bingley to shake his hand and welcome him to the family. Collins also took a significant number of words to inform them that Mr. Bennet had previously provided his consent by letter to an engagement should one be agreed to by Jane, so, they could consider their understanding official.

Darcy shook Bingley's hand in congratulations and looked longingly at Elizabeth. His conversation with Richard was loud in his mind and he redoubled his promise to himself to take advantage of his own moment, or make one happen, soon.

One Proposal and Two Broken Hearts (Take Two)

AFTER BINGLEY AND JANE FINALISED THEIR UNDER-standing, the whole tone of the Bennet sisters' visit to Kent seemed to change. Collins was immensely proud to stand in for Mr. Bennet and be able to provide consent to the engagement for his sister, even though Jane was over the age of consent. However, Collins and Mary insisted on more complete chaperoning of the newly affianced couple, to maintain propriety. Wherever possible, Elizabeth was present at all times while Jane and Bingley were in company, and since the young people from the Hunsford parish and Rosings were ever in company together, Elizabeth seemed to be physically attached to Jane at all hours of the day. Even Elizabeth's typical solitary morning walks had been curtailed for her to be present in the parlour and dining room when Bingley called for Jane each morning. It was no true hardship for Elizabeth, but Darcy was finding himself quite put out.

It had also been determined that Jane and Bingley would curtail their time in Kent and return to London to obtain Jane's trousseau.

Mrs. Bennet had the wedding plans in Hertfordshire well in hand and required little input from her eldest daughter. Elizabeth would have been beside herself worrying about what her mother had planned if this was her own wedding, but Jane was much too sweet and easy going to object to anything that their mother wanted for her wedding. All Jane truly cared about was the groom, and that had already been arranged to her satisfaction.

Originally, Collins had insisted that Elizabeth go with Jane in Bingley's carriage since neither Bingley nor Collins had a female maid to send with Jane. Elizabeth was a bit disappointed to cut her time with her friends, but understood it was the right course of action and was resigned to leaving a full three weeks earlier than originally intended.

Darcy was not at all happy with the arrangement. He had been trying to find some way of engaging Elizabeth in private for weeks, but to no avail. Also, he was certain that his chances of a private conversation would evaporate as soon as she left Kent. There was nothing else to do, he had to find some way to get Elizabeth to stay in Kent at least until her original departure date.

Georgiana unwittingly provided the perfect solution to his dilemma. Her companion, Mrs. Annesley, was desirous of visiting her sister in London who had been recently delivered of a son. Georgiana was more than willing to send her to London for a very nice visit, especially since there was plenty of female companionship to be had at Rosings this year. So, Darcy suggested to Bingley and Collins that it would be a great favour to himself if they would permit Mrs. Annesley to ride with Jane to London, and if Elizabeth would, perhaps stay and then ride back to London with Georgiana, and himself of course.

Collins was inclined to give Darcy anything he designed to ask, and so it was very satisfactorily decided that Elizabeth would remain in Kent while Jane went back to London to shop for her wedding clothes.

On the final night before Jane and Bingley were to leave Kent, Anne hosted a very grand dinner for all of their friends and family as a celebration of their engagement. The night was a wonderful success and even Lady Catherine was convivial and congratulatory. At least as much as the great lady was ever able to be.

"Mr. Bingley, I congratulate you on your engagement. It is a good match for you to be married to a gently bred woman whose father owns a well-respected and long-standing estate. Now, you *must* purchase your own estate in which to install this young beauty as that is now your purpose as shown to you by God."

Anne, Darcy and Richard all tensed at Lady Catherine's tone. This was a most inauspicious opening line for a discussion which might quickly go downhill if allowed to roll in the direction that Lady Catherine was wont to move.

Before any of her family could intervene, however, Bingley responded with his usual good charm and naiveté. "Your Ladyship, I do not take your meaning. Though I am not opposed to purchasing my own estate, and have been making direct progress towards this very goal, I am unfamiliar with any directive from the Almighty."

"Yes, of course this is what has been decreed by God. It is the way of our lives and the foundation of our society. God has given you the money and success from the lower ranks of society to purchase your way into the more refined and genteel ranks of society. Now, He has provided you with a wife of little fortune, but connection to land. God uses land, money and connection to His chosen monarch to order society. Sometimes, someone who is not worthy shall be set to inherit these implements of our Lord, and in His infinite wisdom, He will make a change in inheritance through those means which are only available to the Almighty. You can see it clearly in the Bennet family. Something in the past must have befallen your father as he has no sons, however your father has been rewarded now with the wisdom to marry one of his daughters to the man who will inherit the estate. God has also awarded Mr. Collins with the inheritance and such a well deserving wife for his adherence to God's dictates and the great respect he shows to his betters. Some men are not granted sons, some are struck down, and others see the waste of their estates to such an extent that they are required to sell off their land to pay their debts. These tragedies befall men of lesser quality and elevate men who are worthy in His eyes. It has always been so in our family. Do you not agree, Fitzwilliam?"

Darcy was uncomfortable with his aunt's long held beliefs regarding land and money. "I am not sure I can fully agree with you, Aunt.

I cannot claim to know anything of God's ineffable plan or the ways in which He provides for the world, but I would not say that the men in my family's past who have perished to redirect the inheritance of Pemberley towards my father and myself were unworthy or somehow of lesser moral quality than those who have been given much. Also, many men, women and children die each year of those things which are not in anyone's control. War, pestilence and famine are chief among the killers of humankind, and I do not believe that these are necessarily implements of God so much as nightmares emanating from the human condition and maybe even the human mind. We shall never conquer death, as it is an inextricable part of the human condition, however we can and should do what we can to help those less fortunate instead of lord over them and pretend we are better for having money or a connection to power."

"Well! I never imagined that I had a *Quaker* in my home!"

Darcy shook his head and nearly laughed. Only his aunt could evoke the name of God in her argument, then deride someone for espousing charity and peace. "Now Aunt, be reasonable. I am as devoted to the Anglican church as any man can be, but it is hardly heretical to say that the inheritance of land and money are not so much the dictates of God as the whims of the universe. The Lord gave us free-will and so we must take responsibility for the good and the bad in our lives without losing sight that some of life is luck."

Lady Catherine had heard enough of such nonsense from her relations and fully turned her back on Darcy, then spoke directly to her loyal minister.

"Mr. Collins, I expect that you shall give us all good instruction on the role of God in the nobility, and our duty, as good *Anglican* men and women, to follow His divine plan for not only ourselves but for our country."

Collins bowed deeply. "Of course, my lady. I shall start writing this evening and bring my first draft to you tomorrow after luncheon for your review and approval."

"See that you do!"

In the weeks that followed Bingley and Jane's departure for London, life for the remaining inhabitants of Rosings and Hunsford became much less exciting. By some unspoken agreement, the daily outings slowed to only one or two per week, and the invitations to dine at Rosings dwindled to only one evening per week plus the usual Sunday tea and cold meats. Elizabeth and Georgiana had become grand friends and chose to spend many mornings walking the grounds together when Elizabeth would have normally been at peace to take such walks in solitude. Darcy was loath to discourage such a close relationship between his sister and the object of his heart, but wished that Georgiana might give him some privacy to converse with Elizabeth outside of the watchful eyes of their families.

As days turned into weeks, Darcy was nearly desperate to find some time alone with Elizabeth to make his declarations.

Richard had also not forgotten Darcy's promise, and, on the last day before Darcy, Georgiana, Elizabeth and Richard were to go back to London, the good Colonel was willing to help Darcy create a diversion if needs be. The Collinses and Elizabeth were expected for tea and then dinner at Rosings, and Richard made plans to introduce some diversion or an early evening walk for the unmarried people, then walk swiftly with Georgiana on his arm to make some separation for Darcy.

However, when the time came for the Hunsford party to appear, only Collins and Mary were shown into the parlour. Mary instantly delivered Elizabeth's excuses. "My lady, pray please excuse my sister for not attending to you this evening. She has been up and down the stairs all day packing away all her things and was taken of a headache after luncheon. Remembering your admonishments from early in her visit not to bring any sickness into Rosings, my husband believed it was safer for Elizabeth to spend a quiet night at the parsonage and allow her affliction to recede."

Lady Catherine nodded regally from her high wingback chair. "That was wise of Miss Elizabeth and considerate of her to remember my direction from so long ago. I do appreciate a young woman who takes direction from her betters. Yes, I would say that I have been much impressed with your family, Mrs. Collins. I believe that Mr. Collins has made a very wise choice indeed."

A discussion, which was in no way short, between Collins and Lady Catherine began then, with one laying endless fawning praise at the feet of the other and such other accepting the praise in as self-important a manner as possible.

Darcy heard none of it. He was despondent at the thought of missing this last chance to have a private discussion with Elizabeth. He sank into a seat near one of the windows facing towards the park between Rosings and the parsonage and looked out with a sour expression. Richard, ever the strategist, decided to intervene.

"Say, Darce, you are looking quite pale yourself. Do you think you might be feeling the same effects as Miss Lizzy and require a bit of a rest before we set off for London in the morning? It is nothing to admit that one needs a bit of healthful rest now and then."

Darcy looked sharply at Richard and was about to retort that he was perfectly fine to spend an evening sitting indoors and drinking tea when Richard gave him a significant look and nodded out the window. Understanding started to dawn on his face and Darcy decided to take this last moment and finally seize it. "You know Richard, I believe you are correct. I am feeling a bit overtired today and might excuse myself from the company. Aunt, Anne, please excuse me. Mr. and Mrs. Collins, I hope you have a wonderful evening. I look forward to seeing you tomorrow as we come for Miss Elizabeth to depart to London. If her condition worsens this evening, please do not hesitate to send word and we shall delay our departure until she is well enough for the trip. Georgie, I shall see you in the morning."

Without waiting for anyone to respond, Darcy bowed to the assembled company and turned to swiftly walk out of the parlour. Richard maintained his position at the window looking across the park and smiled to himself when he spied a well-dressed, tall gentleman walking swiftly in the direction of the Hunsford parsonage.

After her sister and brother were gone, Elizabeth, with the intention to distract herself from her exacerbation with Collins for making her stay away on their last night in Kent, chose for her employment the examination of all Jane's letters since leaving Kent for London, which were very many for such a short separation. They contained such expressions of happiness in every line of each that Elizabeth's spirit was buoyed.

Elizabeth noticed every sentence conveying the idea of contentedness, with an attention which it had hardly received on the first perusal. It was some consolation to think that this trip to Rosings was to end on the next day and she would be back in her sister's glowing aura. Though she was gratified to be in Georgiana and Anne's company, and had experienced a most wonderful holiday with her friends and family, it was difficult to spend every day in Darcy's presence and know that her personal happy ending was not coming.

While settling herself to this point, Elizabeth was suddenly roused by the sound of the door knocker and not two minutes later was she stunned to find Darcy being announced to herself.

In a hurried manner, he immediately began an inquiry after her health, imputing his visit to a wish of hearing that she were better. She answered him with flushed cheeks and as much civility as she could muster. Elizabeth was not quite sure how to act.

Darcy sat down for a few moments, and then got up to walk about the room. After a silence of several minutes, he came towards her and in an agitated manner he thus began.

"I have been waiting for the moment in which to beg a private audience with you, but my shy nature and natural reserve have given me such struggles, but it will not do. My feelings will not be repressed any longer. You must allow me to tell you how ardently I admire and love you."

Elizabeth's astonishment was beyond expression. She stared, coloured, doubted, and was silent. This, he considered sufficient encouragement and the avowal of all that he felt and had long felt for her immediately followed. He spoke well, but there were feelings besides those of the heart to be detailed, and *Elizabeth* was determined to speak of them.

"Mr. Darcy, might I ask you a question?"

Her tone stopped Darcy's fevered pacing. She sounded almost… sad. He immediately took a position in the chair closest to her perch in the window seat. "Of course. It is my most fervent wish to hear what you might have to say about this subject."

Elizabeth took a shaky breath, then closed her eyes against the emotion shining in his. "Tell me sir, how will your aunt take the news of an understanding between us?"

This took Darcy completely by surprise. "Of which of my aunts do you speak?"

"Either, truthfully. What would either Lady Matlock or Lady Catherine say to hearing news that we are to be married?"

Darcy looked out the window and twitched in his seat. "Well, I cannot say for certain, of course. However, I am sure that each member of my family would care for my happiness above all else."

Elizabeth sighed. "But that is not the question I asked you. How do you believe they will resign themselves to your engagement to someone so wholly beneath you as myself?"

"Do not say that! You are not…"

"Please sir! Do not be blind. It will do neither of us any good to ignore these objections which your family and friends are sure to voice. Could you expect them to rejoice in the inferiority of my connections or to congratulate you on the hope of relations whose condition in life is so decidedly beneath your own? How can you expect an earl to socialise with a country attorney?"

"This means nothing to me! I care not if my noble relations cast me aside, you must believe me!"

Elizabeth again closed her eyes, this time to try and stop the flow of tears going down her cheeks. It was as good an admission that she was correct, and their union would be derided by his relations and those in his circle. Darcy began to truly fear that he would be unsuccessful in his endeavour.

"Sir, I implore you, please let me be and do not importune me anymore. I am decided. You may say now that you would care nothing for being cast off by society, but you have never been the scorn of anyone. We must also think of Georgiana. Her prospects would be much diminished if we were hated by society and your family. I will not accuse you of lying, for I can believe that *you* believe yourself in declaring that the scorn of your family will not alter your feelings, but I fear a union so marred by adversity. You would come to resent me, I am sure of it." Elizabeth wrung her hands in her lap and stared out the window, watching the sun fall behind the trees. "I have watched my mother and father grow more apathetic each year as my father regrets her nerves and my mother regrets his neglect.

I do not wish such a marriage for myself, one which is filled with much repining."

Darcy was having a difficult time controlling his disappointment, which was making him angry. "And this!" he cried as he walked with quick steps around the room. "This is your opinion of me? This is the estimation in which you hold me? I thank you for explaining it so fully. My faults, according to this calculation, are heavy indeed!" Darcy looked back at Elizabeth who was silently weeping into his missing handkerchief, great sobs lifting her shoulders and causing her head to hang with a great weight. Shame, regret, and a great need to go to her and provide a comforting embrace became almost overwhelming. Before he did anything to shame himself and compromise her, Darcy moved towards the door.

"You have said quite enough madam, and so have I. I am sorry to have brought you such grief with my ill placed declarations. I perfectly understand your feelings and have now only to be ashamed of my shouting here today. Forgive me for having taken up so much of your time and accept my best wishes for your health and happiness. May God bless you, Elizabeth." With these last words, nearly whispered into the room, he hastily left, and Elizabeth heard him the next moment open the front door and quit the house. The tumult of her mind was painfully great. She knew not how to support herself and, from actual weakness, she laid down on the sofa and cried for half an hour. Her astonishment, as she reflected on what had passed, was increased by every review of it and she was in such grief that she could not contain herself. That he loved her enough as to wish to marry her, in spite of all the likely objections of his family and the obvious inferior position of her own, was most incredible and it was gratifying to have inspired so strong an affection. It was exactly as her sisters and aunt had been saying for many months now.

However, Elizabeth was firm that her rejection was correct. Everything she had seen of Lady Matlock in London and Lady Catherine here in Kent told her that their marriage would be doomed. He would come to resent her quickly. And then he would begin to feel trapped by her presence. He might even begin to leave her at Cresselly Park while he visited London to escape her presence.

She would always love him desperately. But love alone was not enough to make their marriage a success.

She loved him in such an overwhelming manner that it felt like she would die from this heartache.

Finally, after calming her tears, Elizabeth made her way up the stairs to her bed to rest for the coming day's journey to London. She would have to be calm and well rested so as to endure the ride in his carriage with his sister and cousin. And him. Maybe her brother would allow her to travel by post in another day if she feigned sickness the next morning. No, it would be better to face the world in the morning and try to continue as casual acquaintances. She was determined not to treat him any different for knowing what had transpired between them. She would not be the destruction of his life or his peace of mind.

She loved him too much for that.

Anne had taken Richard's place at the window looking towards the parsonage shortly after Darcy departed the drawing room. She correctly guessed why Darcy had left in such a hurry and wanted to be the first to spy her cousin coming back with good news to share. Instead, Anne had seen Darcy arrive back to the house in a terror and walk quickly towards the stables. She excused herself from the parlour and walked to catch up to her cousin.

"William, what are you doing at this hour?"

"I am leaving immediately for London. I have had an express and must away immediately," Darcy said tersely.

"Good heavens! Is Uncle George all right?"

"What? Of course, Father is fine. What are you talking about?"

"Well, that is a relief, but I assumed that anything you received by express that has you risking your neck to ride three hours in the dark back to London must be life or death. Or else you would wait until the morning." Anne watched his frenzied buckling of the horse's bridle with confusion. "You are supposed to go back in the carriage anyway tomorrow. I'm sure that Lizzy, Georgiana, and Richard would not mind waking early to leave at first light instead of after breaking their fast."

"No!" Darcy shouted. "I am going alone. I shall not bother Elizabeth again."

Now Anne was extremely perplexed. "What do you mean you 'shall not bother Elizabeth again'? I am sorry to say that if you want an heir you are going to have to be a bother to her, however I am certain she will not mind in the least."

Darcy whirled around and stared at his cousin in shock. "I shall never hear you again say such disgusting things in my presence! You cannot speak of her that way! I will not countenance it."

Anne raised one eyebrow, to borrow an expression from the lady they were discussing. "You will not hear me insult her, but you insist you will never bother her again? I know you too well to be under any false impression as to your feelings for the young lady. I have known since your first letters arrived from Hertfordshire in October that you were smitten. Now, I might go so far as to say you love her unyieldingly. I have been waiting for you to announce that you are engaged to her for many weeks. I thought it might happen in London, but surely after the wonderful time we have had here you cannot be considering abandoning her without declaring yourself?"

Darcy turned back to his horse and began again to fit the fittings. "You know not what you say. Leave me be, I shall off to London and if I break my neck on the way, so be it."

"Fitzwilliam George James Darcy, you will do no such thing! Turn around and face me this instant. I may not be a man and physically able to restrain you, but I will go inside and have Richard put you in chains if that is what it takes to stop this madness."

Darcy finally stopped and hung his head.

Anne stepped up and placed her small, pale hand on his shoulder. "Tell me what has happened, William. We are family, and I promise that I will do what I can to fix whatever has happened."

"She will not have me. I declared myself to her, asked her to be my wife and she has refused."

"What? Why ever would she refuse you? She loves you as much as you love her."

Darcy looked at his cousin with tears in his eyes and something else. A mask of some sort which was beginning to form around the edges of his expression. Anne did not like this look one bit. "Perhaps she does. I certainly thought she did. And her refusal did not mention any specific dislike for my person. But she fears how she will be treated by some members of our family as well as London society. She points out that we are very different people with very different social expectations, and I might harm Georgiana's prospects with a marriage so far below myself. She also fears that I shall come to resent her if society shuns us. Perhaps she is right. I should stick to the original plan and let Aunt Matlock choose my bride."

He dropped the reins and stepped away from the stall. "I will not risk my life to away to London this moment, but I shall not ride back in the carriage. I leave at first light, and I must ask you to make my excuses to Georgina and Richard. Starting tomorrow, I shall do what our aunt asks of me and find the strength to marry the woman which is expected."

Joy and Tears

"**O**H COME NOW, LIZZY! THIS IS FUNNY." MR. Bennet tried to engage his favourite child to share his favourite pastime, laughing at the folly of others. "You always used to enjoy the absurdity of the gossip pages."

Elizabeth was sitting in the high-backed chair in front of her father's desk, as she could often be found after breakfast, looking down at the society pages of the most recent edition of *The London Times*. Right there in black and white was printed:

> *F.D. seen dancing at Almack's again with Lady F.F. TWICE! This unquestionably means that he has made his choice and we expect to have an official announcement to print very soon.*

"If only the publisher of this column knew that you had danced with the man thrice last November here in the country." Her father chuckled while Elizabeth sat completely still with the paper in her hands.

It had long been their habit that Elizabeth and her father would marvel over the gossip column in the *Times*. Or it had been until Elizabeth had overheard, oh so many months ago now, a particular conversation between a certain gentleman from Derbyshire and his happy friend at the public assembly in Meryton.

"William, calm down. I know that the London Times gossip columnist has a special obsession with you, but we are not in London."

While Elizabeth had decided not to indulge in reading social pages in the daily newspaper since meeting Darcy, her father still very much liked to amuse himself with the diversion. That morning, he began to chuckle to himself while reading his paper and Elizabeth asked what had caused such mirth. Mr. Bennet simply smirked at his daughter and handed her the page he was reading.

It was not like his social calendar was a surprise to Elizabeth. She and Jane had experienced the craze of the first few months of the season and spent many more nights at home than Darcy had, even when the entertainments before Easter were fewer than during the full season. With the season now in full swing, it should not be a surprise that he would be dancing with heiresses every other night and attending the theatre on the others. Georgiana's recent letters were also full of the dinner parties, dances, balls, plays, and daily visits to London attractions.

Also, it was not a secret that he *was* looking for a wife. He had said as much at the Meryton assembly last autumn and was resigned to take the wife that Lady Matlock had chosen for him, which appeared to be Lady Fiona. Elizabeth remembered meeting the lady at several events in London, which seemed like a lifetime ago now. Lady Fiona was tall and thin with silky blond hair and stormy grey eyes. She was pleasant to look at, if a bit hawkish in the face. Perhaps a bit reserved and shy, but at the few events they had attended together, she had been welcoming and kind to Elizabeth and Jane. She also came with a significant fortune and close connections to at least two earldoms. She was everything expected of the match Fitzwilliam Darcy was destined to make.

Elizabeth knew better than to take the gossip column as truth, but it was a logical conclusion based on the social conventions of London. Additionally, she knew that marriage to Lady Matlock's favourite niece had been his plan before they became introduced. Their winter/spring diversion had been fun, but it was time they both moved past childish notions of love. Darcy was obviously moving forward with his original plan. Elizabeth should move forward too.

It took all of Elizabeth's strength of mind to hand the paper back to her father with an air of indifference. She waited an interminable ten minutes before excusing herself, leaving the house through the back door and then running all the way to the small clearing near the bourn which marked the boundary between Longbourn and the Netherfield estate. There was a large colony of aspen trees near the water and a bright sunny spot. Years earlier, Elizabeth had dragged a fallen log into the sunshine to be used as a natural bench. Though the decaying process had some-what shrunken her seat, the log was still a pleasant place to escape to.

Today, Elizabeth barely noticed the sunshine or the calming sounds of the bubbling water above her own gasps and tears.

"Oh, my sweet, dear Lizzy."

Elizabeth looked up and felt instantly distraught that her sister had followed her out of the house in such a state.

"Jane, please do not distress yourself with me. I shall be back to rights in a moment." Elizabeth pulled out the handkerchief adorned with Sweet Williams, the same one Darcy had lent her back before everything fell apart.

"Of course I am going to distress myself. You are my most beloved sister and you are upset." Jane sat beside Elizabeth gently and pulled her into a warm hug. "I would do anything for you dearest."

"But, you should be back at the house with Mamma enjoying the chaos, joy and frivolity." Elizabeth wiped at her eyes again. "You should not have to be here with my dour moods."

Tomorrow was to be Jane's wedding day.

All the plans had been made, the dresses and bonnets trimmed, and the cakes were cooling in the larder. Mary and Collins had arrived the day before and the Gardiners were due that evening before dinner. Jane's room and all her clothes except her wedding dress and the clothes on her back, had been packed into trunks waiting to be taken to Netherfield on a cart. When the Gardiners arrived, they would stay in Jane's room and the whole family would be tight indeed, but the Bennet house was used to bursting at the seams. So, it would not be an inconvenience to anyone really.

No matter how much she chastised herself and vowed not to shed one more tear over Darcy, Elizabeth invariably cried herself to sleep each night and at odd times in the day when something would remind her of him. She was determined not to show Jane the full scale of her sorrow on her sister's last day before marrying the man she loved. It would not do to have Jane upset over Elizabeth's own heartbreak. There would be many years to discuss what had happened between herself and Darcy when Elizabeth, as an old maid, lived in the Bingleys' home and helped care for their brood of beautiful and good-natured children.

"I am well acquainted with your moods and am not burdened at all with providing you with love and comfort. Even on this, the day before my wedding." Jane gave a small, then held out a letter for Elizabeth to take. "I was on my way to find you when I saw you run across the back garden. It was obvious you were upset and heading for your clearing."

"You know me so well, dear." Elizabeth took the paper from her sister. "What is this?"

Jane looked at the note with a sad face. "Dear, Charles received a note from Mr. Darcy yesterday. He will not be coming to the wedding and sends his regrets. It was a surprise to him, though I said that I was sure only something extremely important would have kept him away."

"Jane, I am sorry that the Darcys will be absent tomorrow. Has Mr. Bingley decided on a witness in Mr. Darcy's stead?"

Jane nodded "Yes, his father shall stand as his witness. Though, I did not come out to the woods to find you to tell you about Charles's father. You see, here near the bottom of the page is most distinctly a tear stain. I suspect you might know why our dear friend is not going to come to Hertfordshire. And I also suspect you have many items which are just as tear stained, though you have been hiding it from me. Please, dear Lizzy, will you not tell me what has you so out of sorts?"

Elizabeth was quiet and hung her head. "I did not want to bring any clouds to your wedding day. I have not been myself these past few weeks, but I am sure it will pass soon. I promise I am not so burdened that it needs to give you grief during these bright and happy days."

Jane took back the letter, folded it, placed it back in her pocket, then took both of Elizabeth's hands in her own. "Elizabeth Frances Margaret Bennet, I have been your confidante since you could speak your first words. I would never wish for you to keep your own confidence simply to keep me from information which might cause me some pain. I shall not force you to tell me what has been in your heart lately, but I would like to know. *A burden shared is a burden halved.* Please dear, tell me what is wrong."

It was too much. Elizabeth rubbed the embroidered flowers on Darcy's handkerchief and finally told Jane everything she had been keeping inside. Starting from her overhearing Darcy and Bingley talking at the Meryton assembly, through her dance with Richard at the Finchs' ball, divulging Darcy's marriage proposal, and finally the latest gossip news from London that had him attached to Lady Fiona.

After the tale was finished, Jane and Elizabeth sat on the log for a long time in the sun. Not much else was said, as there was nothing left to be discussed.

"Lizzy, I do believe that your mother could not have prayed for a better day to celebrate Jane and Mr. Bingley. I am so very happy for our friends." Charlotte Lucas came into the beautifully decorated dining room and took the seat directly beside Elizabeth.

"You are correct Charlotte, however I do believe that my mother has been praying extremely hard for quite some time for the event which provided the cause for today's celebration and I would not put anything past her notice to include in those prayers if it would increase the grandeur of today, even the weather."

Mary came to sit on the opposite side to Elizabeth. "While we should not deride dreary days, for the Lord gives us the rain to allow life the nourishment required to flourish, I believe He also shows us his favour and lifts our spirits with bright and sunny days."

"Very true, Mary." Charlotte smiled. "I see you have settled quite well into the life of a parson's wife. The occupation suits you well."

"Thank you, Charlotte. I believe I am very well pleased with my husband and our flock." Mary turned to Elizabeth. "I was sorry to bring Anne's regrets with me, Lizzy. She very much wished to come, but with Colonel Fitzwilliam away in Newcastle and Mr. Darcy unable to attend, she did not have a suitable escort."

Elizabeth was sorry to miss her friend, even more sorry than Mary could know. After crying many hours the day before and unburdening herself with Jane, Elizabeth believed she might begin to heal from her broken heart. With so many guests, it had so far been easy to ignore that there were several of their closest friends absent on this day. However, every mention of Anne or the Darcys brought a sharp stab to Elizabeth's heart.

"Thank you for bringing her letter dear." Elizabeth forced a smile. "I was not very surprised by her absence. It is a long way from Kent to come for the wedding of her parson's sister. We would have enjoyed her company but in no way expected her to go to so much trouble to attend."

"Mary, you say that Mr. Darcy was unable to attend today, I must admit I was surprised by his absence." Charlotte looked between the two sisters. "We all expected that Mr. Darcy would stand for Mr. Bingley today. I trust everything is alright with the gentleman?"

Elizabeth squirmed in her seat, which neither of her companions missed. She stumbled over her words, "Well, no, of course nothing is wrong. He merely had some business in town and his sister has just returned to their estate in Derbyshire, and of course he is busy with the social engagements of the season. He is a very important member of the *ton* and has already been away from town for a long time this season. I was surprised that he stayed so long in Kent instead of going back to London. You know, because of all his business interests and social... um... obligations."

Mary and Charlotte were, neither one, fooled by Elizabeth's feigned air of indifference regarding Darcy's absence. However, neither could argue what she was saying, and it was not the right place or time to begin an interrogation of Elizabeth and Darcy's relationship. Mary had been greatly disappointed when Elizabeth left Kent without an understanding with Darcy, and Charlotte had been convinced that both Jane and Elizabeth would catch wealthy husbands during their London travels, however neither knew quite how to start a conversation about Elizabeth's marriage prospects without seeming very rude.

"Mary, I do love your gown. That lavender satin very much compliments your complexion," Charlotte said.

"Oh, thank you," Mary blushed. "My husband purchased this for me as a gift for today's festivities. He feels very proud to have been able to provide Jane and Charles with the location of their courtship. I believe that he even went so far as to ask Anne to help him speak to the modiste in the Hunsford village, and she picked the colour."

Elizabeth smiled widely at her sister and patted her hands. "My first brother is truly a generous and humble soul."

"And how well all of your sisters looked today, each of you in a different shade of the spring flowers," Charlotte teased lightly. "Your mother shall be getting many congratulations from the ladies on how well each of you looked in your finery."

Charlotte continued. "Two persons whom I was surprised by this morning have been Mr. Bingley's sisters. I thought that Miss Bingley had spoken about receiving their new gowns for today from their London modiste last week, but both were wearing older day dresses which we have all seen before. Do you think something unfortunate has happened?"

It had been mentioned by several of her mother's friends that the Bingley sisters were not dressed to their normal level of distinction. During an extremely infuriating carriage ride from London to Longbourn with the Bingley siblings, Elizabeth had been subjected to a painfully detailed discussion about the quality of the silk, the fashionable colour, orange of course, and how it was modelled after the very latest dress designs for the summer season printed in *La Belle Assemblée*. There must be some reason for her not wearing the new gown, but Elizabeth was not interested enough to try and muddle it out.

"I have not heard that something was wrong with the delivery," she said, "but I am sure Miss Bingley will make her displeasure known to everyone if there was some difficulty."

Mary swatted her sister in a scolding gesture, but was herself hiding a smile.

"Ah! Lovely." Bingley interrupted the three friends' conversation. "Please excuse me, Miss Lucas, I need to borrow my new sisters as my lovely bride does not wish to depart without saying all of her goodbyes."

"Of course, Mr. Bingley." Charlotte rose from her chair and reached for Elizabeth. "I must insist on also seeing Jane out on her way. Come dears."

The carriage which would take Bingley and Jane for a short stay in London before leaving for their wedding trip, was waiting in the front drive. The newlyweds would start in Bath, then travel north on a tour of the Lake District and finally ending in a visit to the Bingley family home in the seaside town of Scarborough.

For many years, the Bingleys had lived in a beautiful home just down the street from St. Mary's church, which overlooked the shore and sea. Being so far north, the typical season for entertainments and sea bathing started in July and August. Many of the wealthy northern families went to Scarborough for summer holidays after the London season was complete, and stayed at the Scarborough Spa Resort to partake in the horse racing on the beach, boating and sea-bathing. Scarborough also held the title as one of the first places in England to use bathing machines. Jane had never been to a seaside resort and was very much looking forward to her extended holiday with her new husband.

Walking out to the garden, Bingley spotted his own sisters sitting on a bench. They were sitting facing away from the house, and as he approached to call them to the front drive for the farewells, he could hear the conversation coming from them.

"I am mortified Louisa, just mortified! To think that he actually went through with this travesty of a marriage. How are we to show our faces in London now? We have been deserted already by our dearest friends! Mr. Darcy would not even show his face here. It is as I have been trying to tell Charles for a while now, the Bennet family is so far beneath our notice and our formal connection to them has ruined all our plans." Caroline was not regulating her voice at all, growing in volume and pitch as she went. "We must pray that this backwater country wedding is not interesting enough to garner much gossip in town or else all my hopes are dashed. Well, all my hopes are dashed anyway since Mr. Darcy obviously knows about this connection and has not come to wish Charles and Jane joy. How am I to catch him now? At least I was right to save my new, best dress for London instead of *wasting* it on the people here."

"Caro, you were never going to catch him anyway." Louisa looked bored with what was no doubt the hundredth reiteration of her sister's complaints about this wedding. "Have you not seen the gossip column lately? He is all but engaged to Lady Fiona Finch, who is Lady Matlock's niece. She was also dancing with him at Sir James's ball, you know the one *you* determined was beneath us because the Finch's only have a bestowed title. You clearly do not have a clear understanding of his family and close connections."

"Yes, yes, we have discussed at length how I was wrong about Sir James and Lady Finch, but I would not put too much stock into that gossip column. Last year *The London Times* had my dear Mr. Darcy all but engaged to that horse-faced dullard, Lady Grace Hervey." Caroline waved her hand dismissively. "*Poor* Mr. Darcy has been followed by the *Times* gossip man for so long and since he never behaves in an indecorous manner, the man has started making up nonsense with which to provoke him. I heard from Celia Howard that there was some trouble when both were at Cambridge and Mr. Darcy came out on top. The man has been relentless ever since.

Caroline flicked a bit of imagined dirt from her sleeve, then went back to ranting without a care that they were currently seated in a very public place and surrounded by guests of the very people she was deriding. "If we can survive the *humiliation* of being connected to this dreadful family and dreadful little town, then I plan to force the issue with Darcy before the Prince Regent's ball."

"What are you saying Caro? How do you mean to 'force this issue' with Mr. Darcy?" Louisa looked around the garden to determine who might be within earshot.

"Well, you know that he always needs some fresh air in the middle of the evening at Almack's and usually takes a step onto the rear balcony. I will simply follow him for a private conversation. I can make my openness to an understanding known. I will also be able to assure him I would never expect him to acknowledge the Bennets in the future. I am sure we will have to entertain Charles and Jane at some point in the future, but at least she is pretty enough with pleasant manners. I will have to supervise her dress choices for any events hosted at Darcy House, but that should not be too much of a burden. With all of my pin money, I can probably just purchase her the dresses she should wear and have them available at my home so she can change in and out of them at Darcy House instead of risking that she might bring them here to become filthy in the muddy gardens." Caroline's last sneered words were accompanied by a side look around the beautiful formal gardens at Longbourn, where not even one noticeable puddle of mud was in sight.

Charles, who had been listening at a short distance directly behind his sister's backs for some time, was unfrozen at the degrading way his sister was speaking of his new wife. He marched straight into Caroline and Louisa's line of sight and was not temperate in his reaction.

"Caroline, I am ashamed of you! Here you sit, holding one of Mrs. Bennet's fine crystal glasses filled with punch, eating the wedding cake supplied by my new mother-in-law and you have the atrocious manners to speak so poorly of your hosts! I shall speak to Father about your disrespect and your plans to disgrace yourself in London. I will not let you return to town if your main purpose is to throw yourself at my friend."

With all the rage she had been keeping under relative control for the past six weeks, Caroline vaulted from her seat and nearly spilled her punch all over her skirts. "Your *friend*! You think that Mr. Darcy still counts you as one of his *friends*? If you have not noticed, he has abandoned you to this disastrous decision and refused to come to your wedding. And mark my words Charles, he may be the first, but he will not be the last. I have tried to tell you over and over how poor a choice you were making, but you did not listen to me. You may have ruined your own life, but I will not let you ruin mine. I will return to London, pretend that I have no idea what anyone is saying about the Bennets, and make every effort to catch myself a wealthy gentleman husband before the truth about our connections can be the ruination of all my hopes."

Caroline was properly shouting now. Many of the guests had sought refuge from the heat of the day in the cool breezes flowing through the garden and everyone stopped to stare at the groom being so thoroughly abused by his sister. For anyone who was too far away to hear the actual words being said, it was not hard to guess at the direction of the conversation.

Jane, who had stepped out of the door to the garden in time to overhear a great deal of the ranting from her newest sister, took a fortifying breath. Elizabeth was, mercifully, waiting for them on the front drive and had been spared this scene.

With the grace and serenity that only Jane could summon in the face of such a disturbance, the new Mrs. Bingley decided to calmly cross the garden and retrieve her husband.

"Husband! There you are, I was just about to send out the hounds to track you down. Come dear, the carriage is ready to away and my mother wishes to send you off with a happy wave from the front porch." Jane then turned to her new sisters to take her leave. It was not in Jane's nature to be unkind, even in the face of such provocation. "Caroline, Louisa. Thank you for being with us today. I am so glad to now call you my sisters. I do hope we will see you in Scarborough for you shall have to show me the bathing machines and the best places to shop. I am also looking forward to the horse races. I am sure we shall be a very happy party this summer."

Caroline, Bingley, and Louisa just stared at Jane after her interruption of the heated argument taking place. Bingley recovered first and was eager to sweep his new bride off to their wedding trip. "Of course, darling, I came out to say a fond goodbye to my sisters and it is now time to depart." He turned back to Caroline and Louisa. "Sisters, I trust I will see you at the seaside earlier rather than later this year, where we will indeed, make a very happy party. And as to any of our acquaintances or former friends who would view my family or connections with derision, well, to them I say, a very good riddance."

Summer Plans

WITH THE DEPARTURE OF THE LAST WEDDING guests, life at Longbourn returned to the daily humdrum that had always marked the hot summer days. One might expect, with Jane and Mary gone, the level of noise inside the parlour would drop, however that was not the case. As Elizabeth was learning, though there were five Bennet sisters, only one was responsible for the vast majority of all the chaos which marred the Bennet family house.

Shortly after Jane and Elizabeth had arrived home from London, the militia regiment quartering in Meryton for the winter moved on to their next assignment in Brighton. Many of the young ladies of the neighbourhood were dropping pace with the news, but none more so than Lydia and Kitty. Very frequently Elizabeth reproached them for their insensibility, but Lydia and Kitty insisted that their own misery was extreme and could not comprehend such hard-heartedness from their sister.

Two days after Jane's wedding, Lydia received an invitation from Mrs. Forster, the very lately married, and fairly young, wife of the colonel of the regiment, to accompany her to Brighton. A resemblance in good humour and good spirits had recommended her and Lydia to each other and the two ladies had become very intimate friends in the short time that the militia was stationed in Meryton.

Mrs. Bennet saw no harm in Lydia having a bit of a holiday at the sea since all of their family festivities were complete. Mr. Bennet was less inclined to send another daughter off to some adventure with persons of so little acquaintance, but Lydia would not be gainsaid. She worked on her father every day until, finally, he gave his permission for her to go.

The rapture of Lydia on this occasion, and the mortification of Kitty, were scarcely to be described. Wholly inattentive to her sister's feelings, Lydia flew about the house in restless ecstasy, calling for everyone's congratulations, and laughing and talking with more violence than ever, whilst the luckless Kitty continued in the parlour repining at her fate in terms as unreasonable as her accent was peevish.

As for Elizabeth herself, this invitation was so far from exciting in her the same feelings as Lydia, that she considered it as the death-warrant of all possibility of common sense. As detestable as such a step must make her, were it known to Lydia, she could not help secretly advising her father not to let her go. Elizabeth was sure that if Lydia was left only to the guidance of the Forsters, she would show the world what a determined flirt she was and make herself and her sisters ridiculous.

Her father was not moved. "Lydia will never be easy till she has exposed herself in some public place or other, and we can never expect her to do it with so little expense or inconvenience to her family as under the present circumstances."

Elizabeth could see that her father was in no mood to be worked on, and so she was resigned to the fact that Lydia would go to Brighton. She hoped that at least nothing would come of the scheme that would have long lasting consequences to the rest of their family.

As Lydia packed her trunk for Brighton, she spoke endlessly of all the balls and assemblies she would attend with the officers and how glad she would be to see her *dear* Wickham again.

Kitty, in a poor mood from not being invited, decided to provoke Lydia. "He is not *your* dear Mr. Wickham. I hear that he is Miss Mary King's *dear Mr. Wickham.*"

Lydia put down the bonnet upon which she was placing new ribbon roses and threw a pillow at Kitty. "Do not say such things! He is not going to marry her. I will not believe such stupid rumours. I know that Maria Lucas has filled your head with some gossip that he has been courting her, but I cannot believe there was any strong attachment on his side. Who could care about such a nasty little freckled thing? And besides, she is gone now and he is away with the militia. We will certainly not see her again in his company."

Elizabeth chastised her youngest sister's uncharitable words. "Now Kitty, what is this about Mr. Wickham and Miss King?"

Kitty lit up at being the centre of attention. "Oh! But of course, you would not know! It happened after you and Jane went away. Miss King has come into an inheritance of more than ten thousand pounds. Shortly after that, Mr. Wickham was given to often sitting by her during evening parties, and he asked her to dance twice at the public assembly given in February. It was all but sure that he would ask her to marry him and even a few of his friends did say they had an understanding. Maria told me that Miss King confessed she was much in love with Mr. Wickham and wanted nothing better than to follow the drum as his wife. But her legal guardian, an uncle on her mother's side, was not in Meryton to consent to the engagement. When he came to see her a few weeks later, suddenly she was whisked away to Liverpool. Given that Mr. Wickham cannot leave his post, he has not been able to follow after her, but he was very much heart-broken. Maria and I agree that we are sure they are exchanging letters and must be planning some way to renew their romance. Her uncle cannot keep them apart forever, can he?"

Elizabeth was astonished at this story. Mary King was barely sixteen years old and a bit of a wallflower. No one had ever paid her the smallest bit of mind. Now, the sudden acquisition of a fortune of ten thousand pounds was the most remarkable charm of the young lady and had caused such a marked change in Wickham's attentions. It was unbelievable, except Lydia's vulgar reaction to the story was proof enough that it was true. If Elizabeth was not convinced before this moment that Wickham was the most detestable liar, she now had proof of his character. His exit from the neighbourhood was a blessing Elizabeth would not soon forget.

"Kitty, I do not need to tell you how damaging it would be to Miss King if you spread rumours about her exchanging letters with a man, especially as you have no actual knowledge that they are in fact writing to each other," Elizabeth scolded. "I expect you shall not repeat that again. As for the rest, Mr. Wickham is certainly showing his true colours as an inconsistent acquaintance at best and a fortune hunter at worst. We should take care that we do not become involved in the man's grievances, lest our neighbours believe we are too interested in the man. I for one am glad he is gone with the militia."

Lydia merely stuck her tongue out at her sisters and went back to putting her bonnets into her trunk.

Madeline Gardiner set down the letter she was reading on the side table of the north parlour. It was from her favourite niece, Elizabeth. Perhaps it was not kind to have one niece above the rest that she loved, but it was hard not to feel a kindred spirit in Elizabeth. Madeline was more reserved than her niece, but when they were in company together, Elizabeth's lively attitude often allowed the older lady to engage and become more lively herself. Even in her letters, Elizabeth was often effusive and teasing which left her aunt in a good mood after reading them.

It was that lively spirit which was now lacking in the letter just arrived. But in all, and in almost every line, there was a want of cheerfulness which had been used to characterise her style, and which, proceeding from the serenity of a mind at ease with itself, and humorously disposed towards everyone, had been scarcely ever clouded. Madeline noticed every sentence conveying the idea of unease and sadness.

It was not hard to discern the cause. Darcy appeared more disposed to society than he had ever been before and was often seen attending two social gatherings each day, three if one counted the mid-day meal at his club as male socialising. Sir James Finch was a member at Whites and would take his best friend, Edward Gardiner, to luncheon at the club once or twice a week. It was a very lucrative way for Edward to discuss his business with potential investors and make connections with the gentry for the best agricultural exports that were often sent to India, Canada, and the many other portions of the empire.

Edward had recently seen Darcy at the club on two specific occasions. They had even once discussed a new agreement to distribute the wool coming from Darcy's Wales estate. However, while he was always polite and made the expected inquiries after their shared connections, the taciturn young man had seemed to have lost much of the lustre in his demeanour.

Then there were those few occasions where the Gardiners had been present at some society event with Darcy. Most notably, Sir James and Lady Finch had hosted an art exhibition at their home one afternoon and much of the same guests who had come to their anniversary ball were in attendance. Darcy came with his sister, Georgiana, and spent the entire event at her side, not speaking to anyone even though many of his friends and members of his family were present. The prior week, Edward and Madeline had attended a ball hosted by a mutual acquaintance where Darcy was again among the guests. This time he was without his sister, and when Madeline asked after the young lady, he revealed that she was gone home to Derbyshire for the remainder of the summer.

That evening he danced several times, but only when he could not avoid the activity. Mostly, he was induced to dance after his aunt, Lady Matlock, came up to him in between sets with a well-dressed lady in tow. Most of the rest of the evening Darcy stood against the wall in oddly dark locations between the wall sconces. On more than one occasion, Madeline thought he must be following herself and her husband around the room as he could often be found within a few paces of them while they were conversing with their friends. However, he was always facing away from them with his arms crossed. There was one time when the conversation turned to their nieces, and Madeline thought she saw Darcy's head turn at the mention of Elizabeth.

Though she would like to be of use to the young man, it was not her place to offer any observations or start a conversation about his new social discomfort with someone who was not her family.

However, Elizabeth was her family, and she was determined to be of use to one of these star-crossed lovers.

"Edward, might I disturb you for a bit?"

"Of course dear, come in. What is on your mind?"

Madeline handed Edward the letter from Elizabeth. "I have had a letter from our niece today. She seems much out of sorts and I believe we both know why. I was hoping we might offer her the means to relieve her melancholy."

Edward looked down at the letter for a moment then back at his wife. "I am not sure that it would be a good idea to bring her here, Madeline. Mr. Darcy seems determined to entertain the marriage minded ladies of London, especially Lady Fiona, if *The Times* is to be believed. Lizzy would surely find more to be melancholy about in London than at Longbourn."

"I am not suggesting we bring her here, though I disagree that Mr. Darcy is going to make any kind of offer to Lady Fiona, I am certain he does not mean to attach himself to Lizzy or it would have already happened."

"Why do you say he is not going to offer for Lady Fiona? The gossip is all over town that he means to marry her!"

Madeline sighed. "Yes, I know, however he did not seem too enamoured of her when we were in company with them both at the Griffiths' several days ago. Also, my cousin, Lady Miranda, saw Mr. Darcy at Almack's shortly before Jane's wedding while chaperoning to her own niece, Winnie Craven. Mr. Darcy approached my cousin and her niece in between sets and carried on a very polite conversation, then asked Winnie to dance. During their dance, Lady Matlock came over to Miranda and struck up a very animated conversation. It was most out of the ordinary. We have often observed that Lady Matlock sees Miranda as below herself and they are polite, but not friendly. Well, after the set ended, it became clear exactly why Lady Matlock pretended such a grand friendliness. Lady Matlock was acting as chaperone to Lady Fiona that evening, so she was returned to Lady Matlock at the same time Mr. Darcy returned Winnie to Miranda. What happened next was quite embarrassing as Miranda tells it. Lady Matlock kept the whole group engaged in conversation for so long that as the next dance set was starting, Mr. Darcy was forced to take her out to the floor for a second time that evening. After the set was over, Mr. Darcy returned Lady Fiona to Lady Matlock, bowed to the assembled group, and left the assembly without another word, though there were several dances yet."

"To what end does Lady Matlock force these dances upon him?"

"Miranda says that the Finch family is extremely aggressive in arranging matches for the younger set and is also *very* sensitive to gossip regarding understandings. From certain things that Miranda has said in the past, it is not unheard of for the Finch's to use gossip in their favour when going after an advantage match. The next day, it was reported in *The Times* that they shared two dances and there is a general expectation of their understanding." Madeline pinched the bridge of her nose. "It seems unpardonable to me to force the issue with an unwilling gentleman, but I know many in the upper set see it as a necessary evil."

Edward nodded. "I am sorry for Mr. Darcy if he has been selected by the Finch's to marry Lady Fiona where he is not inclined. He will certainly have a hard time of it without some support, but we can surely do nothing about that situation. What did you have in mind for Lizzy's reprieve?"

"Well, you and I were thinking of taking a trip to the peaks and maybe the lakes this summer, were we not?" Madeline came around her husband's desk. "Kitty could be trusted with the children, then we can take Lizzy with us on our travels. She must be feeling the loss of Jane most acutely. No, I believe that a trip to the north is exactly what Lizzy needs to be well again. We might even stop at Pemberley and see Miss Georgiana Darcy for some time."

"Do you not think that going to the man's estate would be another reminder of all that she has lost with his abandonment?" Edward raised one eyebrow.

Madeline thought for a moment, "No, I do not believe it will pain her. Mr. Darcy Senior is still master at Pemberley. Young Mr. Darcy's estate is in Wales somewhere. Lizzy has a great friend in Miss Darcy, and in her letter, Lizzy says she has been exchanging correspondence with Miss Darcy who has extended an invitation to visit at Lizzy's leisure. I would not expect the younger Mr. Darcy to come to the family estate while his own will need attention at the close of the season."

"Very well wife, I shall bow to your insights here as I am wholly unqualified to judge what may or may not be of use to our young niece's heart. We shall take a trip to the peaks and bring Lizzy along. I know we had originally said we might go so far as the lakes, but I will be unable to leave now until the middle of July, so we cannot go so far." He kissed his wife's cheek and turned back to his ledger book. "Set up the arrangements with my sister and brother."

Travelling North

ELIZABETH, AS SHE DROVE ALONG IN HER AUNT AND uncle Gardiner's carriage, watched for the first appearance of Pemberley Woods with some perturbation, and when at length they turned in at the lodge, her spirits were in a high flutter. It had been decided between Madeline and Georgiana that the three travellers would spend a whole three weeks of their tour of the peaks as Georgiana's guests at Pemberley, using Pemberley's unique location nestled against the edge of the start of the mountains as the perfect point from which to see all the wonders of the region.

It had been expressly inquired of Georgiana whether her brother was expected to come to Pemberley during the summer. Elizabeth wished to spare them both the mortification of such a meeting. A most welcome negative followed her questions, and in fact Georgiana confided in Elizabeth that her brother was expected to be enjoying the London season until at least the Prince Regents Ball, which would be held on the last Friday in July, then at a minimum he would stay in London for another week or so to pack up their town house before leaving for his own estate, Cresselly Park, in Wales. Georgiana was not sure when Darcy was expected to next come to Derbyshire, but she wrote that it might not be again until after the harvest. With Elizabeth's hesitation being removed it was decided very happily that to Pemberley they would go.

Georgiana was truly excited for her friend to come, and had planned many wonderful excursions for them all. The Devil's Arse caves were a favourite of visitors to Pemberley as well as a climb to the top of Kinder

Scout. A full day of relaxing or shopping at the Matlock Baths was also high on the list of excursions for young gently bred ladies. Any days that they were not scheduled to be out exploring the sights generally obliging summer tourists, the extensive sights of Pemberley would also serve as most welcome entertainment.

After nearly a fortnight in the carriage, and country inns of varying comfort levels, Elizabeth and the Gardiners were extremely glad to pass onto Pemberley's lands. The park was very large, and contained great variety of ground. Elizabeth had never seen a place for which nature had done more or where natural beauty had been so little counteracted by any awkward taste.

As soon as their carriage crossed the bridge over the river, Georgiana came out of the front door and stood, bouncing slightly on her toes, to greet them.

"Welcome to Pemberley!" Georgiana embraced Elizabeth with great enthusiasm. "Come, come. Mrs. Reynolds shall show you to your rooms to refresh yourself and rest after your long journey."

"Thank you Georgie!" Elizabeth returned, with equal fervour, then followed the elderly housekeeper, a very respectable looking woman who was much less fine and more civil than Elizabeth had any notion of finding a servant in such a grand house, to her rooms.

"Here you are, miss. The young mistress specifically requested that you have the room adjoining her own. This door leads to a shared parlour which connects the rooms." Mrs. Reynolds was very effusive to welcome Georgiana's good friends into the home. "If you are well enough, a small tea will be available in the music room in half an hour."

Thanks to the extreme efficiency of the Pemberley staff, their trunks had already been placed inside their rooms before Elizabeth could even ascend the grand staircase. A young maid laid out a dress for Elizabeth to change into and informed her that a small bath had been drawn if she would like to wash off the dust from travelling. A short half an hour later, Elizabeth was clean and dressed in a sweet, green striped muslin summer day dress.

The maid who helped her dress obligingly guided Elizabeth to the music parlour to join Georgiana. It was a large, well-proportioned room, handsomely fitted up. Elizabeth, after finding the room to be empty, went to a window to enjoy its prospect. The hill, crowned with the woods from which they had descended, receiving increased abruptness from the distance, was a beautiful object. Every disposition of the ground was good, and she looked on the whole scene, the river, the trees scattered on its banks, and the winding of the valley, as far as she could trace it, with delight. Elizabeth could not wait to cover as much ground as was possible in the weeks they planned to stay with their friend.

Soon, Elizabeth's musings were interrupted by Georgiana entering with two maids in tow. They each carried a tray laden with tea things and cold meat sandwiches for a very refreshing meal.

"Come Lizzy, have something to refresh yourself after the long travels here. Your aunt and uncle have requested to retire in their rooms for the time before dinner, but you and I may take a walk around the grounds after we have eaten something. I know how desperate I am for a ramble after travelling for so many days. I shall take you down to our stables and let you meet the riding mares we have available. You should choose one to use while you are here so we may visit many of the prospects of Pemberley that are only available on horseback. The decision of a mount is of course up to you, but I might suggest Saphed. She is quite a beautiful animal. All white except for a grey flame across her back legs and a grey jewel mark on her forehead. When she was foaled, my brother had been learning all about the culture of the native peoples of India. Apparently, the women there often wear adornments on their foreheads and the marking on our horse reminded William of those women. Since the word for the colour white in the language of the Indians is 'saphed', he decided to name her thus. My father was not well pleased to have one of his breeding mares named in such a strange tongue, but it had already stuck before he could object."

Elizabeth was startled to find that she was not gutted to hear of Darcy from his sister. Most everyone of her family and friends, save for her mother and Lydia, had been keen to never mention his name in front of her these past months. Thoughts of the man she loved and had lost were painful, but sitting here with his sister in the place he was born and grew up, it seemed the most natural thing to hear stories about him. It was a relief that Elizabeth would not need to hide a pained expression every time one of her hosts inevitably mentioned the third member of their family. Perhaps they could one day meet again as indifferent acquaintances. For now, she would eat a small something and then take a refreshing walk in the mid-morning sunshine with her good friend.

The sun was hanging low in the sky when Darcy finally crested the final hill leading to Pemberley. The last mile from there was all downhill towards the manor house by the lake. Darcy was weary, both of body and of soul. His horse knew these roads better than Darcy himself did, so he gave the beast his own head and allowed his mind to replay the torturous months since leaving Kent in April.

At first, he had done exactly what he had told Anne he would do. Darcy accepted every appropriate invitation he was physically able and had escorted his sister to all the London entertainments. Together, they had attended countless balls, plays, musical exhibitions, art installations, garden parties, and everything in between. He had also attended Almack's every single Wednesday and danced with all the insipid, young unmarried ladies London had to offer.

He knew he was not the best company for his sister. She often looked at him with something akin to pity when she was not alarmed at his taciturn and rude disposition. On many occasions, Georgiana had asked him what was bothering him so. Finally, when she had pestered him so many times, he had, in a not so kind way, told her to stop treating him like a child.

Richard had berated him for causing Georgiana so much heartache and demanded to know what the devil was wrong. But no matter how much he wanted to unburden himself, he would not speak of his troubles to anyone. It was bad enough that Anne had dragged the story out of him moments after his doomed proposal had unfolded, but he knew she would not betray either of them. His encounters with Elizabeth, both in the St. Paul's churchyard and her sister's parlour in Hunsford, might be construed as compromising situations for Elizbeth and he would not like to cause her any additional pain by harming her reputation or forcing her to marry him.

Eventually, Richard was required to return to his regiment for the summer training in the north and Georgiana was so upset over Darcy's behaviour, she begged to be allowed to return home with more than half of the season left. Darcy did not even voice any resistance to the scheme and instead stayed behind in London to continue his own personal torment.

Evening after evening, he made conversation, he ate dinner, and he met lady after lady who met the definition of a 'good match' based on the standards of the London *ton*. Each had a dowry of at least twenty-thousand pounds, spoke multiple languages, painted tables, played an instrument, and sang very skilfully.

None of them had any spark behind their eyes. No wit and absolutely no humour.

The worst of all these torments had been Lady Matlock. She was determined to see him matched with Lady Fiona. Suffering her attentions might have been less agonizing if he thought she cared in the smallest part about him personally, but he knew she did not. She was often shy and distracted and when she initiated conversation it was often about his estate in Wales or the various Pemberley holdings in Scotland. Once he had initiated conversation about her favourite book and she could not answer with any book she had read since leaving finishing school. They were so poorly matched, but his aunt seemed not to care for his feelings on the matter.

The whole game disgusted him.

The last week had been the worst yet. His aunt had manipulated him into dancing with Lady Fiona twice at Almack's.

Again.

The first time Lady Matlock and Lady Fiona forced him into dancing twice at Almack's had been a few days before Bingley's wedding. Darcy had decided it was just too much to travel and stand witness for his best friend, probably former best friend as they had not exchanged any letter in the two months since the blessed day that joined Bingley and Jane together in holy matrimony. Darcy was distraught he missed the event. He was very happy for his friend and desperate for even the smallest glimpse of Elizabeth, but she would not have wanted him there.

Truthfully, he knew he could not have stood in the church, listening to the holy words of matrimony and not dropped to his knees to beg Elizabeth to take him as her husband. It was better that he had stayed away.

That first time she tricked him, Lady Matlock had forced his hand when she engineered a moment in which he and Lady Fiona were both without partners as the music began to play. He could have refused and maybe he should have in hindsight, but it seemed much too rude at the time. This past week, his aunt caught him in a maudlin moment missing Elizabeth, so he had barely danced at all and spent two full sets against one wall where the shadows were particularly wide. He was already beginning to wish he had left town with Georgiana back in May.

Lady Matlock finally had pestered him to dance to dispel the frightening look on his face, and Lady Fiona was proffered, much like how the footmen brings around punch in glasses for guests to take. He had been halfway to the dance floor before he remembered they had already danced once that evening.

This time he did refuse to go through with the dance. Darcy turned to Lady Fiona, bowed a deep bow, apologizing profusely that he was feeling suddenly unwell, and headed straight for the entrance calling for his carriage. He even decided to wait outside the front door so that he could claim a need for fresh air if anyone decided to question him.

A few minutes into his wait for his carriage, Lady Sefton had approached Darcy.

"Mr. Darcy, I trust that your premature departure this evening has not been precipitated by anything untoward."

Darcy bowed low to the grand lady who had presided over the Almack's revellers for many seasons. "Of course not, my lady. Nothing untoward could ever happen under your excellent care."

"Oh posh! That is absolutely not true. Many young people have tried to take advantage of the atmosphere and expectation of finding romance to behave badly. Most upstanding gentlemen and ladies, like yourself, would be very surprised at some of the events I have witnessed, and many by the so-called *ladies* who come here. I have no tolerance for one person putting another in an uncomfortable or compromising position for the sake of 'winning' the game."

Darcy could only blush and nod his head.

Moving on to another topic, Lady Sefton broached a question she had been curious about for many weeks. "Tell me sir, have you seen much of the Bennet sisters in recent weeks? I confess I was surprised to hear they had gone back to their family estate instead of continuing their season here in town. I would be happy to sponsor them with invitations to Almack's and extend that invitation to their aunt, Mrs. Gardiner. Many of the titled debutantes could learn about style, class, and pleasant conversation from those country ladies. Especially the younger sister, Miss Elizabeth. She was all that was engaging and kind, in addition to being one of the handsomest ladies of my acquaintance."

Darcy had hung his head for a moment hearing Elizabeth's name, but he could not argue in the slightest with Lady Sefton's characterization of the excellent lady. Clearing his throat, Darcy remembered he had been asked a question. "Yes, my lady. That is, I mean no, I have not had the pleasure of seeing the Miss Bennets lately. The eldest, Miss Jane Bennet has been lately married to Charles Bingley. The announcement was not in the papers as might be expected of a society wedding, but I have heard that it was much attended by the people of the county of Hertfordshire. I was, um, unfortunately detained and unable to attend." Darcy continued to blush a deeper and deeper shade of red under the thoughtful and penetrating gaze of Lady Sefton.

"Well! I must say I have not often heard of two more matched persons as Mr. Bingley and Miss Bennet. In fact, only one pairing seems more obvious to me at the moment. I do wish them much joy."

"You certainly have the right of it, my lady. I believe Charles and the new Mrs. Bingley shall be happy and content all the days of their joined lives."

"And when shall I be able to wish you joy, Mr. Darcy?"

Panic, sudden and pure, overtook Darcy's countenance. He was unable to respond at all sensibly and looked around hoping that there were no other persons within hearing range.

"Peace sir! Please!" Lady Sefton raised her hand placatingly. "I never meant to make you so uneasy. Please, I shall retract my question. I was just hoping that perhaps you might have come to your own understanding with a young, beautiful, country miss with pleasant manners and a lively wit. I should have known that you would take recent talk as my meaning. I assure you, I have no expectations that you shall become attached to any of the young ladies currently circulating in London."

At that moment, Darcy's driver appeared and came to the rescue, bearing Darcy's hat and cane, and announced his carriage was ready to take him home. Letting the last question hang between them unanswered, Darcy simply bowed to Lady Sefton and took his leave.

Though he did not read the social page of the paper himself, it was hard to ignore the rumour of his impending engagement to Lady Fiona, especially when he was greeted at his club with well wishes and jeers about plucking the largest of all the dowries available this season.

In order to put an end to this talk, Darcy went to the wages master and asked to see any bets placed on his own wedding. It was normally not done to look upon one's own pages, however, whenever a gentleman placed money on his own actions, it sent a clear message to the rest of the gentlemen. The page had many bets surrounding the date of Darcy's future wedding and, more recently, there were many bets as to the lady who would ultimately be chosen. Lady Fiona was favoured nearly five to one and most were betting on a wedding day to fall between the end of parliament and Guy Fawkes Day. Darcy laid down a crown as a symbolic bet and entered his own name in the ledger. He simply wrote '*never*' as the bet.

With many of his friends and acquaintances watching, Darcy had laid down the pen and quickly walked out of the club.

For the following three days, he had declined to attend any outings and barely left his rooms. The situation and his mood had deteriorated too much to return to London society. Thinking on Lady Sefton's parting words, he was somewhat heartened that perhaps he was not doomed to a sad life. But then he would remember Elizabeth's pained face and her determined attitude, and he would lose heart all over again.

Without making any excuses or taking his leave of any of his family or friends, Darcy packed his things and left town before dawn four days ago. Originally headed for his estate in Wales, once he reached Oxford, Darcy changed his mind and decided he very much needed to see his sister and father. When Darcy woke that morning at the last posting inn before reaching home, he left a note for his valet that he intended to ride ahead of the carriage.

Still not in the right frame of mind to face his father and sister, Darcy rode all around the perimeter of Pemberley. He looked over the fields filled with the summer crops, chased a fox through the southern woods across a deer trail, and watered his horse where the river thinned and was shallow enough to cross near the apple groves. Considering the lateness of the hour, and Darcy determined it was good manners to arrive before his servants, he steered his horse towards the Pemberley stables.

He knew his father would get the truth out of him in a way no one else could. It would be cleansing to hear his father's advice, even if the tale would be embarrassing.

Darcy finally breached the woods and came into the south garden of the manor house. Across the lawn, Darcy saw two women walking arm-in-arm towards the stables. One of the women was probably his sister, but all Darcy's attention was on the other, who could only be one lady.

For as long as he lived, Darcy would never forget the light and pleasing figure of Elizabeth Bennet. Slight in stature and build, but with a strong gait which easily kept pace with those significantly taller than herself. She was even wearing one of his favourite dresses of hers, which she had often donned for her morning walks around the countryside of Hertfordshire.

Like a man lost in a desert, drawn towards a mirage, Darcy steered his mount toward the women. His rational mind kept yelling at him that this could not be, but his heart knew better. Suddenly, both women turned back at the house looking directly towards his position and, as they were within twenty yards of each other, it was impossible to avoid their sight. Darcy looked directly into Elizabeth's deep chocolate eyes and was overcome. He was so startled to find her really there, that he pulled to roughly on the reins, triggering the animal to stop all at once. The jerking motion of the stop coupled with his inattention to his seat, caused Darcy to fall squarely onto his shoulder at his horse's feet.

Elizabeth, acting on instinct and feeling, swiftly ran towards Darcy and easily reached him first, being a much more accomplished runner than her friend. Without any thought towards his embarrassment and only worry over his potential injury, Elizabeth reached for him and helped him to stand while Georgiana came and took the reins of his horse.

"Mr. Darcy! Are you alright? Please come have a seat here on this bench and let me call for your housekeeper to bring ice from the box. I am sure your arm is smarting terribly."

Once she had taken his arm to lead him to a seat, Darcy was not inclined to allow her to leave again. "No, Miss Elizabeth, please do not trouble Mrs. Reynolds. I am unharmed. Please just let me sit for a moment and I shall be perfectly alright. How could I be otherwise with such solicitous attentions to my injury?"

"Well, only if you are certain that you do not need to attend your arm. I would hate for it to swell."

"I am certain. Please come and sit with me and tell me how you have come to be here." Darcy looked at her with bright eyes and a large smile. "Are you visiting with Georgie for a while or just passing through? Are Bingley and Mrs. Bingley with you?"

"No, Charles and Jane left immediately after their wedding for an extended trip to Bath before heading to Scarborough. They have been enjoying the seaside attractions there for nearly three weeks already. I am travelling with my aunt and uncle Gardiner on a tour of the peaks. Georgiana graciously agreed to host us here while we explore the local attractions. We only arrived today." Elizabeth looked around for Georgiana and any other persons who might be attending their conversation. Finding her friend leading Darcy's horse back towards the stables and no one else within hearing distance of their conversation, Elizabeth lowered her eyes and her voice. "Sir, you must allow me to apologise for being here. Georgiana assured me you were not expected to leave London until the first week of August at the earliest, and then it was more likely that you would visit your own estate in Wales instead of coming here. I had no notion of imposing on you so. I will of course depart if that is your wish. I would never be so improper as to force my society upon you after all that you have endured."

Darcy looked at the blush crawling its way down to Elizabeth's décolletage and the way she was now wringing her hands together.

Placing his finger under her chin, Darcy lifted Elizabeth's face to his own and looked back into her fathomless eyes. "Do you wish to leave, Miss Elizabeth? Do you desire a reprieve from my company so much that you would like to end your holiday and leave my sister's company before your trunks can even be unpacked?"

Stunned by the emotion flowing out of Darcy's tender eyes, Elizabeth was momentarily stuck without the ability to speak.

Seeing something in her eyes that gave him hope, Darcy continued. "I no more wish for you to leave than I wish for the sun to stop rising or the rain to never come again. Please stay and allow me to show you the beauty of my home."

Elizabeth simply nodded her acquiescence for, in truth, she wanted nothing more herself than to follow him around to see the wonders of Derbyshire, and beyond, until the end of her days.

The Sun Also Shines

DARCY TOOK ELIZABETH'S HAND AND HELPED HER make the final climb over the rocks to come to the small plateau at the end of the trail leading to Kinder Scout Point. The Gardiners and Georgiana had accompanied them in the landeau up the mountain as far as the horses and buggy could make it, but eventually they could not ascend any further. Knowing his niece's preference for high vistas, Edward allowed Elizabeth and Darcy to take two of the horses and continue up the path towards the summit. It was a clear day and there were several groups of people about the scout, but those who made it to the summit were few. The final climb of about a quarter mile had to be completed on foot but it was well worth the effort.

Elizabeth finally looked up from the trail and was completely breathless at the sight before her. They could see for miles and miles across the Derbyshire land. To the north a short distance, she could see the spray from a waterfall creating a rising mist. In all directions there were other, smaller peaks visible which Elizabeth knew stretched from Wales to Yorkshire. It was the most awe-inspiring sight she had ever witnessed.

"Mr. Darcy, I believe I owe you an apology."

"Whatever for?"

"For all the times I argued with you last autumn about the suitability of Oakham Mount. I see now, it is nothing, nothing at all, to this." She swept her arm across the vista. "I am at a loss as to why you would ever indulge me to climb to its pitiful peak."

Darcy smiled at Elizabeth in a most besotted way. "Really? I cannot see any difference in the view from the top of either. To my eyes, they are the same."

Elizabeth looked over at him, incredulous, but noticed his gaze was not on the landscape before them. Instead he looked directly, and most affectionately upon her. She blushed very deeply. "You are too kind."

"No, I fear I am woefully unprepared to be kind enough to repay all the joy you have shown to me this past year."

Elizabeth thought this was untrue, certainly, and they both knew exactly how wrong his words were, but through some unwritten rule, neither was able to breach the topic of their parting last April.

During her holiday at Pemberley, Darcy had not been direct in his purpose of romancing Elizabeth, but he had also not been subtle. He had asked Mrs. Reynolds to ensure there were freshly cut flowers each morning in Elizabeth's dressing room and he had also procured lavender scented bath oils for Elizabeth, knowing it was the fragrance she preferred.

Each day before breakfast, Darcy had a small basket with new breads and fruit ready for himself and Elizabeth to take on a walk about the Pemberley grounds. They had meandered all around the southern gardens, the apple orchards, the river path, and on one wonderful morning, Darcy had taken Elizabeth on the ridge path by horseback to a small lake with a beautiful waterfall. They always returned before anyone else was received for breakfast, but it was no secret that the young couple ventured out together. Though Madeline was extremely curious, it was not her wish to force a communication from Elizabeth. For many years, Elizabeth had learned to keep her own counsel since neither of her parents were very reliable confidants. Her father being too quick to make a joke out of his daughters' concerns and her mother too prone to flights of hysteria.

However, it was evident that Elizabeth was much better acquainted with Darcy and shared a much deeper affection than they had any idea of before, which was quite the revelation. It was also evident that he was very much in love with her.

Today's excursion to the scout had been specially planned by Darcy for Elizabeth's maximum enjoyment.

The rock falls and spectacular woods available on the road to the Scout were sure to be of keen interest to Elizabeth. After about three hours, Darcy planned for the whole party to stop for a small luncheon picnic at the lake near the bottom of the road leading up the mountain. It was a popular stopping spot for locals who knew it was there but since it was not visible from the main road that travellers took, it was never crowded. Today, there was only one other family enjoying the lake with several young children flying a kite near the water.

Darcy had also schemed with Mrs. Reynolds to find as many strawberries and blackberries as possible, for Elizabeth loved them. The day before, several of the maids and two of the stable hands had been sent out into the Pemberley woods looking for the largest and ripest of the wild berry patches that dotted the estate. The endeavour had certainly borne fruit, and Cook now had five large baskets full of lush berries to incorporate into their meals. A fresh basket of strawberries with the best sweet cream was packed into a small basket that Darcy had carried up the final trail to the scout point. Darcy opened the basket, spread out a small blanket onto the ground and offered Elizabeth his hand to come rest a moment and enjoy their treat.

The two sat in comfortable silence enjoying the sweetness of the fruit along with the magnificence of the view in every direction. It was nearly too much for Elizabeth to take in.

"Sir, I feel I must give you a great thanks for today and truthfully for each day of our stay here. It has been so wonderful, and I shall always treasure my memories of this holiday, no matter how long my life or where it leads. It is unimaginable to me that we must go back home in only a few days."

Darcy was overjoyed with the sentiment of Elizabeth wishing to stay longer at Pemberley. He wanted her to never leave his side again. Going through his thoughts and searching for the right reply, Darcy took too long and Elizabeth continued with her own thoughts.

"Do you believe you will depart soon for your estate in Wales? I understand you have not been there since before Michaelmas last. It seems a great long time to be away from one's estate."

"Well, you are correct that I have been absent from my new estate since before joining Bingley at Netherfield, however I do not currently have plans to return. The estate has a very proficient steward and land manager who looks after it. He has been with the property since before I inherited it upon my aunt's passing." Darcy thought for a moment. "In fact, I believe he has been caring for that property since I was not more than five years old and he requires very little input from me. Cresselly Park House is a fine situation, however it cannot take the place of *home* in my heart, which is here at Pemberley."

All the talk of home and heart caused Elizabeth to blush a deep rose colour all the way to her fingertips.

Darcy had been arguing with himself for several days over renewing his proposal to Elizabeth. They had not addressed her original concerns regarding a relationship between them, and the potential scorn of the *ton* in general and his aunts in specific. Darcy felt keenly that he needed to find some moment of relative privacy to have this conversation explicitly with Elizabeth. So far, though they had enjoyed many lovely morning walks and quiet moments, it never felt right to impose such a heavy conversation into the light-hearted moments.

He was determined though, and thought that perhaps tonight, after supper, he might introduce a walk in the garden and hope that Georgiana would make herself scarce while still providing an appropriate chaperone for an evening stroll. After they were able to talk calmly about their fears and the future, Darcy intended to drop to one knee and present Elizabeth with his mother's Derbyshire Spar earrings and finger ring. Georgiana had been left most of their mother's personel jewellery collection, but a few pieces had been set aside for him to give as gifts to his future bride. He loved how the blue and purple veins of the Derbyshire Spar gems sparkled in the sunlight. It was the perfect set to give Elizabeth as a token of his devotion.

Too quickly for either's preference, Elizabeth and Darcy arrived back to their party. Edward and Georgiana were enjoying a short game of draughts while Madeline read a book. Once the game had been completed and the horses were watered then re-hitched to the landeau, the travellers climbed back in and started the journey back to Pemberley.

After arriving back at the manor house, everyone had about an hour to refresh themselves before dinner.

Darcy took a short bath, shaved, and donned his finest clothes, hoping to look his absolute best for Elizabeth during what he hoped to be his successful proposal. With nervous energy, Darcy finished his ablutions in a very short time then began to pace in his rooms. Finally able to master his emotions, Darcy descended the stairs to wait for the rest of the dinner party in the usual front parlour. As soon as he reached the bottom of the stairs, he turned and caught a glimpse of something out of the corner of his eye. Looking back up towards the second-floor landing, he saw Elizabeth wearing the most beautiful sunshine yellow evening dress beginning her descent towards the parlour.

She was a vision conjured directly from his dreams, and she was smiling demurely at him as she descended the grand staircase.

Darcy quickly ascended the bottom five steps and offered his arm to Elizabeth.

"Thank you sir, you are very kind."

"It is my pleasure, I assure you. We still have more than half an hour before dinner will be announced, would you like to take a stroll through the garden and enjoy the last of the day's sunshine?"

"You know me all too well. I could not forgive myself if I missed even one opportunity to take in the out of doors while I am here, for one day soon I shall be required to journey home and I cannot say when I shall be able to see the wonders of Pemberley's grounds again."

Darcy beamed at Elizabeth then whisked her out of the double doors of the front parlour and started a sedate pace around the paved garden path leading to the lake at the front of the manor house.

Elizabeth, being the more inclined to speak of the two generally, began their conversation with a pleasant inquiry about their mutual London acquaintances, which perhaps not surprisingly, had not yet come up in conversation.

Darcy took this moment to begin his plan to address some of Elizabeth's fears surrounding London society and his social obligations in general. "Yes, I must say that all our shared acquaintances were very well the last time I was in company. One of my last evenings in town I attended the weekly ball at Almack's. I saw your aunt's cousin,

Lady Finch, and her niece, Miss Craven, who were both enjoying the evening. I hope I do not speak out of turn when I say that Miss Craven is much attached to a Captain in His Majesty's army who is the second son of a Baron from Wales. Lady Finch let me know that Miss Craven was being formally courted by this young chap and perhaps by now they have come to an understanding."

Elizabeth smiled. Even when Darcy gossiped, he only did so with kindness and verified, actionable information. "I have known Winnie for several years. She and I are of an age and we would often play as children when her parents were visiting London. I am glad to hear that she has had a successful season."

"Yes, she seems a kindly sort of lady, one I would not mind an increased connection to. Her intended's family is close in proximity to my Wales holdings, so I anticipate that I shall have occasion to host them at Cresselly Park if she does indeed marry the Captain."

"They would be enjoyable company, I am sure."

Darcy tried again to bring up shared acquaintances. "I must say that many of the Almack's regulars were surprised that you and Mrs. Bingley were absent from the season."

"Really!" Elizabeth laughed at such an unfathomable notion. "I rather doubt that anyone who would garner an invitation to Almack's would have any memory of myself or my sister, but you are kind for saying so."

"Truthfully! Lady Sefton herself inquired about you both and said she had invitations for you to come to the dances if you resumed your season in town."

Elizabeth looked at Darcy with shock on her face. "Lady Sefton told you she would like to provide me an invitation to Almack's?"

"Yes, explicitly. I could not have been mistaken as to her meaning."

"Why would a paragon of the London society, a countess, provide invitations to the most exclusive London high society dance club or choose to champion two country misses?"

Darcy gave Elizabeth a kindly but pointed look. "Perhaps because she sees in you what all people of good sense and breeding see: a kind and generous young lady whose worth is much more than a dowry or noble title."

Had Elizabeth been able to encounter his eyes, she might have seen how well the expression of heartfelt devotion diffused over his face became him. They walked on without knowing in what direction they were headed. There was too much to be thought and felt for attention to other subjects.

After a moment to screw his courage to the sticking place, Darcy began the discussion he had so desperately wanted to have these past few weeks.

"Miss Elizabeth, I must say how surprised and delighted I was to find you here enjoying the hospitality of my sister and my home. Indeed, I am sorry that we had not been in company since we both left Kent in April, which is entirely my misdeed."

"No sir!" Elizabeth cried. "I cannot let you take such blame to yourself, not after I abused you so abominably to your face."

"What did you say that was not deserved? You expressed your fears and criticisms of London society as a whole and certain members of my family specifically, and those fears were well-founded, formed on your own accurate observations of how some in the *ton* treat others." Darcy shook his head. "My Aunt Catherine's behaviour to you at the time merited the severest reproof. And I did nothing to ease your fears or discuss my own feelings on the issue. I just walked out and ran away. I do not know if Anne would have broached the subject with you, but I tried to leave Rosings that night, right after leaving you in the parsonage. I was reckless and she stopped me before I could harm myself. It was unpardonable and I cannot think of it without abhorrence."

Elizabeth shook her head vigorously. "We will not quarrel for the greater shame of the blame annexed to that evening. The conduct of neither, if strictly examined, will be irreproachable, but since we have both, I hope, improved in understanding."

Darcy stopped and turned towards Elizabeth, bringing them to look at each other directly. "Have we improved in understanding, truly, Elizabeth? Do I dare to hope? You are too generous to trifle with me. If your feelings are still what they were last April, tell me so at once. My affections and wishes are unchanged; but one word from you will silence me on this subject forever."

Elizabeth, feeling more than common awkwardness and anxiety of his situation, now forced herself to speak. "I believe that my *feelings* have never been the dilemma, for those are as inclined in your direction as anyone can be, and have been since the beginning of our acquaintance. I must admit it has always been my logic that has presented me with such intimidating future scenarios that I have been unable to follow my feelings. But I have always known my future happiness lies with you."

Before anything else could be said, Darcy and Elizabeth were interrupted by two riders barrelling up the lane towards the main house. The first, whom she recognised as one of the warehouse clerks who worked for her uncle, called out to Elizabeth; and the other, whom he recognised as his father's stable manager from London, called out to Darcy.

Tell Tale Letters (Take Two)

DARCY AND ELIZABETH TURNED TOWARDS THE riders coming up the lane at a full gallop. The Darcys' London house stable manager reached the pair first and dismounted.

"Carlton, what is the matter man?"

"Forgive me Mr. Darcy, sir, is your father home? I have an urgent letter for him from London."

"Of course, he is getting ready for dinner now." Darcy held out his hand for the missive. "I can have it delivered to his rooms. Hand it to me and I shall take care of it. You can take that horse to the stables and go have some rest and a meal in the kitchens. Might I ask who this fellow following you might be?"

Elizabeth stepped up with the answer. "I can attest to this man. Mr. Darcy. Please may I present Mr. Joshua Butler. He is my uncle's warehouseman. He has worked for Gardiner Imports as long as I can personally remember. Mr. Butler, this is Mr. Fitzwilliam Darcy. My aunt and uncle Gardiner, and myself, are Mr. Darcy's guests here at Pemberley." Both men bowed at the introduction, and Butler made a very low and proper bow before turning back to Elizabeth.

"Miss Lizzy, I am sorry to be coming and disturbing your holiday, but this letter needs to be getting to your uncle post haste."

Darcy looked between the two riders. "How have the two of you come to be in each other's company?"

Carlton answered. "Mr. Darcy, Butler and I were both at the inn just north of Hampstead Heath the first night of our journeys from London. He was asking the coach drivers for the best way to come to Pemberley when I overheard the conversation. Since we were both headed here, we decided to travel together for safety and efficiency."

"Very good." Darcy nodded. "Please, take Mr. Butler with you to the kitchens for something to eat and I am sure Mrs. Reynolds can find rooms for you both in the servants' hall. Please plan to stay, at least for the night or two, before we have decided if these messages require anyone to return to London. We can take you back with us if indeed my father or Mr. Gardiner are required to travel immediately."

Another round of bows then Butler and Carlton left to take the horses to the stables and get a much deserved meal.

Darcy finally turned back to Elizabeth and found she had wandered a few steps away and had already opened the seal on the letter delivered for her uncle.

"Miss Elizabeth, what is wrong?"

"This is from my father, I recognised the handwriting on the direction. It is extremely unusual that my father would be in London and sending off my uncle's best and most trusted employee all the way to Derbyshire unless something of extreme import has happened."

"What does it say?"

Elizabeth went back to the letter and began to really read the missive.

Suddenly all of the colour ran from her face and Elizabeth frantically cried, "Oh! Where is my uncle?" Elizabeth darted towards the front door in eagerness to find her relations, and without losing a moment of the time so precious; but as she reached the door, Mr. Darcy caught her around the middle and pulled her into the garden path. Her pale face and impetuous manner made him start, but he tried to stop her from making a scene in front of the staff.

"Elizabeth, whatever is going on? Please talk to me before you go dashing around in the house."

She, in whose mind every idea was superseded by the contents of her father's letter detailing Lydia's elopement, hastily exclaimed, "I beg your pardon, but I must leave you. I must find my uncle this moment on business that cannot be delayed; I have not a moment to lose."

"Good God! What is the matter?" he cried, with more feeling than politeness, then recollected himself. "I will not detain you a minute; but let me or Mrs. Reynolds go after Mr. and Mrs. Gardiner. You are not well enough; you cannot go yourself."

Elizabeth hesitated, but her knees trembled under her, and she felt how little would be gained by her attempting to dash up the stairs and down the halls of the large house. Allowing Darcy to guide her back into the front parlour, she took a seat on the settee by the double doors while Darcy went to ask one of the servants to go fetch the Gardiners as instantly as possible. When Darcy returned to the room, she was looking so miserably ill, it was impossible for Darcy to leave her, or to refrain from saying, in a tone of gentleness and commiseration, "Let me call for your maid. Is there nothing you could take to give you present relief? A glass of wine? Shall I get you one? You look very ill."

"No, thank you," she replied, endeavouring to recover herself. "There is nothing the matter with me. I am quite well, I am only distressed with dreadful news which is in this letter from my father."

She burst into tears as she alluded to it, and for a few minutes could not speak another word. Darcy, in wretched suspense, could only say something indistinctly of his concern, and observe her in compassionate silence.

At length, Elizabeth spoke again. "It cannot be concealed from anyone. My youngest sister left all her friends and attempted to elope with Mr. Wickham. They left Brighton on the first of August and were discovered in London by soldiers who have now arrested Mr. Wickham for desertion before they could be married. She is lost forever."

Darcy was fixed in astonishment. He stood and started to pace the room. "I am grieved indeed, grieved and shocked. But is it certain, absolutely certain? What has been done to recover her?"

"My father writes that she is at my uncle's home in London, where my father is also staying. He had gone to look for them when Colonel Forster told him about the elopement, but had no luck in discovering them on his own. Apparently, Lydia showed up on my uncle's doorstep a few days after my father went to London. She was allowed to return to her family after Mr. Wickham was arrested. Father begs my uncle's immediate assistance with how to salvage the situation. But nothing can be done. How can we ever hope to retrieve her respectability? She can never return home as a ruined woman. Thankfully, Jane and Mary are settled. I only pray that my brothers will be merciful with Kitty and myself. I have not the smallest hope. It is in every way horrible!" Elizabeth hung her head.

Darcy had not stopped pacing for the entire story and the look on his face was so hard it was difficult to see any of the kind and happy features of the man she had known for three quarters of a year. She now understood that her power was sinking, everything must sink under such a proof of family weakness, such an assurance of the deepest disgrace. She could neither wonder nor condemn, but the belief of his self-conquest brought nothing consolatory to her bosom, afforded no palliation of her distress. It was, on the contrary, exactly calculated to make her understand her own wishes, and never had she so honestly felt she could have loved Darcy, as now, when all love must be in vain.

Darcy looked back to Elizabeth and came back to kneel in front of her. He carefully took both of her hands into his and waited for her to look into his eyes.

"My dearest, loveliest Elizabeth. I cannot lie to you and say that this situation is not indeed concerning, but I can promise that you and your sisters will be taken care of for their whole lives."

No more was said before Edward and Madeline Gardiner hurried into the room and discovered Elizabeth and Darcy sitting very close and holding hands, with visible tear tracks down Elizabeth's cheeks.

"Lizzy, whatever is the matter dear?" Madeline went directly to sit beside Elizabeth looking between the two young people.

Darcy stood and strode to the window to give Elizabeth some measure of privacy to tell her aunt and uncle what had happened.

"Aunt, Uncle. This letter from my father just arrived. He requires your assistance with a situation that Lydia has created. She left Brighton with Mr. Wickham intending to elope to Gretna Green. They made it as far as London before he was arrested by the army as a deserter. Now, we must endure this scandal, and my father does not know how he will remedy the situation and restore our family's respectability." Edward and Madeline were understandably horrified.

Darcy continued to look out of the window to give them privacy in which to digest the gravity of the information that had just been received. After a moment, he placed his hand into the pocket holding his watch and felt the other letter which was recently delivered, but entirely forgotten in the melee of Elizabeth's news. Fearing what might be on this new page, Darcy pulled the letter sent for his father out of his pocket and broke the seal.

In an unknown feminine hand, Darcy read a separate account of Wickham's misdeeds, this time from the owners of a respectable boarding house in Covent Garden London, who were demanding payment for lodging and meals for the disgraced officer and his young companion.

Into the middle of all of these revelations, Mr. George Darcy and Georgiana entered the parlour dressed for dinner. Instantly seeing that something was wrong with her friend, Georgiana went straight to Elizabeth's side.

"Lizzy, what has happened? Why do you look so distressed?"

Hoping to spare her young friend some upset, and delay the spread of her family's disgrace as long as possible, Elizabeth tried to demur. "Oh Georgie, it is nothing to concern yourself with. We have just had some news from London which I fear will take myself and my aunt and uncle away sooner than we had planned. In fact, I am sure we will want to leave today as soon as possible. If we pack only what is required and beg your kindness to send our trunks later, we might make it three hours before we lose the light."

"Leave? You cannot leave yet! There is so much unsettled," Georgiana exclaimed, looking quickly between Elizabeth and her brother, "and we have the best day planned for tomorrow at the lake with a picnic at the old folly."

George Darcy decided to take some charge of the situation. "My dear, it seems that Miss Bennet is trying to tell you politely that they have heard bad news and might wish for some privacy to plan their departure. Come dear, come son. Let us give Mr. Gardiner, Mrs. Gardiner and Miss Bennet some privacy in which to discuss this business which does not concern us."

"Unfortunately, Father, we are all too concerned with this business already." Darcy turned from his perch at the window and held out the letter meant for the elder Mr. Darcy towards his father.

Elizabeth jumped up and went directly to Darcy while the other adults in the room looked at them with alarm and curiosity. Darcy allowed Elizabeth to take the letter and read it, for there were no additional private details in there, and also because he did not wish to keep anything from her.

While Elizabeth read the direct account, Darcy addressed the rest of their relations. "Wickham has already dragged the Darcy name into this affair. Apparently, Wickham tried to pay for his expensive tastes in London with a forged cheque on my father's account, but the bank refused to cash the note. The owner of the lodgings where he passed the forged cheque called the army to report a deserter when Wickham tried to pay his bill with his red coat. He has been arrested and deemed to have deserted his post."

Elizabeth suddenly exclaimed, "Sent to fight on the front! He is already gone to France to face Napoleon!"

George Darcy interrupted, "I am sorry, I fear we may need to start from the beginning. How are our two events related? Son, please start from the beginning."

Elizabeth and Darcy looked at each other. Elizabeth nodded and signalled for Darcy to go ahead. Taking a large inhale, Darcy relayed the full story starting with Wickham taking an officer's commission with the militia quartering near the Bennet family estate last autumn, and his elopement with the youngest Bennet sister from the militia in Brighton. The new details from the demand letter revealed that Wickham had a stack of cheques from George Darcy's Royal Bank account and had gotten himself arrested for desertion. Lydia Bennet was identified as the young lady travelling with Wickham and the landlord noted that she had been sent back to her family.

After Darcy finished the whole tale, everyone in the room was quiet for several moments.

Surprisingly, Georgiana spoke first. "Poor Lydia! She is only just turned sixteen and has been very deceived in the character of a charming man with no good morals. Even if Mr. Wickham had planned to take her all the way to Scotland, he was a deserter and a thief. Perhaps fate has been kind to make it impossible that they should not now wed, for if they had been discovered by her father, he would have surely forced them to move directly to church, and she would have been bound to a degenerate all her life or faced being widowed so young."

George Darcy looked at his daughter with kindness and some sadness at this first intrusion into her sheltered childhood. "You are right my dear, it would not have been a good life to be so bound to one who is so lacking in every good feeling as George Wickham. Unfortunately, I did know that a stack of my bank draft cheques had been stolen last summer and I suspected it was Wickham, but I did nothing to sensor him. I simply called at the bank and requested that they refuse to cash those cheques. If I had done something more, I might have been able to stop this from happening. Gardiner, we are at your disposal. Whatever might be in our power to do, shall be done."

In very short order, the men retired to the study to plan what might be done for Lydia while the ladies were dispatched to the family wing to start preparations for their departure in the morning. The whole group sat down nearly an hour late for dinner, but the food was none the worse for waiting. Pemberley's cook was too efficient and proficient a manager to have anything so silly as a family crisis disrupt the quality of a meal placed on Pemberley's table.

After the last of the dishes were cleared, everyone agreed to retire early so that they might all have ample rest ahead of the morning's journeys. Elizabeth and Madeline were going to take the Darcy's carriage back to Longbourn where Elizabeth would be left and Madeline would retrieve the Gardiners' children and take them home to London. Four of the largest, most loyal male servants were assigned to accompany the women who would be travelling alone for the final day of the journey where the road diverged towards Longbourn. The Darcy men and Edward Gardiner would go directly to London in the Gardiners' carriage to assist Mr. Bennet with planning how to salvage the situation.

Before everyone left the table, Darcy requested a short, private, audience with Elizabeth in the library.

"Yes of course. Lizzy, your aunt will be waiting for you in your rooms to ensure that everything is packed for the morning. Do give Mr. Darcy your attention, but do not tarry."

Elizabeth merely nodded and took Darcy's arm as he led her out of the dining room, across the foyer into the library. Taking a seat on the small sofa near the fire, Darcy launched into his speech before any more interruptions might come to dissuade his purpose.

"My dearest, loveliest Elizabeth. I know that now may feel like the wrong time for declarations, but I cannot leave your company without some understanding between us."

"Mr. Darcy, you cannot mean to tie yourself to me now that my family is so disgraced?"

"I do and I will, if you will have me." He took both of her hands in his. "I care not for whatever scandal your sister might create, or the reaction from the world for it. I am sure you will see one day soon, if not now, how little this matters to me, truly."

Elizabeth was too shocked to say anything for several moments. "Mr. Darcy, this is ludicrous! Many formally engaged couples where there had already been an announcement in the papers, or even where the banns had already been read, might consider breaking off their understanding in the face of something like the scandal we are confronting. There is no guarantee Lydia will be able to be saved nor if she is to suffer consequences from her time with Mr. Wickham. How can you even think of becoming engaged now?"

Hoping to avoid a repeat of the scene from Hunsford, Darcy decided to listen to Elizabeth and take her concerns to heart. "Perhaps we might be able to come to some compromise. We are short on time, as your aunt is awaiting your return to your rooms, and tomorrow we must both go into uncertain situations and emotions. Instead of my asking for your hand here and now, might you consent to a formal courtship? This way we can send each other letters while I am required to be away from you and there might be some ray of light in this situation. Once this business with your sister is resolved one way or another, I shall come see you at your father's house and we can do the thing properly. Will you grant me this honour Elizabeth?"

How could she deny him anything he designed to ask when he looked at her with such kind and beseeching eyes? "You are determined,

I can see that. Truthfully, it is more than I could have ever hoped for and much more than my current situation warrants. I cannot find it in myself to demur. Yes, Mr. Darcy. I would be honoured if you would court me."

Darcy felt his whole body become flushed at her approval. "Will you not call me by my name, Elizabeth, when we are in private like we are here?"

"What would you like me to call you?" A light and teasing glint shown in Elizabeth's eyes. "William, as Anne and Georgie do, or perhaps Fitz like Colonel Fitzwilliam does when he is trying to make you mad?"

To hear her tease him again, when everything else of their current situation had her close to tears, gave Darcy great joy and such hope that he could not keep his sombre countenance. His answering smile was wide and bright. "I believe that you could call me anything and I would love it, but how about Wills? My mother used to call me that as a younger man. You remind me of her so much in your demeanour and kindness that I believe I would like to have you adopt that name."

Elizabeth was touched. "Wills it is then. We should retire now, but I shall see you at breakfast… my Wills."

Respectability

"ELIZABETH BENNET! WHATEVER SHALL BECOME of you!" Mrs. Bennet's shrill voice broke through the crunch of gravel following the carriage taking Madeline Gardiner and her four children back to London.

It had been only three days since receiving the letters detailing Lydia and Wickham's elopement, and travelling south in haste. The road had thankfully been dry and in good repair, giving the weary travellers an advantage in making good time. At the last moment, Edward Gardiner and the Darcy men continued on the Great North Road though Meryton to reach London just past sundown on the second day of travel. Elizabeth and Madeline had steered to Longbourn to support Mrs. Bennet and Kitty.

At first, her mother had only been piqued with Elizabeth over having been away when such tragedy befell them, enjoying a holiday without any compassion for her mother's nerves. Elizabeth knew it was useless to try and reason with her mother, even though there was no way Elizabeth could have foreseen Lydia would cause such a large scandal during a trip on which her mother was all too eager to send her. Blessedly, that first night, Mrs. Bennet had whipped herself into such a state that she took to her bed shortly after they arrived and did not emerge until shortly before Madeline and the children were ready to depart.

Now, though, it seemed like Elizabeth was to be subjected to a bevy of new complaints.

"Mamma, I do not know what you mean, I plan to become nothing more than myself." Elizabeth managed to keep most of the frustrations from her tone. But just. "I am here with you and Kitty, safe and sound. We came as fast as the horses could carry us and even left most of our trunks at Pemberley for Georgiana to send later so that we could travel faster with reduced weight."

Mrs. Bennet waved her white handkerchief in Elizabeth's direction and stomped into the house, calling to the housekeeper for her smelling salts.

Taking a moment to herself to calm her nerves, Elizabeth followed her mother inside the house and began to head for her father's book room. Yesterday and this morning she had spent nearly all her time dealing with household and estate matters that continued to require attention without any consideration to the crisis happening inside the house.

Unfortunately, her mother was not ready to give up on her complaints.

"Do not try to escape me, child!" Mrs. Bennet cried from her chaise lounge in the parlour. "I demand you come attend me in here."

"There is much to be done today. The midsummer crop harvest is under way and the rents are due." Elizabeth pointed towards the book room and her escape. "I shall have to review the ledgers and any invoices before going around to the tenants tomorrow."

"Collecting rents are not for daughters! La, it is no wonder you are not married yet. Come in here at once, I have much more important business to discuss with you than tenant rents."

Elizabeth bit her lip to stop her angry retort. There should be nothing in their lives which was more important business than collecting the quarterly rents. It was their entire income. Debating with herself for a moment, Elizabeth decided to give her mother the attention she demanded and to look over the ledgers after dinner.

"You have always been my most troublesome child. I am certain that your bookishness and insistence on handling estate matters is why Mr. Darcy has not come up to scratch." Mrs. Bennet cried and wafted her salts below her nose. "How can you be so obstinate and headstrong! How many times have I told you that gentlemen of means want a *silent* and supple wife. Someone who is easy going and docile. Just look at Jane."

Silence was her only response. Elizabeth knew that any actual discussion would only make her mother's diatribe lengthier. It was better to let her rant and get it over with. She was also not yet willing to divulge her tentative understanding about a courtship with Darcy. Lydia's reputation was still too tenuous and her mother would likely make the situation more complicated if she suspected Elizabeth had any chance of becoming engaged.

"How many weeks have you been enjoying his sister's company now? And you have made no progress there. If you cannot catch him at his estate where there are no other eligible women to compete for his attention, then I wash my hands of you." Mrs. Bennet sat up slightly and wagged her finger at Elizabeth. "When your father dies, and we are thrown into the hedgerows, I shall not support you! There shall be less than enough for myself with just my small portion. I shall not be able to pay for ungrateful and disobedient daughters!"

"My brother Collins is a kind and generous man. Remember the gown he gave Mary for Jane's wedding? He will not throw us from the house."

"Let us hope that after Lydia's elopement that will still be true." Mrs. Bennet cried again and fanned herself with her handkerchief. "I cannot understand what has happened! She was always such a good girl, no trouble at all. Lively and happy, such a favourite of the officers."

Kitty entered the parlour with a tea tray and began to pour their mother a cup of Cook's special calming tea. Elizabeth took the opportunity to escape, locking the door to the study behind her.

Several days later, when all the matters of business were finally concluded, Elizabeth sat in her favourite chair in her father's study, in too much emotional turmoil to rest in her bed. Late that evening, Mrs. Hill entered the study with a fresh pot of tea, lemon biscuits from the cook, and an express letter in her father's hand. It took all of Elizabeth's internal strength to sit quietly as Mrs. Hill poured and prepared her cup of tea and wait until she left the room to tear into the letter.

Lizzy,

I know you have been waiting only three days for this news, but it must feel like a lifetime. I, myself have only just begun to feel the weight of all my failings as a father, and the burden is great indeed. Now my child, I know you and your generous heart too well to imagine your reaction to my old maudlin self, yet who should suffer but myself? It has been my own doing, and I ought to feel it. You may warn against being too severe on my own self, but my little Lizzy, let me for once in my life feel how much I have been to blame in this affair. I am not afraid of being overpowered by the impression. I am sure it shall pass away soon enough. Let me say now while I have your undivided attention, child. I bear you no ill will for being justified in your advice to me last May in begging that Lydia not be allowed to leave us, under so little protection. Considering what has come to pass, your passion and plea shows some greatness of mind. I also fear that too much is fallen on you my dear. I can only imagine your mother's reaction to all this business and so I assume the running of the house and the estate has fallen on your shoulders. I am sorry my dear, as little as you might believe it owing to my indolence in the past, I do not wish for you to have to bear the burdens which should be mine.

Now, dear, in contrast to all those evils I have just apologised for, I shall commit one more. I understand from your uncle Gardiner that you have agreed to receive letters from a certain young man of our acquaintance. He has written you quite a long one here and I am sure that its contents shall have all the particulars of our last few days involving your sister, Lydia. Instead of exerting myself to add more ink to this page, I shall allow him to say what has transpired.

Your appreciative father,
T. Bennet

Elizabeth's heart jumped out of her chest. Her courtship with Darcy had been left in a bit of limbo as her father was not present to give his consent. She had not expected that he would press his suit with him before they all returned to Hertfordshire. Additionally, she was anxious to make any additional steps towards their potential future engagement until the Lydia situation had been finally resolved. But here was the evidence that Darcy was serious about their courtship, and that her father approved of their corresponding directly.

Taking a deep breath, Elizabeth opened the second set of pages, which was sealed with the signet ring from Cresselly Park that she knew rested on Darcy's right first finger.

My dearest Elizabeth,

I hope that these pages find you well in body and that the words within shall soothe your soul. It has been only three days since we parted on the north London road, but I feel that it has been an eternity without your smiles and gentle teasing to ease my mind from the chaos of the days. I believe that your father will most likely tell you of these events from his own perspective, but I cannot help giving you my thoughts. I wish in the future to never keep anything from you, so please indulge these pages filled with accounts of our days. I write them only for your eyes, but also to send you my heart in the pages.

My father and I escorted your uncle directly to his home and met your father and sister in the parlour. I am sorry to say that we found your youngest sister a much changed person. No matter her behaviour before, she is still much too young to know such evil. Her demeanour was very contrite and quiet. You know that my own personality is not one given to boisterousness or overt displays of emotion, however I would have much rather seen the same young lady who laughed loudly with her friends at Bingley's ball than this one who seems afraid of her shadow. I cannot help but see much of Georgiana in your sister. They are quite different in many respects, but that girlish and youthful spirit is still alive in my baby sister. I hope that nothing befalls her which shall rob her of her happy demeanour.

It was with these heavy thoughts that we four gentlemen retired to Gardiner's study after dinner. Your father had not been able to conjure a solution to what should happen to Lydia now, except that she cannot come home for fear of consequences from her time with Wickham. Many thoughts were shared that night, but no resolution presented itself immediately.

That evening, my father and I returned to Darcy House and much to our surprise, found my cousin, Richard, residing in the house. He is, of course, always welcome at Darcy House, however I was under the impression that he was still in Newcastle for the summer training. He informed me that he was on some mission or another to London and decided he would rather not face his mother after yet another season where none of her sons, nieces, or nephews had found matches. When he arrived, he believed me to still be in town and sought refuge here. Since he planned to go back north in only a few days, he decided not to change house. I am sure that hiding from my Aunt Matlock and not wishing the inconvenience of packing his things were happy inducements to continuing his residence at Darcy House, but I know my cousin much better than all this. His real reason for staying was that my father and I keep a much better stock of brandy. My uncle prefers sherry.

While my father excused himself after the long travel, Richard and I took a decanter to the game room and tried to thrash each other at billiards. While we are well matched in fencing, horse riding, and darts, I hope you will forgive my boast when I say that I am the far superior billiards player. Nearly half of the decanter and four lost games of billiards later, Richard finally became a useful freeloader. He told me the story of a good friend of his from university, a Captain with the Royal Navy. His name is Captain Henry Wordsville. He has performed admirably in the wars and was recently given his own command of a mail ship bringing correspondence between England and the continent. The man lost his wife in childbirth while gaining a daughter. He is heartbroken, but also now in desperate need of a new wife to help raise the babe.

All that Richard said led me to believe that Captain Wordsville was a good man, a worthy officer, and in a position to take on a wife with a small portion of her own money. His biggest concerns were with finding someone who would be willing to follow the sail and raise a child who was not her own. After delicate inquiry of Richard, I determined that this might be the perfect solution for Miss Lydia. The next morning, I went straight to your father to see if he was amenable to the situation. I believe his heart was heavy at the thought of putting his youngest daughter at the mercy of a man none of us knew and send her off to lands unknown with a babe to care for, but it was a most respectable situation. In another stroke of luck, Captain Wordsville is presently in London and was available to come to dinner yesterday evening on very short notice.

Richard made the introductions and Miss Lydia was allowed to have some time to talk with Captain Wordsville after dinner. I cannot say for certain, but I believe she discussed her present situation with him and the events of the last few weeks. I did not overhear their conversation directly, but I did witness that he gently placed his hands over her own and spoke softly with her. In the short time I have known him, it seems that his is exactly the kind of man whom we might wish to care for Miss Lydia. It eases my own mind that Richard has known him for many years and also believes that he is inclined to be kind to a young woman regardless of any foolishness in her youth.

This evening, we are due to have your family, Captain Wordsville and his daughter for dinner at Darcy House. I hope we shall come to an understanding and begin the marriage settlement. It has been decided that if the Captain and Miss Lydia are agreeable, they will be married by common licence from your aunt and uncle's house as soon as the bishop will allow the ceremony, so that we might avoid having to read the banns.

I know it is not perhaps the best solution to Miss Lydia's situation, however, she shall come out of this as a respectable married woman with a widow's portion and a family to care for. It might be much too simple of a characterization, but I imagine that this is what all people hope for, a family and some security. Children to love and care for and someone to share their lives, no matter what the ups or downs might be. I know that is what I have always wanted.

Before I give you more ammunition for your biting wit and teasing tongue, I shall stop with these maudlin thoughts. In closing, let me say that I am hopeful for a successful restoration to your sister's respectability and also a happy conclusion to what has been a very trying ordeal for her. As soon as I can, I plan to come to see you at Longbourn. I have spoken to your father about our courtship and hope to discuss the matter further soon.

Forever Yours, Wills.

Elizabeth sighed and sat back in her chair. It was too much. Lydia was very likely to be married and to a respectable man. The letter was dated that afternoon. The express rider must have come from London as soon as the ink was dry.

It broke Elizabeth's heart to see her baby sister wed to a man she could not yet love, but perhaps it was better for Lydia to be placed with a man who would have the discipline to deal with her foolish ways and the compassion to do so with kindness. She would have to trust Darcy and Richard's judgement of this man until she could see her sister for herself, but there was little else for it but to trust.

Looking to the mantle, Elizabeth debated whether she would share this news with her mother and Kitty. Inevitably, her mother would demand to see the words on the page for herself and Elizabeth was not inclined to share her letter with her mother at this time. Elizabeth was hoping to keep her understanding with Darcy from her excitable mother just a little longer. Mrs. Hill had come back from clearing the dinner tray from her mother's room more than an hour ago and it was likely that she had already taken some laudanum to lull herself to sleep. So, no, this news would wait until there was confirmation that Lydia and the Captain would be married.

The bell pull to Mrs. Hill was right behind her father's desk, and Elizabeth called for their housekeeper to come back.

After entering, Elizabeth asked if the express rider was still present.

"Yes miss. He is finishing some food in the kitchen. Do you need to speak with him?"

"No Hill, thank you. Am I correct that the rider was a Mr. Carlton?"

Hill nodded. "Yes miss. I believe he said he was a servant in Mr. Darcy's London home."

"I would like to ask that he be given a bed here for the night, then he can return in the morning to Mr. Darcy carrying letters from me for my father and sister." *And one for Darcy*, Elizabeth added in her thoughts.

"Of course, miss. We have plenty of room. I will go tell him your wishes. Do you need anything else for the night, miss? Sally has just come back to the kitchen from helping Miss Kitty into her night things. She can come help you plait your hair, and dress, miss."

Elizabeth waved off the offer. "I believe I will stay here and write my letters, then I shall retire. I do not know how long it should take me, so please do not bother Sally."

Mrs. Hill shook her head hard. "No, miss. I will just have her wait for you in the parlour. You have been doing the work of the master and the mistress of this house for days now and you deserve to be treated like the lady you are. It shall be no burden to wait for you to write your letters and finish any other business that keeps food in all our mouths."

"Thank you, Hill." Elizabeth smiled. "I do not know what I would do without you here to keep me well cared for."

"'Tis no trouble at all. I count myself lucky to have such a fine young lady to serve. I will just run along now and make sure Mr. Carlton is well situated for the night and we will have scones and tea ready for you in the morning before you go for your ramble. Cook has a full bushel of blackberries from the grove by the bourn and was looking to make some sweets from them. I am sure that blackberry scones and clotted cream will be just the thing to help you make the best of whatever comes tomorrow."

Darcy looked at his gold pocket watch and surmised that Carlton should have made it to Longbourn by now, so Elizabeth should have his letter and the one from her father bringing news that Lydia might shortly be married to a good man. That same man was, at this moment, sitting in the Darcy House nursery with Lydia, his six-month-old daughter, Caroline, and the wet nurse whom Captain Wordsville had hired in the wake of his first wife's death.

Truthfully, Darcy was extremely surprised at how well Lydia had already taken to the child. As soon as the nurse brought Caroline in the door, Lydia came to life again. Her shy demeanour, which did not suit her at all, melted away in the face of a sweet little babe. She had asked Captain Wordsville if she might hold and play with his daughter before dinner was served, instead of shuffling her off to the nursery. Everyone was amenable to having the baby in the parlour since this dinner visit was solely about Lydia becoming comfortable with the father and daughter. So, it was with great satisfaction, and some jealousy, that Darcy watched the young lady play with Caroline, giving her silly faces and baby kisses.

The wet nurse took Caroline for her own dinner above stairs while the adults sat in the dining room. Lydia and Captain Wordsville sat next to each other, with Madeline Gardiner on the other side of Lydia and Mr. Bennet on the other side of the captain. Dinner was a pleasant affair, and though Darcy was at the other end of the table so could not hear their conversation, he was hopeful that Lydia would be engaged by the end of the evening, and at least moderately happy with the prospect.

Mr. Bennet broke Darcy out of his private musings.

"My boy, come sit with me. I believe that we might need to have some conversation regarding another of my daughters whom I believe is much on your mind."

Darcy nodded and invited Mr. Bennet to sit in one of the large wingback chairs by the window. He then moved to the sideboard and poured two glasses of the best brandy for fortification. Darcy handed one glass to Mr. Bennet and then gingerly took a large sip before seating himself.

Mr. Bennet waited a few moments before speaking his mind, watching the younger man squirm under the silence. "So, my brother tells me that you and Lizzy had a very eventful holiday at your father's estate. Morning walks around the grounds, evening strolls in the garden, and many afternoons spent together exploring the hills and caves of the Peaks. He also tells me that you have asked for a formal courtship, to which my Lizzy has agreed. My real question is why are you taking so long a time with the conclusion to this story?"

Darcy choked on his brandy.

There was a considerable amount of time required for Darcy to clear his own throat enough to speak again. When he was able, not much sense came out. "Mr. Bennet, I assure you we have not… I mean, I have not… I mean," *cough*. "Sir, I never meant to disrespect you or your daughter in any way."

Mr. Bennet lifted one eyebrow and looked sideways at Darcy. "Are you saying that you have disrespected Lizzy?"

"*What?* No! I promise you I have not caused her any disrespect."

Mr. Bennet chuckled and took some pity on Darcy. "Young man, I did not intend to make you so uncomfortable." The twinkle in his eyes and smirking smile belied his words. "I just wanted to be sure that you plan to bring this understanding to its natural conclusion, either by letting my daughter free to lick her wounds and move on to greener pastures, or to finally make her an offer of marriage and put the rest of us out of our misery. You were not around in the late spring, and she was quite put out by your antics in London which were reported in *The Times* gossip column nearly every day. I find it hard to believe, from your behaviour in Hertfordshire and these past few days, but it seems that you were playing quite the field during the season. Are you going to leave again now and forget us country bumpkins, or will you come to Longbourn and be honest?"

Darcy considered his answer for a moment. It was clear that Elizabeth had not confided in her father about his proposal from April. It was also clear that he had some significant atonement to attend to before he could put the last five months behind them.

"Mr. Bennet, let me first say how sorry I am that my behaviour this past spring at the society events has caused you, Miss Elizabeth, or any other member of your family distress. I do not know what was reported, though I did know that many in London expected me to make an offer of marriage to Lady Fiona Finch, who is my aunt's niece. I found myself twice in a position where politeness dictated I dance with Lady Fiona twice in one evening." Darcy frowned and stared into his brandy glass. "Truthfully, I *was* taking advantage of the season to try and see what my options were for a marriage partner. The entire endeavour was a mistake. You see, I made an ill-fated offer of marriage to Miss Elizabeth last April when we were all still together in Kent." At his revelation, Mr. Bennet's eyes grew large and he was unable to maintain his usual calm demeanour. "Miss Elizabeth rejected me based on her anxiety regarding her reception by the social elite of London. She also expressed that she was worried I might come to resent her if my own family fell in standing because of her lower social status."

Darcy hung his head in retelling the tale and continued. "I am sorry to say that I was very upset with her refusal and what I felt was a slight to my feelings and character. Instead of trying to reassure her that my affection would stand the test of time, I fled. I went to London determined to put my heartbreak behind me. I am also ashamed to admit that I did not come to the Bingleys' wedding purely because I could not dare to face her."

Mr. Bennet remained silent and waited for Darcy to finish his thoughts.

"I failed spectacularly at putting Elizabeth behind me while dancing with other young ladies. Each was dull compared to her wit, humourless compared to her teasing, and homely compared to her bright smile. I cannot promise you that I will never make another mistake or that my anger and pride will never again overwhelm my good sense, but I do promise that I will make every effort to be a good husband, and father if we are so blessed. My intentions are fixed. I will marry Elizabeth or I shall never marry."

Mr. Bennet took another moment after Darcy's declaration to look at this man. In many ways, at twenty-seven and still waiting on his full inheritance, he was already a more prominent man than Mr. Bennet had ever been. He was already master of an estate worth at least three times Longbourn, and the heir to an estate which was far larger. He was spectacularly well educated, well thought of by his friends, generous and kind, and most importantly, willing to own up to his mistakes. It also spoke well of him that he had such refined taste in a life partner. Though it was not polite to say so, Elizabeth was Mr. Bennet's favourite child, mostly for her bottomless wit and intelligence. There was only one response to such a declaration by Darcy.

"Well, I see then. You have given me much to think on, but I will believe you sincere, for I have never known you to be a dishonest young man. On the matter of any additional understanding between yourself and Lizzy, do you remember what I told Bingley when you and he came to dinner while Jane and Lizzy were first in Kent?"

Darcy nodded. "You told him that you would give your permission for him to call, but that any permission for an understanding would be reserved until you could speak to your daughter to ensure her happy consent."

"Good memory, yes. I said that to Bingley and I will stick by that idiom. Gardiner tells me that Lizzy has accepted your courtship, so I shall not curtail your letters. However, I will not agree to give you my daughter until I can speak to her and be sure of her choice."

"I would expect nothing less, sir. As soon as may be arranged, I shall follow you back to Hertfordshire and give Miss Elizabeth the attention she deserves."

"Very good."

Both men sat in quiet contemplation for a few minutes while they finished their brandy. Before either was ready to rejoin the other guests, Lydia and Captain Wordsville entered the parlour. The shy smile from Lydia and the broad grin from the Captain confirmed to everyone present that there would be a wedding to celebrate in the coming days.

Return

"MY DEAR, WE ARE HERE." BINGLEY GENTLY shifted his napping wife as the carriage stopped in front of the large front doors to Netherfield.

Jane gave a small sigh at the sight of her new home. It seemed impossible that only twelve weeks had passed since her wedding, both in that it seemed like such a short time and that she felt she had always been destined to be married to the excellent man by her side. Their honeymoon trip had been wonderful – so many exciting things to see and do. Jane's favourite new experience had been the sea bathing machines. There were machines for married couples which Bingley had reserved for several days of their stay at the Scarborough Spa Resort. At first, Jane had been reluctant to get so undressed in the out of doors – and to have her husband present! But it had ended up being a wonderfully freeing experience.

And quite amorous.

Jane blushed even thinking about how Bingley had held her in his arms while the gentle waves rocked them up and down under the canopy of the machine. He had been everything that was gentle and kind while introducing her to her new duties as his wife, and Jane was at a loss as to why women bemoaned the marriage bed. Perhaps their husbands were just not as knowledgeable or patient as hers.

Jane was eager to see her family again but also to speak with her mother about certain *particular symptoms* she had been experiencing as of late.

That would be for tomorrow. Today, she intended to take a bath to rid herself of the dust from the long journey, eat a light meal with her husband in their sitting room, and then retire early. She was quite tired after so many days in a swaying carriage.

It was very good to be home.

Bingley was also extremely glad to be home for a host of reasons. Most notably, they had left Caroline behind in Scarborough. His father had agreed that Caroline was not to be trusted in London and took her home to their family house in Scarborough directly after the Bingleys' wedding. She had been encouraged to visit the shoppes, engage with friends, attend society events, and enjoy the entertainments available in the seaside town. However, Caroline had been in a severe snit for the whole summer. She was determined to see her return to her father's house as exile and punishment. It was not up for debate that the society in the north was smaller and less wealthy than the London set, however, it was by no means a threat to anyone's reputation to be seen enjoying the fashionable society in Scarborough.

But it was for nothing. Caroline was sulking and unfit to be seen in public. She would not yield. So, when the time came for Bingley and Jane to return to Netherfield, Bingley refused to allow Caroline to accompany them. It was unfortunate that Caroline had acted in such a way as to force their father's hand, but it was no longer Bingley's problem to keep her in check.

After bathing and eating, Bingley tucked his tired bride into the master's bed, then went to his secretary desk in the sitting room attached to the master suite and began to write the letter that was twelve weeks too late to his dearest friend, Darcy. In fact, it had been so long since a letter was exchanged between them that Bingley did not know where Darcy might be staying at the moment. So, Bingley wrote three copies of the same letter, one to send to London, one to send to Pemberley, and one to send to Cresselly Park.

Darcy,

I believe that it has been too long since we have spoken. Jane and I have returned from our wedding trip and visiting with my father and are this evening instilled in Netherfield again. As you are not one given to lengthy letters, and I have uniquely poor penmanship, as you have reminded me on many occasions, I shall keep this letter short.

Come to Netherfield. No matter what has kept us apart this summer, it is all forgiven. I desire to see you again. No need to reply. I shall have your rooms prepared, and whenever you ride up, you will be welcomed. In case you were worried, my sister does not join us. However, I expect that we shall see much of my wife's family.

Your friend,
C. Bingley

Darcy slammed down the morning edition of the *Times* on the desk. He had not really been anywhere around London except for one night at the theatre with his father and a trip to his tailor to have a few new summer coats and breeches made. But somehow, his shadow, the pernicious gossip columnist, had managed to find him. After Mr. Bennet had mentioned the pain Elizabeth experienced in reading the gossip surrounding his person last spring, Darcy decided he should at least keep one eye on the gossip and society pages to know if there was anything he needed to address with his intended directly. He certainly did not want her to go on worrying about his affections or intentions.

"Cousin, what has you angry with the furniture this morning?" Richard sauntered into the breakfast room and plucked a plum from the sideboard.

"The gossipmonger at the *Times* has been following me again. He has printed a lengthy column this morning dedicated to my particular movements in recent days." Darcy tossed the paper across the table towards Richard. "He goes too far! Even bringing the Gardiners and Lady Fiona into his ridiculous vendetta against me."

Richard skimmed the paper. "Oh! He names Captain and Mrs. Wordsville specifically and has given significant details about their wedding, including that you, me, and your father were in attendance."

He looked up with raised eyebrows. "He must have been in the church or watching the door."

"I did not see him, but perhaps he sent some lackey."

"Or you have a servant on the take." Richard leaned in and lowered his voice. "Perhaps you should speak to Timms about this."

Darcy chewed on his bottom lip and crossed his arms, then sighed and shook his head. "No, I do not believe that a servant is spying. Timms is vigilant, and so many of our staff are from families that have served us for years. It is more likely that he has been following me and I have not noticed."

"Well, hopefully it will not matter soon. After you are married to Miss Lizzy, your life will not be of such great interest to anyone in London." Richard smeared a large amount of jam onto some toast and took a great large bite.

Darcy rolled his eyes. "Do the King's finest not teach basic table manners?"

Richard only answered by taking another heaping bite of his breakfast.

"Addlepate." Darcy shook his head affectionately. "I am anxious to get back to Hertfordshire. I hope that Mr. Bennet is not cross about this report."

"Why would he be cross?"

"Mr. Bennet had specifically decided not to make an announcement regarding Miss Lydia and Wordsville's wedding, to keep the timing of their relationship vague. He had hoped he might be able to tell their neighbours she was staying with her aunt and uncle in London when she met Wordsville and they married after a month or two of courting. Now that will be impossible, as the wedding date is printed here." Darcy went back to worrying his bottom lip.

"You worry too much. Some might talk about the speed of their wedding, but his profession and the imminent departure of his ship is all the excuse they need." Richard took another pass at the sideboard, returning to the table with a full plate and more jam toast. "I would be more worried about what he says about your expected engagement to Lady Fiona."

"Yes, I must admit I am not looking forward to seeing your mother."

Several invitations, bordering on outright summons, had been delivered for dinners at Matlock House. Darcy had let his father send back their regrets each time.

"Mother is certainly fearsome, but I would be more worried about Uncle Nottingham. If he thinks that your honour has been engaged, he will be relentless. You would do well to announce your engagement to Miss Lizzy *soon*." Richard punctuated his words with a hard look, then rose to leave the room, taking with him one final piece of toast, heavy with jam.

Darcy sighed and leaned back in his chair. It had been five days since Lydia's wedding, and a letter had gone between Darcy and Elizabeth each day. His stableman, Carlton, was being used as the express go-between until Darcy could manufacture an invitation to Netherfield. Elizabeth insisted that the Bingleys would be returning to the area in the next few days, and he should wait until he could stay with his friend, but Darcy's patience was wearing thin. He was determined to wait another two days, but then he would go and stay at the inn in Meryton if he had to in order to see Elizabeth again.

A soft knock at the breakfast room door announced George Darcy entering the room.

"Son, how are you this morning?"

Darcy sighed again. "I am fine, Father. I have just been reviewing today's gossip in the *Times*."

George chuckled. "What has that man come up with now? More descriptions of your new summer coat? He is certainly relentless." George looked at his son with understanding. "I honestly came to see how you are faring. I know you wish to be somewhere else."

"I cannot deny that I would rather be with Elizabeth, but I shall practise my patience. Bingley will be back to Netherfield soon, and I believe that Elizabeth means to mention to Mrs. Bingley that I should be invited to come stay. They are close, and I am sure that even if I must apologise profusely to Bingley for missing his wedding, the sisters will prevail in allowing me at least one night's lodgings so that I may make my declarations to Elizabeth."

"I am sure Carlton will be happier to send you with your love letters instead of having to make the journey between here and Hertfordshire every day." George gave his son a hard look but swiftly smiled to soften the admonishment.

Darcy looked chagrined and nodded his agreement.

"Well, I did have other reasons for coming in here." George held out several letters for Darcy to take. "It seems that Georgiana will be upon us here in London soon. She has been reading between the lines, and I believe she wishes to be close at hand when you announce your engagement."

Darcy blushed but smiled at his sister's antics. "I am sure that both Georgiana and Elizabeth will be happy to spend time together. Perhaps Bingley will extend an invitation to you both to join us at Netherfield. That is, if you plan to stay for a while."

George looked at his son and saw a moment of the long hurt his hermit-like actions had caused his children. It was not right that his son would question whether he would want to stay for his wedding. The father stood and put his hand on his son's shoulder. "Of course I shall stay and join you in Netherfield if I am issued an invitation. I am truly sorry for keeping so much of myself hidden away these past years and expecting you to take on the burdens of Georgiana's introduction into society. I know that the expectations of London are as painful for you as they are for me, and as your father, I should have been helping you instead of allowing you to suffer without me."

"It has not been too terrible of a trial, Father. I know why you preferred Pemberley and wished to stay away from London. There have been too many attempts to entrap you. It was disgusting how the young ladies, some younger than even myself, tried to capture your fortune. I was particularly angry with one young lady who implied she could keep us both entertained."

"Who in the world said that?" George exclaimed.

"She does not merit mentioning except to say she is the daughter of a peer and recently married one of the Prince Regent's inner circle." Darcy shifted in his chair. "Hopefully, she does not fall victim to the French disease. I understand it is particularly unpleasant for women. I cannot understand how so many in society see these people as the 'best of us.' Aunt Catherine's opinions have always been particularly baffling to me. Her own life must be a contradiction to her beliefs."

"Catherine will always see the world as she wishes. And your Aunt Matlock is hardly better. She might not be as much of a hypocrite as Catherine, but there is enough evidence in her own family that the pursuit of connections through marriage often brings lifelong unhappiness."

Both Darcy men sipped their coffee and spared a thought for the silly and painful things their relations believed.

After a few minutes, a large bang was heard coming from the front hall, and a booming male voice drifted down the corridor. Father and son both rose quickly from their chairs and exited the breakfast room.

"Where is that scoundrel? I demand to see Fitzwilliam Darcy!" Lord Nottingham bellowed at the Darcy House butler, Timms.

"Uncle! What a surprise." Richard came around from the billiards room with haste. "You are well ahead of the usual calling hour and in a fine mood, are you not?"

"Do not try me, boy. I will not take your cheek this morning." Nottingham zeroed in on the younger Darcy, who was standing behind his father, but as he was several inches taller than the older man, there was nowhere to hide. "Fitzwilliam Darcy, I demand satisfaction!"

George spoke first. "Lord Nottingham, there will be no duelling with my son, not while I still have breath. Now, what in the world is this about?"

"Darcy, I should have known you were encouraging your son to act disreputably." Nottingham sneered down at George and poked him in the chest.

"I do not care for your tone. You may be a peer, but this is my house." George raised his chin and gave Nottingham a hard look. "My son has acted in all ways a gentleman and done nothing to elicit your demands for satisfaction. His honour is not engaged."

Nottingham scoffed. "Your son should have come up to scratch for my daughter ages ago. Now she is ruined forever!" Nottingham took several threatening steps towards Darcy and raised his hand as if to slap him.

Richard stepped between them and grabbed Nottingham's arm. "Uncle, calm yourself. What do you mean Lady Fiona is ruined?"

"She is completely ruined!" Spittle flew from his mouth as he bellowed. "She has run off with the second son of the Marquess of Winchester!"

"Run off? With Ingoldsby Paulet?" Richard said. "When was this?"

Nottingham looked back at Richard, who was holding his arm in a tight grasp, keeping him from advancing on the Darcys. "She left three days ago. Her mother believed she was travelling with Lady Celia Howard to Brighton for a short holiday, but my wife saw Lady Celia shopping yesterday on Bond Street and came home in quite the state. My men have been able to confirm that she was travelling north with a man matching Paulet's description."

"And how did you know to provide Paulet's specific description? He is not a particularly unique young man. Medium height and build, brown hair, no discernible scars or such." George eyed Nottingham suspiciously. "A man meeting that description could have been anyone."

"He came to ask for her hand last week, so it is logical that he is now her abductor."

"Abductor!" Darcy cried out. Then he laughed. "Let me hear you correctly. The son of the longest-standing marquess in the whole peerages of Britain came to ask for your daughter's hand and you refused him because he is a second son?"

"Of course I refused him!" Nottingham exclaimed. "He is a solicitor with a paltry share of his mother's estate. My daughter was to marry the son of the richest man in all of Derbyshire, and Matlock promised me you would be given the Earldom of FitzWalter if you married Fiona."

"So, you began negotiating with my brother when I refused to sign a marriage contract over my son?" George looked agog at the irate earl in his front hall. Darcy whipped his head around to stare at his father. This was the first he had ever heard of a contract for his marriage to Lady Fiona.

"When you never responded to my letters last winter, I decided to pursue a different avenue."

"I thought my nonreply would have been enough of an indication of my feelings without having the insult of committing them to paper."

"At least Matlock is a reasonable man." Nottingham leaned back and crossed his arms, giving the Darcy men a sneer. "He knows the value of continuing beneficial connections for the next generation."

"I am sorry, but how is the Marquess of Winchester not a beneficial connection?" Darcy was absolutely dumbfounded that Lord Nottingham considered him a better match than Ingoldsby Paulet. "I may have more annual income than Paulet, but in all ways, the other man is much more well connected inside the royal circles."

Nottingham sniffed and did not deign to answer Darcy's question. "You have publicly jilted my daughter. I want recompense, or I shall take this to the King's bench for breach of promise."

"Now that is wholly ridiculous!" George interjected. "Your daughter is the one halfway to Scotland with another man. She will be married very shortly. No court would entertain such a case as a married woman being jilted by a man with whom she had no contract."

"It has been all over the papers this season that your son is courting my daughter!" Nottingham spat. "I do not need any formal promise, the gossip column in the *Times* shall sustain my case. It was all anyone could talk about the other night at Lady Derby's ball – how you had bought a new green waistcoat in which to make your declarations to my daughter."

Darcy looked up sharply. He had indeed purchased a new green waistcoat. It was the exact colour of his favourite day dress of Elizabeth's, the one she had been wearing when he had unexpectedly arrived at Pemberley. He even had half a mind to be wearing it when he finally asked her to marry him again. But the detail of the colour of that garment had *not* been in the paper. Darcy had even remarked out loud to Richard that at least the gossip was not so exact as to mention the colour of his new wardrobe.

"You have been having me tailed." Darcy said in a calm and even voice.

"What?" Nottingham exploded. "How dare you –"

"Do not now deny it. That is how the reporter has been getting such complete information about my daily activities. You have been having me tailed, probably by one of your servants, then sending detailed reports to the *Times* of my movements." Darcy looked directly into Nottingham's eyes. "I assume that you have also been having him print any time I have been in company with Lady Fiona and our dances at Almack's. You meant to trap me."

"I do not have to take this slander!" Nottingham turned to leave, but his way was blocked by Richard.

"Has my mother been privy to your schemes? Or was she just employing the normal female pressures on the marriage mart?"

George stepped up and placed a hand on Richard's arm. "I believe that this conversation is now at an end. Lord Nottingham, I must ask you to leave. If you choose to take your demands to the King's bench, we will be happy to answer any charge you wish to lay. My coffers are quite full, and my retainer with Scoones & Associates is up to date."

Lord Nottingham sent a hard look to all three men opposing him, then roughly shook off Richard's hold. Grabbing his hat from the footman, who had been holding it through the entirety of the shouted conversation, he stormed out of Darcy House.

"Timms, please gather the staff and issue the gag order. Though this gossip is truly nothing to us, I will not have Lady Fiona's reputation harmed by talk from my house," George said as soon as the front door was closed and bolted.

"Right away, sir." Timms bowed and shuffled away as fast as his aged legs could take him.

"Well! That was exciting, don't you agree, Fitz?" Richard slapped Darcy on the back and laughed off the harrowing encounter with his uncle.

Before either of the Darcys could gather enough thoughts or wits to move from the front hall, Mrs. Timms came through the servant's entrance from the back garden.

"Excuse me, sir, but I have just received this morning's royal mail delivery." She held out one letter separated from the others. "This one is marked urgent for the young master."

Darcy took the letter extended to him and smiled widely. It was Bingley's handwriting, postmarked from Netherfield. He had travel arrangements to make.

The Countess

ELIZABETH, KITTY, AND MRS. BENNET WERE SITTING in unaccustomed silence in the parlour of Longbourn. In the morning hours after breakfast, without Lydia's chatter, Mary's playing, or Jane's polite conversation, the remaining three Bennet women were often found in quiet pursuits. So, it was easy to hear the crunch of horse hooves and carriage wheels the moment they came upon the drive. Elizabeth gave little thought to their visitor until the parlour door was thrown open and, to Elizabeth's great astonishment, it was Lady Matlock.

Mrs. Bennet, all amazement, though flattered by having a guest of such high importance, received her with the utmost politeness.

After sitting for a moment in silence, Lady Matlock said very stiffly to Elizabeth, "I hope you are well, Miss Bennet. That lady, I suppose, is your mother."

"Yes, my lady."

"And *that*, I suppose, is one of your sisters."

"Yes, madam," said Mrs. Bennet, delighted to speak to Lady Matlock. "She is my youngest girl but one. My youngest of all is lately married in London. My eldest, Jane, I believe you had made the acquaintance of this past winter and is now Mrs. Charles Bingley, and my middle daughter was married last Christmastide and resides with her husband in Hunsford parish, of which I believe you are familiar as your sister's community."

Though it would have been the polite thing to acknowledge all their shared connections, Lady Matlock barely acknowledged Mrs. Bennet's speech.

"You have a very small park here," returned Lady Matlock after a short silence.

"It is nothing in comparison of Rosings or Pemberley, my lady, I dare say, but I assure you it is much larger than many in our neighbourhood."

"Miss Bennet, there seemed to be a prettyish kind of a little wilderness on one side of your lawn. I should be glad to take a turn in it, if you will favour me with your company."

"Go, my dear," cried her mother, "and show her ladyship about the different walks. I think she will be pleased with the hermitage."

Elizabeth obeyed and, running into her own room for her parasol, attended her noble guest downstairs. As they passed through the hall, Lady Matlock opened the doors into the dining parlour and drawing room and pronounced them, after a short survey, to be decent-looking rooms.

As soon as they entered the copse, Lady Matlock began very abruptly in the following manner: "You can be at no loss, Miss Bennet, to understand the reason of my journey hither."

Elizabeth looked with unaffected astonishment. "Indeed, you are mistaken, madam. I have not been at all able to account for the honour of seeing you here."

"Miss Bennet," replied her ladyship, in an angry tone. "You ought to know that I am not to be trifled with. But however insincere *you* may choose to be, you shall not find *me* so. A report of a most alarming nature reached me several days ago. I have lately travelled to my sister's home in Kent to visit with Lady Catherine and Anne. There, I met your sister and her husband, that ridiculous parson, taking tea with *my* relations. It was then that I was told that you, Miss Elizabeth Bennet, would, in all likelihood, be soon united to my nephew, my own nephew, Mr. Fitzwilliam Darcy. Though I *know* it must be a scandalous falsehood, though I would not injure him so much as to suppose the truth of it possible, I instantly resolved on setting off for this place, that I might make my sentiments known to you."

Elizabeth was dumbfounded. "If you believed it impossible to be true," said Elizabeth, colouring with astonishment and disdain, "I wonder you took the trouble of coming so far. What could your ladyship propose by it?"

"At once to insist upon having such a report universally contradicted."

"Your coming to Longbourn, to see me and my family," said Elizabeth coolly, "will be rather a confirmation of it. If, indeed, such a report is in existence."

"*If!* Do you then pretend to be ignorant of it? Has it not been industriously circulated by your relations? Do you not know that such a report is spread abroad?"

"I have not been to London in many months, and we are not privy to such gossip here."

"This is not to be borne. Miss Bennet, I insist on being satisfied. Has he, has my nephew, made you an offer of marriage?"

"I do not pretend to possess equal frankness with your ladyship. *You* may ask questions which *I* shall not choose to answer."

"Let me be rightly understood." Lady Matlock pointed her finger at Elizabeth's nose. "This match, to which you have the presumption to aspire, can never take place. No, never. Mr. Darcy is engaged to *my niece*, Lady Fiona Finch. Now what have you to say?"

"Only this: that if he is so, should not an announcement have already been run or the bans begun?" Elizabeth raised one eyebrow. "He has not seen Lady Fiona since leaving town for the summer, and both Nottingham House and Darcy House are as yet silent on the matter."

Lady Matlock hesitated for a moment, then replied, "The understanding between them is, for now, one of duty. His attentions to her this past season have been observed by all members of the *ton*, reported in the *Times* society pages, and all are now expecting their engagement. I will not allow their marriage to be prevented by a young woman of inferior birth, of no importance in the world, and wholly unallied to the family! Do you pay no regard to the wishes of his friends? To his tacit engagement with Lady Fiona? Are you lost to every feeling of propriety and delicacy?"

"What is that to me? If there is no other objection to my marrying your nephew, I shall certainly not be kept from it by knowing that his aunt and the gossip columnist at the *Times* wished him to marry Lady Fiona. You both did as much as you could in planning the marriage. Its completion depended on others." Elizabeth's voice was slowly rising in both volume and pitch. "It seems a flimsy argument that a few dances would see a man engaged or a lady so ruined that she could not marry elsewhere. Did he ever call upon her at home or send her flowers? Was he seen escorting her on walks through Hyde Park? I cannot see how his honour has been engaged, and if Mr. Darcy is neither by honour nor inclination confined to your niece, why is not he to make another choice? And if I am that choice, why may not I accept him?"

"Because honour, decorum, prudence, nay, interest, forbid it. Yes, Miss Bennet, interest; for do not expect to be noticed by his family or friends, if you wilfully act against the inclinations of all. You will be censured, slighted, and despised by everyone connected with him. Your alliance will be a disgrace; your name will never even be mentioned by any of us."

"These are heavy misfortunes," replied Elizabeth. "But I do not believe you. I have *already* been accepted by his friends and family. Your own cousins, Sir James and Lady Finch, are cousins to my aunt and uncle Gardiner. We were welcomed guests at their ball last winter and fully in company with your family on several occasions. My sister is married to Mr. Darcy's dearest friend, and I am on intimate terms with Miss Georgiana Darcy. We are also very well connected to Miss Anne de Bourgh by both affection and marriage. It seems that we are not so 'wholly unallied to the family.' Also, if the world did decide to punish us for our attachment, the wife of Mr. Darcy must have such extraordinary sources of happiness necessarily attached to her situation, that she could, upon the whole, have no cause to repine."

"My brother's daughter and my sister-in-law's son are formed for each other. They are each descended from noble lines and from respectable, honourable, and ancient families. The whole of London expects their attachment, and what is to divide them? The upstart pretensions of a young woman without any fortune. Is this to be endured? Who was your mother? Who are your uncles and aunts? Do not imagine me ignorant of their condition."

"How can you continue to object to them?" Elizabeth exclaimed. "Those same aunts and uncles which you deride are connected, by marriage, to yourself! Must I repeatedly remind you that your cousin and my aunt are related by marriage. We are actually quite closely connected already, and their *condition* cannot be of any concern to you."

Lady Matlock looked at Elizabeth as if she had been recently sucking on a lemon, then jumped to her next assault without acknowledging the truth of their mutual connections. "Tell me once and for all, are you engaged to him?"

Though Elizabeth would not, for the mere purpose of obliging Lady Matlock, have answered this question, she could not but say, after a moment's deliberation, "I am not."

"And will you promise me never to enter into such an engagement?"

"I will make no promise of the kind."

"Miss Bennet, I am shocked and astonished. I expected to find a more reasonable young woman. But do not deceive yourself into a belief that I will ever recede. I shall not go away 'til you have given me the assurance I require."

"And I certainly *never* shall give it. I am not to be intimidated into anything so wholly unreasonable. Your ladyship wants Mr. Darcy to marry your niece, but would my giving you the wished-for promise make their marriage at all more probable? You have widely mistaken my character if you think I can be worked on by such persuasions as these."

"Not so hasty, if you please. I am no stranger to the particulars of your youngest sister's infamous marriage. I know it all – that the young man she left Brighton with is not the same man who has married her, and even that marriage was a patched-up business, at the expense of your father and uncles. Shall Georgiana be tarnished with such infamous relations before she even makes her debut? Are the shades of Pemberley to be thus polluted?"

"This is nonsensical, your own *son* was Captain Wordsville's groomsman! Your family was the introduction of Wordsville to mine. You can now have nothing further to say," she resentfully answered. "You have insulted me in every possible method. I must beg to return to the house."

Her ladyship was highly incensed. "You have no regard, then, for the honour and credit of my nephew! Unfeeling, selfish girl! Do you not consider that a connection with you must disgrace him in the eyes of everybody?"

"Lady Matlock, I have nothing further to say. You know my sentiments."

"You are then resolved to have him?"

"I have said no such thing. I am only resolved to act in that manner which will, in my own opinion, constitute my happiness, without reference to *you* or to any person so 'wholly unallied' with me."

"You refuse, then, to oblige me. You refuse to obey the claims of duty, honour, and gratitude. You are determined to ruin him in the opinion of all his friends and make him the contempt of the world."

"Neither duty, nor honour, nor gratitude," replied Elizabeth, "have any possible claim on me, in the present instance. No principle of either would be violated by my marriage with Mr. Darcy."

"And this is your real opinion! Very well. I shall now know how to act. Do not imagine, Miss Bennet, that your ambition will ever be gratified. I take no leave of you, Miss Bennet. I send no compliments to your mother. You deserve no such attention." The incensed lady then turned on her heel and stormed back to her waiting carriage.

Elizabeth stood for a moment before quietly returning to the house. She heard the carriage drive away as she proceeded upstairs. Her mother impatiently met her at the door of the dressing room to ask why Lady Matlock would not come in again and rest herself.

"She did not choose it," said her daughter. "She would go."

"She is a very fine-looking woman! And her calling here was prodigiously civil! She is on her road somewhere, I dare say, and so, passing through Meryton, thought she might as well call on you. I suppose she had nothing particular to say to you, Lizzy?"

Elizabeth was forced to give into a little falsehood here, for to acknowledge the substance of their conversation was impossible.

After a few additional minutes in her mother and sister's presence, Elizabeth excused herself, walked into the back garden, and kept her ladylike pace until she reached the shade of the wooded path leading to her favourite grove.

Then she ran.

A Tale of Two Families

"**R**EALLY, LIZZY, YOU MUST STOP RUNNING AWAY into the woods at every minor inconvenience." Jane's voice was calm and fondly exasperated as she walked into the aspen grove where her sister often found refuge.

"Jane, what are you doing here?"

"What am I doing here?" Jane laughed. "You know exactly what I am doing here. You ran off from the house hours ago and no one could find you. Mother sent Johns to Netherfield to ask Charles to form a search party."

"Oh no!" Elizabeth groaned. "I did not mean to make anyone uneasy about my whereabouts. I just needed some time to myself."

"I know, dear sister. That is why I came here." Jane adjusted her skirts and sat upon the old log near the edge of the clearing. "It has been quite an exciting day at my own home. We have a number of new visitors."

"I am nervous to ask."

"Oh yes, I can well understand your nerves." Jane said. "Just before luncheon, we had a lone rider come seeking lodging, which was much anticipated by my husband." Jane raised one eyebrow.

Elizabeth groaned. "I presume that Mr. Fitzwilliam Darcy has come to Netherfield at last."

"Yes, he has." Jane smiled. "And his arrival is most welcome. Then, to our great surprise, not thirty minutes later, a coach carrying Lady Matlock arrived at our door."

"Oh no!"

"Well, she took poor Mr. Darcy into the music room and had a very . . hmmm . . . spirited discussion."

"Did every servant hear their argument about me?"

"I am sure that the stable boys were not privy to the shouting."

Elizabeth hung her head. "Oh dear."

"Quite." Jane cleared her throat. "Curiously, after only a few minutes, Lady Matlock bolted from the house, shouting at her carriage driver to make haste back to London and straight to Nottingham House. I have no more details on that particular problem, but her ladyship did seem very agitated and quite pale."

"Was Mr. Darcy very angry with me?" Elizabeth asked in a voice so small, Jane had trouble hearing her.

"I cannot say with certainty. He has been locked in his room since her ladyship left. But, our string of unexpected visitors is not yet done."

"What?"

"Very shortly after Lady Matlock left, yet another carriage pulled into our drive. This one bearing the senior Mr. Darcy and Colonel Fitzwilliam." Jane tapped Elizabeth's arm with the fan attached to her wrist. "The elder Mr. Darcy was very anxious through our introduction because he had passed Lady Matlock's carriage in Meryton and was distressed about what mischief she might have caused us all."

"Where are Mr. Darcy and Colonel Fitzwilliam now?"

"Oh, they plan to stay in Hertfordshire for a while yet and will continue to reside with us at Netherfield. However, at this moment, both the elder Mr. Darcy and Colonel Fitzwilliam are having tea with our mother in the blue parlour."

"*What?*" Elizabeth exclaimed.

"Yes." Jane smirked.

"Jane Margaret Bennet!"

"Bingley."

"That is wholly not the point." Elizabeth pointed her finger at her older sister. "Do you mean to tell me that you have left Mr. Darcy's relations in the Longbourn parlour with Mother and did not lead with their visit?"

"Yes."

"I must return at once!" Elizabeth stood abruptly and brushed a few leaves from her skirts.

"Yes."

"Oh, tosh you! Come, it is time I faced everyone."

Elizabeth and Jane entered Longbourn's blue parlour to a most bizarre sight. Mr. George Darcy was engaged in conversation with Mr. and Mrs. Bennet over tea, and they were all laughing heartily over some anecdote one of them had just shared. Colonel Richard Fitzwilliam and Kitty were sitting a bit apart from the older adults, having a lively discussion about fashion on the continent, Richard having spent a good deal of time in France over the past several years fighting Napoleon's war. A casual observer might believe that these two were regular visitors at Longbourn instead of first-time guests.

Richard was the first to notice Elizabeth's entrance.

"Miss Lizzy! Oh, thank heavens. Mrs. Bingley said she was certain where you had gone off to, but I still worried you might be in need of someone to verbally spar with and unable to find your way back to the house."

Elizabeth chortled under her breath. "I am deeply sorry to have caused you any stress, Colonel. Have you brought with you someone of sufficient intellect with whom I might engage in a fair battle of wits?"

"Lizzy!" Mrs. Bennet scolded.

But Richard just laughed loudly. "No, certainly I have not come adequately prepared for any battle with you."

Mrs. Bennet harrumphed. "Well, it is good that you are back, Lizzy, as we now have dinner guests. It would be unacceptable to hold the meal for your ambles."

George Darcy answered with all the civility of a man with great manners, "Madam, I thank you for your invitation. As we have come lately from London this morning with no prior invitation, I do not wish to impose on yourself or your daughter's hospitality."

"It is no imposition at all, sir! My cook is too well inured to my habit of inviting guests to dinner on short notice that she always has plenty to serve the whole neighbourhood." Mrs. Bennet waved her handkerchief about the air. "We need only to send a note to Netherfield for Mr. Bingley and your son."

Both George and Richard squirmed a little in their seats at the mention of the younger Darcy. "Yes, my son has arrived at Netherfield but was of a poor constitution this afternoon. I am not sure that he would be disposed to come to dinner."

Jane interjected, "Mamma, our guests have travelled much today. I believe it would be better for us to plan on an early dinner at Netherfield without any after-dinner entertainment so that everyone might have an early evening."

"Jane dear, you are correct. That will be best for everyone's constitutions." Mrs. Bennet nodded her head and picked up her teacup.

"Mrs. Bennet, I've often heard Lizzy speak of the beauty of Longbourn's natural gardens. We had a slow ride from London, and now that you have provided us with much-needed refreshment, I would dearly love a walk in the fresh air. Uncle, shall you join us?"

Elizabeth's eyes shot to Richard with surprise. She was well used to interference from her friends for finding time to walk about and have quiet conversations with Fitzwilliam Darcy, but it seemed quite strange to be pushed towards walking with *George* Darcy. What in the world could the elder man have to discuss with her? Before Elizabeth could demure, a vociferous agreement from Mrs. Bennet had the three young women, Richard, and George Darcy with their outer things quickly donned and out the door to the back garden. Richard held out an arm each to Kitty and Jane, then started asking questions of Jane's recent travels. This left Elizabeth to take George's arm, which bore too much resemblance to that of his son for Elizabeth's composure, and she allowed him to escort her about the garden.

"Miss Bennet, I believe it is time we had some conversation. It is unpardonable on my part to have ignored such an intimate friend of my children, but as an old widower who always detested the London scene, I have chosen to keep myself locked away at Pemberley for the better part of the last several years. I hope you will forgive me for only now coming to pay my respects to your family for the kindness and hospitality they have bestowed upon my son and daughter this past year."

Shaking off her feelings of unease, Elizabeth replied with as much humility and politeness as she could muster. "Mr. Darcy, I do believe that if we are to speak of gratitude and forgiveness, it is I who owes you the larger share. Hosting your children at our dinner table was easy and always full of happy company for my family. I believe I must beg you accept my gratitude, and the gratitude of my entire family, for taking Lydia's life in your capable hands. Without you and your son, I'm sure she would have been utterly lost to us."

"I can accept only very minimal thanks for your sister's situation. In fact, I should accept none, since my own indulgences and blindness created the spoiled man who could devise such schemes against the world. George Wickham should never have been allowed to hurt a cockroach. But I cannot change the past. Only, I hope he learns something of dignity and honour while facing Napoleon's forces before he meets his maker or comes back to England with battle-worn eyes." George signed heavily. "I must say, in the moment when I agreed to help, I was thinking of only my son. And surly he was only thinking of you."

There were no more words that came to Elizabeth's mind, and so she contented herself with companionable silence until George composed his own mind to break into the topic he clearly came all the way to Longbourn to discuss with her. Elizabeth guessed in that moment that the two Mr. Darcys were much alike in their need for a certain amount or quiet before broaching important subjects.

"Would you indulge an old man for a bit more and allow me to tell you the story of two families? There are many among these families today who would regale you with talk of how respectable and noble their bloodlines are, how important their positions, and how that makes them somehow better than the rest of society, more qualified to rule over everyone else and demand we all fall into line behind their grand plans. Personally, I believe that the privilege of station is mostly random chance and of little importance. But my relations have likely painted a very different vision of the upper set than upstanding and dutiful land managers."

George paused for a moment and took a deep breath. "My father was a tenant farmer on one of the largest farms at Pemberley until he unexpectedly inherited the manor house and all the ancestral lands of the Darcy family at age thirty-one. He was a Darcy by blood but so far removed from the primogeniture line of inheritance that my grandfather did not even believe it was worth the expense of giving him a formal education. Though in recent generations there has only been one Darcy male born to inherit, at one point, my family was quite large. My great-grandfather had two sons and four daughters. His oldest son married the daughter of a baron and had two sons of his own. The second son of my great-grandfather, my grandfather, took the living at Krypton and had two sons and five daughters. My father, Henry Darcy, was the second son. I was born in the little cottage on the edge of my father's tenant lands.

"In the summer when I was three years old, scarlet fever came to Derbyshire. It devastated the county, and my family in particular. Richard Darcy, my grandfather's older brother, was the master of Pemberley at the time with, as they say, an heir and a spare. But both of my second cousins, plus their mother, died of the fever, so there were no heirs left to my great-uncle. Richard invited my father's older brother to live at Pemberley and learn something of estate management. My father became the heir apparent a few years later, after a fire on the estate took my uncle and several of the most trustworthy and dedicated footmen in our household."

Elizabeth laid her free hand on George's arm. "I am very sorry to hear of so many losses to your family, and in such a short time."

"Thank you, I was seven years old, but I still remember the funerals and how many people came to pay their respects." George looked straight ahead for several moments, gathering his thoughts. "So, after the mourning was over, my family was brought to the manor house from our tenant cottage as the next heirs. My mother was a wonderfully warm person. As the daughter of the Lambton haberdasher, she had no formal education, but here she suddenly found herself the mistress of one of the oldest and largest estates in the whole of England."

George looked sideways at Elizabeth. "I remember being terrified. I was used to chasing the chickens around our little garden or climbing all the trees I could manage around Pemberley's woods. As we walked up to the main entrance of the house, I asked my mother how I should act. She stopped walking and came to her knees in front of me. And do you know what she said?"

Elizabeth shook her head.

"She said I should always be respectful to the servants, mind what my tutors tell me, and never speak to my great-uncle unless spoken to."

Elizabeth nodded. "Sensible advice for a child."

George stopped them and looked at Elizabeth directly. "Then she told me to never forget that this was to be my house someday and I shall be the master. So above all else, I was to hold my head high and ignore anyone who would speak against our family's connections. For what need have we, the Darcys of Pemberley, for others' connections? We are the ones to whom people shall want to be connected. My grandfather, the haberdasher, does not bring down the Darcy name, rather the Darcy name uplifts the haberdasher."

Elizabeth was stunned. That the wealthiest man in Derbyshire should have been born in a tenant cottage, the son of a tenant farmer and a haberdasher's daughter, was the opposite of what she expected to hear from George.

They walked on in silence for a few paces.

"The second of the two families," George continued, "revolves around those persons who, I am sure, have recently left the most memorable of impressions. My wife, Lady Anne Darcy, died as the sister of the 8th Earl of Matlock, but she was born the daughter of a country barrister. The 5th Earl of Matlock, my wife's grandfather, had two sons, and as you can probably guess, my father-in-law was the younger."

"Truly?"

"Quite true, yes. My wife's uncle inherited the earldom young and married the fabulously wealthy daughter of the Earl of Wessex. They were much in the London *ton* and miserable at home. The 6th Earl of Matlock had three daughters by his wife and a number of other children by, well . . ." George cleared his throat. "Anyway, he died of the French disease while his youngest two daughters were still in finishing school."

"Oh dear."

"Before the 6th earl became visibly ill, his oldest daughter was presented to society at the same time as my Anne. Matlock wanted an alliance between Pemberley and the earldom. He hoped to foist his daughters off on the richest men he could to secure their futures. I was thrown into Lady Eleanor Fitzwilliam's path at least three nights a week for her entire first season. Her mother even orchestrated a situation where I was forced, out of politeness, to ask Lady Eleanor to dance a second dance at a high society ball. It was rumoured in every drawing room and in several days' worth of the society pages that I was on the verge of proposing to her."

"London has not changed much since, I understand." Elizabeth laughed in order to stave off frustrated tears.

"No, it has not. The 6th Countess of Matlock and her daughters were mercenary and shrewish. The Matlocks of a generation past valued money and land above all else. Each of the earl's daughters had a dowry of more than thirty thousand pounds but little else to recommend. I truthfully wanted nothing to do with any of them. In comparison, their sweet-tempered cousin, who came with only two thousand pounds, caught my eye the moment we were introduced. In fact, I had already proposed to her before that fateful ball where I was forced to dance twice with the earl's oldest daughter, but the announcement had not yet been run."

"I am sorry I will not have the pleasure in this life of knowing Lady Anne."

George smiled down at Elizabeth with sad eyes. "She would have absolutely adored you, my dear."

"I am sure the feeling would have been mutual." Elizabeth said.

"Well, the countess was incensed when our engagement was announced, but I was unmoved by her shrieking. When female persuasions did nothing to change the direction of my marriage, my father-in-law and I both had to stand firm against the earl promising to use his considerable power to make London a very unfriendly place for all of us if I jilted his daughter for the relatively poor daughter of his younger brother. It mattered not to me." George looked very pointedly at Elizabeth. "For what need have I for others' connections?"

Elizabeth laughed and George continued. "Anne and I married only a few days after her seventeenth birthday, and it was the most joyous event of my life."

"That is a lovely story." Elizabeth smiled.

"Yes, I am partial to it, but it is not over. After all the turmoil and tittering and gossiping surrounding my marriage, can you guess what actually happened to myself and my wife?"

Elizabeth shook her head slightly.

"Even before the 6th Earl went to his early grave, we were welcomed by London society. When we arrived in town for the season, we received invitations to all the most exclusive parties. As we only accepted those invitations that we desired to attend and issued invitations only to people we wished to have in our home, soon it became said that 'it was not truly a grand event unless the Darcys graced it with their presence.' Our dinner parties and balls were always a crush. I believe it was Anne's bright smile and unassuming manner that put everyone at ease."

George stopped their walk and looked at the honeysuckle bushes growing along the path. "The very day that the 6th Earl passed from this earth, we were greeted by the *ton* with a renewed sense of respect. We were in town for the holidays when the sad event happened. Anne's father had written us an express letter from Matlock which was delayed, so we were sitting in our parlour, unprepared, that afternoon when one of the worst gossips that ever graced our door came calling at the tea hour. She was announced and immediately went to my wife and said, 'My *dear Lady Anne*, please accept my condolences upon the passing of your uncle.' From that moment on, my wife was the daughter of an earl and titled in her own right. In private, sometimes she would ask me to call her simply Mrs. Darcy, but not one person of society ever did so again."

Several moments of silence fell between them.

"As both my daughter and my son have assured me that you are a uniquely intelligent young woman, I am sure that I do not need to elaborate on all of the reasons I have imposed on your time in order to tell you this extremely long story, but if you will indulge me a little more, I shall highlight some of my private thoughts surrounding the events which have very likely left their undeniable impression upon you involving my sisters-in-law."

George continued down the garden lane. "Lady Catherine was elevated on the same day as my wife to the daughter of an earl, but she was as of yet unmarried. Her near spinster status was due to her own highbrow opinion of the Fitzwilliam family and refusal to look at the numerous young gentlemen with distinguished careers as suitors. She was determined she would marry into land, and she had rightly guessed that her philandering uncle would neither produce a legitimate male heir nor outlive her twenty-second birthday. Sir Lewis de Bourgh was a good man, and Catherine looked no further than the size of his entry hall before accepting his suit. They were married one week after our family put off our blacks.

"If you asked her, she would say that God himself had appointed her father as the rightful heir." George punctuated his speech with a grand gesture towards the sky. "This is how Catherine neatly gets around the incontrovertible truth that, on the day of her birth, she was born in a modest townhome in Derby and her father owned no more land than the ten-foot-square patch of grass on either side of the sidewalk leading to his front stoop. Do not be fooled, Miss Bennet, the formidable Lady Catherine de Bourgh was born much lower than you and has spent her entire life trying to make everyone forget that fact.

"Lady Matlock is another story entirely. I know that my brother-in-law and his wife are well suited, affectionate, and married for what I would consider the reasons that bring happiness. But I also know that Lady Josephine Finch, at sixteen years old, was given a list of families from which she could choose a husband. Her own father directed the whole matter in a businesslike manner, with scripted dinner parties and Almack's dances to narrow her choice of husband. Her father approached Anne's father about a contract for the marriage after their second night of dancing. My wife's father was horrified by the prospect of contracting for his son's marriage, but fortunately for everyone, Henri and Josephine were both inclined in the same direction.

"I believe that Lady Matlock very much loves my children and has always been a wonderful surrogate mother for them, especially Georgiana, who was too young when my wife died to even remember her mother outside of portraits and stories. But she is very much a product of her upbringing. I know that her brother approaches the matter of marriages for his children much in the same way that their father conducted their marriages. I was approached by Lord Nottingham for a contract over William several years ago, when he was still at Cambridge, but I flatly refused. And now it seems that the lady has taken matters into her own hands."

Elizabeth was completely drained by the time George stopped walking to shake his head at the fate of Lady Fiona. Two more steps took her to the bench on the edge of the garden wall near some lilac bushes, where she rather ungracefully sat heavy on the wood. George kept a few paces' distance and remained silent for several moments.

"Miss Bennet, I will leave you with just this. My son loves you wholly, and without reservation, but you still harbour some hesitation, which after today is wholly justified, over the potential negative reaction of London society and members of our extended family. If my tale has revealed nothing else to you, Miss Bennet, I hope you came to realize that, as far as society in general is concerned, they may express some indignation upon first learning of your marriage, but the world in general will not care for long."

George took the final few steps towards Elizbeth, sat down on the bench and took one of her hands into his own. "My dear, the past two mistresses of Pemberley were born as the daughter of a country barrister and the daughter of a haberdasher. To have the next mistress be the daughter of a landed gentleman with a respectable estate will be a significant step up for Pemberley. All of London forgot the size of my Anne's dowry in under a fortnight. They shall forget yours too."

Dialogue

ONCE THE CARRIAGE WITH LADY MATLOCK LEFT Netherfield's drive, Darcy could take no more and hid himself away in his room with a decanter of brandy. He was angry with himself for another failure. If only he had pressed the issue about Lady Fiona earlier, instead of letting everyone's expectations continue to build. He had failed to protect his beautiful Elizabeth from his aunt's tirade, and Darcy was as disgusted with himself as he was with Lady Matlock.

The whole encounter had been dreadful.

Though it was not, perhaps, the best idea he had ever had, Darcy tried to finish the decanter in his rooms in one sitting. An hour later, Darcy's valet had come to insist that he eat something of substance. After two strong cups of black coffee and nearly half a loaf of plain bread to soak up the remaining alcohol, Darcy was being choked into a new cravat and dinner waistcoat.

Hanging his head in shame, Darcy decided he should go to the study and prepare an apology for his behaviour to Bingley and Jane.

After quickly penning a letter to be placed in Bingley's rooms, Darcy turned towards a letter for Elizabeth. He wanted to express how much he regretted leaving her exposed to Lady Matlock's vitriol and beg for her forgiveness. He was also prepared to release her from their courtship if she wished to be divorced from him and his objectionable family. Darcy promised himself that he would leave the decision about their continued relationship to Elizabeth alone, but he could not resist the urge to beg her not to leave him. Each attempt at a letter would inevitably devolve into a plea for her to return his love and relieve his suffering. In his frustration, Darcy kept crushing the offending papers into his hand and starting again with a renewed commitment to not pressure Elizabeth to maintain their courtship.

After about an hour, and many crumpled pieces of paper thrown into the fire, there was a knock at the study door.

"Come."

The door opened slowly, and someone with soft footfalls entered the room.

Several moments of silence followed, and without looking up, Darcy said, "Yes, what is it?"

"Hello, Wills."

Darcy's head snapped up from his papers at the sound of Elizabeth's voice. It was the most wonderful, unexpected, calming thing he had ever heard. Without thinking, he stood too fast, knocking over his chair and the ink holder.

"Elizabeth!"

Rushing forward to try to stop the ink from flowing over the side of the desk on the floor, Elizabeth was surprised when Darcy caught her around the waist and engulfed her in a tight hug. After a moment, he released her, then immediately sank to his knees.

"My dear, I cannot believe you are here! I have spoken with my Aunt Matlock and am horrified by her abuse of you. Please, my love, I will do anything if you forgive me for not dealing with her interference with Lady Fiona earlier. I promise that she is no longer an issue, as she is on her way to be wed in Scotland. I will stand against my aunt if needs be. You will never be subjected to her vitriol again."

Looking up from him, Elizabeth took in the scene they presented – the ruined pages on the desk, the overturned chair, the ink dripping onto the floor, and Darcy on his knees begging for forgiveness – then started laughing. Her mirth brought Darcy back to the present, and he looked himself at the state of the room. Finding much less humour in their situation, he looked back up at Elizabeth with a question in his eyes.

"Come, Wills. Do you have an old handkerchief on your person to stop the ink from ruining the rug? I only have one handkerchief on me, and it is a personal favourite which was given to me by a gentleman I happen to favour very much, and I do not wish to ruin it."

Darcy nodded and fished a cloth out of his pocket to take care of the mess on the desk. After throwing the soiled cloth into the fire, along with some of the discarded papers which had not quite hit their mark, Darcy gingerly sat on the sofa, physically as far from Elizabeth as the space would allow. Finding the distance between them not to her liking, Elizabeth moved closer to him and laid a hand gently on his arm. She was disconcerted by his skittish behaviour but buoyed by his initial reaction of embracing her tightly.

"Miss Elizabeth, I am very glad to see you here."

"Wills, are we back to such formality? Please, I would prefer if you use just my name when we are alone." Elizabeth ducked her head to catch Darcy's eyes. "I have come to see you. I hope that is not too forward of me. However, I just now decided that it was more important for us to speak than for me to remain missish."

Guarded hope took over Darcy's visage. "Do I dare to hope? Can you really forgive me for being so dismissive of your fears last April? I am devastated by Lady Matlock's treatment of you today. It was everything you told me in April that you feared. I have never been so ashamed of myself for never really believing that your concerns were reasonable. Do you truly wish to continue to expose yourself to people like Lady Matlock?"

"I will not lie and tell you that the *encounter* with your aunt was of no consequence to me. She was mean and said hurtful things about myself and my family."

Darcy hung his head in shame. "I should have protected you from this. You told me in April that you did not think my aunts would approve, that you feared their reaction, that you worried how their reactions might affect our relationship. I only heard that you believed I would come to resent you and took offense. Then during the season, I was painfully aware of Lady Matlock's wishes regarding my marriage to her niece. However, I did nothing to head off this disaster. I should have confronted my aunt before leaving London."

"Oh, Wills. You and I have had a difficult time, have we not? We both allowed our fears and self-doubt to interfere with what we owe to each other. I most assuredly forgive you any missteps along our journey so far, as long as you will forgive me mine."

"How can you overlook Lady Matlock's treatment of you?"

"You know, the funniest thing happened while your aunt was using such ridiculous arguments against our marriage. I realised how hollow these arguments truly are and how little they will change my heart." She smiled widely. "Anyone who chooses to turn their noses against us for such shallow reasons are not of real consequence to our lives. Also, she insulted you in her ranting, which, perhaps strangely, led me to believe her actions are being directed by something else other than true malice for our relationship. It also seems that she is perhaps worried for her favourite niece, Lady Fiona, who is now perhaps in some disagreement with her father."

"Yes, I dare say she and her new husband will not be welcomed by Nottingham, at least not straight away."

"Well then, we should be kind to her in the future. I enjoyed her company well enough this spring. Perhaps we shall host a dinner party in celebration of them next season."

"Your generosity and compassion never cease to amaze me, Elizabeth. How can you take no mind to the wounds so unkindly inflicted on you by others?"

Elizabeth reached over and finally took Darcy's hand between her own. "It is easy to be compassionate with people who are unhappy when I, myself, find such joy in my situation."

"Elizabeth . . ." Darcy was unable to speak for a few moments and instead tried to put all his joy and love into his eyes. "You are too generous. If the most recent events have not made you wary of our alliance, then will you please make me the happiest of men and agree to share this life with me? Will you be my wife?"

Happy tears gathered and glistened in Elizabeth's eyes.

"Yes!"

Unable to stop himself for even one moment more, Darcy put his hands on either side of Elizabeth's face and pulled her into a kiss which was just over the line between chaste and something more. With only a second of surprise, Elizabeth moved her own hands and arms around Darcy's neck and leaned into his kisses.

Breaking for a much-needed breath, Darcy stared into Elizabeth's eyes and lost himself again. One of his hands wound around her waist, and before Elizabeth could object, Darcy pulled her slight body to sit in his lap for another round of heated kisses. This time, Elizabeth was a bit more prepared for his attack. She allowed him to kiss her for only a few seconds before pulling back.

"Wills! We cannot continue in this attitude. I am sure my sister and brother are on their way to this room shortly." Elizabeth's admonishment was firm, but the laughter in her voice was enough for Darcy to know she was not truly upset with his behaviour.

"If Bingley finds us in this attitude, then surely he will tell your father, and they will then insist on an immediate wedding. I see no reason to separate."

Tinkling laughter flowed through Elizabeth. Darcy relaxed his hold on her waist, but instead of removing herself from his lap, Elizabeth tightened her hold on his shoulders and rested her head in the crook of his neck.

"Far be it from me to argue with my future husband. I shall start learning to rely on you for all things and keep myself here."

Darcy let himself revel in the feeling of holding Elizabeth in his arms for a long moment. After taking a few steadying breaths, Darcy gently released Elizabeth and helped her return to sitting on the couch in an appropriate position, though still much closer than strict propriety would have dictated.

Suddenly, a thought came into Darcy's mind when picturing the moment he would place a delicate gold ring on Elizabeth's finger. "I have something for you! I have been keeping it with me at all times." Darcy fiddled with the inside pocket of his waistcoat and pulled out a small silk pouch. "Here, dearest, please accept this gift for our engagement!"

Elizabeth gingerly opened the drawstrings and found earrings and a finger ring set with the most impressive Derbyshire spar gemstones in a dark, luscious blue colour and small flecks of gold veins. Gently, Darcy lifted the ring from the box and placed it on Elizabeth's third finger on her right hand. It was slightly too big, so he moved it to the second finger, where it fit just perfectly.

"These are so beautiful, Wills! I cannot believe you would get such an extravagant gift for me. I am sure I shall be terrified of losing them."

Darcy laughed. "I do not believe you in any danger of losing these items; you are far too conscientious for that. On the matter of cost, the earrings originally belonged to my grandmother Darcy, and the ring was made for my mother upon her engagement to my father. They were all made from stones that my father found in the hills and caves of Derbyshire on our lands. They were expertly set in London, but the pieces are far more valuable in sentiment than they cost to acquire. I have more items with which I wish to spoil you; however, these are purely for my personal enjoyment of seeing you wear something that my grandmother and mother loved and which is tied so closely to my home. The home I wish to share with you for the rest of our lives."

"I am honoured to have such beautiful pieces of my new home."

Darcy was unable to contain his happiness and reclaimed Elizabeth's lips in a sweet, all-consuming kiss.

A few minutes later, Darcy and Elizabeth were interrupted by Georgiana bursting into the room. "Goodness, have you finished discussing your understanding yet? I have been waiting as patiently as possible for nearly an hour! Please put me out of my misery and tell me that you have set a date for your nuptials!"

"Georgiana, whatever are you doing here?" Darcy looked at his sister, very much perplexed at her sudden appearance.

"I wrote to Father that I intended to come to London and break my journey here at Netherfield for a day or two. Jane had sent me an open invitation to come whenever I wished. From what I understand, I arrived just after Father and Richard."

"Father and Richard are here too?"

"Yes, keep up," Georgiana scolded. "They left London in the carriage just after you sprinted away on your horse. We have all been here for a few hours, waiting on you to come down from your rooms."

Elizabeth laughed and jumped up to take her friend's hands, while Darcy scowled at his sister. "Oh, Georgie! We have not set a date for the wedding, but we have decided to stop letting silly things keep us apart." Elizabeth looked back at Darcy and smiled impertinently, then gave him a small wink. Georgie squealed and jumped up and down in front of the sofa where Darcy was still seated.

Unable to keep his severe mien in the face of Georgiana's joy and Elizabeth's mirth, Darcy gave in and laughed himself. He held out his hand for Elizabeth to come back to him. "I suppose we should inure ourselves to this reaction. I believe many of our closest family and friends shall express the same frustration at the pace our relationship has taken and heartache it has caused."

"Yes, brother." Georgiana pouted. "You have been quite insensitive to my delicate constitution. I am sure I have suffered mightily waiting on you to bring me a new sister."

"I apologise, dear. It was especially rude of me not to take your feelings into greater consideration when conducting my relationship with Elizabeth."

"Well, I suppose I shall have to forgive you, as long as you promise not to keep her locked away for most of the year at Cresselly Park. I will need a friend and female chaperone next year as well for my coming out. Oh!" Georgiana turned back to Elizabeth. "Perhaps we can both be presented to the Queen together!"

"Me! Presented to the Queen? Surely not." Elizabeth scoffed. "I will be happy to accompany you as your sister anywhere, but I cannot imagine I shall be provided an audience with the Queen. Who would even be my sponsor?"

Darcy gently patted Elizabeth's knee. "My dear, of course you should be presented, as is appropriate for a newly married woman of our social status. When a lady marries into *le bon ton*, it is usually her new mother-in-law that does the honours, however, as my mother is no longer with us, you have abundant options for a sponsor. From the Fitzwilliam side of our family, I am sure Anne would be more than happy to be asked to act as your sponsor. Lady Matlock was going to be Georgiana's, however that plan is not currently fixed. There are also your own family's connections. Lady Finch comes to mind as someone who would be both an appropriate choice and an enthusiastic participant. If those options are not available or satisfactory, I believe that Lady Sefton might do the honours. It would be quite an introduction into society to have the great Lady Sefton act as your sponsor."

Elizabeth was flabbergasted at the suggestion that Lady Sefton would act as her sponsor for presentation to the Queen. She was also quite surprised to realise she had at least one close family connection with a bestowed title who would be in a position to introduce her to society.

Georgiana interrupted Elizabeth's thoughts. "We can discuss the particulars of our joint presentation and society introduction ball later. Now, it is time to dress for dinner. Come, Lizzy, Jane had a maid come with a dinner dress for you. I cannot wait to tell Jane of our big news!"

"*Our* big news, sister?" Darcy looked at Georgiana, with a bit of scolding in his voice.

"Yes, brother, *our* news. This is a joyous moment for both our families. I shall have my share of the celebrations."

Elizabeth laughed at the siblings' attempts to stare the other into submission. "I see I shall be spending a great deal of time moderating arguments between you two in the future. Come, Georgie, I agree it is time to change for dinner, and I would be very much appreciative of a short bath to wash away the dirt and leaves which are no doubt clinging to my hair after my run through the woods earlier."

The two ladies walked out of the study arm-in-arm, with their heads close together, whispering something or other that Darcy did not catch. Darcy was struck with a sense of serenity. He was very much looking forward to more days and evenings where he watched his wife and sister laugh together.

Less than one hour later, most of the Netherfield inhabitants were assembled in the front parlour when the Bennets were announced. Mrs. Bennet went straight to Elizabeth and began to loudly express her joy at being back in the company with Darcy.

"Mr. Bennet, I was hoping I might have a moment of your time before dinner."

Mr. Bennet bounced lightly on the balls of his feet. "No need, Darcy, no need! Elizabeth's smile is all I need to give you my permission for your engagement. Unless that is not what you wanted to discuss, in which case, I instead challenge you to a duel in the form of a chess match in the public game room of the Fox and Hound in Meryton tomorrow at sunset."

Elizabeth nearly spat the sip of wine she had just taken from her mouth. "Father, no!"

Jane attempted to hide a smile behind her fan, while Kitty and Mrs. Bennet groaned loudly.

Bingley looked perplexed. "That is an interesting challenge, most peculiar. I have never heard of someone being challenged to a chess match before."

Darcy looked around the room and, noticing the mirth from Elizabeth's sisters and father combined with the indignation of Elizabeth, concluded there was some highly entertaining story here related to his fiancée.

Before Darcy could comment and ask for the tale, Richard was announced to the room. "Good evening! Cousin, it is most gratifying to see you and have this opportunity to say very loudly and in the hearing of our good friends that it is about time you extracted your head from your horse's rear end." Richard came up to Darcy and smacked him on the back of the head. "Did no one tell you it was abominable manners to keep a lady waiting so long?"

Richard then went straight to Elizabeth, clicked his heels, and bowed dramatically over her hand with a whispered kiss to her knuckles. "Madam, I give you my joy and welcome you into the family. I pray you shall always have the patience for my oblivious cousin which you have graciously bestowed so far."

Elizabeth laughed heartily. "I thank you, Colonel. You have impeccable timing."

"What? Have I interrupted something?"

"No!" cried Elizabeth.

"Absolutely," declared Jane. "Lizzy, for shame. You did not think you would get out of your teasing so easily did you?"

Elizabeth groaned and placed her face in her hands. When she looked up, everyone in the room was looking at her with some combination of mirth and expectation. Sighing heavily, Elizabeth nodded and waved her hand at Jane in acquiescence for her sister to continue with the tale.

Jane smiled widely and cleared her throat in preparation. "When Lizzy was eleven years old, our neighbour John Lucas, declared he was going to marry Lizzy one day. Well, Lizzy was wholly disgruntled with the idea and let my parents know she was not interested in John one bit. The situation became slightly out of hand when he began talking about his 'betrothal' in the churchyard after services. Lizzy marched over to him and the group of young men and demanded he stop saying such things. John laughed and told her that she would come around someday. So, in the fashion of the types of silly novels that young girls love to read, Lizzy challenged him. There was much laughing by the boys, but John decided to engage in a challenge to save face. He asked Lizzy what challenge she would lay at his feet. She chose a chess match where the stakes stood that if she won, he could never speak of any betrothal ever again, and if she lost, she would concede to his boasting, though any actual engagement would have to wait until she was of age and with the approval of our father. So, it happened that an eleven-year-old Lizzy played a game of chess in the Fox and Hound, essentially for her own hand. Father took Lizzy to the game room and even supplied the chessboard."

The whole room was chuckling, except for Darcy, who was sporting a deep frown. Richard looked over and laughed even harder. "Jealous, cousin?"

Darcy checked himself and looked down, embarrassed to admit that he was, in a small way, jealous. "I assume, since we find ourselves in this current state of understanding, that you won the challenge?"

Elizabeth laughed at herself and nodded. "Yes, I won the game of chess. Quite handily, I might add. He was woefully underprepared for my level of obsession with chess as an adolescent. I believe that if I could somehow find myself today in a chess match with the eleven-year-old version of myself, I would lose to her superior skill." Elizabeth looked at her father with mock indignation. "I am still mortified that you would make such a challenge as a threat to Wills."

"Would you rather pistols at dawn? Would that appease your feminine sensibilities?" Jane teased.

Elizabeth sniffed and raised her nose in the air. "Of course, does not every delicate female wish to inspire such recklessness from the men in her life that they are driven to fighting over her affections?"

Bingley was the first to react to such ridiculousness. "My dear wife, I am deeply disturbed that you have not yet apprised me of my duty to fight for your affections. Please point me in the right direction of who to challenge, and I shall immediately fulfil my duty."

"Oh, you silly man." Jane laughed and tapped Bingley on the arm with her fan.

Darcy smiled widely at the scene in the drawing room. His family, friends, and future family all together and in good spirits. It was more than he could have ever imagined wanting. A profound feeling of peace moved through him, and he realised that all the pieces of his life had finally come into focus.

This was always meant to be.

Acknowledgements

Number two! When I started seriously writing in the summer of 2015, I could not have imagined that I would actually finish and publish *two* novels. It has been an absolutely bonkers adventure which has taken me to some amazing places – literally! This spring I actually got to visit another indie published author in my writers' support group who lives in *Bermuda*. So, above all else, I want to say thank you to my husband, Don, for always giving me the space and support to try new, crazy things. It's you and me against the world, and we always seem to come out on top, together.

I've also become part of an amazing collective of Jane Austen pastiche authors who love one another and support one another's projects. I'm so proud to be part of the Always Austen bloggers (https://alwaysausten.com/) and the Women in Publishing School Author Pod #9. Big thanks to Regina, Corrie, Don, Riana, Tiffany, Alexa, Lynn, Kimberley, Rebecca, and Trish!

Next, to my dear friend Katie, without your guidance and example, this would not have happened, certainly not twice. I have watched you write your stories with confidence and excitement for nearly ten years. In every way, you gave me the roadmap to publish my own.

Finally, to all my friends and family who supported me on this journey, especially my mom, Mary Ann – my sister, Allison – and my cheerleaders: Bernadette, Chase, Debbie, Jenn, Jessica, Julie, Miranda, Rosa, and Tina. I love you all!

About the Author

E.M. Storm-Smith is a mother, wife, attorney, former engineer, and literature lover. A lifelong obsession for books drove her to create stories of her own. Several years into the journey of writing about characters she loved, E.M. decided to take her passions to the world and see what happened. When she's not writing, E.M. is spending her time reading others' books – preferably somewhere with lots of sunshine, traveling (a global pandemic notwithstanding), and cooking things with chocolate as a primary ingredient. Come find out about all of E.M.'s projects at https://www.stormhauspublishing.com.

Other Titles by E.M. Storm-Smith
Reputation, An Easy Thing to Lose

Please Leave an Honest Review
The best way to support independent authors is by leaving a review on your preferred platform. On most, you don't even have to have a verified purchase! If you liked this book (or not) please consider leaving it a review. You can find links to various distribution review pages on the Storm Haus Publishing website. Also, if you want to get the latest from E.M. and Storm Haus, you can follow us on social media or sign up for our newsletter. Just follow the link to get all the latest information: https://www.stormhauspublishing.com

9 781737 403937